NATIONAL ACCLAIM FOR
PAINKILLER!

"A KNUCKLE-BITING MEDICAL THRILLER!"
—*Dallas Times Herald*

"Spruill shows tremendous talent with this first novel."
—*West Coast Review of Books*

"Rivals the best of Robin Cook in medical terror and psychological suspense . . . a real page-turner that will keep you reading until the end!"
—*Tulsa World*

"It's scary and medical enough to be a Robin Cook novel!"
—*Troy News*

Painkiller's "central idea is as intriguing as they come . . . It shows a real talent for illuminating character."
—*The Washington Post*

"A scary medical thriller, Spruill deftly creates viable characters while setting the stage for a chilling climax."
—*Booklist*

More . . .

PAINKILLER

STEVEN SPRUILL

ST. MARTIN'S PAPERBACKS

PAINKILLER

Library of Congress Catalog Card Number: 89-27056

ISBN 0-312-92497-6

Printed in the United States of America

St. Martin's Press hardcover edition published 1990
St. Martin's Paperbacks edition/June 1991

10 9 8 7 6 5 4 3 2 1

I dedicate this novel
to my clinical psychology faculty
at Catholic University—
except for the ones who won't think
I mean them.

ACKNOWLEDGMENTS

I'd like to thank the following people for their help as I wrote this novel: my good friends Richard Setton, Ph.D., clinical psychologist, and F. Paul Wilson, M.D., for their expert technical and editorial help; Marc Hertzman, M.D., for his kind assistance, and Connie Dunlap, M.D., for sharing with me some of her experiences as a psychiatric resident in a major Washington hospital; Jeanne Kamensky, M.L.S., Gary Edwards, M.A., J.D., Marcia Eggleston, R.N., and Bill Eggleston, M.D., for their excellent feedback on earlier drafts.

I also want to thank my wife, Nancy Spruill, Ph.D., for her untiring effort and many insights as she helped me get *Painkiller* into shape; my brothers, Tim Spruill, M.A., and John Spruill, nurse anesthetist, for their careful reading of the manuscript; Maureen Baron, executive editor at St. Martin's, for her invaluable editorial contributions, and Al Zuckerman, D.F.A., my agent, for his help at every stage.

And finally, my heartfelt thanks to Jocelyn Knowles, M.S., for her splendid suggestions just when I needed them most.

AUTHOR'S NOTE

Adams Memorial Hospital in Washington, D.C., is a fictional place, but it is as real as I could make it, based on a number of different hospitals in which I have served as everything from dishwasher to orderly to doctoral intern in clinical psychology.

1

A S SHE EMERGED from the hospital, Sharon Francis realized with a mild shock that it was night. Disoriented, she checked her watch: ten thirty! Where had the time gone? Last time she'd looked, it was only six.

Sharon peered up at the dark sky, feeling an eerie sense of slippage. Night, but still hot. The heavy, baked air settled on her face, stealing away the chill of the hospital air-conditioning. Morning, noon, sunset, hot day or cold; they were all the same back in the cool fluorescent catacombs of outpatient psychiatry. A mistake, trying to hide out in there. She had caught up on her charting all right, but when she'd tried to slip back out, Denise had spotted her.

"Sharon, thank God! We've got a DV and Mike's still up in traction. I'd handle it, but I got a guy who took himself off his lithium and is practicing Brownian movement in room C. I know you're off duty, but would you . . . ?"

As chief resident, Denise could have ordered her, but Denise had made outpatient chief by being, on top of damn good, so darned nice. So, the DV, yes. Domestic violence: a woman who had walked in with a fresh reddish bruise spreading under one eye. No fracture; it was Tylenol III, then holding her hand and telling her about the shelter that would get her and her daughter away from her husband, but the poor woman had argued, as they usually did, and that was where the time had gone.

Sharon stalled, undecided, gazing down along the hospital's west wing toward the Mental Health Unit annex. The glass-fronted lobby was still lit, glowing into the night. But visiting hours were over, and Mom was probably asleep.

Heavy with disappointment, Sharon trudged to the bike rack at the edge of the front parking lot. She straddled her ancient Schwinn, settling on the seat and glaring at the hospital. What do you want from me? she thought. Don't I get any time of my own?

She watched a couple of residents spill out the emergency entrance. They staggered and laughed, pointing at each other, acting giddy with relief over finishing shifts that had probably, like hers, been "officially" over since three thirty. The huge central bulwark of Adams Memorial towered over the two doctors in the darkness, glaring down with a hundred molten eyes, as though it resented their escape: *Get back in here. I need you.*

Sharon felt a wave of weariness. Closing her eyes, she became conscious of the city of Washington murmuring at her back, a constant background hiss of tires on pavement. Car horns blared; a bus rumbled by with a rising pneumatic wheeze. In the distance a siren rose and fell, growing louder. She opened her eyes and checked the ER entrance. Two ambulances were already parked there. An attendant dozing against one came to life, got in, and pulled forward, making room.

Listening to the siren come closer, Sharon felt her stomach tighten. With eight hundred beds, Adams Memorial was the grand dame of the city's private hospitals, but there were a million and a half people out there in the D.C. metro area. They kept pressing in: old ladies who fell and broke their hips, frightened women with lumps in their breasts, sweating, scared executives with pains in their chests, stabbed pimps, beaten prostitutes, drug dealers shot down

2

in the night, United States senators who wanted the kind of checkup only a top teaching hospital could offer.

A hundred residents slaving around the clock would not be enough. The hospital does need us, she thought, depends on us, craves us like a drug.

Her resentment faded. Being needed wasn't such a bad feeling—most of the time.

But Mom needed her too. And she needed Mom.

The hell with visiting hours, Sharon thought, getting off her bike. I'll go just for a minute, tuck the sheets up around Mom's chin, plant a little kiss on her forehead.

Sharon cut across the parking lot and started up the broad stone steps of the MHU annex. Thunder grumbled sullenly in the distance. She glanced up at the sky again, noticing its heaviness, the lack of stars. The hot air felt suddenly electric. On the sandstone piers that flanked the steps the fake gaslights sputtered and buzzed, their yellow halos fuzzy in the humid air. Moths circled the lights, butting the glass, as if fleeing the coming storm. Bits of mica in the piers glinted under the flickering lamps, and Sharon had the sudden thought that this was where the stars had gone, fallen from heaven.

She didn't like having that thought just now. Too loose—the kind of thing her mother would think.

She faltered to a stop, staring up the steps. The empty foyer of MHU blazed down on her, making her think of a vast, blank theater screen where the film had suddenly snapped. What now? Did she really want this movie to go on? She felt a sly twitch of nerve in the pit of her stomach and realized what had really been holding her back: not how late it was, but the fear that her mother might not be any better than last time. That her face would have that faraway look, that she would speak in riddles.

Okay, Sharon thought. You're afraid. Now go on in.

The entry foyer was cool and smelled of floor wax and wood polish. As she mounted the steps to the mezzanine the coolness thinned, and she felt a prickle of sweat. At the top she pushed the lit button beside the steel door and waited. Her throat ached; she massaged it gently. Probably be hoarse tomorrow. She would have to stop pouring so much time into the charts, learn Denise's knack for dictating compressed histories and case summaries.

Sharon heard a soft tread; the door swung open, revealing Chuck Conroy, the night orderly. He seemed startled to see her.

"Hey, Doc. Good timing."

Sharon had a sinking sensation. "My mother? Is something wrong . . . ?"

Chuck's Joe College face looked solemn. "She's kind of confused and agitated right now. Taylor is giving her a shot."

Sharon pushed by Chuck and hurried down the vast, semidark commons area to her mother's room. A shot, damn it. As she got close she heard her mother pleading, "No, no, I'll be good." The humiliation in her voice made Sharon feel sick. She pushed inside. Nurse Taylor was sitting on the side of the bed, holding the needle in one hand, patting Ellen Francis's shoulder with the other. Sharon was glad to see that the syringe was still loaded. Taylor turned, her weight wringing a squeak from the tortured bedsprings. Her round face creased in a relieved smile. "Dr. Francis! You must be an angel from heaven."

Ellen Francis sat up straighter in bed, looking hopeful. "Honey, don't let her give me any Haldol."

Taylor got up and waddled over to Sharon. Squeezing her arm, she whispered, "See what you can do. Maybe we won't need the injection. I'll be down in the station if you need me."

"Thanks." Sharon went to her mother, slipping into her outstretched arms and hugging her tight. She could feel her trembling; her nightgown was damp with sweat. "It's all right," Sharon said soothingly. "It's all right." She leaned back, taking her mother's hands, smiling. "So. What's the matter?"

Ellen Francis sagged back against her pillows. "They got Meg."

It took Sharon a second to place the name. Meg Andreason. Suicide attempt; cut her wrists after her college boyfriend dumped her. Her parents had brought her in a week ago, and Mom, in her own disjointed way, had taken her under her wing.

"Who got her?" Sharon asked, then wished she hadn't. It sounded like some paranoid fantasy, and she shouldn't encourage it.

Her mother swallowed hard. "Please, Sharon. I know what you think, but this is real. Reel the truck in and paint its tires for the prom. It's a big spring, and if you're not ready they won't be steady. . . . "

Sharon felt herself tensing up inside, clenching her teeth, tasting an acid surge of fear on her tongue. Altered states of consciousness, breakdown of neurotransmitters, dissociated speech—none of the fancy terms could change the way it felt to look into Mom's eyes and see madness sitting there on its haunches, giving you its toothy, panting smile.

Sharon got up and walked around the room, trying to blot out the thick mesh that covered the window, the small desk bare of anything sharp, the eyelets at the head and foot of her mother's high, narrow bed where they could secure the strap restraints. Even shutting her eyes, Sharon could see them all with perfect, scorching clarity.

"Honey . . . honey, listen."

Sharon turned back. Her mother was staring at her with intense earnestness, the cords of her neck standing out in furious effort. "Meg was my friend. She was a good girl, pretty and sweet, just like you. She needed to be here. I knew about signing out AMA; I've been in enough places like this, so I should. But Meg didn't know—I know she didn't. And I never would have told her." She took a deep, shuddering breath.

She's not talking crazy now, Sharon thought, just having

trouble organizing what she wants to say. "Meg signed out against medical advice?"

"Yes. And she shouldn't have, believe me. Most people in here don't even know they have the right to sign out AMA, you know that."

Sharon nodded. That part was true enough. All voluntary patients signed a form at admission agreeing, among other things, that if they requested discharge they must wait another seventy-two hours for evaluation before release. What was *not* explained was that, in actual practice, doctors rarely tried to enforce this delay unless the patient presented a clear danger to himself or others. Staff didn't like to advertise AMA, or patients would start taking off the minute things got rough.

"And I'm almost sure Meg didn't know she could do it," Mom said. "The reason I'm suspicious, I saw her and Chuck having a deep dark talk late last night, at the table outside the staff kitchen. I don't trust Chuck. He's too smooth. He watches you too much. I think he told her about AMA and convinced her to do it. And now she's gone."

Sharon's heart sank. Mom's sentences were tracking now, but edging toward delusion; more coherent than the gibberish, but just as nonsensical—

Sharon caught herself. She wasn't listening to her mother, she was diagnosing her. Realizing it gave her a dread, trapped feeling. She couldn't—and shouldn't—ignore the fact that her mother was a paranoid schizophrenic, but at the same time, Sharon could see and feel herself in her mother's place, very clearly. Sitting there some day, feeling sure that what she was saying was true and important and urgent, and knowing, because she had been on the other side, that no one would believe her. It would be the worst thing about being in this place.

"Tell me more," Sharon said. "What are you afraid of?"

Her mother chewed at a fingernail. "I think Chuck put

the idea in Meg's head to leave, and when she did, they were waiting to kidnap her."

Sharon felt the words dragging her down inside, making her feel weary and strangely detached. She fought the feeling, reaching across to squeeze her mother's hands.

Ellen Francis looked at her daughter with hope and gratitude. "Will you call her parents? I'm so worried about her. I have the number, they live right here in D.C. The nurses won't dial it for me." She took a rumpled scrap of paper from her robe and pressed it into Sharon's hand.

"Mom, it's after eleven. I'd be waking them up."

"Please. I'll go to sleep right now. No shot. You can tell me tomorrow. I just need to know someone's checking to make sure she's all right. I can't trust the staff here . . ." Her mother looked suddenly miserable. "Okay, I'm paranoid. I suppose it's crazy, but I can't help it. I've always trusted you, though, even when I'm really sick. *Please,* honey."

"Sure I will." Sharon felt her spirits lift as she took the paper. It was a reasonable request, and a good sign. Mom was willing, even hoping, to be proven wrong. That was not characteristic of paranoia. "I'll call as soon as I'm off the ward."

Ellen Francis sighed and relaxed against the pillow. Sharon watched the worried expression smooth out into the gentle, beautiful face she loved so much. Mom was almost forty-five, but she looked more like thirty-five, her face unlined, as if the gods wanted to atone for the deep, torturous wrinkles behind the smooth forehead.

"So how are *you* doing, honey?"

"I'm fine, Mom."

"Do you have a boyfriend yet?"

"I don't have time."

Mom gave her a severe pout. "Pish tosh. All the fine young residents at Adams Memorial, not just here in MHU but all through the hospital. You could marry yourself a nice pediatrician or a surgeon anytime you wanted."

Sharon laughed, but she also thought about Jeff Harrad in neurology, who was paying a lot of attention to her lately, asking to borrow her texts, dropping into the next seat at the caf. "Let's talk mental health," he'd say, and then they'd talk about anything but. He seemed very interested in her, and she had to admit that she'd been doing some checking on him, too. His father was a surgeon, an attending down at G.W. Hospital. His mother sat on the board of the Kennedy Center. She was a Merriweather, daughter of one of the grand old families of Washington. According to the nurses, who knew everything and made up what they did not know, Jeff was rich, but he tried to keep it a big secret.

Sharon didn't know how she felt about that. Mom's fondest fantasy was that her daughter would escape a lifetime of poverty by marrying a rich man. Mom never stopped to consider what a Mrs. Merriweather-Harrad type might think of her son marrying a young woman who owned a one-speed bike, a black-and-white TV that had been thrown away by the apartment janitor, and a mountain of medical school debt.

Sharon suppressed a smile. Forget rich; when a man looked like Indiana Jones only taller, who needed money?

And Jeff was funny, too, something she really liked. He could make her laugh in a second—once she'd laughed so hard over something he'd said in the cafeteria that she blew milk out her nose.

He was a little cocky, too. There was a story going around Adams Memorial that he had taken on Nurse Morgenthal down in ER one of the cold nights last winter. Morgenthal had been shooing a couple of vagrants out of the waiting room chairs. Jeff had told her to get back behind her counter and leave them alone. Residents did not talk that way to senior charge nurses, especially to Morgenthal, who ruled ER like a Valkyrie in her paper-horned nurse's cap. But Jeff must have had something on her, because she got back behind her counter, huffing, and the bums stayed warm.

"What are you thinking?"

Sharon came to with a start to see her mother smiling coyly at her. "Nothing."

"Don't nothing me. I haven't seen such a dreamy look on your face in ages. Who is he?"

Sharon wanted to drop it; this was making her really uncomfortable. Sure, she liked Jeff, would like him a lot if she could let herself. But she couldn't, and there was no way to explain that to Mom. What could she say? Because you're here, I'm twenty times more likely than the average person to land in the room next to you? The hard, statistical truth. It wasn't her mother's fault, any more than it would be Sharon's, if it happened to her. But Sharon knew she could never stand to feel that thing lunging from its haunches inside her, driving away the man she loved, the way it had done to her mother.

Another two years, Sharon thought, and I'll be well past the window for onset. Then we'll see about falling in love.

"Is he one of the residents?" her mother prodded.

"Mother, really. I don't have time."

"You're done with your internship, aren't you?"

Sharon held back a sigh. When was Mom going to get this straight? "That was just the first year of residency. Now I'm in my second year, doing just psychiatry, with two more years to go after that."

"But you're not as busy this year, are you?"

"In some ways I'm busier."

Mom pouted. "Well, you should make time. Romance doesn't wait. You're pretty and you're smart. You'll never have a better chance."

The lights flickered suddenly, flaring white, then the room was plunged into blackness for a second. Sharon smelled ozone and felt a tremor under her feet as emergency generators cut in and the lights came back on, dimmer than before. Thunder cracked and rolled to a booming crescendo, rattling the windows. A chill ran up Sharon's spine, and as she looked at her mother she was swept up in a powerful moment of déjà vu. Once when she was a little girl there had been a storm right on top of them like this, hideous explosions of thunder, louder and closer than she had ever heard before. Terrified, she'd run to her mother's bedroom, and Mom had wordlessly lifted the sheet for her to crawl in next to her. Her mother, who was afraid of so many things, had given her a calm, reassuring smile and a hug. Sharon could remember precisely the feel of Mom's arms around her, the sweet, lavender smell of Mom's skin. Her fear had vanished. She had understood suddenly why Mom spent so much time in bed: it was safe there; nothing bad could happen to you in the secure, tented warmth.

Rain slashed at the window outside the mesh and the tight, electric smell dissipated, freeing Sharon from the memory. Her mother was looking at her wistfully, and Sharon had the uncanny feeling that she'd been remembering the same thing.

Not tonight, Mom, she thought. It isn't safe anymore—not this bed. A feeling of loss swept over Sharon, sharp and bitter.

Then the rain settled into a lulling rhythm and she was all right again. She kissed her mother, pulled the blanket up, and turned off her light.

"Don't forget to call Meg's parents," Ellen Francis said.

"I won't."

Chuck Conroy was hanging around outside the room, almost as if he were waiting for her. Sharon felt a little sheepish, wondering if he'd heard what her mother had said about him. If so, he gave no sign of it, nodding pleasantly at her.

Sharon made her way back down the ward, tired and drained. Her face had that greasy feel, as though she had just biked a mile uphill. She turned into the staff women's lounge. The stopper in the sink wouldn't quite settle in. Waiting for the leaky basin to fill, she caught sight of herself in the mirror and laughed. Her hair had fought a day-long battle with its barrettes and was now sweeping up on either side of her head like the wings of a crow about to take off. Her face looked like chalk. Either a vampire had been sneaking bites or, once again, her makeup hadn't made it.

Where does Mom get the idea I'm pretty? she wondered.

Exasperated, she prodded some color into her cheeks, trying to think what to do about the chronic makeup problem. Even with its red undertones, her hair was so dark that her face usually looked white in contrast. Maybe more makeup, except that she hated to smother her face from six A.M. to nightfall. If she could grab a minute around noon to touch up—but that was dreaming.

Okay, maybe a darker shade, then. That might help with her eyes, too, which could look too bright when her face got pale. Suddenly, she remembered Higley's remark to her when she'd come to get the charts: "Sharon, you sure you don't wear green contacts?" One of the other nurses had meowed, and Higley had flushed. The whole thing had gone right by Sharon at the time, but now it came together as she realized that Ellis Winter, the handsome new attending, had been standing there too. Higley *had* been making a catty remark.

Sharon flushed, feeling a belated blip of indignation. Where did Higley get off? She was too gorgeous to be jealous of anyone, with her blond hair and great figure.

And who cares anyway? Ellis is all yours, Higley.

Sharon gazed at her face, her cheekbones and then her throat. Her throat was nice, long and smooth. She'd always liked her neck. Higley wore the size D bras, but she had the neck.

Sharon groaned and pushed her face down into the basin, savoring the cold shock of the water. She held her face under until she had to exhale, bubbling the water up around her ears. Feeling revived, she dripped and groped her way to the paper towels. The door creaked open behind her and she turned, patting her face, to see Taylor waddling in.

"How's your mom?"

"Much better," Sharon said. "She calmed right down and promised to go to sleep."

"Good. I hate giving her that p.r.n. shot. You know that, don't you, Dr. Francis? But sometimes we just have to."

"I know. What's the story on Meg Andreason?"

Taylor bent over the next basin, washing her chubby hands, shaking her head sadly. "Signed out AMA."

Sharon felt a small relief. So Mom had at least that much right. "I thought her parents brought her in."

"They did, but she showed us her driver's license. She's over twenty-one. We had to let her go. I just hope she's not out there somewhere slitting her wrists again."

A little shiver ran up the insides of Sharon's arms. "Who's her doctor?"

"Valois. He came in, but he couldn't talk her out of it."

Valois. Just the sound of his name gave Sharon a feeling of distaste. "Couldn't he at least have persuaded her to wait for her parents to pick her up?"

"She wanted out right then and there. No, Dr. Francis, when they're bound and determined like that, there isn't a thing anyone can do. Your mom will realize that, now that she's calmed down. She's a smart lady, even if she does have trouble sorting things out because of the . . . because of being ill."

"Yup," Sharon said, knowing Taylor meant it and wasn't trying to patronize her.

Taylor turned and gave her a searching look. "You know, living with this for so long like you have, I'll bet you could do some crackerjack work with our schizophrenics. Not with your mom, of course, but with some of the others. Since you rotated onto the ward, I've kind of been waiting for Valois to assign you a couple of his patients. . . ." looking up at Sharon's face in the mirror, Taylor trailed off.

"I'd like that too," Sharon said in a neutral voice. Like it? She would kill for it. It was the whole reason she had scrambled for the residency at Adams Memorial. But thanks to Valois, it was on hold. It would not go off hold until Valois changed his mind, and in the meantime, Sharon didn't want to think about it.

"You get on Valois's blacklist or something?" Taylor asked shrewdly.

"Something like that."

"Well, for what it's worth, I think they're wasting your talents."

Sharon realized she still had the paper towel wadded up in her fist. She tossed it into the wastebasket and patted the nurse's shoulder. "Thanks for all you're doing for Mom. She likes you and appreciates it, and so do I."

Taylor beamed. "Well, she's a real sweet lady, and she's got a nice daughter, too. I wish my daughter was half as close to me as you are to her."

Sharon didn't know what to say to that. She wanted suddenly to be out of the bathroom, out of MHU, even if it meant biking home in the rain. In fact, the way she felt right now, she might enjoy that.

But first she had a call to make.

"Gotta run," she said, and squeezed past Taylor out the door. She left herself out the front entrance and went to the phone in the foyer, hoping she wasn't being foolish. Meg had probably gone straight home and presented her parents with the fait accompli. Sharon would be waking them up after a rough day, and there would be the awkward introductions and questions. But a promise was a promise.

The phone was picked up after only one ring. "Meg?" A woman's voice, high, tremulous with fear.

She didn't go home, Sharon thought, and felt a sharp sense of dislocation, as though the foyer had shifted around her. "No, this is Dr. Francis, from Adams Memorial—"

"Has she come back there? Have you heard from her? Please God, say yes." The woman began to sob.

A lump rose in Sharon's throat. She groped for words of reassurance, finding them, feeling her training take over as her mind raced ahead to the unpleasant conclusions: one, Meg hadn't come home yet; two, it was going to fuel Mom's paranoid delusion.

And what *had* happened to Meg Andreason?

2

SHARON WAS DRIFTING down the short exit hallway of MHU toward the steel door. The passage swam
with a syrupy half light. Her eyes were almost closed. She
tried to force them open and couldn't. Still, somehow she
could make out the elaborate wood moldings around the
door. She felt a dim surprise. Why had she never noticed
them before? They must date back to when the door had
been wood and MHU had been called an insane asylum.

Reaching the door, she stood, inches from it. A draft
chilled her legs and naked back and she realized she was
wearing a hospital gown slit up the back. The tile floor was
cold beneath her bare feet. She was terribly frightened. She
could feel her heart pounding, and her throat was very dry.
She pressed a shoulder against the door, but it was solid
as rock—she couldn't move it even a millimeter. A mewling
whine bubbled up in her throat. She had to get out of here.

You work here, she thought. You have a key. Use it.

Somehow the key was already in her hand. She slid it into
the round cylinder lock. It glided in smoothly, but it
wouldn't turn. She twisted frantically; it resisted, the edges
cutting into her fingers.

Footsteps clacked up the hall behind her, and she knew
it was Nurse Taylor. Kind, fat Taylor. Sharon struggled
harder, desperate to force the key over. It would not turn.

"Come on, Sharon," Taylor said in her sweet voice. "Back to bed."

"No. I don't belong here. This is my key, see?" She turned to show Taylor the key, but her hand was empty. The nurse took her arm and pulled her back along the hallway. Sharon tried to fight, but Taylor was strong, implacable, murmuring in her ear, "You don't want a shot, do you?"

Sharon tried to scream, but only a breathy, whuffing noise came from her throat. She fought to get her eyes open. If she could just get her eyes all the way open . . .

She did. She was lying in bed. She sat up, twisting around to peer at the window. There was no mesh over it. She was in her apartment. Relief rushed through her. Only another nightmare, one of the endless versions. Taylor had assumed the keeper's role this time because Sharon had seen her last night when she went to visit her mother.

The sky outside the window was pink with the first touch of dawn. Hungry for the light, Sharon watched the sky brighten, waiting for the terror of the nightmare to dissipate. She had the strong urge to get up and run, to *do* something. She made herself sit in bed and think calmly and rationally about the nightmare and why she'd had it. Clearly, it was the business with Meg. Her mother's paranoia about an MHU plot, compounded by the fear and desperation of Meg's mother, had infected her. And, of course, the part of her that was always afraid had spotted the paranoia and gone into a terrified spin, bringing on the nightmare.

But it's Mom's paranoia, she told herself, not yours. Meg may or may not be all right, but there's no plot within MHU to get her. You know that.

She hoped her subconscious was listening.

Sharon dreaded telling her mother about Meg. She biked to the hospital early to get it over with, checking her watch as she walked in the front entrance. Seven fifteen, good.

Austin wouldn't be in the office yet; she could use the phone in privacy. She would rather tell Mom in person as soon as she got on the ward, but visiting hours didn't start till noon.

Could she make an exception this once?

No. If other patients saw her breaking the rules, taking advantage of her position on the ward, it would undermine her and make trouble for Mom. A patient would surely bring it up in the community meeting, and with good reason.

Sharon took the elevator up to four, getting off at psychology services. The corridor was still on night lighting, every other light turned off. In the dimness, the deep blue carpet ate her shadow and rejected the sound of her feet, giving her the familiar sense of alienation, of not belonging. She wished she could shake the feeling. All the other second-year residents had offices on MHU. But she and Austin had drawn the short straw, and that was that. If the hospital hadn't added two more training slots in 1986, she might not have landed the residency in the first place. Too bad they hadn't added office space, too. Psych services had the nearest available space—a whole wing away. She probably wasted two hours a week just walking back and forth between her office and MHU.

But the worst part was not belonging.

Most of the psychologists and psychology interns went out of their way to be nice, but this was their turf, and there was always that feeling of strangeness, that wariness behind the smiles, because a psychiatrist and a psychologist thrown together were like two cats trying to sit the same fence.

Sharon unlocked her office, turning on the light and settling at her desk. She started to pick up the phone, then hesitated. Still pretty early. Mom might not be up yet.

Sharon's pager beeped. She called in and was rung through to Rod Weyrich, her chief on MHU. One of his R-3s had called in sick; he needed someone pronto to handle some overnight consult requests—an agitated, confused

17

patient on orthopedics and a couple of depressions on thoracic.

Sharon put off the call to her mother and headed back to the elevator, pleased. Her chief had just given her work usually reserved for R-3s. He must have a pretty good opinion of her.

Or maybe she was just the first R-2 in this morning.

Well, that didn't hurt, either.

On eighth-floor orthopedics, Sharon stepped into the minor bustle of the shift change. At the station the morning charge nurse was being briefed by the night nurse. She pointed at Sharon. "You here about Keefer? I want to see you."

Sharon nodded and motioned that she was going on down. The long corridor beyond the station was populated only by parked wheelchairs, aluminum walkers, and a linens cart. The hall wouldn't stir to life until the breakfast trays came and nurses aides started getting patients ambulatory.

Mrs. Keefer was a tiny old woman in the first bed of a semiprivate room. Sharon said good morning and got a wide-eyed, quizzical look in return. Mrs. Keefer's white hair stuck out in disarray, giving her a wild look. According to her chart, she had undergone total hip replacement the day before. During the night, she'd buzzed for a nurse five times, "talking crazy" each time.

Putting the chart down, Sharon saw that the leg on the repaired side had been strapped down for wide adduction, as was normal, but the nurses had tied the other ankle too.

"How are you feeling?" Sharon asked.

Mrs. Keefer pointed to a silver birthday balloon that floated on a string tied to the foot of the next bed. "That's the manager," she said. "He's looking down at me and saying who let that old bird in here?"

Sharon saw a red comb on Mrs. Keefer's bedstand. She ran it through the old lady's fine hair, chatting with her, working in the usual questions. Mrs. Keefer knew where she was and why, but not the date. Pleased, Sharon wrote *Oriented X 2, continue observation* in the chart. When she went back out in the hall, the charge nurse was waiting. "Did you prescribe a tranquilizer?"

"It would only make her loopier," Sharon said. "Keep the restraints on, give her another day to clear up from the surgery, and I'll check back."

"Thanks, piles."

Sharon walked away, pretending she didn't hear. She could appreciate the nurse's problem: orthopedic staff had enough to do meeting the physical demands of totally immobile patients without having to cope with abnormal or demanding behavior too. But this woman was only mildly confused. There was a good chance she had broken her hip in the first place because of medication. Almost fifteen percent of broken hips suffered by older people were caused by drugs like tranquilizers that made them lose their balance and fall. The woman was scheduled for her first physical therapy session that afternoon and her legs would be shaky enough without a load of tranks.

The other two consults were patients on thoracic, facing major heart surgery the next day. They needed someone to hear out their fears without cheerily brushing them aside, someone to help them clothe their terror in controlling words. Sharon spent half an hour with each patient. By the time she finished with the second, the hospital's morning routine was in full swing, the hall crowded with nurses, aides, and breakfast carts. Sharon wended her way toward the elevator, feeling drained but good. Most doctors would rather have root canal than talk to a patient about the fear of dying. What made her different?

Face it, Francis: you're a ghoul.

Woolgathering, she almost ran into a couple of wheelchairs, the occupants leaning toward each other for a chat. She squeezed around them, then had to back into the wide wall rail to make room for a patient being rolled in from surgery. Sharon smiled down at the young woman as she passed, getting back an unfocused, barbiturate blink and a stringent whiff of Betadine antiseptic.

Above her a speaker crackled to life with a tense female voice: "Code RT, three four six seven—repeat, RT, three four six seven." Sharon felt her heartbeat surge inside her. She saw one of the thoracic residents pounding down the hall toward her. Scanning door numbers, she got a fix on where she was—3467 was behind her. Turning, she saw the two wheelchairs still blocking the way. She grabbed the one with its back to her and pushed it sharply forward out of the way, ignoring the patient's indignant squawk.

"Thanks," the resident said, running by.

Sharon followed him into 3467 and saw a man of about fifty sprawled on the side of his bed, his face waxy and cyanotic around the ventilator bag. The crash cart was in place, and more thoracic people were crowding in, so she backed out to give them room and headed for her office again, feeling her knees compress squishily with each step. Her heart was banging as if she'd just chugged three coffees. Dear God, she would never get used to resuscitation codes. All the frenzy as the vital seconds ticked away, your hands squeezing the bag or loading the syringes or pumping over the stalled heart. So dramatic!

And, in a way, so easy.

If only it could be that way in her specialty. But when a mind stalled, no one got on the speakers. There was nowhere to dash to, nothing for your hands to do. You fought back with your own mind, and even when you were lucky or good enough to bring back what was lost, it sometimes took months or years.

Back at her office door, Sharon took a deep breath and eased it out. Okay, she thought. Time to call Mom and tell her about Meg. When she slipped inside, Austin was sitting at the other desk. His shaggily bearded face swung toward her and he gave her his grave, Aleksandr Solzhenitsyn look. "Good morning, Dr. Francis."

Damn! "Good morning, Dr. Demaris." She dropped her

voice in a teasing imitation of his. Poor Austin, he could never forget that he was Harvard Med and that the world, though his oyster, was still a very serious place. It made him unintentionally funny, which was okay most of the time. But not now.

"It's good to see you easing up a little," Austin said.

"Huh?"

He held up his watch. "Coming in on time instead of early. I've been saying all along that you'll have more of yourself to give your patients if you—"

"I know. You're right. Austin, could you excuse me for a few minutes? I've gotta make a personal call."

He leapt from his chair. "No problem." At the door he paused and eyed her. "I hope it's nothing serious."

Sharon forced a smile and shook her head, wondering what he had seen in her face. When the door closed behind him, she dialed MHU. The nurse said she would see if Mrs. Francis was in occupational therapy yet. Sharon waited, fretting about how to handle this without fueling her mother's delusion.

"Hello, this is Ellen Francis."

"Hi Mom."

"Did you call them?" Her voice was high with stress.

Sharon hesitated, dismayed.

"She didn't come home, did she," her mother said flatly.

"Not as of last night." Sharon tried to sound upbeat. "But listen, Mom. I've seen this happen before. Sometimes when a person checks out AMA, they're afraid to go home for fear their family will try to make them go back."

"Not Meg."

"She could have hitched a ride to college."

"No. They've taken her. I knew it."

Sharon's heart sank. She knew there was no sense arguing with her mother. She tried to think of something to say.

"Thanks, honey. You tried. I appreciate it," Ellen said.

She sounded really depressed. Sharon felt awful about it. It might be a delusion—it was a delusion—but to Mom it

21

was terribly real. "I'll call them again as soon as I get a chance. She'll turn up and be fine, you'll see."

"I've got to go, honey. They're making us do macramé. I wish they'd let me have my cross-stitch."

"I'll ask them," Sharon said, but she knew it would be useless: needles were contraband for all patients on the ward. Once that door locked behind you, you were not an adult anymore, no matter what your age. Sharon felt a claustrophobic tightness in her chest.

"Bye," her mother said.

"I love you, Mom. See ya later."

As soon as she hung up, Sharon dialed Meg's parents. No one answered. The office door opened and Austin gave her a look of wincing apology. "Sorry—I forgot to tell you. Weyrich wants to see all the R-twos at eight forty-five, something about a new policy on committing ER walk-ins to the psych wards at St. Elizabeth's Hospital."

Sharon checked her watch. "Yow! That's in five minutes!"

But Austin was already gone. She scrambled after him.

The next time Sharon got a free moment it was evening and almost time for her pain group. She had ten minutes. Grabbing a cup of coffee, she dialed the Andreasons again. This time Meg's mother picked up after one ring. She said, "Hello?" instead of "Meg?" but her voice held the same discordant resonances of fear and hope. Something about it spooked Sharon—she almost hung up without saying anything but realized how cruel it would be. She gave her name and asked after Meg. Mrs. Andreason's voice turned heavy with disappointment. No, they hadn't heard from her. They were worried sick. The police seemed sure Meg had run away, but the Andreasons knew she would never do that to them.

Then a male voice came on the line. "This is Bud Andreason, Meg's father. What's your interest in this?" His voice was harsh, stinging Sharon, but she reminded herself how miserable he must be, and how much easier men found it to be angry than to be scared.

"I'm a psychiatric resident at Adams Memorial," she explained. "My mother is a patient in MHU and—is a good friend of Meg's." Sweat popped out on her face. She had almost said "was a good friend."

"I see." His voice was gentler, edged in sympathy, now that he knew they were both members of the same sad club. "If you'll give me your number," he said, "I'll call you when we hear from Meg."

"I'd appreciate that, sir. I'm very sorry for all the pain this must be causing you and your wife."

"Thank you."

Sharon gave him her home and office numbers and rang off. Crap. Not only did she not have any good news for Mom, she was starting to get involved emotionally with Meg, whom she didn't even know.

She checked her watch. Eight twenty-seven. In three minutes, a dozen people she did know would be waiting for her. She got up and headed for the group room, determined to put Meg from her mind.

Most of the patients were already seated in the circle of chairs. Dr. Irwin Jenkins was enthroned in his usual spot, gazing up at the cone lamp that hung low above the middle of the group. His cane was slung beneath his chair. Cherry-scented smoke crept from his pipe in thin whorls, drifting through the slanting mantle of light into the darkness above. He shot Sharon a cool look, but she knew she still had a minute to go, so she gave him a pleasant smile. Poor Jenkins. Probably worried that he might have to run group tonight. Many of the pioneers of group therapy methods were clinical psychologists, but you wouldn't know it from working with Jenkins.

Sharon sat down and glanced across the circle at Brian, trying to get a quick read. He was staring at her, his little way of warning her that he would be going after her again tonight. She suppressed a sigh and reminded herself what the poor kid had working against him. When you looked at his chart, it was easy to feel sorry for Brian Gifra: only twenty years old, he suffered terrible migraines. Like most members of the pain group, he was an outpatient, but unlike the rest of them he lived all alone, in an apartment a few miles from the hospital. His job wasn't much either—he worked stocking shelves at a Safeway from midnight to six. His father had left his mother when he was only a baby and his mother, a diabetic and grossly obese, had died two years ago, just after he left home. He never talked about either parent or about his job. Only about his pain. His migraines were intermittent, but his obsession with them was constant. He seemed to have no friends. Small wonder, Sharon thought. As tragic as Brian's life was on paper, in the flesh it was hard to feel anything good about a guy who kept slapping away every outstretched hand.

Sharon glanced over at Dr. Jenkins, wondering how he would take it if she started pressing him again to put Brian in a group with more general goals, and people his own age.

Badly, she decided.

But it was worth another try anyway. If Brian could learn how to make some friends, he might not be so obsessed with his pain.

Jenkins leaned forward in his chair. "I believe last time the group was sharing personal techniques for dealing with pain." He settled back again, and Sharon knew it would probably be the last thing he'd say for an hour.

"This group is a frigging waste," Brian snarled, staring at her.

There it was, the opening salvo. She struggled to get hold of her concentration. Brian's face was red. A vein bulged on his forehead. He'd like to punch me, she thought. "You seem really furious, Brian."

"How would *you* feel? We sit here on our duffs, week after week, *jawing* about our pain, and it's still just as bad as when we started. This hospital isn't doing anything for any of us. Neither is our medicine. Either it doesn't dent the pain, or it knocks you dizzy and you get hooked, so your life is down the toilet anyway. I got a right to be angry."

"Okay," Sharon said. "Let's say you have a right, but is it what you want? Or might it be a problem, too, along with the pain?"

"The pain *makes* me angry!"

"Ah. So there's nothing you can do."

Brian glared at her, his mouth working. "I'm not a frigging doctor or a scientist. You want to do something for us, Sharon, forget psychiatry and go become a chemist. Go find a painkiller that really works, then boogie on back to Adams Memorial. We'll all be glad to come to group that night." He went on staring at her, his eyes narrow with malice, arms tightly crossed, fists pinned under bulging biceps. He made her think of a maddened bull on the verge of charging. She could feel her pulse tripping in her throat. She realized she was sitting up very straight and had shoved herself back in her chair, putting extra distance between them. She was afraid, but what was more important, that was how he made other people feel too. He had probably been doing it ever since he grew up, repelling and scaring people, and maybe he wasn't even aware how big, dangerous, and brutal he looked.

So make him aware.

Sharon said, "You're saying a lot, and I'm trying to listen, but my feelings are getting in the way. I feel that you're very angry with me personally right now."

She thought she saw a glint of satisfaction in his eyes. He does know, she thought. He wants you to be afraid of him. She felt a stir of anger and suppressed it.

"Do you like how you're feeling right now, Brian?"

He stared at her, tight-lipped.

"If there was a medicine for anger, would you want that, too?"

"If I could get rid of the frigging pain, I wouldn't need the anger medicine."

Sharon thought of the landmark study of pain and aggression: 1964; Azrin, Hutchinson, and Sallery put a rat and a doll in a cage and electrified the floor. When they gave the rat a shock, it attacked the doll. Did that sum up Brian? His terrible migraines were the shocks, group was the trap, and she was the doll? Or was there a deeper problem hiding beneath the pain: Brian Gifra hated women.

Suddenly she felt she was in over her head. She glanced over at Jenkins, but he tamped his pipe, refusing to let her catch his eye. She wished she could call time out, pull him into the hall with her and say, "Look, what do I do next?" But these were real people, not a circle of practice dummies; she couldn't just pound on their chests, breathe into them, and then toss them into a corner. They were watching her, waiting to see what she would do, and the clock was running.

"Nothing to say?" Brian prodded scornfully. His gaze was still fixed on her; he was up to his old trick of trying to shut out the rest of the group and go one-on-one with her. Time to get some of the others involved. She looked around the circle, hoping, but it didn't look promising: Frank Greene was bent forward, stiff-backed, staring into his clasped hands; Edith Heurlich tugged her sweater tighter around her arthritic shoulders. The rest just sat there with expressions of distaste. The low-slung light cast a looming Stonehenge of their shadows on the walls behind them, making Sharon think of some ancient druidic circle of elders. They really can't stand Brian, she thought, and felt a pang of sadness for him. If she could just figure out a way to get them to help him. Somehow she must help them understand how Brian had missed out on most of the nurturing the rest of them had gotten in life. If they could realize that and start making allowances for Brian's general obnoxiousness, they'd have a lot to give him, and it might help distract them from their own pain.

Sharon waited, but nobody would speak. Looking around the group, she said, "It's a real problem, isn't it? No one has a cure for pain, and the pain makes us angry."

26

"Us?" Brian snapped. "What's this 'us' bullshit, Sharon? I bet you've never had real pain in your life."

She thought of her mother. A lump rose to her throat, surprising her. "I'm afraid most everyone has pain at one time or another," she said. "Physical or emotional. Sometimes we can't make it go away. But we can learn to master it through our attitude toward it."

"Bullshit. Pain is physical, not mental. Anybody who says different is a witch doctor."

"Brian." Frank Greene spoke up, finally. "Shut up. You're always going after Dr. Francis, and the rest of us are sick of it."

A couple of the group members clapped or murmured agreement. Sharon tensed, expecting Brian to explode. Instead, he hung his head, blushing a bright red.

Hmmm, she thought, looking at Frank. Despite the sharp words, there was kindness in his eyes. At sixty, he was old enough to be Brian's grandfather.

Might he also care enough to act like one here in group?

Until this session, Frank hadn't said much. Like a lot of men his age, he probably had some trouble with the idea of therapy. He was a sheet metal worker, retired by the same fall that had put him in this pain group. The men he had worked with all his life were a tough, physical bunch, not the sort who sat in a circle and shared their feelings.

But there was more to Frank than the chronic vicious back pain and the forearms that bulged from years of squeezing tin snips and wrestling ducts into place. He had been married to the same woman for forty years. Mrs. Greene had had four miscarriages. There were no children.

Sharon's pulse quickened. Four miscarriages, she thought. You two must have wanted kids very badly. . . .

She became aware suddenly of the heavy silence around her and knew with a sinking feeling what she must do. She struggled to find the right words.

"Frank . . . okay. You wanted to let Brian know you didn't like what he did. That's good. We all need feedback, good and bad, to help us see how we're coming across. That's what group is for. But we have to be careful not to shut each other up, because then it's over—no more feedback. Right?"

Frank gave a chastened nod and returned his gaze to his hands. Damn! She had done her best to soften it, but now it looked as if she had shut *him* up, and that was the last thing she wanted. Why did this have to be so damn tricky? If only she could be working with MHU's schizophrenics like Nurse Taylor had said, something she knew about, something she had prepared for, not just in medical school but almost her whole life.

"You think you're so noble, don't you," Brian said in a low, tight voice. "Pretending to stick up for me after I stick it to you. But I don't need you defending me."

"Just listen to yourself, kid," Frank said. "She's the best friend you've got in this group and you—"

"Don't call me kid," Brian mumbled. He looked down again, avoiding Frank's gaze.

Now we're getting somewhere, Sharon thought.

"Then stop acting like one," Frank said more gently.

Brian stood, knocking his chair over backward. "I don't need this. I'm quitting this bullshit group."

He hurried out, slamming the door behind him. Sharon felt an instant of relief, then regret. This time he might not come back. There was so much he needed; she wasn't ready to give up on him.

The minute he was gone, the group stirred to life, shifting in their chairs, talking and joking. "Sorry, Dr. Francis," Frank said. "But that boy's got what the army used to call a serious attitude problem. You've bent over backwards to help him."

"I think group can now be declared a success," Barbara said. "We just got rid of our biggest pain." Most of the group laughed; Sharon noticed that Frank didn't join in.

"I just hope he means it this time," Edith said. "Remember, he's quit twice before."

Listening to them made Sharon feel frustrated. They just couldn't see past Brian's anger to his need.

The group got busy with each other, and ran for a while under their own power, doing decent but shallow work. Sharon took some deep breaths and felt calmer, more accepting. Brian probably *would* be back next session, and she'd have another chance.

From the corner of her eye she saw Dr. Jenkins moving at last, lifting his arm and checking his watch. His other hand settled on the curved handle of his cane. Sharon had the urge to lip-synch the words she knew were coming and caught herself just in time.

"Well," Jenkins intoned, "I'm afraid the hour's up, people. See you next time."

He stood, leaning heavily on the cane, and limped from the room, trailing puffs of smoke, as though the effort of walking had stoked a furnace in his chest. Sharon stayed in her seat, watching him go, sweating a little. She had almost done it. She had almost made fun of Jenkins. I have to stop hanging around with Jeff Harrad, she thought. It was just the sort of thing Jeff would do on neurology rounds.

Damn Jenkins! Why wouldn't he pitch in? Jenkins *knew* pain. He must feel it with every step, stabbing through the spliced bone and wasted muscle left by the car accident. He bore it bravely, never complaining, even when his face was white and pinched. What was the secret of that bravery? If he were any other man he might be entitled to keep it inside. But he was a psychologist, and the senior therapist of this pain group. He owed the group everything he could give.

Sharon sighed and trudged back to her office. Luckily Austin wasn't in. He always wanted to schmooze, and she was too worn out. She just wanted to change into her slacks and get home to bed.

Except that she had planned to put in an hour at the university library first. So go, she instructed herself. Sit, read, learn new stuff.

But her legs refused to stand her up.

There was a little coffee left in the Norelco. No cups, so she sipped it straight from the pot. It was tepid and sludgy, biting strong. Making a face and shuddering, Sharon choked it down. The caffeine hit as she changed into her slacks and sweatshirt, flooding her with a perky optimism. How could she even think of skipping library now that she had finally crawled up from the primordial ooze of the waiting list into a nice carrel? And tonight, waiting for her in its cozy privacy, was a juicy new article on schizophrenia, a sweet hour of uninterrupted time.

She took the elevator down to the basement. As usual, a light was on in Dr. Pendleton's office. On impulse Sharon tapped on the frosted glass.

"In."

She opened the door enough to put her head in. Dr. Pendleton was bent over some papers, his white hair mussed, as though he had been running his hands through it. His nose was a touch red; she remembered hearing the slide-clunk of a file drawer just before he'd told her to come in.

Pendleton looked up, then checked his watch. "Sharon! What have I told you about all work and no play?"

"I'm outta here. You want me early in lab tomorrow?"

"Nine will be fine. You tell that twit Valois he's not to work you so hard. Leave something for me."

Sharon laughed. "Ri-i-i-ght." She felt a little guilty for laughing. Hearing the chief of psychiatry called a twit by another department head should have offended her.

If this were the best of all possible worlds.

Ha! she thought bitterly, then cut herself off before thoughts of Valois could go any further. She eased Dr. Pendleton's door shut. Turning away, she became aware suddenly that the air of his office had held a mellow hint of sour mash. But his speech had been clear, hadn't it? And anyway, the only way he would get stuck with surgery this late was an emergency with no residents around—

Sharon realized she was defending him to herself and laughed. Who was she, Carry Nation? Pendleton was the best neurosurgeon in the city, and a hell of a nice man, too. The other chiefs would be sipping their nightcaps at home about now, safe from the sniffing noses of their acolytes.

Sharon pushed through into physical therapy, wending her way through the silent warrens, her Reeboks squeaking on the tiles. One of the lights was out at the head of the last hallway. She hurried through the well of darkness, easing up again between the rows of examination booths as she felt the reassuring increase of light, white curtains picking up the dimmed night cycle of the fluorescents.

Ahead in the shadows at the door to the back parking lot, she saw a man slouched against the wall, waiting. She tensed: physical therapy was closed for the night, a shortcut for staff, not a place where anyone should be loitering. As she got closer, she saw that it was Brian and knew from the way he straightened that he was waiting for her. The hairs stirred on the back of her neck. Was he still pumped up with his private rage?

Maybe he wanted to get back into group.

Sharon walked toward him, hopeful but keeping her face noncommittal. It had to be his decision, reached without any pressure from her. Before she could get to him he stepped in front of her, blocking her exit. His face was a hostile mask. She felt suddenly hollow inside. She was hyperconscious of the silent, deserted corridor behind her. Her mind flooded with contingency plans: run back to Pendleton's office; scream—but if she had to scream, it would be scattered to nothing in the burrowlike side rooms, the curtained booths.

Calm down, she told herself. He's all bluff and bluster. You can handle him. She swallowed, resisting the urge to back away. "Yes, Brian?"

He glared down at her. "I didn't like the way you treated me in group tonight."

"I'm not sure what you mean."

"You'd better be nice to me, or I'll—"

"Don't threaten me." Fear twisted in her stomach, but somehow her voice stayed calm. "This isn't group now. You can't say whatever you please out here. If you want to rejoin group, you'll be welcome. Now please step aside."

Brian held his ground, leering down at her. The pitting of old acne scars around his thick neck looked white against the redness of his skin. She put her hand against his arm and pushed past him, shuddering at the touch of his sweat-soaked shirt, the soft nudge of his belly. Pulling the door shut behind her, she strode across the parking lot to her bike. Her heart was hammering and she was breathing too fast, dragging air into the top inch of her chest. Easy, she thought. You're fine now.

She looked around the parking lot. It was reassuringly bright under the security lights; a man in a suit was getting into one of the cars in doctors' parking. She glanced behind her to see if Brian had followed her out, but the door to PT was still closed, and there was no sign of him.

She fumbled the lock off her bike, jumped on, and headed out fast, using the excess adrenaline in her legs to push her lingering fright out through the pedals. The night was warm and smelled faintly of tar; they must have finally patched those potholes ahead on Fremont Avenue. A fat moon floated in a dense, dark sky. She slowed as she pedaled past the park behind the hospital, listening to the chirr of crickets, incongruous amidst the hiss of traffic and the scattered honking of cabs. City or no city, the night was soft, the warm, humid air sweet on her tongue. She thought again of the article awaiting her at the library: "Sentence Modeling with Hospitalized Schizophrenics," by Coult and Leatherman, the latest issue of *Clinical and Consulting*. Would it hold out some promise, or was some element of the statistical analysis flawed, as all too often happened?

She became aware of a crunch of tires on the street be-hind her, headlights washing past her front tire, and real-ized that the car had been there for several seconds; it was matching her speed, not passing. Probably just someone looking for a street sign or an address.

She glanced behind her and was half blinded as the car switched on its brights. Thanks a lot! Annoyed, she pedaled harder, trying to draw ahead. The car speeded up to keep pace. She had pulled over as far as possible; the car had plenty of room to pass, but it stayed close behind her, its tires crackling on the pavement. She waved it past. It con-tinued to tail her.

Sweat sprang out on her face, running down her forehead and stinging her eyes. Feeling her front tire shave the edge of the curb, she veered out a little. The car accelerated, its left headlight tracking her.

It's going to hit me!

She felt a frozen instant of disbelief, then her front tire struck the curb and she had to fight the handlebars. As the car pulled even with her, a dark shape leaned toward her from behind the wheel. She turned to see who it was. A flash went off in her face as a terrible jolt tore through her, and then she was falling, down and down.

3

S HARON SMASHED down hard on her side, blinded and terrified. *I'm shot!* The night spun above her. She tried to draw a breath and couldn't. She sucked at the air, desperate, getting a trickle, and then her lungs expanded and she gasped, over and over.

She realized she had not been shot, that the jolt had been her bike wheel hitting the curb, throwing her down. Tires spun suddenly a few feet from her head, shrieking, then biting into the pavement as the car sped away down the street.

Fury slammed into her. Get up! she thought. Get the license number! She pushed herself up to a sitting position, but her eyes still swam from the flash. All she could make out were two shimmering red dots of taillights, dwindling to nothing.

She sat a moment, probing gingerly for bruises. Fortunately she had fallen onto the narrow strip of grass between the curb and sidewalk. At least she had missed the concrete. The pain receded. She got to her feet and examined the bike, fingering the frame in the darkness. The front tire was hanging, deflated and useless around the rim. Bastard! She felt her hand shaking on the tire rim. The flash went off again, in her memory. A camera—someone took my picture. Fear percolated up her spine, dousing her anger.

Who'd want to take a picture of me—and why?

She heard the crackle of car tires again, turned and saw the headlights. He was back; he must have gone around the block. The car pulled in to the curb. Fear swelled in her as she saw the driver's door swing open. Her mind went dim; she felt herself stalking toward the car, raising her fist. What was she doing? She should run, get away.

"Most people wave with their hand open," said a familiar voice. Sharon blinked and focused on the man who was looking up at her from the driver's seat. Jeff Harrad! She felt dizzy with relief. She wanted to grab him, pull him from the car and hug him.

"You okay?" he said. His hair was mussed on top, and he needed a shave; he must have just finished a marathon shift.

"Sure—" Sharon's voice broke. She cleared her throat. "I just hit the curb and demo'd my front tire."

"Sure you're not hurt?"

"I'm fine."

His eyes held hers. In the glow of the streetlight they were a deep brown, rich as bourbon. She became aware of a hot tingle in the skin of her face, a rush of warmth around her heart. She was desperately glad to see him.

"How about a ride home?" he said. "Or better yet, we could go up to the doctors' lounge and watch pro wrestling."

"Sounds delightful, but I've got to go to the library."

He gave her a pained look. "You'd rather study than watch someone get their legs wrapped around their neck? What kind of psychiatrist are you?"

Jeff got out, opened the trunk and went to put her bike inside. The trunk was huge. She studied the car. It was an old Buick, late fifties probably, and in mint condition. Under the streetlight its smooth maroon surface gleamed almost black, like patent leather. She loved it at once. It fit perfectly with what she had heard about Jeff, that he didn't like to flaunt the family money. Jeff could be driving a Vette or a Jag; instead it was this nice old car that even a high school kid could afford, if he bought it cheap and fixed it up himself.

"Don't take this wrong," Jeff said. "But you look pretty well narked. And if you're too tired to watch pro wrestling, you're too tired to study. I'm taking you home."

Sharon started to argue, then realized he was right. She was tired, almost punchy. The article on schizophrenia could wait until tomorrow. She slid gratefully into the seat beside him, keeping her distance, settling back as he drove.

"So what really happened back there?" Jeff's voice was serious now.

"Some jerk drove too close to me. Probably just a drunk sophomore from Catholic U out on a lark." She decided not to tell Jeff about the flashbulb going off in her face. She didn't want to think about it. She just wanted to sit there and let her neck muscles unwind against the plush leather of the seat. As the car rolled along, the darkness, the faint smell of car wax and gasoline, Jeff's closeness made her feel a little drunk, set the nerves in her stomach tingling. She squared her shoulders, trying not to think of the fine, strong body next to her. But she could smell him—a musky tang of sweat mixed with Old Spice. It gave her a warm sense of safety; she remembered suddenly that her dad had worn Old Spice.

The car pulled up to her apartment; she didn't want to get out. Jeff idled the engine and gave her a searching look. "Want me to see you up?"

Yes, she thought.

"No, I'm fine. Just let me get my bike."

At the door she waved him on his way, feeling a somber regret as the long, slick Buick pulled away from the curb and vanished down the street. She roll-lifted her bike up the stairs to the second landing, careful not to wake old Mrs. Birdsong. Inside her apartment, Sharon felt the emptiness at once, the silence. She wished Mom were there. Tonight she really wanted to hear her voice, listen to her disjointed recitations of the TV soaps as she got ready for bed. Sharon felt lonely tears prickling at the backs of her eyes and told herself to straighten up. She'd had her chance for company tonight and turned it down.

Sharon left the lights off, reluctant to illuminate the emptiness of the apartment. And anyway, its sparse shapes and threadbare carpets looked better in the soft sheen from the streetlight outside the kitchenette window.

Standing the bike in the foyer, she hurried to her bedroom and pulled her father's old barbell from under the bed. Its coolness shocked her hands pleasantly. Already, dust had begun to coat it, filling in the light scoring worn down over the years, and she realized she hadn't worked out in almost a month.

She pulled her hair into a ponytail and hurried through the warm-ups and stretches. Sliding a five-pound weight onto each end of the bar, she twisted the bent locking pins tight. She picked the barbell up with a knee bend. Standing in front of the window, she curled the thirty pounds, counting silently. Eight, nine, ten—it was not some kid on a lark—seventeen, eighteen, nineteen—because kids on a lark didn't take your picture—twenty-four, twenty-five. Feeling the long, slim muscles in her arms hardening, starting to ache. She welcomed the pain, the resurging sense of strength inside her as she slipped gradually into the old, metronomic mantra. After thirty reps, she eased the barbell down and sat on the edge of her bed, staring out her window.

Was it Brian?

If only she had been able to get a good look, but she hadn't even really seen what kind of car it was. It was some dark color . . . she thought. Terrific.

She stood again and added twenty more pounds to the barbell. Fifty for a standing press, ten reps, that ought to be about right. She pushed the weight up, wondering what Brian would think if he knew she lifted weights. She would like him to know, but there was little chance he would ever guess it. She weighed only a hundred fifteen pounds and wore a size six. But she was not weak. She was strong. And she was going to *stay* strong.

You *had* to, that was the sad truth. She had known it from the time she was a little girl and life had started to go wrong, but she had almost let herself forget it. She mustn't do that again. There was never a time in your life when you didn't have to stay strong.

Sharon pressed the fifty pounds above her head over and over, until tears spilled from her eyes, mingling with her sweat.

Morning began with the rats. Sharon squeezed through the maze of big rolling carts in Dr. Pendleton's animal room, mouth-breathing the gamey animal smells that hung in the room's stagnant warmth. Deep among the carts, she found the study she had agreed to observe. The top row of cages was well above shoulder height; she reached up gingerly, testing, and felt a sharp, warning twinge in her shoulder. Too many curls last night, too many clean and jerks, too many bench presses.

Too much falling off bikes.

Sharon's neck tightened with anxiety. She rolled her head back, forcing her neck and shoulder muscles to relax. Forget it, she thought. Just some nut with a camera. He's long gone. It's over. You're fine.

She reached up and pulled at the first cage. It stuck on its runners. She jerked at it, and pain knifed through her elbow, making her wince. If she could get a more level pull on the cage . . . She stood on tiptoes, and agony flamed in her calves. Sharon groaned, then looked around, feeling sheepish. She hadn't heard anyone else in the rat room, but someone could be back in the maze of carts, writing quietly in a protocol book or something.

Going over to the bare wall, she straightarmed the cinderblock and walked her feet back out, gritting her teeth as the calf muscles stretched.

Feeling a little better, she went back to the cages and

began working her way down from the top row. She lifted each cage down, observed the rat inside, stuck the cage back in and wrote *Appearance and behavior normal* in the proper square in the protocol notebook.

She felt a lingering spot of tension in the middle of her back where the car had been aimed. What if Jeff hadn't come along? Would she have disappeared, just like Meg Andreason? Two days now, and Meg's father had not called her or left any messages. As of this morning Nurse Taylor was quite sure Meg was still missing. Meg had gone out the door of Adams Memorial and vanished into thin air. Was the last thing she heard the roar of a car engine, the last thing she saw a flash of light in her face?

Sharon felt the tension rising again, winching her neck muscles tight. Relax, she told herself.

She went back to work, forcing herself to concentrate on the rats. They all seemed exceptionally tranquil this morning. What were they on? Thumbing to the methods page of the protocol, she read the first few lines and found that they were getting endorphin, directly in the feed. She laughed. No wonder they looked so mellow. They all probably had a nice buzz on. Endogenous morphine, the brain's very own painkiller. Sharon rubbed gingerly at the bruise inside her thigh, where she had hit the crossbar of the bike going down. She could use some endorphin herself about now.

She pulled out the last cage and found the rat curled up nose to tail inside its mason jar of feed. A familiar sight, but something about it touched her today. Gently, she grasped the rat by the nape of the neck, lifted it from the jar and set it on the floor of its cage. It blinked its red elfin eyes at her and she stroked its back, letting her own shoulders slump, breathing at last through her nose. The rat's malty perfume rose to her nostrils on eddies of feed dust stirred up by her stroking fingers. The rich carbohydrate scent was oddly pleasant, reassuring. She understood suddenly why the rat slept on its feed: it was aware how precarious existence was; it knew what it needed to live and stayed as close to that as it could. Sharon felt a sudden bond with the rat.

If I want to feel safe, she thought, all I have to do is put a couple hundred pounds of cereal in a huge jar and sleep on top of it.

Sliding the cage back in, she brushed her fingers off and wrote in the protocol *Appearance and behavior normal.*

She carried the notebook from the animal room back to its shelf above the files in the main lab. As she shoved it into place, she saw Dr. Pendleton coming out of his office. Someone was with him, a younger guy, medium height, but his leanness made him look taller. He was deeply tanned, with thick dark hair and the rugged, chiseled face of a model in one of those L. L. Bean ads. Sharon felt a pleasant tingle in her stomach. Definitely the kind of man who made you look twice.

She heard Dr. Pendleton call him Mark and realized it must be his son, whom she had heard about but never met. He sure didn't look much like his father. They both had thick hair, though the father's was white and bristly as a polar bear's. Grant's face was square while Mark's was a fine oval. And Grant's bulgy red Tip O'Neill nose was about as far from Mark's fine straight one as you could get. Maybe Mark took after his mother.

Pendleton put his arm around Mark's shoulders. Something about the sight triggered a snippet of memory: Dad hugging her at the circus. The moment flashed back to her so vividly that she felt her breath catch: bright spotlights crisscrossed the arena, playing over the backs of the marching elephants. She could smell their strong, eye-watering odor all the way up in the grandstand. She was awed at their size, the slow weight of their movement, the tiny side-set eyes that seemed to look piercingly straight at her. She had begun to be afraid. What if one of them broke from the ring and moved up through the grandstand on those mighty, crushing legs? She felt Dad's arm around her shoulders and snuggled against him, warmed and reassured. Dad was stronger than the elephants. Dad would never let anything happen to her. Dad would find whoever ran her off the road and—

A piercing scream made Sharon jump. She stared across at Dr. Pendleton and Mark, a cold aftershock rippling along her nerves. Then the location of the sound registered. The baboon room. The scream came again and she ran for the room, past a technician who had stopped in his tracks. She pushed through double doors into the arena of big stacked cages.

The baboons were all crowded to the front of their cages, hooting and jumping around, their coats erect with aggression, making them look huge. Harry, one of the animal care men, was on his knees in front of Bogart's cage. Bogart had him by the wrist. Harry's face was white. Sharon gasped with fear—Bogart was the biggest of the baboons, ninety pounds of bone and muscle. His muzzle was peeled back, exposing two-inch daggerlike fangs. Harry struggled vainly to pry Bogart's grip open. The baboon started jerking Harry's hand against the feed opening. In seconds, the hand would either fracture or Bogart would wrest it into the cage and start slashing with his teeth.

Sharon lunged to Harry's side, planting her feet and grabbing Bogart's furry wrist, prying at the long, sinewy fingers. Bogart grunted at her and clicked his wicked teeth in warning. The hairs on her neck bristled with fright; she held on, and put everything she had into peeling the powerful fingers back. God, the animal was strong! For a second, she couldn't budge the fingers, then they gave way and Harry jerked his hand free. She let go at once; Bogart squealed and jerked his hand back into the cage.

Sharon crouched, frozen, stunned by what she had just done. She was dimly aware of Harry sitting beside her on his rump in the middle of the floor, holding his wrist and saying "Jesus" over and over. Then she realized she could not hear the baboons anymore. She looked around the encircling walls of cages and found them all staring mutely at her, as though she had just landed in a spaceship. It struck her as hilarious and she burst out laughing.

"Bravo!"

Sharon turned and saw Mark Pendleton standing in the doorway in front of his father. Mark applauded her, his handsome face alight with admiration. He was very good-looking, but his eyes were odd, a strange, light, transparent gray. Or perhaps it wasn't so much the color but the contrast with his darkly tanned face.

"I've never seen a woman so strong," Mark said.

Sharon blushed furiously. Terrific—he thinks I'm an Amazon. The adrenaline drained from her suddenly and she felt woozy. Mark was at her side in a second, helping her to the door, grabbing a stool from the lab table so she could sit down.

"You'll be okay," he said. "It's just the reaction. Do you know how strong those animals are?"

"Now I do." Her voice came out in a dry croak.

"I've seen one of those ugly brutes take on a lionness and send it packing. An outsize male like that one can throw a man ten feet. What did you have for breakfast?"

"Raisin Squares." She felt instantly stupid.

He didn't laugh. "Well, you ought to call up Kellogg's and offer to be on the box—give Wheaties and Mary Lou Retton some competition."

"Hear, hear!" Dr. Pendleton chimed in. "That was really incredible. I'm sure when Harry here recovers his wits he'll want to thank you."

Harry stood and ducked his head to her, mumbling something. He gave Bogart a dark look, then hurried out, muttering. Sharon looked at Mark, found him giving her a strangely private smile, as though they shared some delicious secret. The pleasant heat returned with a tingle to her stomach.

Pendleton gave her a shrewd look and glanced at Mark. "I guess you two haven't been introduced. Sharon, my son,

Mark. Mark, this is Dr. Sharon Francis, one of our second-year residents up in psychiatry. Psychiatry's letting her grab some hours down here to get the hang of my methods, see if she can get some ideas for a joint neuropsych study."

Mark took Sharon's hand. His grip started out firm, and got firmer. She realized he was looking for a reaction from her. She had no particular patience for that and let her hand collapse. He inclined his head in a slight bow, and she had the feeling she had just passed some kind of test.

Pendleton cleared his throat. "I've got a meeting, so I'll leave you two to wrestle apes or whatever."

Sharon was suddenly aware that Pendleton had just given her a verbal nudge, ever so slight, toward his son. The warm, dry pressure of Mark's hand lingered, sending an electric tingle through her fingers. Her awareness of him sharpened, crossing a threshold inside her, triggering old warnings.

Time to rein this in.

"I've got to get back up to MHU."

"I think you should take the rest of the morning off," Dr. Pendleton said. "That had to take a hell of a lot out of you. I'll call your chief resident if you want, what's his name? Weyrich."

"No thanks. I'm fine."

"This hospital damn well owes you. If Bogart had bitten Harry or broken so much as his pinky, Harry would have sued me, Bogart, Adams Memorial, and the city of Washington. You sure you don't want to go home, maybe rest up for my party tonight? You are coming, aren't you?"

She remembered the invitation he'd sent her last week. She had already told him she couldn't come, but apparently it hadn't taken. "Thanks, but I'm afraid it's a little far to bicycle."

"What? Only twenty-five miles?" Pendleton gave her a look of mock incredulity, then shook his head. "Don't be ridiculous, I'll take you. You're one of my star staffers. Can't have you missing it."

She felt Mark looking at her. She wondered if he would be there. What could she possibly wear? What would she do if Mark asked her to dance? No, forget it.

"All right," she said.

As Pendleton drove, Sharon gazed out the passenger window, enjoying the enforced rest, the chance to just sit and do nothing. She had raced like crazy on her lunch hour to buy a dress for the party, and then the ward had hopped all afternoon. Weyrich had handed her an emergency admission, a guy coming down off angel dust, so twitchy she had to sic the orderly on him, and now all she wanted to do was sit and let the convolutions in her brain unclench. Pendleton seemed to understand, keeping a companionable silence, heading south from the hospital. He picked up Route 50 at Constitution Avenue, battling late rush hour traffic as he drove west over the Roosevelt Bridge. Sharon let her eyes follow the broad glittering curve of the Potomac toward Key Bridge and beyond, where Georgetown shimmered in a humid haze.

On the Virginia side of the river, towering high rises crowded against each other, peering hungrily back across at the forbidden, monument-hallowed ground of the District. Sharon's interest quickened. It had been years since she had ventured into the Virginia suburbs. Pendleton stayed on Route 50, following it west through Arlington and Falls Church. She watched as landscaped apartments and tidy houses slid by, alternating with carefully zoned commercial tracts—Hardee's, McDonald's, Exxon stations, and shopping centers.

After the Beltway overpass, the traffic began gradually to fall off as the outer suburbs gave way to rolling farmland. At a little burg called Gilbert's Corner, men in bib overalls and Caterpillar hats sat around the screen door of a weathered "deli," their heads panning in unison as Dr. Pendleton's silver Mercedes glided past. Pendleton glanced at the men and smiled. "Now we in the *real* Vuh-ginia," he said in a bad imitation of a southern drawl.

The car wound through lush woodlands. Sharon rolled the window down an inch and set her face into the warm evening breeze, letting it cleanse her lungs of the bus fumes of the city, the sharp, hospital smells of disinfectant, medicine, and sickness. She felt herself relaxing, getting a little hungry. What was Pendleton planning for eats? A barbecue maybe? Or suth'n fried chicken, crisp and juicy. Sharon's mouth began to water.

The woods thinned a little and a white rail fence appeared on the right. Pendleton drove through a gate onto a long gravel drive. As the trees fell away, Sharon saw the house at the end and caught her breath. It was magnificent, a big southern colonial. Tall white pillars dominated the center, creating a formal veranda. The high arched windows of the two symmetric wings of the house looked out onto acres of smooth manicured lawn. As the Mercedes swept closer, Sharon saw that even the eaves of the house were gorgeous, trimmed with intricate sculpted moldings.

"It's beautiful," she breathed.

Pendleton smiled. "Yeah, but the commute's murder."

He parked the car in front and escorted her through the veranda into the house. She got a brief look at a huge curved staircase of gleaming wood, and then Pendleton led her through a back foyer and outside again, to the house's rear portico. She was surprised to see that a number of people from the hospital were already there. Pendleton made a small gesture and a handsome black man stepped from the crowd, bringing over a tray of champagne. The man was coatless in the evening heat, dressed in black tuxedo pants, a pleated shirt and a gold brocade vest. There was a fine sheen of sweat on his high forehead.

"Isaiah, this is Dr. Sharon Francis," Pendleton said. "Take good care of her, and watch she doesn't shrink your head." Pendleton excused himself to go change; Sharon took a glass of champagne and sipped. "Delicious!" she said.

"I'm glad you like it, ma'am." Isaiah kept his eyes down. In this setting, his deferential manner raised a twinge of discomfort in her. It reminded her of a household slave's, as if he had time-traveled through some portal straight from the gardenia-scented mists of antebellum Savannah.

"I'm Sharon," she said. "I'm only twenty-seven. Call me ma'am again and I *will* shrink your head."

Isaiah met her eyes. "Some of my ancestors shrank heads. They weren't M.D.s, either."

"In that case, you can call me anything you want."

Isaiah, at last, rewarded her with a smile. "If there's anything I can get you, Sharon, you let me know."

She watched him navigate smoothly through the crowd, tray held high. She hadn't imagined that Grant Pendleton would have a household staff. Or that he lived in a place a tsar might envy. She had heard the jokes around the hospital, of course, about his first name turning out to be prophetic—Grant Pendleton had indeed brought millions of dollars of grant money to Adams Memorial. No doubt he had been well compensated for his value to the hospital, but this house went beyond salaries and bonuses. It was a mansion of blue blood and old money.

Sharon drifted to the stone rail of the portico, savoring the warmth of the setting sun on her face. A hundred yards from the house the sectioned glass of a greenhouse glowed like mother-of-pearl. The woods on the surrounding hills were dark except for a thin rosy crown. A sudden emerald brilliance blazed up from the swimming pool as lights flicked on across the patio and along the edge of the canopied tent that had been pitched on the back lawn. More guests were arriving by the minute; the party was getting into full swing. Sharon saw with dismay that everyone else was dressed to the nines: medical chiefs and administrators wore tuxedos and evening gowns, and even the residents had abandoned their usual jeans and sports jackets for suits or dinner jackets. Sharon resisted the self-conscious urge to glance down at her dress. It was navy blue cotton with a saucy red bow at the neck, and expensive for her. Even with the sale price, paying for it would mean two months of light lunches. And she had worried she might be overdressed.

Overdressed, hell. She was definitely underdressed. A light flush rose up her neck. She had the urge to duck out, find some shadows to hide in, but that would just draw attention to herself. It was like one of those silly anxiety dreams where you're sitting in church and suddenly you realize you're in your underwear, and you try to act like nothing is wrong, because getting up and leaving would guarantee that everyone would see you—

"Ah, Dr. Francois, isn't it?"

Sharon turned, preparing to smile at the play on her name, then realized with a little shock that it was Judith Acheson, chief administrator of the hospital. Acheson glanced at her dress, then instantly looked back at her face. Sharon swallowed, unnerved. "Uh, Francis."

Acheson smiled indulgently. "Francis, of course. From the ancient tribe of Franks, who gave their name to France. So I guess it's French either way."

"I never looked into it."

"But you should. It's fascinating. Your very own chief, Dr. Valois, is of French extraction too, of course. So you must be getting along very well."

Oh, heavens yes. Sharon searched for an innocuous reply. Her mind fumbled, dazzled a little by the woman she was facing: Judith Acheson, Columbia University M.B.A., former assistant secretary of health and human services, now in charge of the biggest hospital in the nation's capital. Grand dame of the Grand Dame. She looked it, too, fifty and heavy-shouldered in a slimming gray gown, diamonds sparkling at her neck. Tales of this woman's exploits could be told at campfires to scare little children. There wasn't an intern or resident in the hospital—except maybe Jeff—

who wasn't afraid of her, and that went for a lot of the attendings.

So? It was kind of nice to see her here, in a place where it counted. More power to you, Sharon decided.

Acheson gave her a shrewd look. "On the other hand, the French are not known for getting along, are they? Even with each other. Tell you what, I like to stay in touch with my residents. When you get a free moment, why don't you come on up for a chat, Dr. Francis."

"That would be very nice," Sharon said.

Acheson moved off. What was that all about? Sharon wondered. Has she heard rumors that Valois and I don't get along? Nerves stirred in the pit of Sharon's stomach. God, I hope not.

Unless she's on my side.

Sharon heard the sweet strains of a Mozart concerto below her and saw that a small orchestra, also in formal dress, had set up beside the striped canopy. The music soothed her. You haven't done anything wrong, Sharon thought, so don't worry about Acheson.

Another server approached, holding out a tray with rolled bacon pastries, little quiches, cheeses, pear slices, and some mushrooms stuffed with crabmeat. Sharon watched her hand waver over the tray, overwhelmed at all the choices. The movie *Heidi* flashed into her mind, that scene where the poor little urchin, awed by a table of food beyond her dreams, had started stuffing rolls into her dress.

She took some cheese and one of the mushrooms and retreated into the house, hurrying through the rear foyer past a cloakroom, looking for a place she could hide out and survive the evening. She passed through a long, hushed hallway, carpeted in red. The light in the hall was very low. Every few feet along the walls hung paintings in huge baroque frames, murky hunt scenes or portraits she could barely make out through their sheen of cracked varnish. She felt herself slipping back in time even further, past the Civil War to colonial America.

On impulse, she turned into a side room and found herself in a study. A huge, intricately carved desk sat across from a marble fireplace. Above the fireplace the head of a magnificent buck deer gazed down at her. She turned away, repelled. The severed head did not seem to fit with Dr. Pendleton. He was known for his respectful treatment of his lab animals. He made sure all animal cages were clean and as roomy as possible. He tolerated no abuse, no carelessness. According to Jeff, Pendleton had flown into a red-faced rage at one of the other neurology residents for handling a rat too roughly.

Could this same Grant Pendleton have gone out and shot this beautiful, innocent animal for sport? No, she couldn't imagine it.

"There were too many of them that year," said a voice behind her. "They were starving."

She felt a twinge of irritation at being discovered so quickly—and at having her mind read, from the rear, no less. "People are starving around the world, too," she said without turning. "But we don't feed them bullets."

"Not bullets. An arrow."

Suddenly, she recognized the voice. Mark. She turned, flustered, but he was smiling at her, obviously not offended. She saw that, unlike most of the people at his father's party, he was dressed casually, in khaki slacks and a tan corduroy sports jacket. His shirt was open at the neck. Suddenly she felt much more as if she belonged.

"I'm sorry. I didn't mean to preach."

"No, you're quite right," he said. "I hate the way most people hunt. Big guns. Packs of drunks in loud jackets, blasting anything that moves, leaving it there, half the time. Showing no respect. That stag had every chance. I tracked him two days, saw him four times. He saw me too, but got careless. Finally I got close enough for a shot I knew would kill. After I removed the arrow, I apologized and explained the need to the stag's spirit."

Sharon was intrigued despite herself. "That's an old Indian ritual, isn't it?"

He nodded, looking impressed.

"I know that the herds get too big at times," she said, "and someone has to thin them out. But I'm afraid it still leaves me cold, no matter how it's done."

He raised an eyebrow. "Aren't you squeezing in some hours on one of Pop's neuropsych studies, so you can learn the ropes? I'm sure you realize you'll be killing some animals, cutting them open, popping their brains out."

The graphic way he put it unsettled her. "That's different," she said, determined not to show her discomfort. "In a lab, you're not reaping what you didn't sow. Those rats were bred for it. They would never have been given life in the first place if it weren't for research. We feed them and protect them. They don't have to worry about a cat or dog jumping on them. And they're living pretty well. The rats you're talking about are riding a semipermanent high, with all that endorphin floating around in their bloodstreams."

"So are you ready to trade places with them?" he asked dryly.

His sarcasm irritated her. "Would you care to trade places with that head on the wall? Everything living dies. At least your father's rats will be sacrificed in a good cause: to relieve human suffering."

"Wouldn't it be fairer to sacrifice humans?"

Sharon started to get indignant, then saw his half smile and realized he meant it as a joke. She didn't smile back, but he did not seem perturbed.

"Pop said you're a psychiatric resident. Why all the interest in his neurology lab, anyway?"

Relieved at the change in subject, she settled into a big leather chair beside the desk. Mark sat on the corner of the desk, facing her, with a serious, attentive expression that flattered her. Her irritation with him faded. She said, "I'm interested in schizophrenia."

"In rats?"

"If they get it, sure. But regardless, it's becoming pretty clear that there is a biochemical or neurochemical side to schizophrenia. I feel that to have any hope of understanding the disease, I need to learn all I can about neurology, too."

"Very commendable. Even so, wouldn't you prefer to be working with actual human schizophrenics? There must plenty of them up in MHU. Your own chief of psychiatry is always using his patients as guinea pigs for various research studies."

Sharon sighed, depressed at having to think about Dr. Valois. "Sure. I'd like to be working with Valois's patients, research *or* treatment. But so far he's been keeping me away from them."

Mark did not seem surprised. "Do you know why?"

"My second week as an R-2, I was at a joint staff meeting for psychiatry residents. One of the R-3s from outpatient was holding forth on the uses of individual psychotherapy. He said it was basically useless in treating schizophrenics. I don't agree, so I spoke up, citing some studies showing that certain types of one-on-one therapy can be very effective with schizophrenics."

Mark winced. "And Valois was there."

Sharon realized Mark already knew the significance of what she had done.

"You really trod on a land mine that time," Mark said. "When it comes to his schizophrenics, Valois has no use at all for psychotherapy. His thing is pills."

"Yeah, I know that—now. I wish someone had told me before I walked in. The resident was only parroting Valois's cherished beliefs, so when I spoke up I guess Valois took it as an attack on him personally."

Mark shook his head. "That S.O.B. He's done that before. You aren't the first, and you won't be the last, but it's still a damn shame."

Sharon was pleased by his sympathy and a bit surprised at how much he knew about Valois. "You seem pretty up on hospital lore."

"Pop and I are close. I keep up with his life and he keeps up with mine." There was pride in Mark's voice, and an odd, wistful quality.

"And what *is* your life?"

"I'm a cop."

She looked at him, surprised, wondering if he was joking. This guy, this terrific-looking bronze man with the strange, light gray eyes couldn't be a cop. "I don't believe it," she said. "We've been talking almost ten minutes and you haven't said 'vehicle' once."

"And you haven't said, 'What do *you* think it means?' "

She laughed. "Touché. A cop where?"

"Red Falls. It's a little town about five miles south of here, not far from Haymarket. About two thousand people, mostly farmers. I'm chief of police, got six whole guys and a crusty old woman named Blanche working for me."

Sharon was both intrigued and repelled. Here was a man who looked like an angel but who shot deer with a bow and arrow for pleasure and worked in a dangerous profession where the prey was human. She wanted to ask him why, but such a question was too personal on such short acquaintance.

Mark cocked his head. "I think the orchestra has dropped the Mozart. Would you care to dance?"

Sharon hesitated. She had both dreaded and anticipated this. Now the moment was here, and the dread was in command. Talking was one thing, safe, pleasant. But touching? Her stomach twisted inside her. She could feel already what his hands on her might do, the wishes they would invite, the needs they would arouse. No. Don't even start.

And then she realized that there might be something else behind his offer: Mark had followed her into the study, and now he had found a pretext to ask her to leave. It made perfect sense. It was a private sanctum after all, and she had no business there.

She stood. "Okay."

She got herself in hand as she followed him back out to

the portico. Surely dancing with him would not lead directly to his marrying her and then leaving her when she began talking in circles and refusing to drink from previously opened milk containers.

Sharon felt a strange, dizzying lift of surprise. She had just come very close to joking with herself about it. Was that good or bad?

If it broke down her determination, bad.

Walking down the steps to the flagstone patio with Mark, she noticed the greenhouse again, a ghostly white shape in the darkness beyond the party. "Your dad likes flowers?"

"Yeah. Pop spends hours out there puttering around."

She smiled. *That* did fit with Grant Pendleton.

So how had his son become the last of the Mohicans?

She let Mark guide her onto the dance floor. A number of other couples were already dancing. Mark turned Sharon smoothly, keeping his hand properly in the middle of her back. He held her with a light touch, each movement of his fingers along her back warming her, sending little ripples of pleasure through her. She found herself wishing he would pull her closer. Over his shoulder she saw another couple bearing down, the man overstepping. Before she could warn Mark, the man bumped into his back, and Mark stumbled forward. Sharon felt something hard under his arm beneath his jacket and knew with a shock that it was his gun. The other man mumbled, "Excuse me," and Mark nodded without turning. He grinned at her, and it made her think of Bogart's bared teeth that morning.

Oh, great, now I'm really getting paranoid.

She gave herself over to dancing. Once she stopped running her mind, she started to enjoy herself. Other couples made way for them and clapped appreciatively after they had danced through a fast number.

"You dance beautifully," Mark said. "Who taught you?"

"My mother."

"Is she as beautiful as you?"

Warnings went off in her mind, but she saw he was not

53

looking into her eyes. He had not tried to draw her closer. His voice was simply conversational.

"Much more beautiful," she said. She gazed over Mark's shoulder. A face in the crowd at the edge of the dance floor registered: Jeff Harrad. He was looking at her, and she had the feeling that he had been watching her and Mark dance for some time. As her eyes found his, he gave her a little wave and turned away. She felt suddenly awful. She tried to reject the feeling. What did she owe Jeff? What did she owe either of these men?

The dance ended and Sharon slipped into the crowd, escaping from both Mark and Jeff. Her heart was beating very fast. Forget me, she thought. Both of you.

But she knew she didn't mean it. She did not want them to forget her, and that was dangerous, terribly dangerous, because the walls were there for a reason, and she must keep them up. In just another year or two, she could be sure she was past the likely age for onset of adult schizophrenia, the age when it had invaded Mom, like a clawed hand thrusting into a soft puppet, forcing Mom to play out a tragedy Sharon knew she herself could never bear.

Just a year or two more, Sharon thought, and I can stop worrying.

Where will Jeff be then? And Mark?

She broke away from the party, striding across the vast, darkening lawn toward the greenhouse, trying to flee the ache inside her and knowing she couldn't. As she walked, Meg Andreason popped into her mind. Meg, who had cut her wrists because her boyfriend had left her. Sharon realized suddenly why she kept thinking about Meg. She didn't really know her, but Meg Andreason had had to watch the man she loved walk out of her life forever. Just like Mom.

And just like you, if you're not careful.

Sharon gazed into the darkness. Where are you, Meg? she wondered. Are you running? Or is it something else?

A chill ran up Sharon's spine. She turned back, hurrying back toward the warmth and light of the house.

4

MEG ANDREASON WEPT from the pain. She sat
on the table they had given her for a bed, cradling
her arm. It hurt so much she could hardly think. But she
must think, or she would never escape.

If she could just do something about the pain, maybe rig
a splint or something. Except her elbow wasn't just cracked,
it was shattered. If she moved even a little, she could feel
the loose pieces of bone grinding together in there. And anyway, the room was bare, not a thing in it to make a splint
with.

Blinking back tears, she stole a look at the elbow. It
looked even worse. The patch of purplish black had spread,
and a round yellow spot had appeared in the middle. The
spot was about the size of a hammerhead. She looked away,
sickened.

It made no sense. Why would they smash her elbow?

They're crazy, she thought. They're going to kill me.
Coldness rushed through her, and she shuddered. The tiny
movement sent pain knifing up into her shoulder, clawing
down into the bones of her hand; sweat poured from her
forehead. She could smell herself suddenly, a damp, chalky
smell of fear.

Chuck, you bastard!

Pain flared in her elbow and she realized she had

clenched her fists. She made them relax. Chuck. If she could, she would kill him! She imagined her fingernails clawing into Chuck Conroy's face, gouging his eyes . . .

A hopeless feeling swept over her. Who was she kidding? Even with two good arms, she couldn't overpower Chuck Conroy on her best day.

Why were they doing this to her, hurting her so? She hadn't done anything to them. Tears poured down her cheeks and she began to sob, gasping as her elbow jerked. She tried to stifle the tears and hold herself still. It will be all right, she told herself. This is just a nightmare.

She shut her eyes. In a moment she would wake up. She would be in her bed in Damson Hall. If she opened her eyes, Donna would be sitting at her desk studying: Donna's sketchbook would be near her hand, as always. Her funky round glasses would have slid to the end of her nose. She would turn, see Meg was awake, and crack one of her dead-pan intellectual jokes. Meanwhile Kitty would be making her usual racket out in the hall, goofing off in her daft way, bouncing through one of her dance routines or uncorking a handspring. Heaven!

Soon, I'll have missed too much work to make up, Meg thought. Donna and Kitty will graduate without me.

A terrible ache swelled in her. The sobs returned. Stop it! she thought fiercely, hiccuping. But she could not stop. As she cried, she caught herself rubbing at the itchy line on her wrist. She stared with revulsion at the thin white scar. It seemed to wiggle and blur. The cut was almost healed now, the blood safely sealed back up inside. She shuddered. How could she ever have done such a thing? *Gesture*, that was the word Dr. Valois had used: a suicidal gesture. How she had hated that word, with it's implication that she hadn't really been serious about killing herself. But Valois had been so right. Look at her now. How precious life suddenly seemed.

The door to the cell opened. She turned and saw Chuck

Conroy backing in. He was pulling a medical gurney with straps hanging from the sides.

"Hello, Meg."

She made a furious effort to choke off her tears. She would *not* let Chuck see her like this. "Let me go," she said. "I won't tell anyone, I promise."

"We're going to give you something for the pain now. Come on, onto the gurney."

Something for the pain. Need swelled in her. To lose the pain—oh yes, please! If she could kill the pain, then she might have a chance against Chuck. She let him help her from the table onto the gurney. As she lay back, he gripped her smashed elbow and she screamed. Blackness lapped at her eyes. She gritted her teeth and hung on. Pain rebounded through her, making her sick to her stomach; Meg clamped her jaws to keep from throwing up.

"Sorry."

His voice seemed to come from very far away. Dimly she felt a sudden constriction across her chest and thighs and realized he was strapping her down.

"Why?" she sobbed. *Damn* him, he'd made her cry again.

"Don't worry. They're just safety belts. The bed's pretty narrow, and we don't want you rolling off while I'm wheeling you around. Relax, Meg. Everything's going to be just fine."

Something in his tone terrified her. He was lying. She could not stop the sobs. Her eyes stung with tears and her throat was hot. Dimly, she saw the arched door slide past over her head and then they were in a hallway. The concrete ceiling above her was braced every few feet with thick steel beams. She smelled mildew; the gurney passed under a stained section of concrete, and she realized that they were underground.

"Wh-what is this p-place?"

"Don't worry."

Dread mushroomed inside her. This was all wrong. She was supposed to go back to college, see her friends, her parents. She wanted to graduate and get a job—a career job, for the first time in her life—and buy a car.

She strained against the straps, gasping at the fierce pain that flared in her elbow. The foot of the table bumped something; she saw two steel doors fanning aside as the cart passed through. A blurred green shape swung into view. She pinched her eyes shut and shook her head, trying to throw off the tears. The shape came closer. She saw that it was a man dressed in green surgeon's clothes.

They're going to cut me!

Desperate strength surged through her. She thrashed against the restraints, barely feeling the pain in her elbow. The straps held her tight. She lay back, gasping. Her eyes were suddenly dry and cold, her throat so parched she could barely swallow. Her mind spun with terror.

Behind the surgeon she saw a sink like the ones they washed your hair in at the beauty parlor. The image jarred her, refusing to add up. What were they going to do to her? Who was the man in surgeon's clothes? Did she know him? She had to make contact somehow, make him listen.

"Please," she rasped, "Who are you?"

The man did not answer. She stared at his face, but all she could see between the mask and cap were his eyes. They seemed familiar. She fought the straps again, feeling them bite into her, holding her fast. The swaddled head bent over her, terrible eyes gazing into hers, the pupils small as pencil points.

"I'm sorry. Get her in position." The mask muffled the man's voice; she could not recognize it.

"No, listen to me, *listen*—"

The cart swung in a dizzying half circle and Meg felt a jolt above her head. Chuck pulled her up along the gurney, grasping her elbow again, not letting go even when she screamed at the pain. Dimly, she felt the back of her head bang against the hard front of the sink. A surgery light blazed on above her face, dazzling chrome, half blinding her. Fingers twined into her hair, pulling her head out and supporting it above the sink.

The man in surgical dress leaned over her once more, and the eyes winced. "I'm sorry, Meg," he said, "but we can't do it any other way. Your sacrifice will count. I'll see to it, I promise you."

"Don't, DON'T—" She heard a sudden, high-pitched whine, steady and mechanical. Panic tore through her in cold waves. She screamed, out of control.

"Hold still!" the man shouted. "HOLD STILL OR IT WILL HURT MORE!"

But she could not hold still. She bucked and jerked on the cart. Hot wires of pain stabbed from the roots of her hair. She couldn't shake free. *Oh, please, dear Jesus!* She tried to scream again; a powerful jolt of pain ripped through her body, a million volts of her in one final flash and then Meg was gone.

5

SHARON PEDALED toward the hospital, enjoying a delicious sense of freedom. The street stretched before her, open and fresh in the pink dawn. In another hour the morning rush would choke the pavement in both directions, but now Washington was all hers. She steered down the middle, fantasizing that she was the first, that no one had ever ridden there before her.

From the corner of her eye she saw the sun, red and hazy, swelling up above the roofline of the row houses on Michigan Avenue. There wasn't a breath of wind. She pedaled faster, creating the illusion of a breeze as she plowed through the still air. But the false wind was too warm and the extra effort brought a prickle of sweat to her forehead. She eased up again. It was going to be another of those beastly "three H" days—hazy, hot, and humid.

She thought of Meg. Still no messages from Meg's father. Sharon had a bad feeling about it. Too much time had passed. If Meg were going to show up or call, she would probably have done it by now.

Something bad had happened—she knew it. A chill rippled through Sharon, tingling unpleasantly under the heat of her skin. You *can't* know it, she told herself.

But the sense of foreboding persisted.

Why hadn't Dr. Valois tried harder to keep Meg in

MHU? Valois could have stalled her while he tried for an emergency commitment order based on her being a clear danger to herself. Maybe he hadn't believed Meg would really kill herself. That would be violating one of the cardinal rules of treating "suicidal" patients. Therapists did it, of course, and sometimes it was justified. But knowing when to gamble—that was the rub. By letting Meg leave, Valois was playing chicken, betting that she wouldn't head for the nearest tall bridge.

It was starting to look like a very bad bet. The fact that Meg had vanished without a word and had been gone so long made suicide the number one probability. Her body might be floating in some backwater of the Potomac right now.

Or she might have been murdered.

Sharon remembered the roar of the car accelerating behind her and shuddered. The feel of Mark's gun came back to her, its hard pressure between them as they had danced last night. A police chief. Maybe he could get the D.C. police moving on Meg. And while I'm at it, Sharon thought, I could ask him about the flashbulb creep.

Right. After the way I ducked out on him last night, I'm sure he would be overjoyed at a chance to help me hassle the Washington PD. And if I, a psychiatric resident, have no clue why someone would want a picture of me falling off a bike, what could Mark add?

Sharon pedaled into the hospital parking lot, feeling stymied, suddenly eager to give her mind over to her morning routine. In her office she changed into her dress, hoping Austin wouldn't come in early. She put coffee on and picked up her library book on primate brain biochemistry. A note fluttered off the top of the book: *Please see me when you get in—Grant Pendleton.*

Sharon looked at the note with mixed emotions. Pendleton probably wanted to have one of his fatherly chats: how are things going, are you getting enough rest, so on. Nice, but not before her morning coffee. She checked her watch:

7:00. She wasn't due on MHU until eight. She looked hopefully at the Norelco, but the water was just starting to trickle through. Another few minutes, at least.

She marched herself out before the first whiffs of brewed coffee could destroy all reason. At least Pendleton was close by, thanks to the new breezeway that had been built between psych services and the research labs. If Pendleton was brief she could still get back in time for a boost of caffeine.

Hurrying across the breezeway, she kept looking up, wishing they hadn't run the glass walls right to the floor. Jeff liked to gaze down the six stories to the concrete alley, but it made her dizzy. Safely enclosed again in the research annex, she decided to cut through the oncology lab and save half a minute. That meant going through the dog quarters. She tried slipping in quietly, but the door squeaked and twenty beagles yammered in welcome. She hurried through, wincing as the yelps tore along her uncaffeinated nerves. This better be good, Pendleton.

She found him in his lab, puttering with some petrie dishes. He looked up. "Sharon! Good to see you. Thanks for stopping by." He smiled happily, as though the sight of her had just made his day.

How could you be mad at the man?

"I really enjoyed your party," she told him.

"Oh, good, good. Glad you came."

Sharon followed him into his office, marveling at the spring in his step. By the time she had left the party last night, his eyes had been bloodshot and droopy. He had looked unsteady pushing himself up from his lawn chair when she'd gone to say good night. Apparently he approved of his champagne too.

But he had got himself back together pretty well this morning.

"Sit," he said, settling on the other side of his desk. "I wanted to talk to you about one of my patients who's in your pain group," he said. "Mr. Greene."

She nodded. "He's responding very well to group therapy. He's also beginning to reach out to one of the other patients, a young guy who's very hostile."

"Yes, but don't you think it's strange that Greene's still complaining of back pain? I operated on him nearly four months ago. We've had him back as an inpatient for three days now. I've gone over him with a fine-toothed comb, every test in the book. Results: nada. Damn it, there's no way that man should still be feeling pain. I wonder if he's a hysteric." Pendleton eyed Sharon. "What do you think?"

I think you just put me on the hot seat. She hesitated, searching for the right words. It was unusual for a man to become a hysteric; more often they were women. But Pendleton must know that; he wouldn't need her to point it out. The problem was that if she said she thought Frank Greene wasn't a hysteric, she would be saying that Pendleton's surgery on him was a failure; if she agreed, she was hanging a very sticky label on Frank. For many of the hospital staff, *hysteria* was just a fancy word for faking. Once patients got tagged with that, they would either be discharged, or passed from department to department, often patronized or humiliated, and rarely helped.

"I don't think he's a hysteric," Sharon said.

Pendleton frowned. "So why is he still in pain?"

Eeeee, she thought. *Don't do this to me.* "Dr. Pendleton, if Frank's pain has you baffled, think what it does to me."

Pendleton laughed. "Damn it, Sharon. For a second-year resident, you're picking up the game fast. You manage to drop it back in my lap and butter me up in the same breath. But I don't buy it. I've examined Greene over and over. I find no inflammation, no structural damage. I think we need a more frankly psychiatric approach—" Pendleton looked nonplussed, then grinned. "If you'll pardon the pun. Anyway, I'm going to transfer Frank to MHU this morning."

Sharon could not keep her dismay from her face.

"Don't get me wrong, Sharon," Pendleton said. "I'm

sure you've done all anyone could do, treating him in pain group. But this way Frank can stay in the hospital a few extra days. Otherwise, we can't keep him here. I've done all I can for him. I want Valois to evaluate him, and we'll take it from there."

Valois. Nod, she thought. Accept it. "Okay, Dr. Pendleton, but I still think we should keep him in the pain group, let him continue through the MHU evaluation and then as an outpatient. As I said, Frank's become a key member. That young guy he's starting to help—" She stopped, realizing suddenly that Brian had quit group. She had no idea whether he would show up again tonight or not.

Pendleton stood, and her heart sank. She had lost.

"I'm sorry, Sharon. I admire the way you're fighting for what you think is right. But you've got to see my side of it, too. It's my duty to make Frank my primary consideration and to do what's best for him. I'm sure someone else in the group will come forward to help your difficult patient." Pendleton took her arm and ushered her to the door, chatting about the party, thanking her for coming.

On the way back to her office, Sharon tried to be philosophical. Despite what had just happened, Dr. Pendleton was on her side, the best friend she had among the ruling clique of the hospital.

Still, she felt he was wrong about Frank Greene.

Back at her office, she pulled up short, startled. Dr. Jenkins was kneeling on the floor, rummaging through the bottom drawer of her file. He seemed startled, too, reaching for his cane, struggling up to face her.

"This file is a mess," he said crossly.

Good morning to you, too, she thought, irked. And what are you doing in my files? She caught herself. These were *not* her files, they were hospital files. A lot of the stuff in them had been there when she came. When she left, the files would stay.

And this was psychology services, Jenkins's turf. Furthermore, even though Jenkins was a psychologist, not a psychiatrist, he still happened to be one of her clinical supervisors. Which meant he had a right to check up on her, to come in here if he wanted and rummage all he pleased.

But it was still a sneaky and underhanded thing to do.

"Can I help you find something?" she said.

"From the condition of these files, I doubt it."

"They're just the rough drafts of our patient intakes," Sharon said. "We keep the final reports in—"

"I know quite well what they are," Jenkins said. "Not very important, perhaps, but what if you need to go back and double-check a datum in your final copy? If you're going to keep these roughs at all, you should be professional enough to keep them in good order, alphabetically filed."

A datum? Sharon's annoyance faded. She had to struggle to keep her face straight.

Jenkins turned, pivoting on his cane, and limped out. Poor guy; the leg must be bothering him today. He wasn't really the curmudgeonly twit he sometimes seemed to be.

Sharon had a sudden brainstorm: Frank Greene was in pain group, which made him Jenkins's patient, too. Jenkins was head of psychology services. Maybe he had the clout to keep Frank Greene out of MHU—

Yeah, and if she sicced Jenkins on the case, it sure wouldn't endear her to Dr. Pendleton. In fact, it might seriously strain their good relationship.

But damn it, Frank didn't deserve the rough time he was going to get once he got tagged as a faker.

Sharon hurried after Jenkins, catching him down the hall. She told him about Frank and asked him if psych could at least override Pendleton on the issue of keeping Frank in group. Jenkins leaned on his cane, giving her a look of strained patience. "Let me enlighten you, Sharon," he said when she had finished. "Psychology services is a very recent addition to this hospital's program. There were . . . elements here that did not want us in the first place, elements that continue to maneuver against our very existence."

Dr. Valois, she thought.

Her spirits sank. Of course. Jenkins and the other psychologists at Adams Memorial basically did two things: psychological testing and therapy. Valois had nothing that she knew of against psych testing. But he considered psychotherapy to be useless in combating schizophrenia. So how must Valois feel about psychology services, who treated nonhospitalized schizophrenics on an outpatient basis? By training, psychologists were Ph.D.s, not M.D.s, and they did not prescribe drugs. The treatment they gave their schizophrenic outpatients was psychotherapy.

"I have to think of all our patients," Jenkins went on, "not just one. Maybe I could win this battle for Greene, but if it set my department back with neurology and psychiatry, it could hamstring me on dozens of future cases."

"So you go down without firing a shot, and Mr. Greene is the one who pays."

Jenkins stared stonily at her, and she knew she had gone too far. "Are you sure, Sharon, that Mr. Greene is the one you're concerned about? Or is it that you can't stand the thought of Dr. Valois taking over one of your patients?"

Damn it, that was unfair.

No it wasn't. "It's both," she said, flushing.

His face softened a little. "Right," he said. "I understand." He hobbled off down the hall.

Gee, thanks.

Sharon stood there, feeling very dejected. Any time now they would be taking Mr. Greene over to MHU. As soon as Pendleton said go, Frank would go. Not many people, especially if they were hospitalized, had the self-confidence or the guts to defy their physicians.

No doubt they'd push Frank over in the inevitable wheelchair, making him feel helpless and dependant. Then Frank would sit in his room or on the ward commons, hurt and confused, unnerved by the idea that his doctor thought he was some kind of mental case. After a while, one of the psychologists, maybe even Jenkins, would come over and administer the Minnesota Multiphasic Personality Inventory. Frank would have to answer endless true- or false-type statements like "I sometimes experience difficulties with my bowel movements," and "My mother sometimes made me go to school when I was sick." He would keep seeing the same statements, reworded, as though he could be fooled so easily into thinking they were different. Maybe he would be indignant, but it would do him no good. By tonight, he would be depressed and afraid.

At least the pain group would have given him a lifeline back into the real world. All the other members, except possibly Brian, liked him. They had given him lots of support—

Sharon cut herself off. Pain group was out. Frank was going to be in MHU, and there wasn't a thing she could do about it.

Except visit him. The thought cheered her a little. Tonight, she decided. I'll go straight there after pain group.

After group, Brian stood in the dim, deserted hallway of physical therapy and waited for Sharon. His head throbbed, and his chest was tight with rage. If he had known she was going to be such a bitch tonight, he wouldn't have come back to group. She had done something different, he couldn't figure out what. But it had been the worst group session ever. At least that Frank guy wasn't there leaning on him, getting on his nerves. That should have made things better, but it hadn't.

In fact, he'd actually missed the old bastard.

Wasn't that a hoot!

Brian peered up the darkened corridor. What was keeping her? She always came out this way after group.

He fumed. The way she'd acted tonight, so cool and collected, always giving him the soft answer, trying to act as if he didn't repulse her. That made him the maddest. As if he couldn't tell. Inside, she thought he was just a beefy slob, an overgrown kid with a potbelly and pimples. He turned her off, and she didn't even have the honesty to let it show. For that, he really hated her.

Well, I've got pieces of you already, sweetheart, he thought. When I go home tonight, I'm going to look at your face and fuck you. And you'll be terrified of me. It's right there in the pictures. Terrified, and nothing you can do about it.

But first I'm going to see you in the flesh, just you and me, right here. I'll tell you how I hated group and watch your face and that will make it better tonight. So come on, come on. Don't keep me waiting.

He stared up the hall, feeling the beat in his head, the anticipatory swell between his legs. But Sharon did not come. At last he gave up and went home to the pictures.

Sharon stared at Nurse Taylor, stunned. "What did you say?"

"I said Mr. Greene has had a breakdown. He's back there in seclusion." Taylor's round, patient face was touched with sympathy, and Sharon realized how her own face must look. "I'm sorry," Taylor went on, "but Dr. Valois said no visitors."

Sharon felt sick. She should have tried harder. Fought harder. "What kind of breakdown?"

The nurse hesitated.

"C'mon, Mrs. Taylor. He's my patient too. You can check his chart if you like. I have him in group."

"Well, you *did* have him, I know. But the chart says that's terminated." She looked apologetic. "Oh, hell. The preliminary diagnosis is paranoid schizophrenia."

A shock went through Sharon. "But . . . he's sixty."

"It happens," the nurse said sadly.

Yeah, it happened. The window in the mid- to late twenties for adult onset schizophrenia was only a set of probabilities. It could crawl into a person at any age. Sharon felt a little pulse of fear in her stomach.

"Can I at least see his chart?"

"Sorry, no can do. Not without Dr. Valois's permission." Taylor frowned at her watch. "Oh, that Chuck. I sent him off to the pharmacy and he's been gone an age. I'd better call down there." She picked up the phone and turned away.

She's giving me a chance, Sharon thought. Her heart speeded up. She walked away quickly, across the commons toward the staff entrance in back—and the seclusion room. Halfway across, she glanced back at the nurses' station. Mrs. Taylor was still on the phone, her back turned, her voice silenced by the glass. Bars of yellow light dropped through the windows and stretched along the darkened floor toward Sharon. The station reminded her suddenly of a squat guard tower in some surreal prison. The hateful image chilled her. Come on, she told herself, it's normal. There probably isn't a staffer here who doesn't loathe the place every now and then.

But she knew she couldn't afford to, not when she was going to be in places like this the rest of her life. One way or the other, doctor or patient, this was where the war would be fought.

Sharon turned from the nurses' station and headed for the seclusion room. Using her key, she slipped inside, leaving the door slightly ajar. Moonlight poured through the wire mesh window, illuminating the padded walls and floor, the bare sink and toilet in the corner, the mattress along one wall. Frank was lying in the middle of the padded floor, his sheet pulled around him. His eyes were open and he looked rigid. For a minute he seemed not to see her, then he scrambled to his knees, the sheet draped over his back. Sharon raised a finger to her lips. He gave a jerky nod, but his eyes stared at her like a wild man's.

"Help me, Dr. Francis," he croaked.

She heard the snick of a key slipping into the staff entrance door outside in the commons. Her heart began to pound, but then she realized it was probably just Chuck, back from the pharmacy.

Frank reached a hand out to her. She took it and squeezed.

"They poisoned me," Frank said. "I'm not really crazy."

She tried to keep her dismay from her face. There it was—the paranoia. "Frank, they'll take good care of you. As soon as you stabilize, they'll put you in a regular room. I work up here on the ward, you know. I won't be your doctor, but I'll be seeing you. For now, just try and relax as much as you can."

The door to the seclusion room creaked open behind her. She turned, but it was not Chuck. It was Dr. Valois.

The air froze in Sharon's lungs. She stared at Valois, appalled. Jesus. What the hell was he doing here? He was going to kill her for this!

Valois stared back at her. "Good evening, Dr. Francis," he said in a soft voice. "May I see you in my office, please."

6

SHARON COULDN'T quite get her breath as she followed Dr. Valois across the commons. Her hands felt cold. Her mind slipped and slid with fright. Dear God, Valois had cut her off from the patients she wanted most to work with just for expressing an opinion he didn't like. What was he going to do to her now?

Damn it, she thought, what is he *doing* here so late at night? An emergency appointment? Peachy luck for me.

"I know you're out there."

The sudden, low voice startled Sharon. It came from the room they were passing, an old woman's voice, trembling at the bottom of its range. The fear in it made her skin crawl. Valois did not react, but suddenly Sharon had to pick up her pace to stay close to him. She followed him past the nurses' station into the short hallway leading to the offices and front exit. After Dr. Valois passed, Mrs. Taylor made a sympathetic face, so lugubrious that a snicker shot up in Sharon's throat. She choked it off, feeling an icy rush along her nerves. You didn't laugh at Louis Valois, in panic or otherwise.

God, she really detested being this scared!

Valois stood aside at his office door, motioning her in ahead of him. He sat behind his desk in his huge, chairman-of-the-board swivel chair. Settling back, he locked his hands behind his head and gazed at her. There was a posed quality to it, like a peacock spreading its tail. As usual, he looked elegant—blue pin-striped suit tonight, with cream shirt and a red tie. The sharp tailoring took away ten or more of his fifty years. His thick dark hair was slicked straight back, gleaming wetly with tonic. Not many men looked good with their hair combed that way, but Valois did—an Arab sheikh with a French name and suits to match. Sharon noticed laugh wrinkles around his eyes and was surprised. Probably got them pulling the wings off flies.

The silence stretched and her nerves began to twang. Her calves were still sore from the workout; she really needed to sit down. Come on, she thought, *say* something. Instead, he let his gaze drop to her body. He stared for a long time at her chest. Anger boiled up inside her.

"You don't think much of authority, do you, Sharon?" He was looking at her face again.

"I try to give authority the respect it deserves."

She saw his expression tighten and knew he was weighing her answer for signs of disrespect, finding nothing he could be sure of. It gave her a small satisfaction, then she caught herself: Jesus, don't try to top him.

"Didn't Nurse Taylor tell you that I'd ordered no visitors for Mr. Greene?"

"Yes. I reminded her that Mr. Greene is my patient."

Valois sniffed. "Sharon, you are a resident; I am your chief. No patients are assigned to you without my say-so. By the same token, if I want to take a patient away from you, I do it. I have taken Mr. Greene away from you."

For a second she disliked him so much that it made her faintly sick. "I have no authority, Dr. Valois. I realize that. But I can still disagree."

"Do you think that entitles you to defy my medical orders."

"No. I'm sorry."

Her apology seemed to catch him off balance, but he said, "I'm afraid sorry's not good enough."

She felt a chill. What *would* be good enough? Her dismissal? "Dr. Valois, would you tell me why you've taken Mr. Greene away from me."

"Frank Greene is suffering from paranoid schizophrenia. That means that for quite some time to come he is not going to be participating in a group—which I do not consider to be adequate therapy in any case." Valois spoke carefully, as though he were explaining something to a child.

"Do you consider it process or reactive schizophrenia?"

"That is not your concern. Since Mr. Greene is no longer your patient, telling you the details of his condition would violate his right to privacy." Valois gave her a pious smile.

"Please, Dr. Valois. I worked with Frank for several months. I came to like him very much, and to care about him. I only want to know—" She stopped, realizing how it would sound.

Annoyance flashed in Valois's eyes. "I know perfectly well what you want to know. You want to know if the shock of being sent to MHU might have precipitated this crisis in Mr. Greene. But if you were any good, you'd already know the answer to that question. As you say, you had him for several months."

Bastard! She kept her voice calm. "I saw no signs of schizophrenia during the time I treated him, Dr. Valois."

He gave her a cold smile. "I'm not sure what that proves."

Her face burned. She was playing straight man for him, and he was loving it. I will not hate you, she told herself. It's too much trouble. "Frank seemed very well adjusted."

"To you, perhaps. I'm sure you didn't want him evaluated here in MHU. You were perfectly sure—no doubt because of your instinct, or perhaps your feminine intuition— that this nice man you liked and cared about couldn't be a hysteric."

"I think you're being unfair," she said as evenly as she could.

"Is that so?" Valois said with perfect indifference.

73

"First you make sure I don't get assigned to any of the schizophrenics in your ward, even though you know very well that's who I most want to treat. Then one of my patients suffers a schizophrenic breakdown, and you immediately write an order keeping me from seeing him."

Valois raised his manicured hands in a gesture of innocence. "You're beginning to sound paranoid yourself, Sharon. That order doesn't single you out; it includes everyone. Mr. Greene is very agitated right now, and I don't want him disturbed."

"Off the record, what do you have against me?"

Valois steepled his fingers and sat for a long moment, as if considering. "Sharon, I've got nothing against you as a human being. In fact, you're an attractive young woman. Very attractive. But I wouldn't be much of a psychiatrist if I didn't know why you're so interested in schizophrenia. You're *too* interested. Science is rational, not emotional. Bleeding through the nose and mouth for our patients does not help them. Logical and dispassionate application of good medical practice does. Schizophrenia is just a disease, not a diabolical entity. But you seem to think you're some kind of secular exorcist. I don't want anyone with a personal vendetta against schizophrenia messing with my patients."

She was almost relieved. There it was. It wasn't just that she had voiced an opinion he didn't like. It was something deeper that Valois, in his infinite clinical wisdom, thought he had divined in her. Now maybe they could deal with it. "I'm neither ashamed nor proud of my personal reasons for being interested in schizophrenia," she said. "They exist, yes, but please don't judge me by them. When I was a medical student, I co-authored two published papers on attentional processes in hospitalized schizophrenics. If you want to assess my logic and passion, I'd prefer you look there."

When Valois tried to cover his look of surprise, she realized she had scored. Of course, he wouldn't know about the papers. Her psychiatry professor's name appeared first on both articles, and neither had been accepted for publication until after she had already gone through the application process at Adams. It gave her a fierce satisfaction to be able to pop it on him here and now.

"Very impressive," he said stiffly. "Especially for one so young. But I'm afraid my reading has suffered lately. I've been rather busy writing articles myself."

"I know."

"You've read one of my articles?"

"All twenty-nine of them."

"Really." His voice sounded suspicious. "What did you think of the one in last June's *Psychiatric Medicine*?"

She smiled to herself at his transparent attempt to test her. "Beautifully written."

He nodded cynically.

"But I'd have been happier to see a larger test group. It's hard to tell much from only ten subjects. Also, I wondered why you didn't set up a blind, so you wouldn't know which subjects were getting the placebo and which the Haldol."

He frowned. "It was only a pilot study. I thought I made that clear in the article."

"It was a very interesting study," she added hastily. "I admire the reasoning behind it." She hoped that did not sound too insincere. The fact was, it was true. In spite of everything he'd said and done to her, she knew she could learn from Valois—if only he would let her.

"Yes, well. Thank you. But this isn't getting the matter before us resolved, is it?"

She realized with relief that the chilling malice was gone from his voice. Maybe he would listen to her now, just a little. "Dr. Valois, I do apologize for what I did. All I can say is, it came out of my concern for my—for someone who had been my patient, and not out of any desire to defy you. In fact, I'd be very happy to be under your supervision on this case."

"Out of the question."

"How about at least letting me monitor the chart as you go along. That way I could learn—"

"No."

"Might I at least review the chart up to this point?"

"You may not." Valois seemed exasperated. "Mr. Greene's chart is strictly confidential. If you had been able to contain yourself tonight, I might have okayed that request. But as things stand, no. Be thankful that's the only action I'm going to take."

Sharon felt a mixture of relief and frustration. She wanted badly to get a look at that record, see if there *was* anything she should have seen, some sign that poor Frank was headed for a breakdown. But Valois was cutting her off again.

"I warn you, Sharon; leave Mr. Greene alone. Cross me again and it won't go so easy for you."

The phone on Valois's desk rang. He snatched up the receiver. "Yes? Oh, right." He looked across at her. "No, take them to the conference room. Do it right away, please, Mrs. Taylor. Yes, I understand. Tell them I'll be right with them."

Sharon got up and went to the door, turning as he hung up, knowing he would expect her to thank him. Being cut off from Frank Greene was bad, but it wasn't as bad as what he might have done. "Dr. Valois, I appreciate your kindness, and—"

"No you don't," he said. "I'll be watching you."

Outside in the hall, she saw Mrs. Taylor showing a middle-aged couple into the conference room. The woman said something to the nurse. That voice . . . it was Meg's mother!

So that was why Valois had come in so late.

Had Meg come home? Sharon felt a sudden lift. Why else would her parents want to talk to her therapist? If Meg had come back, they would need to discuss issues like readmission, or how to handle her at home.

The door to the conference room shut firmly behind

them. Sharon gazed at it, sorely tempted. Why not? She would only listen for a second, just long enough to find out if Meg was back.

Sharon put her ear to the door. She could hear Mrs. Andreason speaking, but her words were muffled by the door, sounds hanging just at the edge of meaning. There was a noticeable gap between the bottom of the door and the doorsill. Sharon crouched down; her heart began to hammer. This was crazy—what if someone opened the door, or came down the hall?

She took her pen from her jacket pocket and placed it on the floor by the door. The hall lighting was dim; now someone might buy her being on her hands and knees. It would have to do.

She leaned down close to the wide gap.

". . . very upset by this, Doctor," Mr. Andreason was saying.

"I can understand that," Valois said in a soothing voice. "But I'm sure you can understand that I have a duty to cooperate with the police."

"What about your duty to Meg?"

"I take that very seriously too, of course," Valois said more stiffly.

"Well, surely you should have known that if you told them she'd run away once before, they'd immediately write her off as a runaway and stop looking for her."

Valois, you weasel! Sharon thought as she realized what he had done.

"I'd think that fact would reassure you," Valois said. "Truth is, it makes it much more likely that this unfortunate—this terrible ordeal you're going through will end happily. Past behavior is the best predictor of future behavior. If you can believe that she's simply run away—"

"She was only fourteen when she did that," Mrs. Andreason snapped. "She was upset because we'd grounded her for a week. She was only gone overnight; she stayed with one of her friends. When she saw how frantic it made us, she cried and promised never to do it again, and she never did. If I'd known it would be used against her like this, I never would have mentioned it when you people were taking all that information in the beginning. . . ."

A door opened just around the corner: the nurses' station. Sharon sprang up with alarm, but Mrs. Taylor's footsteps clacked away into the ward commons. Sharon picked up her pen with a shaking hand and walked the other way, to the front exit, her mind racing. She had heard enough. Meg was still gone.

And Dr. Valois had practically guaranteed that no one was going to look for her.

Sharon slept badly and came in the next morning with a mild headache, which got worse when she discovered Frank was still in seclusion. She popped two aspirin and checked the on-call schedule for last night: Dr. Wallace. She found Brittina in the staff rest room, rinsing her face.

"Hi," Sharon said. "Any problems with Frank last night?"

Brittina gave her a blank look, face dripping.

"The guy in seclusion."

"Oh," Brittina said. "Mr. Greene. No problems, no. But he is still hallucinating, and the man is *very* paranoid." Brittina looked in the mirror and winced. "I don't suppose you have any flesh-colored makeup."

Sharon groaned. "Come on, Wallace, I'm not touching that with a ten-foot pole."

Brittina laughed. "Just a joke, Francis. Sometimes I think *all* you white folks are paranoid." She turned back to the mirror and pinched her smooth ebony cheeks. Sharon wondered what she could possibly be worried about—she looked fantastic.

"You say paranoid. What was the content?"

"Oh, the usual stuff. That someone was drugging him, that he wasn't really crazy and he didn't belong here. Some vitamin H mellowed him out a little."

Haldol, Sharon thought and felt a twinge of irritation at Brittina for dosing Frank. She got hold of herself. If Brittina had done it, it must have been necessary. Poor Frank!

"He started in on me again every time I checked him," Brittina added. "Jeez, I'll be glad when we're R-3s and switch to daytime call. Listen, nudge me if I pass out in morning report."

Sharon checked her watch. "Speaking of report . . ."

After the morning report she went to support group, then supervision, then substance abuse group, chart dictation, and spent an hour priming her medical student, Jack Conklin, who was presenting in walk rounds. During the rounds themselves, with the other R-2s watching and asking questions, Sharon felt more nervous than if she was the one standing up front. But Jack did just fine, and she was able to let her mind go back to Valois, and Frank and Meg. Something wasn't quite right, she could smell it. If she could just have half an hour to sit down and think about it.

Maybe if she skipped supper.

Rounds ended and Sharon checked on all her patients and charted, then ran to the training seminar to hear Dr. Choate, an expert in schizophrenia from the Menninger Clinic.

Afterward, when the other R-2s headed for the caf, she mumbled excuses and veered off to her office. Closing the door, she flopped into her chair. Alone at last! She sat, waiting for her muscles to melt into the chair. Her lungs felt bloated, as if a day's worth of air was pent up in them. She let out a long sigh, rolling her head on her shoulders.

Okay, Valois. What is it with you, Vally, old boy? First you let Meg out without a fight, even though she's in for a suicide attempt, then you undermine any decent search by telling the police she's probably a runaway.

Then you get Frank as a patient and the next day Frank suffers a full-blown psychosis.

Sharon felt her mind slipping into focus. The fact that

Frank's condition seemed so advanced was the biggest thing that felt wrong. With schizophrenia there were usually warning signs for weeks or months, even years. But not with Frank. Not in all the time she had known him, six weeks of group.

And I ought to know the signs, Sharon thought.

All right, she knew the signs, but she couldn't be sure about Frank. Not unless she had a chance to go back over his chart. There could have been little indications that Frank had not exhibited around her, or that she had missed, things charted by nursing or PT.

But Valois had expressly forbidden her to review the chart.

Sharon chewed at the end of her pencil. Was something going awry up in MHU? Something with Dr. Louis Valois at its center?

Her door opened and Austin slouched in. "Hi. Guess I'm not hungry enough for the caf either."

Sharon suppressed a groan and picked up some applications for an outpatient group, pretending to work so that he wouldn't try to start up a bull session. She heard a sudden loud volley of squeaks and crunches and had to look up. Austin was chewing his way around an apple. Gross. The apple was wetting his beard, making it more scraggly than usual. It looked really silly beneath his morose, Weltschmerz face.

Sharon gave the sheaf of applications a firm snap, pretending to look at them again, then actually seeing what they were. Oh yeah, the herpes support group Denise wanted to set up in outpatient. It seemed almost quaint. With AIDS on everybody's mind, it was easy to forget the scare just before it—unless you had herpes.

She looked up at Austin again and found him gazing at her. He raised an eyebrow and she quickly broke eye contact. The last thing she needed was Austin trying to draw her into one of his existential discussions on the illicit power of the psychiatrist, or the immorality of selling ersatz friendship under the guise of therapy.

The office door popped open. It was Jeff. Sharon felt a mixture of relief and pleasure.

"May we help you," Austin said a bit frostily.

"Au contraire," Jeff said. "I've come to help you. This office is entirely too small for two people. Alas, I can only take one of you to dinner." Jeff gave Austin a judicious look. "If you were me, which one would you ask?"

Austin flushed and looked at Sharon.

"Her?" Jeff said. "I agree. Sharon, how about it?"

"Can't," she said with real regret.

Jeff looked shocked. "You would deprive this man of the extra space? And think of his mental health. One gets very tense when one has to sit in a room with another person and act normal. With you gone, he could eat Gummi Bears instead of that apple, or sit around making silly faces."

Dinner, Sharon thought. The idea was tantalizing. Jeff had kept himself pretty scarce lately, and she missed him, his banter, his *interest*. Even if it couldn't lead to anything.

"Okay," she said, and was glad at once. His pleased grin made her feel even better.

On the way out Jeff closed the door behind them, then whipped it open again. Austin was looking at them cross-eyed, with a finger up one nostril. Sharon started to laugh, then saw Austin's embarrassed flush and waited until Jeff and she were safely on the elevator. She said, "I've never seen Austin act silly before."

"He wouldn't let you. He's in love with you."

"Get out of here," she said, astonished. "You don't even know him."

"No, but I know you."

She felt a warm rush of pleasure, and then the old automatic warning mechanism kicked in. Careful, Sharon. It's just dinner. Keep it that way.

In the grand old Buick she relaxed a little, snuggling back into the leather seat, watching out the window as Jeff drove down Capitol Street. The Capitol dome was barely visible from so high up the long slope of the city. It looked a thousand miles away, dwarfed by run-down brownstones, crumbling vistas of brick, harsh orange under the anticrime streetlights. Black kids stood around on the corners looking bored and hopeless. Their frustration penetrated the polished glass of the car window, eating at her. She, too, came from the other side of this glass. They were black and she was white, but she and they were all poor as hell, and that made her a lot more like them than like the man she was riding with.

What was she doing, cruising along with this rich guy?

On the other hand, why be prejudiced?

Jeff drove them south to Constitution and turned west along the broad, straight avenue. She watched, enjoying the awesome view. The curbs were lined with trees, beyond which the federal buildings rose in white-columned splendor. As they passed the towering white spire of the Washington Monument, Jeff said, "what would Freud say about that?"

"Don't drop it on your foot."

He laughed. "Coward."

In Georgetown, the sidewalks in front of the shops teemed with tourists, and kids with purple spiked hair, starving for a little recognition. Jeff drove uphill into the tree-lined streets where stately houses elbowed each other over narrow strips of grass or cobbled alleys. He gave her his own personal tour, pointing out the walled mansions of the great, wealthy families of Washington, the pied-à-terre where an ambitious but reckless congressman had traded a night of sex for his shot at the presidency; the unassuming brownstone that had been a KGB safe house.

Sharon made the appropriate comments, thinking instead of the houses surrounding the famous ones, the elegant homes with quieter, private histories, where the families of the merely rich had nestled together in warmth and security. What would it have been like to grow up in

one of those houses? One with a back staircase and maids'
quarters, twin parlors and a vast dining room with glittering
chandeliers. Where Father stayed with Mother, and no one
ever got sick or depressed. Where even the maid was happy.

And I'm making myself depressed, Sharon thought.

"Egad!" Jeff shouted. "A parking place on P Street!" He
squeezed the Buick into a space that looked barely large
enough for a Nissan. Taking Sharon's arm, he pulled her
along to a bright awning displaying the name MORTON'S
in tasteful black letters. Her mouth watered suddenly in anticipation. She had heard of this place—aged prime beef,
great cellar, expensive as hell. Jeff wasn't just kidding
around tonight.

Inside it was cool and bright, all noise and good cheer,
with colorful Leroy Nieman prints and portraits of various
Kennedys on the walls. Coatless young waiters and wait-
resses dodged each other between widely spaced tables. Jeff
urged her to go for broke, but she ordered a filet mignon
and no side dishes. After a steady diet of plain pasta at
home, too much rich food all at once would make her sick.
Jeff ordered a Haut-Médoc to go with the steaks.

Was this how people like Jeff ate all the time?

"You look kind of pensive," he said.

"I've had some weird stuff on my mind," she said. She
told him about Meg and then about Frank.

He laughed. "I love it. Valois is making people disappear
and poisoning his own patients."

Sharon started to get annoyed. He wasn't taking her seriously. He saw her expression and held up his hands. "No,
no. I've felt for a long time that something wasn't quite
right about that man. For one thing, he doesn't own a
cat—"

"Jeff—"

"Jeffrey!"

Sharon looked up, startled, and saw a short slip of a
woman with a cherubic face leaning over Jeff from behind,

putting her hands on his shoulders. The woman winked at her. "Don't worry, dear, I'm just his momma."

Jeff looked embarrassed and tried to get up.

"Sit. We're just passing through."

Behind Jeff's mother stood a tall man in a sportsjacket. Except for the fact that he was bald, he looked just like Jeff, even to the embarrassed expression. Jeff succeeded, finally, in turning around inside his mother's tight clutches. He kissed her on the cheek and waved to the man behind her. "Mom, Dad, this is Dr. Sharon Francis."

"Pleased to meet you, Mrs. Harrad, Dr. Harrad."

Mrs. Harrad waved Sharon back into her seat and held her hand out. "Call me Alice." Sharon shook hands with her, feeling instantly warmed. Alice Merriweather Harrad was nothing like Sharon had imagined. Dr. Harrad offered his hand too, and she saw how like Jeff's it was, large and long-fingered.

"Oh to be a young resident again," Dr. Harrad said, eyeing her appreciatively.

She smiled. "Why don't you join us?"

"There's nothing I'd like better," Alice said, "but we're headed for a celebration party there in the back room. Jeff's dad teaches at Georgetown Med School. One of his friends over on the history faculty just got tenure. You come see us, Sharon. Don't wait for Jeff—he never comes to see his poor momma." She cuffed Jeff's ear and headed off, Dr. Harrad trailing in her wake.

"Phew!" Jeff rolled his eyes.

"Oh, I *like* them." Sharon felt a lingering glow from the contact. What nice people. Meeting them made her feel that she knew Jeff better.

"Before the human tornado came through, you were talking about Valois," Jeff said. "I wasn't being too helpful. I apologize. Would you like me to kill him for you? Prussic acid would be good. Or I could get some curare."

Sharon smiled despite herself. "Nothing so drastic. Just sneak me a copy of Frank Greene's chart."

"Huh? You're a resident up there, you can look at it any time you want."

"Valois expressly ordered me not to."

Jeff raised an eyebrow. "Hmmm. The plot thickens. Still, you don't have to do everything he says, you know. Especially when he's not around."

"There's always someone around those charts. He made his orders plain to all the nurses too. And anyway, I can't get what I need just by sneaking peeks. I need to really go over it."

Jeff gazed at her, nodding, nodding. "Copy a mental patient's chart and sneak it out of the hospital. Sure, why not? What can they do but kick me out?" He flicked a dismissive hand.

"You're right. Never mind."

"No, I'll get you the chart. But it'll cost you." Jeff gave her his lopsided Indiana Jones grin. He looked positively evil. Sharon felt a stir in her stomach, a hunger that had nothing to do with food. She could almost feel his hand touching her face, stroking her cheek. Her heart started thumping in her chest. *Knock it off!* She imagined herself standing in a cold shower—with all her clothes on. It helped a little.

"I'm broke," she said.

"I'm not talking about money."

The waiter brought the steaks. They were huge and gorgeous, each sizzling in a plate of juice. Sharon forked a tender bite into her mouth, savoring the explosion of flavor. "Ahh-h-h-h. Delicious."

Jeff said, "You gotta come to my beach cottage Saturday."

"Can't, I'm on weekend call." Her mind started to race.

"Get someone to switch with you. You can do that."

She finished chewing, taking her time, stalling. "I didn't know you had a beach cottage." *Think.*

"My folks', actually."

"Would they be there too?"

"Yes," he said. "In spirit."

"I've never had a spirit for a chaperone."

Jeff leaned toward her a little, his eyes narrowing as if he were suddenly concentrating. "Chaperone?"

Sharon felt a little embarrassed, but she was determined not to be put off. He had better understand how things were, and if it sounded juvenile to him, too bad.

"My intentions toward you are entirely pure." His expression was suddenly quite serious. "So pure it worries me. Listen, we'll leave early. I'll get your chart copied and we'll take off. You'll be back before pumpkin hour."

"Okay," she said, and felt butterflies batting about madly in her stomach. Sharon, what are you doing?

I need to study that chart, she told herself stubbornly.

"Great," Jeff said.

For the rest of the meal something new shone in Jeff's eyes. Sharon felt more and more uneasy as he drove her back to the hospital. She had encouraged him, stirred up false hopes in him. And in herself.

As they pulled into the hospital parking lot, Jeff said, "What say we put your bike in the trunk and I take you both home, save you getting run off the road by another crazed sophomore."

Sharon thought of the car bearing down on her, the flash exploding behind the black window and almost said yes. Then the undertone in his voice registered. It would come to asking him up, or keeping clear of it. She wasn't doing too well lately at keeping clear.

"I pass. But thanks for a great dinner."

He got out and stood with her. "Okay, see you Saturday."

She caught sight of Mark Pendleton beyond Jeff's shoulder, striding down the hospital steps, heading straight for them. She had a sinking feeling.

"Sharon—" Mark said. "Oh, Jeff. Hello."

"Mark." Jeff's voice was polite but cool.

"I was hanging around with Pop," Mark said to her. "I decided to drop by your office, but you weren't there."

"She was busy sticking me with the check at Morton's," Jeff said, a trifle too smugly for it to be funny.

Mark gave him a cool smile. "I should have realized such a beautiful woman wouldn't lack for good company."

Jeff gave an ironic little bow.

Their brittle courtliness made Sharon anxious. Any second one of them would take out a glove and whip it across the other's cheek. Beam me up, Scotty.

She turned to Jeff. "Well, thanks a lot."

"Right."

After Jeff had gotten into his car, Mark said, "How about some authentic venison stew Saturday?"

"I'm sorry," she said. "I'm afraid I have plans."

From the corner of her eye, she was acutely aware of Jeff driving off with creeping slowness.

"Another time, then," Mark said.

"Sure." Sharon walked over to her bike, unlocked the chain, and got on.

"Hey, I've got my pickup here. I'd be happy to—"

"Thanks," Sharon said, "But I'd better work off dinner."

"Yes," he said dryly. "Let's get that behind us as quickly as possible."

The presumptuousness of the remark irritated her a bit. But she said good-bye more warmly than she should have, got on her bike, and pedaled hurriedly from the lot, feeling Mark's eyes on her back.

Anxiety welled up, churning in her stomach. Why now? she thought. Not just one guy, but two. I've met other men I knew I could fall for. But I was always able to slip them the message.

Why can't I do it this time?

7

JEFF WAS REACHING for Frank Greene's chart when
he noticed the one just above it: FRANCIS, MRS. ELLEN.
The name leapt out at him through its tab of amber plastic. He stared at it, startled. Some relative of Sharon's? Not
likely. Francis was a fairly common name. And Sharon
would have mentioned it.

Wouldn't she?

Jeff stared at the chart.

It might explain a lot, he thought.

His fingers itched to lift the file from the cart. But he had
told Sharon he would pick her up for the beach in an hour.
That didn't leave a lot of time to copy the Greene chart.

Jeff glanced over at Nurse Reever. She was sitting at the
meds counter, her back to him. She had thought nothing
of him wanting the Greene chart—Greene was still as much
Pendleton's patient as Valois's. But there was no reason for
Pendleton's resident to be snooping into a chart that was
purely a psychiatric case.

Right. Jeff slid the Francis chart up and out, flipping back
the metal hinge. At the top of the admissions page was
typed: "Ellen Francis, 45, white female, widowed. Next of
kin, daughter Sharon, psychiatric resident at this hospital."

Christ, Sharon's mother!

Jeff stared at the chart, stunned. Forget you saw it, he

thought. Put it back, or you won't be able to look her in the eye today. Let her tell you about it if and when she likes.
. . .

His fingers had flipped to the blue diagnosis sheet. He stared at it with dread fascination: "Schizophrenia, paranoid type."

God damn. The big one, the worst. Why couldn't it have been something else—depression, hypochondriasis, hysteria. Anything but schiz.

He felt oddly shaken. Why hadn't Sharon told him?

On the other hand, why would she?

They kidded around a lot, sure. And so far, that was about it. Jeff began to feel depressed and vaguely angry. What's the matter with you? he thought. So her mom's a paranoid schiz. You can get used to that, right?

Right?

He looked through the glass of the nurses' station at the ward commons. Two men and a woman were strolling the ward. The woman was too young. But Sharon's mother was up here somewhere, in one of those rooms. He checked the chart. Room 216, down there at the end. In half an hour breakfast would arrive and then she'd be coming out of that room. He imagined walking down to meet her. The thought shook him. God, how different than anything he'd ever imagined. He should be meeting Sharon's mother the way she had met his, sitting in a restaurant, or going to her home for dinner one night.

And what about Sharon? If a person had at least one schizophrenic parent, what were the odds of that person going schiz too? Higher than normal, but still not terribly high, were they?

Jeff flipped through the chart to the family history, not wanting to see, but unable to stop himself. The summary began with Ellen's childhood and adolescence, which, according to the chart, were unremarkable. At the time of her wedding, Ellen was a normal, well adjusted eighteen-year-old just out of high school. She married Ed Francis, also eighteen, a laborer and amateur weight lifter who had serious prospects of making the Olympic team. . . .

Jeff paused, struck by an odd connection: Mark Pendleton had been a bronze medalist in archery at the Olympics. So?

So maybe it gave Mark an edge with Sharon. Didn't women gravitate to men like their fathers?

But did Mark know Sharon's mom was a schiz?

Jesus! The chart felt suddenly oily and cold against Jeff's fingers, as though a malevolent force was seeping from it into him. He should put it back right now, get the hell out.

He read on: Ellen got a job when Ed started college, but almost at once, Ellen got pregnant. In 1962, ten months after they married, she gave birth to Sharon. Ed quit college and worked in construction jobs six days a week to support his family. He abandoned his plans for making the U.S. Olympic weight lifting team, but he wanted to finish college. He and Ellen agreed that he would join the army so he could take advantage of its education benefits afterward. But he didn't want to leave his daughter until she was old enough for school, so he waited until 1968, when Sharon turned six, to enlist. After basic training, Ed was sent to Vietnam. Ellen coped well during her husband's absence. With her daughter in grade school, she was able to work at a public library during school hours. She did well at her job and was liked by the other staff.

Then Ed came back from Vietnam. He was a changed man. Where he had been cheerful and gregarious, he was quiet and withdrawn. He had trouble concentrating and suffered spells of weeping. He was given a medical discharge for depression, and Ellen quit her job to be with him. He tried to get work as a laborer again. But a Vietnam vet with a psychiatric discharge had little chance in the job market, and he was frequently out of work.

About that time, at age twenty-six, Ellen's symptoms first appeared. She began to feel, for no discernible reason, that Ed was a danger to her and her daughter, then eight years old. Ed apparently did his best to reassure her, but her condition worsened. She began to hear voices warning her about Ed. Also, she refused to eat anything from any container that had been previously opened. Unable to cope with his own depression and his wife's increasingly irrational behavior, Ed took her to the hospital. Over the next few years there were several cycles of hospitalization for Ellen, followed by temporary improvement in her condition and then relapse. Finally, in 1974, unable to endure the situation any longer, Ed left home.

Jeff did the mental arithmetic and winced: Sharon would have been only twelve years old.

The history got worse. Ed began to drink and was killed when his car crashed into an abandoned gas station a year later. There was some thought that he had deliberately smashed himself into the brick.

Jeff felt a stab of pity. Sharon, Sharon. Poor little girl.

Paradoxically, Ellen seemed to pull herself together after Ed's death, perhaps because he had been, however unfairly, a source of her paranoid fears. She was able to comfort her daughter. She was determined to take care of Sharon and see her through the rest of elementary and high school. At times during this period, Ellen was only marginally functional, hearing voices that warned her about numerous imaginary threats. But she clung to the idea that the voices weren't real. Her daughter was able to take care of her; Ellen managed to stay out of the hospital until Sharon's high school graduation in 1980, which she attended and which she considered "one of the happiest days of my life."

However, shortly after Sharon got out of high school, Ellen suffered another full-blown schizophrenic crisis, and these have since continued every few months to this time. Ellen has been in the hospital on the average of two times a year for the past eight years, usually for three or four weeks per episode. This is her first hospitalization at Adams Memorial, arranged on a reduced-fee basis because of her daughter's staff position. When Ellen is not in the hospital, she lives with her daughter, who takes care of her. Ellen feels a very strong bond to her daughter; Sharon's unfailing support and love over the years, have been a vital adjunct to Ellen's treatment . . .

Jeff closed the chart, torn between sadness and awe. The family history was oriented around Ellen Francis's tragedy, but all around the periphery was such tragic pain and suffering for Sharon. What a fighter she must be, to have survived that. Not just survived, triumphed. What would have destroyed many people had made Sharon strong.

So strong she felt she didn't need anyone?

Well, we'll see about that, Jeff thought. Hey, at least Sharon's mother was not an ax murderer. Or a television evangelist.

"I think you've got the wrong chart."

Jeff looked up at Reever. "Miz Reever, ma'am?"

With a look of patient suffering, Reever took the Francis chart from his hands, slid it back into its slot, and handed him Greene's chart. "You can't just browse through any chart you want to, you know."

"I can't? Then what's the fun of being an M.D.?"

Jeff took Greene's chart and headed for the Xerox room. It didn't matter about Sharon's mother. Or maybe it did matter, but he didn't yet understand how. All he knew for sure was that he had awakened this morning hungry to see Sharon, and he was just as hungry now.

Jeff wished he hadn't taken the front seat of the double bike. He couldn't see Sharon behind him without turning around, which was dangerous with all the potholes. He wanted to see her. The day would be too short as it was without his having to spend all this time looking in the wrong direction.

"I can't see the road," Sharon complained from behind him.

Jeff pulled up and grinned back at her. "I guess with these massive shoulders—"

"Your medicine ball head, you mean. How about giving me the front?"

"Wel-l-l, I guess." Thank you, God, he thought—and you can quit reading my mind now.

In front, she set a fast pace, her luxuriant dark hair streaming back at him like a banner. He watched her taut back and shoulders, her slim legs flashing in the sun. She looked so wonderful, so alive. It was hard to believe that she had grown up under the predatory shadow of madness.

"How much farther to this terrific beach of yours?" she shouted over her shoulder.

"You can pull us over any time."

She swerved the bike off the hard packed dirt of the coastal road into the sand and sea grass and jumped off. He pulled the bike into the tall grass, talking happily to her until he realized she had already run off through the low dunes. He watched her go, pleased by her eagerness. She stopped fifty yards from him and peeled off her shorts and top. Underneath she was wearing a black one-piece bathing suit, modest, but the smooth, creamy contrast of her skin took his breath away. He walked after her, intoxicated, pulling the salt breeze into his lungs, listening to the steady roar of the breakers, the cries of the gulls.

At the water's edge he spread out their towels and took out the Frisbee. She flagged down almost everything he threw and flipped the disc back to him with diabolical sweeps and curves, until his legs ached from running in the sand. A golden retriever loping up the beach saved him from collapse by plucking the Frisbee from midair and running off. Sharon chased the dog a hundred yards, her laughter trailing back to him. Transfixed with wonder, he watched her run. Her body seemed to glide effortlessly, her skin gleaming like pale satin in the sun. She was strong, aglow with health. Lust swelled in him; he yearned to hold her, to feel that smooth energy coiled around him. . . .

And if she came back now he'd have to drop face down into the sand to hide the bulge in his swim trunks.

With an effort, he shifted mental gears. He was pleased she was having so much fun. He hadn't wanted her to come just because of the chart; he would have gotten it for her anyway. But she hadn't even mentioned it, all day.

Jeff felt a sudden, formless joy. He let loose a yell at the sun. He wished he could make this time right now last forever.

But it kept slipping by.

She came back and they lay down together in the sun. He could smell the coconut oil on her gleaming skin. He studied her long dark lashes, visible from the side under her sunglasses, and decided they were perfect, like the fine straight line of her nose, the delicate curves of her lips, her sculpted chin, girlish but strong. He wished she would take off the sunglasses and look at him so he could see how her green eyes looked in the sunlight. Her dark hair was wild from the wind, full around her face, feathering in soft fringes along her lovely, long neck. He could see a faint pulse at the angle of her jaw.

A sudden, powerful sorrow for her gripped him. It did not seem right that she should ever have suffered pain. He wanted to hold her, soothe her, tell her he was sorry.

He felt the swelling inside his swim trunks again and rolled over, suppressing a groan. Think of something else. That cranial hematoma yesterday, Pendleton's pointers, the surgery lights hot as this sun on his back. The sand felt cool against his cheek. It smelled of salt and crabs. This was the life. He could stay . . . here . . . forev . . .

"Hey cowboy. Time to get back to the chuck wagon."

He swam up from dimness, spitting out flecks of sand, running the sentence again in his head. Her hand was cool on his shoulder. He had fallen asleep! He sat up and looked at her, dismayed. How much time had slipped away?

And yet, he had a sense of her being with him through the lazy, floating dimness. It felt quite strange and wonderful.

"Chuck wagon?" he said.

"You *do* know how to cook, don't you? Because I don't."

He made his face grave. "What's your position on Tater Tots?"

Sharon sat in the cabin's little living room, the photocopies stacked on the pine coffee table before her, reluctant, for some reason, to begin. Sweet of Jeff to insist on cleaning up the dishes while she took a look at Frank's chart. She listened to the pleasant clinks and sloshes from the kitchen, nice, comforting sounds. It had been a good day. She realized with surprise that she had barely thought of Meg and Frank and the flashbulb creep. And when she had, it had been without the tight knot of worry between her shoulder blades that she was beginning to think had moved in to stay.

Being with Jeff made her feel everything was all right. He had something, an inner stability she could not quite put her finger on. It was something she craved.

And would have to wait for.

A crash came from the kitchen. "Phlogiston!" Jeff shouted.

She hurried in in time to see him picking up pieces of the platter he had served the Tater Tots on. "Phlogiston? Whatever happened to 'oops'?"

"Never say oops," Jeff said. "When you want to be a surgeon, that's the first thing they teach you."

Sharon laughed. Would she ever get used to his weird sense of humor?

Not if she didn't give herself the chance.

She felt a sudden, vague ache in her chest. All right, cut it out.

"The hell with washing dishes," Jeff said. "I can buy new dishes." He toweled his hands off and took her arm, ushering her into the living room. The last rays of sunset slanted through the screen door into her eyes. Through the murmur of the surf she could hear crickets starting their night songs outside the cabin. For a second she felt what it would be like to be content, to stay here with Jeff, day after day, night after night, until . . .

Yes. Until.

"How you coming with the chart?" Jeff sat down beside her, picked up the undisturbed stack and fanned the edge with his thumb. "I hope you realize the deadly peril in which I put myself copying this. At this very moment, Royal Canadian Mounted Police, better known as Mounties, are—"

"Give it here," Sharon said, laughing.

With Jeff beside her, she found she could look at the chart. She started poring over the pages, looking for anything suspicious—anything Louis Valois might not want her to see. As she immersed herself in the chart notes, she felt a strange mixture of eagerness and dread. She wanted to find something that would point to Valois, help her pin down the wrongness she was sensing in MHU. But what if it pointed at her instead? What if she found some sign of impending psychosis in Frank that she should have seen before?

Then so be it. She might know more than the average bear about schizophrenia, but she still had a lot to learn. She didn't want to make any mistakes, not ever, but sometimes mistakes taught you the most.

She concentrated on the daily nursing notes, where any warning sign was most likely to be recorded. Page after page of the chart yielded nothing. According to the nurses, Frank Greene was an unfailingly cheerful patient. No mention of any strange talk, any disturbance by odd noises no one else could hear. Frank had never even refused a meal tray, which in hospital terms made him a candidate for sainthood.

Sharon paused, struck by Frank's dietary habits. They certainly didn't suggest paranoid schizophrenia. Excessive carefulness around food was a common sign, like with Mom. She continued carefully through the chart. Only one other thing looked odd. There was a missing blood workup.

The request was there, signed by Dr. Pendleton before Frank went up to MHU. But the results were not in the chart.

Sharon turned and found Jeff looking at her with an odd expression. "What?"

"Your face," he said. "I was watching you read. Your eyes, they looked different—hard and hungry, like a panther's eyes. And your jaw was really set."

"Come on."

"I'm serious. You were almost scary. As if you wanted to tear into something, kill it, slash it to pieces."

She looked back at him, not knowing what to say.

"Would you like a brandy?" he asked.

"No thanks." She handed him the request slip. "What do you make of this?"

He looked it over. "Lousy penmanship."

She dug an elbow into his ribs. "Be serious. You sure you copied the whole chart?"

"Yes'm." Jeff shrugged. "Maybe Pendleton called up and cancelled the blood test. Or maybe the report slipped out of the chart at some point, like when they transferred Greene to MHU."

"But wouldn't someone have found it on the floor and made sure it got back in?"

"I guess, if they were a good citizen."

Sharon heard a soft thump outside the cabin and looked toward the window. It was dark now, the window a black square softly glazed by the low inside light. She could see nothing, but her mind served up an image of a face staring in at them. A dirty face. The nape of her neck tingled. "Did you hear that?"

Jeff gazed at her. "Yes. You said, 'Did you hear that?' "

"Unless you have a dog, I think someone's out there."

"Probably the Mounties." He got up and went out the screen door to the porch, looking around. He came back and settled beside her again. "It was Geraldo Rivera. He wants us to be on his show. I told him to go away."

Sharon gave a token laugh.

"What's the matter?" he said.

"I want to see that blood test."

"So go by hematology. They've got backups of everything in the computer."

"Good idea. Will you go over it with me?"

Jeff took the chart from her hands and put it on the table. "What are you thinking, Sharon?"

"I saw Frank up in MHU. He said he was being poisoned. The blood test was ordered just before he went up. If hematology didn't get to him until he was in MHU, the test might show something. But it's gone. I don't like that."

Jeff gave her a somber look. "You don't seriously believe Frank is being poisoned, do you?"

She heard something in his tone, another question inside the surface one: *Aren't you being paranoid, Sharon?*

She was suddenly suspicious. Had Jeff been digging into her background?

No, that *was* paranoid.

She slumped back against the couch, confused and a little depressed. "Maybe I will take that brandy now."

"Great," Jeff said. "And I'll light the fire."

Brian crept back to his spot below the porch window. He could feel his heart hammering like gangbusters. Stupid, dropping his penlight. Dr. Dipshit had almost caught him.

Brian eased up into the corner of the window. They were back on the couch—no, Dipshit was getting up! Brian got ready to scuttle away again, then saw that the guy was headed for the fireplace, not the door.

Now's my chance, Brian thought. He raised his Minolta into the corner of the window and aimed it at Sharon. His breath caught as he focused through the lens—perfect! He snapped the picture, knowing that the one-thousand–speed film would bring her to him in sharp clarity despite the low light in the room.

He snapped several more shots, his heart hammering giddily in his ears, his scrotum tightening. Oh, God, yes! With her face down like that, unsmiling and melancholy, she looked like a woman in submission. He would crop out the papers she was looking at, crop out everything but her face, her head. That's all he needed—for now.

Watch it! He dropped down below the windowsill as Sharon started to lift her head. Hunching against the side of the cottage, he breathed deeply, anticipating just where each shot of her face would best fit. It would be great to have new ones. The others from outside the hospital had been good—supreme at first: her look of shock as she fell off the bike, the blood-spots of reflected retina in the backs of her eyes from the powerful flash.

But those shots were worn down now from being used so many times, sort of like smelling something real good, sniffing it in and in until you could barely smell it. He would keep the shots always, of course, and there would be days, moments, when their value resurged.

But now, with these new pictures, he'd get the initial, powerful rush all over again.

Brian's legs began to hurt from crouching. He touched the charcoal he had rubbed on his face; it felt grimy with sweat, but he figured his face would stay dark as long as he didn't wipe it off. He wondered if he dared rise up again. As long as they didn't flip on any bright inside lights, his face wouldn't stand out in the corner of the window.

Maybe she and her dipshit boyfriend would make love on the couch by firelight.

Brian's hand clenched the camera. An almost unbearable excitement filled him. To have her naked body on film, instead of the substitutes! The ultimate prize . . .

Well, not quite the ultimate.

Brian's head began to pound with the migraine, but he was barely aware of the pain.

Jeff was acutely aware of the soft touch of Sharon's fingers as he handed her the brandy snifter. When he settled beside her, she sat forward, cradling the glass in both palms, inhaling the brandy fumes deeply. He took advantage of the moment to slide his arm across the back of the couch behind her so that when she sat back, her shoulders fit against the crook of his arm.

But only for a second. Then she sat forward again and looked at him, her face pale and somber. Abashed, he pulled his arm back. "Right. Sorry."

"No," she said. "I'm the one who's sorry. We've had such a wonderful day. It's only natural."

"Not if it makes you uncomfortable."

She let her head fall back, staring at the ceiling.

"You're so beautiful," he said. "Inside and out. I've never known anyone like you."

Her mouth twitched into a smile. "That last part's probably true enough, but I'm not sure it's for the good."

"I know about your mother," he said, and was astonished at himself.

Her head turned slowly toward him against the back of the couch. Her eyes were unreadable.

"I saw her chart when I was in MHU today. It was right there in the next slot up from Greene's. I had to know if she was related. I'm sorry."

"Don't be."

"I had no right."

"I'm glad that you know. It will help you understand why . . . we can't let ourselves go farther with this."

Jeff had a sinking sensation in his stomach.

She touched his hand, then pulled hers back. "Do you see?"

"I see that you're giving your life to fighting schizophrenia, and I see why. But you don't have to do it alone."

She gave a sad laugh. "No. No, no, no. That's not it at all. You read the history, right?"

"Yes."

"The history lies. Dad wasn't as weak as they make him out to be. Sure, he came back from Vietnam changed, but

I think he was stronger in some ways, *more* ready for what happened to Mom than he would have been before. And still, he couldn't take it. He *had* to leave her."

Suddenly Jeff did understand. "You're afraid it's going to happen to you."

"I can't expect you to understand."

"But I do. For just a second this morning, when I first found out, I felt like running, too."

Sharon looked stricken; fear rushed through him in a cold wave. Had he just blown it? "You want lies? I won't do that to you, Sharon. Yeah, my first impulse was to run—totally selfish, as first impulses usually are. My second impulse was selfish too. I realized what running away from you would do to me. Not to you, to me."

"A child with one schizophrenic parent," Sharon said, "is twenty times more likely than average to become schizophrenic. Mom got it at twenty-six. I'm twenty-seven."

"But the odds are still against it."

"Jeff, if someone offered you a million dollars, would you put a bullet in a revolver, spin the chamber, place it against your head, and pull the trigger?"

"No."

"Why not? The reward would be huge and the odds you'd die only one in six."

"This isn't Russian roulette, for God's sake. And you are worth more than a million dollars."

"Am I?" She gave him a sad smile. "Have you ever lived with a schizophrenic? Tried to talk to one, listen to one, get through to one?"

"No, but I'm sure—"

"Try to imagine it. Then imagine how it would be if you *loved* that person. That makes it harder, Jeff. So much harder. You talk about how selfish you are, but I know you. You care about me, and I'm glad, even though it hurts. You care about everyone. You like to play the joker, but you're really the king of hearts."

Jeff felt suddenly uncomfortable. "Come on, Sharon, I'm

no Mahatma Gandhi. I swat mosquitoes. I cut people off in traffic, I root for Bad News Brown in wrestling—"

"And stand up to Nurse Morgenthal in ER so a couple of smelly vagrants won't get thrown out into the cold. If you turned all that love and caring on me, and then I . . . went—"

"Sharon, stop. You're trying to make a decision that's not yours to make. You're entitled to be loved. If I know the odds and I want to fall in love with you anyway, then it's my problem."

"No. Please, Jeff. Let's not talk about it any more."

He stopped, frustrated.

Sharon hunched forward, pulling away from him, gazing into the flames. "My father was a good man," she said in a faraway voice. "The very best. He was strong and kind and gentle. And he left my mother. I've seen what it did to her, especially in the times when her craziness wasn't as bad, and believe me it was *not* better for her to have loved and lost. I can stand being alone now, Jeff. But I could never stand having what she had and then one night seeing it walk out the door forever."

Jeff took her hand and held on. He felt a choking pressure in his throat; all the words he wanted to say: *Let me help you. Let me love you. Let me try to protect you.* But he knew they were not the words she wanted to hear.

Outside the window, Brian pumped the silent shutter. His breath was ragged, the sweat poured down in rivers through the mask of charcoal. In the flickering light, he caught all the planes and angles of torment on her face, imagining how she would look in the photos when he used them the way he wanted. I love it! he thought.

8

CHUCK CONROY WAITED with mellow patience inside the phone booth. He felt very good, very right; a perfect dose. He would be able to take the call, deal with Hand without feeling nervous or scared.

Deal with Hand—that was a joke, wasn't it? Conroy smiled. An odd code name, Hand, but he was pretty sure he had figured it out. Heads instructed and hands carried out those instructions. When a boss really depended on an employee, he would say something like, "This guy's my right hand."

Yeah, Hand was just the subordinate who did whatever the head ordered. No reason to be afraid of him, no reason at all.

Bull*shit!* Conroy thought, but he smiled. The truth was, at this moment, he *wasn't* afraid of Hand. Everything was in harmony. Even the sidewalk felt soft under his feet. He was sweating, but it was just the heat, and that kind of sweat was no sweat.

He smiled at his little joke. Nothing could bother him right now; nope, not even Hand.

The phone rang, a soft, companionable sound. He picked it up before it could ring again. Yeah, just right.

"This is Amber Jack," he said, savoring the sound of it. Now *there* was an outstanding code name. He pictured a jack in a deck of cards, a unique, gold-robed jack. Hand could be a cold son of a bitch, but he'd shown some respect in assigning him that code name.

"You ready to do it?" Hand's voice grated from the receiver with its usual distorted buzz. Conroy felt a prick of fear, then annoyance that he hadn't got the dose quite high enough after all. He knew how Hand did it, talking with one of those gizmos the people with throat cancer used, so that possible wiretaps couldn't be used for a voiceprint. He expected it, he was ready, half waxed, and still it scared him.

"Amber Jack," the voice buzzed at him.

"Yes. I've got it all lined up."

"Are you high?" The buzzing voice was flat, merciless.

"No sir."

There was a long pause. Sweat rolled into Conroy's eyes. His fingers hurt, clenching the receiver.

"Okay," the horrible voice buzzed. "You know the subject's pattern. Do it after tonight's session, just the way we agreed. And be careful; there's already unrest because of the last one."

Conroy felt a twinge of irritation, very dangerous, and suppressed it. If Hand wanted to forget who had warned him about Sharon and her paranoid schiz mother in the first place, that was Hand's business.

"You clear on it?"

"Yes," Conroy said.

"And Amber Jack. Don't ever be high again when I call."

Conroy's fright returned in a cold rush. "No sir," he said, but Hand had already hung up.

Sharon sat on her bed, picking her soggy shirt away from her chest and dreaming of an air conditioner. The apartment was sweltering. Even with the windows open, she could barely feel the heavy air moving. Only an hour until sunset, but the outside brick was just now passing the midday heat into her apartment. Her own little time machine, dragging her back to the noon sun.

All she needed was one of those little window units to hum away sweetly here in the bedroom.

On her stipend, all she could afford was the hum.

Maybe she should tape record an air conditioner and try to teach herself to feel cooler just hearing it. Right. Classical conditioning might have worked for Pavlov, but she wanted air conditioning.

She realized the apartment was starting to smell of macaroni and cheese. She trudged through the living room, switching on the big fan. It flogged the hot, dead air into motion but did nothing to cool it. In the living room Sharon was more aware of the silence and emptiness of the place. She wished her mother were there, sitting on the old davenport, blurting out her bizarre little observations.

Plodding to the tap in the kitchenette, Sharon ran water over her wrists. The warm flowing wetness made her think of poor Meg trying to cut her wrists open. She shuddered and pulled her hands back, grabbing for the towel. But thoughts of blood persisted. What had happened to Frank Greene's missing blood test?

The log in Hematology showed that the test had been done, but the results were not in the computer. It was hospital policy to always computer-store a backup copy, but not this time. Gone. Erased, or never entered. The clerk said it sometimes happened. But Sharon didn't like the nasty coincidence.

Frank claims he's being poisoned and the blood test that might prove otherwise vanishes into thin air.

Or, as Jeff might put it, into phlogiston.

Fairly apt. Had the blood test merely been lost, or had someone burned it?

Sharon opened the oven and snatched out the macaroni and cheese. The blast of heat started a waterfall of sweat at her hairline. Plunking a plate, fork, and napkin onto the table, she picked morosely at the cheesy noodles. They couldn't compare to steak, Tater Tots, and wine with Jeff. Everything but the wine had been burnt, but it had been wonderful.

Even their talk at the end of the day, painful as it had been, had somehow made her feel closer to him.

And here she was, alone again.

Knock it off!

Sharon got up and switched on the old black-and-white TV the janitor had given them. "Sixty Minutes" coalesced slowly from gray fog. Morley Safer's head looked long and thin, but his grandfatherly voice cheered her up right away. She ate, watching with horrified fascination Safer's wincing, apologetic dissection of a woman who ran a computer dating service. That's where you're going to end up, she told herself, after you've decided it's safe to fall for someone and no one wants to fall for you. A dating service, or maybe the personals in *The Washingtonian*. SWF seeks warm loving man with air conditioner.

She laughed in spite of herself.

Mike Wallace was next, getting ready to dismember the proprietor of an L.A. sperm bank. She switched the set off and cleaned up the dishes. Pain group in an hour. Might as well go on over now, chill out on some of that good, hospital AC.

On the street, she eased through the hot darkness, coasting as much as she could. Why would someone make Meg disappear and then poison Frank so that he seemed psychotic? Even if the someone was Dr. Valois, Sharon's favorite villain in all the world, she had no answer.

She pulled into the hospital parking lot drenched in sweat. Inside a delicious wall of coolness met her. She stopped off in the psych services rest room and patted her face dry, savoring the feel of wonderful machine-cooled air evaporating the dampness from her clothes. Lingering at the mirror, she tried to see what Jeff saw. Her eyes were still very green, her hair very black, her face very pale, but suddenly it all looked different to her. *You're so beautiful,* he had said, *inside and out*. A strange, alien pleasure swelled in her, tingling in her lungs like exotic smoke. She fluffed her hair, trying to bring out the deep red undertones. Jeff, oh Jeff.

Sharon turned from the mirror, blowing out a long breath, bringing herself back to earth. She strolled toward her office, thinking of huge mountains of ice, hearing a phone ringing faintly behind one of the office doors—

Her door.

Hurrying, Sharon unlocked her office, snatched up the phone. "Dr. Francis speaking."

"Working on a Sunday evening. I must say, I'm impressed."

A woman, but Sharon could not place the voice.

"This is Judith Acheson, Dr. Francis."

"Oh yes, hello." The chief administrator! A spot of tension sprang up between Sharon's shoulder blades.

"If you recall, at Grant's party I suggested you come up for a chat." There was an edge of accusation to the smooth voice.

Sharon had a sinking feeling. "Oh, yes," she said again, wanting to say more, to explain. She stopped herself. You did not tell Judith Acheson you had been too busy to see her.

"Would now be a good time?" Acheson asked.

"Yes, of course. I'll be right up."

"Good." The phone clicked dead.

In the elevator, Sharon leaned against the wall, gripping the handrail, thinking furiously. At Pendleton's party, Acheson had brought up Valois, hinted about "Frenchmen" not getting along. Was that what this was about?

The elevator stopped and an orderly pushed an old man in a wheelchair on. Sharon tried to smile at them. Her lips felt tight and strange, but the old man smiled back.

What was Acheson doing in her office so late on a Sunday? The head of the hospital—shouldn't she be off at the opera or something?

The elevator stopped and the orderly wheeled the man off again. Sharon stepped away from the rail and composed herself. Relax, she thought. Acheson will tell you what's on her mind.

Then you can panic.

The door slid open on the executive level. The corridor was hushed and empty, its wine red carpets freshly vacuumed for Monday. Fluffed spots the size of small feet led from the elevator toward the end suite—Acheson's. Okay, Tonto, Sharon thought. Follow those tracks.

All of Acheson's doors stood open: the outer office door, that of a middle anteroom, and way in the back, the final set of oaken double doors to the inner sanctum. As she approached, Sharon could see part of a desk within, a braceleted arm, the hand writing busily.

"Hello?"

"Come," the voice floated back.

Sharon hurried through, catching side glances of potted ficus trees, burnished mahogany desks, lush settees, and recessed lighting, dialed low. Acheson's office was lit only by the reddish glow of sunset pouring through the panoramic bank of windows. In the distance, the Capitol dome glowed like an ivory breast, nursing the fiery horizon. The view took Sharon's breath away. How could a person turn her back on that long enough to get any work done?

By being Judith Acheson.

"Sit." Still writing, Acheson nodded toward one of the chairs across from her desk. Sharon sat, sinking down so low she could see only Acheson's head and shoulders over the edge of the desk.

Acheson stopped writing and looked up, giving Sharon a slightly unfocused gaze. "You've been calling Meg Andreason's parents, is that right?"

Sharon blinked, taken aback. "Yes . . . twice, I think."

"Why?"

Sharon pulled herself forward to the edge of the soft chair, perching straight-backed where she could see Acheson's hands. They held a gold pen at either end, fingers rotating, rolling the pen.

"My mother knew Meg—"

"Knew?" Acheson's voice was sharp. The pen stopped rolling.

"When Meg was on the ward I mean. Mom is a patient here—"

"So I understand."

"—and they were friends. When Meg signed out AMA and disappeared, Mom got worried and asked me to call her folks." Sharon tried to read Acheson's flat expression. What was going on here? Why did Acheson care about this? "Is there some problem?"

"You said 'disappeared.' If you also used that word with Meg's parents then yes, certainly, there is a problem. Meg Andreason has not disappeared, she has simply run away. Cases like this are always very delicate matters for a hospital to handle. Meg was—is not your patient, and whether your mother asked you to call or not, your professional judgment should have told you it was unwise."

Through her anxiety, Sharon began to feel annoyed. "I was very circumspect," she said. "May I ask how you knew I had called them?" The instant she said it, she realized how bad it sounded—*Who ratted me out?*—a backhand admission of guilt.

"How doesn't matter. What matters is that you realize the importance of avoiding such potentially damaging situations in the future. All this hospital needs is for the Andreasons to decide that we were somehow negligent in the care of their daughter. They would be wrong, of course, but in this country anyone can sue anyone for any reason. The sued party, even if it ultimately wins, must go to great effort and expense to defend itself. If you plan on practicing psychiatry for any length of time, you would be well advised not to forget that."

Sharon felt a cold tightness around her heart. Had Acheson just threatened her?

"Do you understand what I'm saying?"

"Yes," Sharon replied.

Acheson's face warmed suddenly with a pleasant smile. "Good." She got up and went to a cabinet on one wall of her office. "Drink?"

"No, thank you. I have a group in a few minutes."

"That's right, Jenkins's pain group."

Sharon nodded, amazed at the woman's knowledge. Was she as well briefed on all her residents?

"I won't keep you then." Acheson came to her and took her hand in a firm grip. "You're doing a good job here. But we women have to be extra careful, extra good at what we do, just to make it. I'm sure you know that. I want to see you do well. So stay sharp and keep up the good work."

"I'll do my best."

"As long as your best doesn't interfere with keeping up the good work." Acheson smiled and gave her hand a final squeeze.

Riding the elevator back down, Sharon rubbed the hand Acheson had shaken. It was cold. She held it to her cheek, feeling a blaze of heat there. Damn! So who *had* ratted her out? Either Valois or Meg's parents. Sharon decided she did not want to know which. Forget it, put it out of your mind. Meg's father will either call you if she comes back, or he won't. Either way, you don't need to call them again, so just forget it.

Heading for the group room, she forced the meeting with Acheson from her mind, preparing herself mentally to do therapy.

As she walked in, she saw that someone else was already there, too, a young, bald-headed man—

God—Brian! He had shaved his head.

Sharon realized she had stopped in the doorway; she walked on in, trying not to stare.

"Good evening, Sharon." Brian smirked at her, a sly disturbing expression. His stripped head gleamed under the low-slung light like a polished billiard ball.

"Hi, Brian." On impulse, instead of taking her usual seat across from him, she sat in the chair next to him in the circle. He got up and stalked to the one across from her, the one she normally sat in.

What was this? More of his anger? Or might he actually be scared of her?

The others began to file in. Dr. Jenkins, of course, gave no sign he noticed Brian's shaved skull, but the other group members, especially the older women, reacted with shocked looks and shakes of the head. When all the group was seated, the chairs on either side of Brian remained empty.

Dr. Jenkins nursed his pipe to life, sending the first tendrils of cherry smoke up, signaling the beginning of the session. He said, "I believe last time we were discussing our fears of addiction to the painkillers that have been prescribed by our doctors." He settled back and folded his arms across his chest as though he had just explained the meaning of life. Sharon suppressed a groan.

"What did you do with Frank?" Brian stared accusingly at her.

She looked back, surprised, and then pleased. Was Brian finally starting to realize his loss? "I'm not sure I understand your question."

"It's a silly question," Mrs. Reddle complained. "What do you think she is, a magician who makes people disappear? What did *you* do with your *hair?*"

"I wasn't talking to you," Brian said without looking at her.

"As I told the group last time," Sharon said, "Frank won't be able to be here for a while. You seem to have some feelings about that. Let's hear 'em."

"This group doesn't give a shit about me or my feelings, and you know it."

"Do you have to use filthy language?" Ida said.

"Would it make any difference if I didn't?"

Sharon could scarcely believe her ears. Brian was talking

to one of the other group members. She held very still, afraid the fragile bridge might shatter.

Ida sniffed. "Of course it would. You think manners aren't important, but they are. Manners is just showing some consideration. If you act like the rest of us don't matter to you, why should we care about you?"

"You wouldn't anyway." Brian was looking at her now, his eyes narrow with malice. Or maybe it wasn't malice but fear, a flinch from the blow he knew would come.

Sharon waited, but the exchange appeared dead. "It doesn't seem you're giving the others much credit, Brian," she said. "Why should they be mean to you if you treated them well?"

"It's the way everyone is," Brian said. "No one really cares about you. They wouldn't even know you existed if you didn't . . ." He stopped and glared at her.

"Yes?"

"You think you're so clever. But that's not why I did this." Brian jabbed a finger at his glistening skull.

"You want to tell us why?"

He gave her his chilling, crafty smile again. "Doesn't it remind you of anything, Sharon?"

She knew suddenly what Brian wanted: for her to accuse him of some sort of phallic motivation, which he could then smirkingly deny. Maybe he thought it would embarrass her. She felt sad for him. Poor lousy kid. You miss Frank and you don't even know it.

"It reminds me of ancient times," she said. "When people had lost someone they loved, they would shave their heads in mourning."

Brian's face paled. His upper lip curled and Sharon thought for a second he might burst into tears. But then he managed to sneer instead. He started to say something, but his voice was too choked. He lowered his head and crossed his arms, glowering down at his knees, the posture he always assumed when he was finished for the session and wanted to close them all out. Sharon made several attempts to bring him back, but he ignored her.

She wasn't sure how to feel about what had just happened. Clearly there had been a sort of breakthrough, but where would it lead? Sometimes if you went too far too fast, the patient would relapse, act out even more wildly than before in a desperate attempt to fend off the hurtful truths that were swimming too close to the surface.

Let it be, she thought. Don't push him.

Despite his downcast eyes, she felt Brian's attention focused on her as the session continued. About ten minutes from the end he suddenly stood.

"If you all will excuse me," he said, "I have another appointment." He walked out with a slight, manic spring in his step.

His politeness alerted Sharon; it was so unlike him that it must mean something. But she could not think what.

Tonight, I'm going to get her, Brian thought. He walked down the corridor between the white-curtained booths, dizzy with excitement. Slowing, he looked at the row of booths, trying to choose one. He could barely think; his head spun, and the air seemed trapped high up in his chest. Be careful, he thought. Do this right.

He remembered that he had seen a light on in the doctor's office just outside the physical therapy doors. And someone was definitely in there, because he'd heard a cough. So he'd better go down the other way, near the outside exit, just close enough to hear if someone came in.

Brian chose a booth in the middle of the row and stepped inside. He felt a swell of anticipation. This was perfect. He would hear Sharon coming, that squeaky sound her sneakers made. When she was across from him, he would jump out and grab her from behind. Or should he punch her first? He didn't want to knock her out, he wanted her to struggle. Let her see his face, know it was him doing this to her. The bitch.

Brian groaned softly, tremendously excited now.

And they couldn't even get him for it, because he was already being treated by a psychologist *and* a psychiatrist. He would get off on being a mental case, right? Unable to help himself—

Brian heard a soft sound, almost right next to him, and jumped. What the hell was that? He stared at the curtain dividing his space from the next booth. Was someone in there? The curtain ended a foot from the floor. He bent down to look under. Probably just a mouse.

As he bent, the curtain swished aside and he saw legs. He straightened with a yelp. Christ, a man, his face all smeared. What was that in his hand—

The man held out a thing that looked like a pen and touched him in the chest. Brian felt a huge shock and then a freezing wave of pain that locked his arms and legs. He couldn't move. He tried to scream, but his lungs wouldn't work either. He felt himself starting to topple forward and was unable to stop himself. The man stepped through into the booth with him, caught him, and slipped around behind. Brian felt numb, as though his whole body had gone to sleep, but his mind was very clear: the man's face was smeared because he had pulled a nylon stocking down over it; the thing in his hand had given him a big shock, like a cattle prod. Jesus, Brian thought, the guy was waiting for me—he knew I come out this way. He's been watching, stalking me, just like I stalk Sharon.

Brian felt a sharp prick in his shoulder, followed by a flood of coolness. A shot. Another scream caught in his throat; he couldn't make the muscles work right to push it out. The man held on to him. He's waiting for me to pass out from the shot, Brian thought. Fear leapt through him, scattering his thoughts. He made a fierce effort to concentrate. The man had only an arm around his chest to keep him from toppling over. The lock on his muscles was starting to break up. If he held still, made the guy think he was still frozen, maybe in a few seconds he could break free.

Brian felt a soft rippling like water sloshing inside his head. The booth seemed to be turning smoky, making it hard to see. Passing out, Brian thought. No, hang on!

Up the corridor, the double doors to PT flopped open. Hope sprang up in Brian. Someone's coming! he thought. Sharon!

The man stiffened behind him, his arm tightening across his chest, the other hand snaking around to clamp his mouth. Brian forced himself to stay still, gathering himself, listening as her footsteps squeaked closer and closer along the tiles. He could barely see. He clung to the tiny sounds of her feet, chirping to him like birds. Closer, closer—*now!*

Brian clawed the hand away from his mouth and lunged against the arm, breaking free, bursting from the booth. Sharon was a blur in front of him. She turned, gasping his name as he grabbed her. They fell together into a deep, black well, dropping down and down, but never hitting bottom.

9

SHARON SHOUTED in fright and then Brian was on her, ramming her backward, his feet tangling with hers. She lost her balance, and as she drew a breath to scream, he smashed her down hard against the floor. Pain slapped back through her spine, her hips, the back of her head. She tried again to scream but couldn't catch her breath. His chest pressed on her, soft, tensionless against her pushing hands, as though he were trying to mold every inch of himself to her. The heavy, oozing contact revolted her, filling her with sudden, animal fury. Get . . . off . . . me!

She pushed him up and yanked air into her lungs. With a shout, she heaved him off to the side.

She scrambled to her knees, sucking the sweet air, afraid he would jump back on her. Then she saw that he wasn't moving. She stared at him, confused, realizing suddenly that he hadn't really struggled with her at all. From the moment he had fallen on her, he had been limp, a dead weight.

Sharon crawled over to him. His mouth was open and slack, his eyes closed. Groping at his wrist, she tried to find a pulse and failed. She scanned him for a wound. Nothing—no bruise or cut, no blood. A cold dread settled in her stomach.

Probing at the angle of his jaw, she tried again to find

a pulse in the thick sheaths of fat and muscle. She detected a faint, thready heartbeat.

She stared at him, still stunned, unable to make her mind work. What had happened here? Had Brian had a heart attack?

A sound whispered beside her. She looked up at the examination booth. The curtain had fallen back shut. It rippled in the wash from the fan.

Beneath the curtain, she saw legs, standing very still.

Fright flashed through her. She leapt up and ran back the way she had come, bursting through the double doors of PT, wheeling wide around the corner to Dr. Pendleton's office. His light was still on. Thank God!

Sharon hammered on the door, looking back the way she had come. No one was there, and she could hear no running steps; the man hadn't followed her. Relief hit with an aftershock of weakness in her knees.

Dr. Pendleton jerked the door open. "What the hell—Sharon!" He stared at her as though he were seeing a ghost.

She pushed inside. "There's a man down in PT. I think he hurt my patient. He was in one of the booths—I saw his legs."

"Wait. Who's hurt?"

"His name is Brian Gifra. He grabbed me and we fell, and then he was out cold. I could barely find a pulse."

Pendleton looked at her, pop-eyed. "Christ!"

"Call the police," Sharon said, "and then let's get someone from ER to go in as soon as we know it's clear."

Pendleton was still staring at her. She reached for the phone on his desk. That seemed to break his paralysis; he picked up the receiver and jabbed at the buttons. "This is Dr. Pendleton. Get someone down to PT at once, and make sure he's armed." He slammed the phone down. "Security," he explained. "They'll get here a lot faster than the police. They can decide whether to call the police." He grabbed his stethoscope and medical bag. He leaned close, looking into Sharon's eyes. "Did you hit your head?"

"No—yes, when I fell." She reached back and felt a knot on the back of her head.

"You might have a mild concussion. Here, sit down." He pulled out his chair for her. She sank into it gratefully. He started out the door.

"Wait," she said. "Give security a chance to get down there first, make sure it's clear."

"You said your patient was in bad shape?"

She nodded.

"Then I'd better not wait."

"Do you at least have a gun or something?"

"A gun? Christ no, I don't have a gun. Wait a minute!" He jerked his drawer open and pulled out something that looked very much like a gun. "Squirt gun," he said. "Took it off one of my lab assistants!" He gave her a slightly crazed grin, and she could see that he was scared.

"I'm going with you."

"No you're not, Doctor. You're staying right in that chair until I get back and check you out." He patted her shoulder. Sharon watched him hurry off, the squirt gun clenched in his hand, his white coat flapping behind him. She felt a surge of affection for him. Suddenly she remembered something from when she was quite young: a couple of bigger boys took her bike, her first, that little one with training wheels that Dad had given her. She had run into the house, crying. Dad had listened to her, patted her on the shoulder, told her to stay put, and rushed out.

Like Dr. Pendleton just now.

It struck Sharon how brave Pendleton was. Going in to help Brian even though the man might still be there. She watched the door, very worried for him, wishing she had tried harder to get him to wait. Now there might be two bodies down there instead of just one. . . .

She heard footsteps outside the door.

"It's me," Pendleton said, walking in.

Sharon realized that it could have been the man from the booth and felt a belated ripple of fright. "Find him?"

"No." Pendleton leaned over her, prying her eyelid back and staring into her eye. "When I got down there," he said, "the place was deserted. No sign of your patient or anyone else."

"But he was there. I saw him. He fell on me. He had a real low pulse—"

"I believe you." Pendleton probed gently at the back of her head, wincing as he found the knot. "Maybe the guy who nailed him was there and dragged him off. Security's checking out the parking lot now, looking for anything suspicious. If need be, they'll call the police."

He sat down across from her. "You got a nasty bump there, but I think you'll be fine. . . . Sharon, you said you saw someone's legs. Was he in one of the booths?"

She heard doubt in his tone. "Yes. I saw his legs and feet behind the curtain."

"Could it have been a pair of pants?" Pendleton made a face and shook his head. "That sounds damn silly. What I mean is, one of the booths had some pants hanging on a hook right over a pair of shoes. Gave me a real shock. I leapt up and pointed my squirt gun at him, told him to come out. Then I saw what it was." Pendleton looked sheepish. He held the squirt gun up and pumped the trigger, making a dry sound. Sharon closed her eyes and tried to see the legs again, make them into a pair of pants hanging over some shoes. They stayed legs.

"No," she said. "I think someone was there. Maybe he hung the pants up afterward, to make it look like . . ." She trailed off.

Pendleton asked, "Is this guy Brian the sort to play a joke on you?"

It would be just like him, Sharon thought. "If that's what it was, I'd like to know how he got himself to look so bad. His face looked like cheese. It took me a long time to find a pulse."

Pendleton nodded. "Of course, when you're as shocked

and rattled as you must have been, you tend to fumble a bit."

"True." Sharon felt doubt creeping in.

Pendleton got up and opened a file, taking out a bottle of Virginia Gentleman and a crystal glass. He poured a shot and handed it to her. "Drink up, kiddo."

"I'm all right."

"You've had a hell of a shock. Doctor's orders." He folded her fingers around the glass. Sharon tipped it back, sipping, coughing as the fiery stuff slid down her throat. As she drank, Pendleton patted her shoulder. His hand felt warm and comforting. "When you're done with that, I want you to go home and go to bed."

"What about security, the police?"

"Is Brian's address and phone number in your Rolodex?" Sharon nodded.

"Write his last name down for me. Security can unlock your office and we'll get the rest off the Rolodex. If they need more, they can talk to you tomorrow." He put a pen into her hand and she wrote *Brian Gifra* on his prescription pad.

"What does security think?" she asked.

"Oh, they're pursuing it. . . ."

"C'mon, the truth."

"They think we're both crazy. They asked me if I had a permit for this." Pendleton brandished the squirt gun. "God, how I wished I had water in it right then."

Sharon laughed, feeling the tension blow out of her.

"You leave security to me," he said.

She drank the rest of the bourbon, feeling its warmth soothe down all the way to her stomach. "Okay," she said. "Thanks."

She stood. He walked her down the PT corridor and showed her the pants hanging over the shoes in the booth. She stooped down and looked at them. They did look a lot like legs. Still, Brian had been in such bad shape—hadn't he?

Mercifully, Pendleton said nothing. She followed him outside. The night air was hot and muggy, softening the outlines of the cars that gleamed under the parking lot lights. A security man was checking car windows. Pendleton called him over and gave him the name she had written down. The man took it with a skeptical nod and went back to strolling between the cars.

Pendleton turned back to her. "You're not going to ride that bike of yours home?"

"Well . . ."

"I think Jeff got called down to ER tonight. You go over there. You can stretch out in the doctors' lounge until he is free to take you home."

"Okay," she said gratefully. Good advice. She wondered if Pendleton would like to rent himself out now and then, in case she needed a surrogate father.

"I'll watch you across from here," he said.

Feeling awkward, she offered her hand and he shook it. However nice the fantasy, he was not her father. He was one of her supervisors, to an intern or resident, far beyond a boss. Closer to "Master." Tomorrow they would have to go back to that relationship.

As Sharon walked toward ER she felt a growing indignation. What if Brian *had* been playing some kind of morbid trick on her?

There was one way to find out: go to his apartment.

The idea appealed to her at once. She imagined Brian there, yucking about his terrifying little joke, and then his doorbell would ring, and she would be there with Jeff, and Brian could start yucking out of the other side of his mouth.

Nurse Morgenthal the Valkerie was the front nurse in emergency tonight. She gave a disapproving frown and said Jeff was with a patient.

"Tell him Dr. Francis will be waiting for him in the doctors' lounge."

Before Morgenthal could say anything else, Sharon swept by her through the door. She flopped into one of the tacky

Naugahyde chairs and waited. After a few minutes she started to get impatient. She got up and paced around the lounge. If Brian *was* okay, he would be home by now. She wanted to know, *had* to know what had really happened.

If he wasn't dead she was going to make him wish he was.

"Hiya."

Sharon swung around and saw Jeff grinning at her. As soon as he saw her face, his grin faded. "You look like you want to drop-kick someone through the goalposts of life."

"Close enough." She told him what had happened.

"Aw-w-w-w." He came over and gave her a big hug. It felt great.

"Would you go to Brian's apartment with me?" she asked.

"What do we do if Brian does answer the door?"

"You and I will have a talk with him."

"And if he's holding a bazooka? You're the shrink, but the guy sounds like a psycho to me."

A siren whooped up to the emergency entrance outside and died in a faltering warble. Jeff plopped into one of the chairs, letting his arms dangle over the sides. His tie was askew, his medical coat bunched around his waist. He let his head sag back, closed one eye, and gazed at her with the other. He looked absolutely dead. Sharon suddenly felt terrible for laying this on him.

"Jeff, you're right. It's a bad idea."

He opened his other eye. "Nah, I'll take you. Sounds like more fun than being dragged backwards nude through a cactus patch."

A nurse poked her head in. "Dr. Harrad, your concussion has arrived."

"Put it right here," Jeff said, pointing at his forehead. The nurse faked a smile and ducked out.

"I don't know how long this will take me," he said. "When I get clear, we'll go."

"No, we won't. When you get clear, you'll go to bed."

He struggled to rise. She gave him her hand and pulled

122

him up from the chair. "Go in there and put Humpty back together again."

He mumbled at her to wait for him. But she gave him a minute to get out of sight, then left ER. She went back to her office and took out her Rolodex to look up Brian's address. She stared at it, frustrated.

Ask Mark, she thought suddenly.

But Mark lived twenty-five miles away. She didn't even know his number.

She got it from information and dialed. Mark answered at once, as though he had been sitting by the phone.

"Mark, this is Sharon Francis. I . . . need help."

"Where are you?" His voice was calm, assured.

"The hospital."

"I'll pick you up out front. Forty minutes, no longer."

"Wait!" she said. "Don't you even want to know—"

"Forty minutes." The line went dead.

She hung the phone up and stared at it in wonder.

"I'm not sure we should be doing this," Sharon said to Mark as he slipped his credit card into the lock on Brian's door.

Mark's hand froze. He gazed at her. "Aren't you?"

"Just because he didn't answer doesn't mean he's not in there."

"Do you want to know or don't you?"

She swallowed. "Get us in."

"Good," he said. He angled the card this way and that in the crease of the door, then flipped it sharply. The latch clicked and the door swung inward. Sharon looked down the dim hall at the other apartments, making sure there was no one to see them. Then she followed Mark in, her throat dry. What if someone caught them?

What if Brian was waiting in the shadows with that bazooka?

A gross smell hit her: old socks, dirty laundry. Mark flipped on the light and she stared around in dread fascination. The walls were filthy, covered with smudgy fingerprints. What a small apartment, even for an efficiency. Dirty dishes in the sink, no rugs on the floor, no curtains either, just venetian blinds.

He's poor, Sharon thought. Just like me. She pushed the thought away. She didn't want to identify with Brian, even a little bit. He might be poor, but he wasn't just like her.

She watched Mark prowl around the main room of the apartment, searching the place with quick, practiced motions. He lingered over the cheap, beat-up dresser, pulling out each drawer all the way and feeling along the back.

"What are you looking for?"

Mark gave her a strange smile. "Spoor," he said.

She felt a little chill. The hunter was stalking not a deer this time, but a man. She felt a sudden powerful kinship with him. For weeks she had circled around Brian's mind, trying to find her way in, see what made him tick, and now Mark was doing the same thing in this apartment, Brian's lair.

We shouldn't be here, Sharon thought, but the knowledge was becoming very small inside her, easy to suppress. She made her own search of the room, looking for a camera with a flash attachment. She didn't find one. Maybe Brian kept it in his car.

Sharon followed Mark into the bathroom. It was even filthier than the rest of the place. She clung to the doorpost, too repulsed to go any farther. The toilet seat was up, the rim of the bowl spattered with yellow stains. Brian is an *animal,* she thought with disgust.

Then she felt a twinge of shame. Brian was gross, but he was a human being—and her patient. And they shouldn't be doing this to him.

"Mark—"

"Wait."

He left the bathroom and circled around to the closet. There weren't very many clothes inside. She looked at the pitiful array, growing more uncomfortable every second.

She did not want to see any more. There was a terrible, aching sadness to this place, an atmosphere of ruination and despair. In her mind she saw Brian as a wide-eyed baby, lying on a pastel blanket, waving clean chubby arms and legs at the universe. Bursting with life and eagerness.

How could he have come to this?

"Bingo," Mark said.

Sharon saw that he had pried away the plumbing access panel above the closet baseboard. He was taking a large manila envelope from inside. He motioned to her, taking the envelope to Brian's bed, spilling the contents onto it. Photos spread like tarot cards on the filthy sheets. Photos full of pink arms and legs, bare breasts. Sharon gasped.

Her arms and legs, *her* breasts.

She sank to her knees, stunned.

"Christ," Mark murmured.

And then Sharon saw that only the face was hers. The bodies had been cut from porno magazines, legs spreading, bodies arched, each of them with her face pasted on it. One face was very white, overexposed, blanched with shock and alarm.

She saw the flash going off in her face again, felt herself falling, falling—

Mark caught her arm. "Easy. Take a deep breath."

"That *pervert,*" she whispered. She grabbed handfuls of the ugly hybrids, shredding the magazine paper, tearing off the taped heads until she had them all gathered in one hand. She clutched them to her chest. It hadn't been just that one time with the car. He had been following her, taking picture after picture. Where had he shot all of these? With her head cut out and the rest of each photo gone, there was no way to tell.

Sharon realized Mark was looking at her. His gray eyes were full of approval. "You're okay. He didn't get you. He wanted to, but he didn't."

She felt nauseous with loathing for Brian. "He did it in his mind. Over and over."

Mark shook his head. "His mind doesn't count. Not at all. He's gutless. You are much stronger than him. You are here. You know him—you've come here and taken him. He hasn't taken you at all, and he never will, not in any way."

Sharon felt tears coming. She battled them back. Yes, she thought. I have to be strong. I always have to be strong.

"Do you want to wait for him awhile?" Mark asked.

"Yes."

"Good." Mark pulled all the sheets off Brian's bed and flung them into a corner. He flipped the mattress over and motioned for her to sit. She could not bring herself to sit on the bed, the same bed where Brian had probably spun his hateful, sick fantasies and dreams. She paced up and down while Mark sat cross-legged on the floor, watching her.

After a while she understood the significance of what Mark had done to the mattress and settled onto it. Mark did not speak but continued watching her. It made her aware again of his strange eyes, those pale irises gleaming from the dark face. In them, she saw great respect. It startled and then gratified her so deeply that she wondered at it. Here was a man who spent days in the woods with his bow and arrow, tracking animals. Who, as a cop, must have hunted, maybe even killed, men. She did not admire such behavior. It frightened and repulsed her, and yet it somehow made his respect at this moment so much more powerful. Seeing his eyes on her like that, she *felt* strong.

Sharon settled in with Mark to wait for Brian. They waited until two A.M., but Brian never came home.

10

S HARON STOOD at her office door, yawning and fumbling in her purse for the key. C'mon, c'mon. So sleepy her fingers wouldn't work right. Shouldn't have hung in so long last night with Mark. Brian's squalid apartment sprang up in her mind—the awful photos. She leaned against the doorjamb, her stomach squirming.

The nausea passed; she felt the sharp edges of her key cutting into her fingers. A pale thread of light shone into her eye and she realized with a start that the door was already open a crack. Goose bumps sprang up on her neck; she stepped back, alarmed. It wasn't even seven yet, too early for Austin. What if it was Brian, waiting for her? She didn't have Mark to help her.

On the other hand, she was a fast runner.

Sharon eased the door open a crack.

A snore fluttered out, homey and harmless, wiping out her anxiety. She pushed the door the rest of the way open. Jeff was sprawled across her and Austin's desks, sound asleep. He looked so vulnerable, so totally relaxed that she almost burst out laughing. His hair was all messed up and his mouth was slightly open. His long medical coat was twisted around him, as though he had rolled over a few times. His shoes sat neatly on the floor, toes pointed toward her, just like the shoes under the curtain last night.

The goose bumps returned; she rubbed at her neck.

Dear Lord, had Jeff slept here all night?

She walked over and tickled the bottom of one stockinged foot. Jeff groaned softly. Easing the top drawer open, she removed her feather duster and brushed it across Jeff's nose. His whole body shuddered. She bit her lip to keep from laughing. She saw her lipstick lying in her drawer and a nasty idea occurred to her.

No, she couldn't be that wicked.

She took out the lipstick and, with careful, light strokes, fashioned Jeff's lips into a huge crimson clown's mouth. She put the lipstick and feather duster away again, and said sternly, "What do you think you're doing?"

Jeff's eyes popped open. He stared at the ceiling, then groaned and sat up. "God what time zit?"

He looked hilarious gazing down at his watch with pouting, painted lips. She thought she would explode with laughter. With a fierce effort, she kept her face straight. "Almost seven. What are you doing here, Jeff?"

He gave her a sheepish look. "I was worried about you. You were gone when I got off at emergency, so I came up here. The cleaning guy was in here emptying wastebaskets, so I sat down at your desk like I owned the joint and dialed your apartment. No answer. Then I really started to worry."

She gazed into his eyes, trying desperately to ignore the garish lips and thinking, I must not laugh.

"I thought you might have gone on over to this bozo's place alone. I was going to go after you."

She felt herself flushing. That would have been all she needed—another person gawking at Brian's sick fantasy montage of her.

Not to mention Jeff finding her with Mark.

Wait a minute. Why should that bother her? She had been up front with Jeff: their relationship had to stay casual. So if she was with someone else, she owed him no explanations.

Jeff was giving her a speculative look. She had the uncanny sense that he had just read her mind.

"Trouble was," he said, "I had no idea where this guy lived and couldn't remember his name. Brian something."

"Gifra."

"Gifra! If I'd remembered that, I could've found his address in the damn phone book."

"Thanks, but you needn't have worried."

He eyed her. "I knew you were too smart to go over there. So where were you when I called?" He narrowed his eyes in exaggerated suspicion, trying to make it funny.

Sharon began to feel a little irritated. What made Jeff think he had the right to check up on her like this? "I was at Brian's."

"I knew it!" he exclaimed.

"I got Mark to take me."

"A-a-ar-r-rgh!" Jeff flopped back down on the desk, kicking his heels and writhing. With a final spasm, he went limp, then cracked an eyelid at her. With his big red lips, he looked much sillier than he knew, and she had to laugh. He sat up again, looking glum.

"We broke in," Sharon said, knowing she was being cruel now but unable to stop herself.

Jeff looked up at the ceiling, then closed his eyes.

"Jeff, you were too beat to take anyone anywhere. I never should have asked you. But I did have to get over there and see if I could find Brian. I know it was risky, but sometimes you have to take risks."

He gazed at her. His face was so serious that the clown lips no longer looked funny to her. "Risks," he said. "I'm glad to hear you say that."

Sharon caught his meaning. He still wanted her; their talk at the beach house had not squelched that desire. She felt glad, and then anxious. She groped for an answer and could find none.

He slid off the table with a sigh and began tucking in his shirt, smoothing out the wrinkles in his white coat. He came to her and took her hand in both of his. "I was out of line," he said, "asking after your personal business. You haven't given me that right. And you haven't asked me, either, to feel that if anything happened to you, the light would go out of my life. But I do." He looked down at their hands, rubbing a thumb softly over her knuckles. She felt a flood of warmth spreading up her arm, around her heart. "Do you know that I'm on a cloud the whole time I'm with you?" he said. "It's a little like being drunk. And when I go a day without seeing you, it starts to ache in here." He brought her hand to his chest. She felt his heart beating. She wanted him suddenly, so much that it made her slightly dizzy.

"I'll never love another woman this way. If you need time, take it. Just give us a chance."

She longed to put her arms around him, but the old fear held her rigid.

Jeff let her hand fall and smiled. "So, on the lighter side, how about us getting married tomorrow night."

"That's your idea of giving me time?"

"Okay, a movie, then. There's a retrospective of old Cagney movies at the Biograph in Georgetown. No—don't answer now. Just think about it, will you? I'll drop by later." He glanced at his watch. "Yama tamama, rounds in five minutes."

He brushed by her out the door.

Sharon sank down behind her desk, trying to unscramble her jumbled feelings. Russian roulette, and yet she was getting closer and closer to pulling the trigger—

His lips! *Oh no!*

Sharon ran out after him, trying to catch him, but the corridor was empty. He had already disappeared. He was going to rounds with great huge clown lips painted on his face.

Sharon went back into her office, her face tingling with shame. What was going to happen to him? Oh, Jeff, I'm *sorry!*

She burst out laughing, then felt sorry all over again.

How would Jeff take it? What if he was furious with her? She realized that it would make her feel terrible.

Jeff loved her. Even if she couldn't love him back.

Oh, bullshit, Sharon.

She felt a thrilling, roller-coaster swoop in her stomach. To let herself go! To love Jeff, to be able to accept his love, to stop being alone . . .

In her mind she saw her mother's face the day Dad walked out the door for the last time.

She emptied her mind. Relax, just relax. Nothing has to be decided in the next minute, the next hour.

Sharon sank into her chair and closed her eyes. As if they had been waiting for the chance, Brian's horrid photo montages popped into her memory—and Mark's face as he had looked at them, the awful intensity of his stare. What had *he* thought, and felt? A mortified heat rose to her face. Those hateful images of her must be indelibly etched in his mind now. It made her stomach crawl.

And yet she could feel it binding her to Mark in some strange way. He had seemed to know what seeing those photos did to her, to know and to understand. She had the sudden urge to call him, ask him to dinner or something. She felt such anger at Brian, such rage at how he had stalked her, used her. She needed to talk about it, and Mark was the only one—

She stopped, startled. What was she thinking? Jeff had just told her he loved her. She could love him back, and that scared her, made her want to run, to use Mark to pull herself away from Jeff. And realizing it didn't do her a damn bit of good.

Physician heal thyself.

Sharon looked at the wall clock, desperate for escape. Seven twenty. Time to head over to MHU for morning report. Physician heal everyone else.

She got up and headed out into the fray.

* * *

Just before noon Sharon went to security and gave them her statement about Brian in PT last night. They said they were calling his apartment. No luck yet, but they would let her know.

She headed back to MHU, pumped up and rolling, feeling as if she had shucked part of Brian off on somebody else. It was after noon and she had a few minutes, why not drop in on Mom. As she walked up the commons, she looked for Frank Greene but didn't see him. He was out of seclusion now, but evidently he was staying in his room. She would swing by there after she saw her mother. Just for a minute, to see how he was, if he was any less paranoid and irrational.

And ask him if he remembered them taking blood.

Her mother's door was ajar, an unofficial rule in MHU. Sharon knocked and waited.

"Come in."

As she entered, her mother smiled and said, "I knew it had to be you."

"No one else knocks?"

"*Everyone* else knocks. And then they come straight in, whether I say to or not." She smiled, showing that she wasn't bitter.

Sharon gave her a hug and a kiss and sat on the bed beside her. "So how's tricks?"

"More tricks than treats," she said. "Halloween is in between and the blades are the fruits of it." Her eyes were slightly unfocused.

Sharon tried not to let her dismay show.

Her mother's eyes focused on her again. "Meg hasn't come back. I haven't seen her. And they don't tell us anything in here. Conroy took her and that was the last of it."

Sharon knew it would do no good to argue. "If I hear anything, I'll let you know."

Ellen Francis patted her daughter's hand. "I know. She was a sweet young woman. A lot like you, only not so cheerful. Depressed over that stinker boyfriend. But she would never run away."

"How do you know?" Sharon asked, despite herself.

"I just know." She sighed and looked out her window, through the steel mesh, at the north parking lot. Sharon wished she could get her a better room; the ones on the other side looked out over the little park behind the hospital. But she had been lucky to get her mother in at all. If they'd charged her, there would have been no way.

"Parkers and barkers," Mom mumbled. "Parkers and barkers, and harkers back. When the time comes the time goes and the hands run round and round."

She went on rambling for almost a minute. Listening to her, Sharon felt all the adrenaline of a morning on the run draining out of her. Her mother had been doing better, getting close to being able to return home. Why had the stress of Meg's disappearance had to come along, setting her back, triggering her paranoia?

Sharon tried to rally herself. Maybe this was only temporary. Mom sometimes got like this when she was tired.

"Are you sleeping okay?"

Ellen Francis turned back from the window. Her smooth, pretty face drew tight with anguish. "I try, but they keep stopping me, crowding into my brain and talking, telling me about Meg and the terrible terrible things . . . things that sing in the night, making fright. . . ." She gave up the effort and her face relaxed.

Sharon felt a sudden, powerful rage at the formless force that hid submerged in the chemical sea of her mother's brain. So powerful and yet so elusive, deadlier than a shark pack, harder to find and kill.

I'll find a way, Sharon thought. I'll hurt it back before I'm done.

She pulled her mother close and hugged her. Ellen hugged back. "I'm trying, sweetie."

"I know." When her mother pulled away, Sharon had her smile in place. "I'll come back tomorrow, all right?"

Ellen nodded.

Sharon went back out to the commons area and stood a moment, feeling listless and deflated, watching a couple of older men play pool. On the other side of the table Brittina stood with one of her patients, a paranoid schizophrenic who believed the CIA was trying to poison him. He was talking earnestly, and Brittina was doing the only thing she could at the moment—listening. Sharon felt a twinge of envy and suppressed it. Brittina was her friend. She didn't want Brittina's schizophrenic patients, she wanted her own. Sharon looked away to the Ping-Pong table, where a couple of the teenage patients had started a game. Beyond, other patients sat in chairs, talking or reading. It was a pleasant, almost homey scene, but Sharon knew she would see it differently if she were sitting in those chairs or batting the hollow white ball.

She looked up and down the commons for Frank Greene. Someone tapped her shoulder; she turned, and there he was.

"Hello, Doc."

"Mr. Greene. It's good to see you." At once she could see the difference in him, and her spirits lifted. He looked much better than he had the other night. And *he* had sought her out. Now Valois couldn't nail her for talking to him. "How do you feel?"

Frank looked around the big ward, his eyes wary. "Right now, pretty good. I managed to fool them this morning at meds. But they watch you like hawks, make sure you take all your pills. I'm afraid they'll catch me next time."

Sharon felt a sharp disappointment. Frank looked better, but he was still irrational. He took her by the wrist, his fingers clenching hard, and she realized he was scared silly. His hand loosened and began to tremble against her arm. She could feel his fear flowing into her and had to resist the urge to pull away. He said, "Listen, please. We may not have much time."

"I'm listening."

"What I said the other night," he whispered. "I know

you probably thought I was crazy, but it's true. They *are* drugging me. Either the meds, or something in my food. I keep seeing things—terrible things. I see Nazis in torn uniforms. Their heads are skulls. I know they're not real, but I see them anyway. I wake up and they're trying to choke me. That's never happened to me, *never*. I'm not crazy, Dr. Francis. That isn't me."

Sharon could feel her heart thudding inside her. "Why would they poison you?" she asked softly.

"Not poison, drugs. And I don't *know* why. I know it sounds paranoid. I can't think of a single reason for it. But it's true. You've got to believe me."

Sharon stared at Frank, chilled, knowing suddenly that he *wasn't* irrational or paranoid. Listen to what he's saying, she told herself. He's making a highly rational distinction between poison and drugs, admitting he sounds paranoid, and offering no reason for what he thinks is being done to him. A true paranoid might hold back his craziness in any one of those areas. But all three?

And another thing: where was the disordered, rambling speech common to schizophrenia?

"It's terrible, Doc. When they drug me, I can't think straight or talk straight."

Phencyclidene, she thought. Angel dust. Probably mixed with something else, blue dots, maybe—LSD. A psychotropic cocktail to make Frank crazy.

Frank's fingers closed on her arm again. "Please, Dr. Francis, you've gotta get me out of here—"

"There you are, Frank."

Sharon turned, startled. It was Chuck Conroy, bearing down on them. "Time for your back therapy," Conroy said, taking Frank's arm.

Frank's face drained of color. "I was talking to Dr. Francis. Go away and leave me alone."

Conroy smiled warmly. "Now, Frank, you don't want to upset their whole schedule, do you? They're waiting for you. Come on now." He pulled Frank along. Frank's steps dragged; he looked back over his shoulder at Sharon in silent appeal. She gave him a thumbs-up sign. She could feel the blood racing through her head. Frank, drugged? Incredible.

And she believed it.

Before Sharon knew what she was doing, she was walking toward Valois's office. She rounded the nurses' station, feeling the noise and activity of the open ward drop away behind her, giving her a sudden sense of isolation. Valois's office door was closed. She knocked and waited, her stomach hollow. This was crazy! What was she going to say? If Frank was being drugged into paranoia, Valois was the number one suspect.

But showing him that she knew might make him stop. Or it might make her next in line.

Sharon started to turn away as Valois's door opened. He stared out at her. "Yes?"

"May I see you a minute?"

Valois glanced at his watch. "About what?"

"Frank Greene."

Valois's eyes narrowed. "I don't think we have anything to talk about there."

"He says he's being drugged."

Valois looked at her, hesitating. "Well, of course he's being drugged."

"He doesn't mean with proper medication. He means that a drug is responsible for his symptoms."

Again Valois hesitated, longer this time. "I thought I told you to stay away from him."

"He approached me. I could hardly turn away."

"That's exactly what you should have done. He's not your patient anymore." Valois's voice was curiously free of anger, as though he was too taken by surprise to feel anything else. "Come in, Sharon."

Come into my parlor, said the spider to the fly.

Sharon forced her legs to move, to carry her into his office.

He pointed to a chair. She glanced at the seat, checking it, then looked back at him, keeping her eyes on him as she sank down.

"Sharon, I'm worried about you."

"About me?"

"Frank Greene is a paranoid schizophrenic. You know that. And yet you let him take you in."

"He's not taking me in."

"Really. This thing about the drugs is obviously a delusion. Can't you see that?"

"I don't think it is a delusion."

Valois nodded, looking very serious, regarding her with avid attention. Her blood ran cold. That is the look, she thought. Clinical. We give it to people when we know they're over the line but we still want to impress them that we're hearing them.

"Sharon," he said gently, "why would we want to make him crazy?"

"I . . . don't know, but—"

"But nothing. You're not thinking straight at all. In fact, I'm starting to have grave doubts about your ability to function in your role here at Adams Memorial."

Sharon felt a jolt of fear. She tried to form an answer, but her brain seemed paralyzed.

Valois came over to her, put a hand on her shoulder. "I know you're under a strain. You work terribly long hours, burning the candle at both ends, what with your residency and the time you're spending in Pendleton's lab. I think you should consider cutting back. One or the other, not both; that would be my recommendation."

She swallowed, trying to martial her thoughts, reclaim the conviction that had brought her to his door. "Dr. Valois, I'm sorry, but I wouldn't have come here if I hadn't thought there was a chance, however slim, that Frank is not delusional. I . . . I just thought you should know what he's saying."

Valois patted her shoulder. "I *do* know, Sharon. Of

course I know. I also know that you've got to get a grip on yourself. I've already got one member of your family up here, and I don't want another."

Sharon felt frozen with dread. She wanted to get up, run out, but she could only sit and stare at Valois.

"I'm sure you're all too aware of the concordance rate between family members for schizophrenia."

She felt herself nod.

"Think about what I've said about cutting back. And if you have any more trouble keeping things straight, I want you to come to me. Will you do that?"

She went on staring at him, unable to speak.

"I know we haven't been on the best of terms," Valois said soothingly, "but I really do have your best interests at heart." He looked at his watch. "And now, I'm afraid I'll have to run. I've got a conference. Remember, if you have any more problems like this, you come to me. And stay away from Frank—for both your sakes."

She realized she was standing, letting herself be ushered out. There was a blank space and then she found herself outside the MHU door, striding through the corridor toward surgery. Jeff, she thought. Go find Jeff.

She walked faster, her mind spinning.

Was it starting to happen to her?

She pushed through the doors into the lab.

Dr. Pendleton was standing at one of the stainless steel necropsy tables. A rat was pinned to the black cork board, its skull cut open, leaking bright ribbons of blood. She stared at it with a distant, sick feeling. Dr. Pendleton turned.

"Oh, Sharon, hi. Jeff was looking for you. I think he's through there, in the rat room." Pendleton winked at her. She stared at him, wondering why he had winked, then registering what he had said. She hurried to the rat room. Jeff was inside, standing in front of one of the drawers, holding a rat up under the light.

"You!" he said, pointing. "Fiend! Thanks to you, I'm the

laughingstock of Adams Memorial and possibly the entire Western Hem—"

Sharon ran to him and threw her arms around him. He grunted with surprise, fumbling the rat to the side, dropping it back in its cage. He held her close and didn't talk. She felt his warmth seeping into her.

"If this is an apology," he said at last, "I accept."

Oh my God—his lips! She had forgotten all about the lipstick. She looked up at him and laughed, feeling it tear through her throat. She stopped, embarrassed at the harsh sound. "Oh, Jeff, that. I'm so sorry."

"Go to the movies with me tomorrow night and all will be forgiven."

"Do we have to wait until tomorrow night?" she said.

He gave her a searching look.

"I don't want to be alone tonight," she said.

"I don't want you to, either," he answered softly.

11

S HARON TOOK the drunk's blood pressure and thought, Hey, I got my wish. I'm not alone tonight. But I'm sure as hell not at the movies with Jeff either.

The refrigerator in the MHU break room next door kicked in with a rattling hum and she had to pump the cuff again. She eased the air out, concentrating. Taylor was right, this guy was murder to pick up. Ah, got it. When the faint beats died away again, she deflated the cuff and turned to the nurse. "I get two hundred over ninety. Let's start Mr. Reigle on twelve point five milligrams of hydrochlorothiazide, see if we can get it down a little that way first. Also a glucose IV with a vitamin chaser."

Mr. Reigle gave her a bleary smile. "You gotta' sensa humor, Nurse. I like that." His eyes slipped out of focus and closed. His breath rose to her, sickly sweet.

She patted his shoulder. "Sleep, Mr. Reigle. We'll talk in the morning."

Outside in the dim silence of the commons area Taylor whispered, "you have all the luck, don't you? Dr. Kamensky was on call last night and slept the whole eight. By the way, what if Reigle gets agitated?"

Sharon rubbed at her eyes. Only eleven, and already she was dead. "I'll write you an order for oxazepam, seven point five milligrams, no more than b.i.d., one week max.

I don't want him switching addictions." Sharon's beeper went off. She groaned.

"All the luck," Taylor repeated sympathetically.

The call was from ER. Police had brought in a man who was running naked down Rhode Island Avenue with a knife. Sharon left MHU by the front entrance and trotted across to emergency, breaking into a sweat in the muggy night air. ER was hopping, the waiting room almost full, including a man in greasy clothes who was groaning and holding his stomach while the others watched him from the corners of their eyes. Sharon pointed him out to the triage nurse.

"I know," the nurse snapped. "He's hamming, believe me, and we have our hands full. Your man's in booth three. Dr. Cagle had to trank him. Look's like angel dust. We need a commitment order to St. E.'s."

"No insurance, huh?" Sharon said.

"Hey, you want to take him up to MHU with you?"

"Not much."

Sharon wrote the order, gave it to the policeman, and took the inside route back to MHU, walking slowly. Taylor waved her past the nurses' station and Sharon plodded gratefully to the on-call room. She sank down on the bed, yawning, thinking about Jeff, telling herself that she would have been no good at the movie, either. That go-around with Valois had taken too much out of her.

Her stomach felt suddenly hollow. She had almost lost it with Valois. Paranoid; she had done a great paranoid gig for the oily bastard. She shuddered. And then she had been so rattled she'd forgotten she was on call tonight, which must have impressed Jeff. So what? she thought. He'll forgive you. You'll go tomorrow night. Quit at three thirty for once, and sleep until it's time to meet him.

If she had any sense, she'd call off tomorrow night and sleep straight through until morning.

If she had any sense, she'd be asleep right now. . . .

* * *

Sharon awoke with a start. She lay on the bed, her heart throbbing, a tinny taste of fear in her mouth. *Where am I?*

On-call room.

Why is it dark?

Taylor must have turned off the lights.

So why did I wake up?

Sharon raised her head and peered at the molten line of light under the door.

It was broken in two places.

The hackles rose along her neck. Someone was outside, standing very still. She heard a soft, steely rasp: the door-knob being turned.

"Who's there!" she called sharply.

The knob snicked back and the light under the door flowed together into an unbroken line.

Sharon got up and hurried to the door, yanking it open. The corridor was empty. A chill ran up her spine. She walked to the nursing station. Chuck Conroy was sitting there, reading a book. He looked up. "Hi, Doc."

"Did you just see a patient walk past here?"

Conroy frowned. "No, but I could have missed it."

"Someone was at the door to my on-call room."

"You sure?"

"Yes, I'm sure," Sharon snapped.

Conroy looked abashed.

Get hold of yourself. "Sorry. Where's Mrs. Taylor?"

"Taking her nap."

Sharon's beeper went off and she picked up the desk phone. ER again, a suicide attempt, could she come down right away.

Walking out, Sharon could feel Conroy's eyes boring into her back. It was him, she thought, then realized it could have been harmless old Mr. Merrill, who liked to wander around quietly at night.

Or it could have been no one.

In which case she was seeing things.

Sharon tried to laugh, but it stuck in her throat.

142

* * *

Eight o'clock came at last, and she was off call.

And back on duty on her regular shift.

Thirty minutes until morning report, time enough to blitz the Norelco. She hurried over to her office and started the coffee brewing, fidgeting while she waited, knowing she had to keep rolling or the fatigue would kick in and start dragging her down.

The rough draft file caught her eye. While she had a few minutes, she could get it organized. Let Jenkins come snooping in here again and he would find apple pie order.

Her fingers brushed Brian's intake; Meg's was right next to it. A nasty coincidence. She looked at the yellow folders, feeling an unpleasant tingle of nerves in her neck. All right, just put Meg under *M* and Brian under *B*. She did it and stood back, wiping her hands on her skirt. She kicked the drawer shut. The hell with the rough draft files.

The door opened behind her and she jumped, but it was only Austin. "Good morning, Dr. Francis," he said.

"Good morning, Dr. Demaris." She was absurdly glad to see him.

When three thirty came at last, Sharon went straight back to the on-call room. No sense going home to sleep when Jeff wanted to pick her up here for the movie anyway. Brittina promised to wake her at seven. Sharon instantly fell into a dreamless sleep. When Brittina knocked, she awoke at once, feeling amazingly fresh.

Brittina leaned in the doorway. "You taking dex or something? Thirty straight, then three and a half of sleep, no one looks that good."

"I'm taking dex."

"Bullshit, Francis. You wouldn't take an aspirin if you had a scorpion nailed to your head." Brittina gave her a speculative look. "You in love?"

"God," Sharon said. "I hope not."

Filled with eagerness, she hurried over to neurology, but Jeff wasn't in his office. Bill Jacques, one of his buddies, was sitting across from Jeff's desk, his feet up, thumbing through one of Jeff's wrestling magazines.

"Know where he is?" Sharon asked.

"Ob-gyn. Said he had to run an eval."

But when she got to ob-gyn, Jeff wasn't in the testing room. One of the nurses waved her through to the nursery. She saw Jeff from behind. He was standing among the tiny cribs with his shoulders hunched over and his head bent forward, swaying from side to side. Sharon could hear his voice crooning. There were three other people in the room, two women around forty, exquisitely made up, wearing chic power suits, and a grandfatherly man dressed in baggy pants and a plaid sweater vest. Like Jeff, all of them were holding babies, rocking them, crooning to them.

Sharon realized suddenly what it was: the part of the nursery where they boarded babies whose mothers couldn't or didn't want to care for them. Drug-addicted mothers, thirteen-year-old mothers, street mothers.

Schizophrenic mothers with no husbands.

The hospital kept the babies there until a social worker could place them in adoption agencies. Some of them—preemies and born heroin addicts—would stay longer than others. While they were here, they needed to be held, talked to, rocked and cuddled, or they would not grow, and some of them would die. The nurses, who already crammed sixteen hours into every eight, couldn't spend enough time with the babies, so the hospital had organized a volunteer program.

Sharon saw a tiny brown foot kick feebly past Jeff's arm. "Grab my finger," he said. "Whoa—you *are* getting stronger, aren't you?"

A warm feeling came over her. She felt a big lump in her throat. She wanted to walk up behind Jeff and put her arms around him.

One of the women in the expensive suits smiled at her. Sharon realized she was grinning. She nodded at the woman and backed out of the room. The babies were obviously a little secret for Jeff. He hadn't told his good buddy Jacques, and he might not be keen on her discovering it just now.

Sharon headed back toward Jeff's office, feeling the smile break out on her face again. Men could be so damn foolish.

And was she in love with this one? Oh, yes, there was a good chance.

Jeff's office was empty now. She sat down at his desk and waited for him. After a few minutes, he hurried in. "Sorry," he said. "Had to run a damn finger-tapping test on a guy, and for some unknowable reason every time the counter got to nine he'd stop tapping and grin at me. I don't know how many times I had to make him start over."

Clearly Jeff didn't realize that his face was glowing.

"That's all right," Sharon said, and kissed him.

Sharon watched the art galleries and yuppie restaurants and punky night clubs of M Street inch by, enjoying the easy flow of Jeff's voice. The traffic stalled completely and he turned, resting one hand on the wheel. "This theater we're going to," he said, "has been around a long time. The Biograph. It's hung in there year after year while other old theaters got bought up or plowed under by the AMC Twelves and the K-B Sevens and the shopping mall clones where you can hear three movies at once while you basically watch TV."

Listening to him, Sharon decided that his choice of theater went with his choice of car: Jeff liked things that lasted. Georgetown, despite its aimless crowds and its tacky overlay of glitz, was a part of that. He kept bringing her back there, where the two-story brick and stone shops leaned on each other as they had for a hundred years, not even an alley to part their embrace. Georgetown had been around for a long time, had endured a lot. Georgetown had lasted.

He won't care if we're perfect, Sharon thought, but he'll want us to last. She put the thought from her mind, determined to let nothing depress her tonight.

Jeff parked in a lot across from the theater. Even from

outside, Sharon liked the Biograph. Marquee bulbs flashed around the lobby windows. Inside it was larger than she expected, but still intimate, with soft, low lighting, and a good-size screen.

The theater was quite full. The murmur of voices, the ambience of happy expectation, gave Sharon a lift. She chose the middle row, middle seats, enjoying the comforting shoulder-to-shoulder closeness of people all around her.

Then the lights went down and the screen lit up with a theater promotion for Friday night "Midnight Madness," two great horror flicks. All at once the people receded into the darkness around her and she felt cold clock hands crawling together inside her. Midnight madness—Ellen and Sharon Francis, two of a kind, folks, and yes, Valois, I am aware of the concordance rate for children of schizophrenics.

Jeff picked up her hand by one finger and kissed her nail gently. A warm shiver of delight ran up her spine, driving out the cold. The promo ended, and for a second a shaft of pure silver light poured down from behind, lighting the screen in moonglow. Sharon heard the babble around them dwindle to nothing in the magical light. Numbers flickered—four, three, two. Why was there never a one? The old movie started with a melodramatic chorus of violins. She tried to watch, but she was very aware of Jeff. He took her hand again, folding it in his. She felt him probing the calluses on the pads of her fingers with a feather touch. Was he wondering where they came from? What would she tell him if he asked? I pump iron, Jeff.

Maybe she could tell him she was a concert pianist.

How marvelous and deft his hands were, large and long-fingered, perfectly proportioned. Sharon could imagine him doing the most delicate brain surgery, never slipping, finding his way into the smallest crannies with unerring skill.

She could imagine those same hands on her breasts.

She felt a thrill in the pit of her stomach. The movie rolled on. She imagined making love to Jeff. I could ask him up, she thought, when he takes me home. The idea made her feel a little dizzy.

The movie ended.

It was hot outside. The pavement radiated its warmth into the heavy night air. Jeff walked her back to the car with an arm around her shoulder, matching the rhythm of his stride to hers.

"Isn't Jimmy wonderful?" Jeff said.

"Huh?"

He gave her an odd look. "Jimmy Cagney. You know, the guy in that movie we just watched, in the theater back there."

"I knew that."

"It's all right," he said, grinning.

"I was watching. I *was.*"

They were back at his Buick. She slid across the warm smooth leather, sitting close to him. Ask him up? she thought. Her mind spun, refusing to give an answer. In what seemed an eyeblink they were back uptown, outside her apartment, and she still didn't know what she would say. He turned and looked at her, his face half in shadow, half bright under the streetlight. "It doesn't have to be all movies and the beach," he said. "I want the rest of it, too, the bad times with the good."

She was touched. He couldn't really know what he was saying, but he meant it, as much as anyone could. She said, "The bad could get *very* bad."

"I don't care how many verys you tack on to it. You're not your mother, and I'm not your father."

She felt a stab of anger. "Be careful, Jeff."

He looked baffled.

She was shocked at herself. The anger shrank away. "I'm sorry. I don't know why I said that."

He looked at her. "I think I might."

Sharon felt a cold, unreasoning edge of fear. "Do me a favor, will you? Don't tell me. Not now, not tonight."

He nodded.

"Would you like to come up?"

He nodded again, then checked his watch. "I'm taking part of Jacques' on-call tonight. I've got to be at the hospital in an hour and a half."

"Come on."

The apartment was baking hot, but Sharon felt the heat only dimly. She went to the couch and sat down, feeling a little breathless. Jeff sat down several feet from her, then leaned over, putting his head in her lap, gazing up at her. "You have exquisite nostrils," he said.

She laughed and slipped her fingers into his hair, combing through the thick tangles, conscious of the weight of his head on her thighs. His cheek nestled against her stomach. "You're warm," he murmured. He turned his face into her dress, inhaling deeply, and she felt his shoulders shiver against her. She put her other hand on his chest, letting her fingers find their way inside his shirt. His chest was warm and damp, matted with fine, curly hair. She dug her nails in a little, leaning her head back, dizzied by a surge of pleasure. She ached with desire for him. *Think,* she told herself, but she didn't want to think—to *hell* with thinking.

"I love your smell," Jeff said. "It's like salt and vanilla. Jesus, it goes to my head."

"Jeff, Jeff."

He slid a hand under her knees, easing her down along the couch, pulling her to him. He held her for a long time. She could feel his heart beating against her. "I love you, Sharon," he said. "And I want to make love to you."

Heat flared in her body where it pressed against him. She pressed herself along him, wanting to feel every inch of him. He hardened against her and she felt an answering surge of desire, like a drug in her veins, filling her with a strange ecstasy.

She backed off the couch and stood, giving him her hands, pulling him up. Slowly, she unbuttoned his shirt, her fingers trembling. He slipped out of his other clothes, then helped her with hers, his hands touching her lightly through the cloth at her breasts, sliding down her hips as her skirt dropped. She sat him down, fingering the hardness of his shoulders, and then lay with him, pressing him back. Reaching down between them, she touched him lightly, excited by the straining of his blood and nerve in desire for her. He cupped her breasts in his hands, fingering her nipples to hard nubs.

"Sharon, my love, my true love."

"Mmmm." She wrapped her legs around him. He entered her, so slowly, so gently, a ball of warmth started in her belly and spread through her. She dug her fingers into his hair and pulled his mouth to her, licking at his tongue, tasting the wet heat of him. Oh, yes, I love you, Jeff, I love you, so beautiful, how can it keep on?

He kissed her ear and murmured into it, the heat of his breath tingling, "You feel so soft, like silk inside."

"Move higher—ah!" She rocked gently against him and he joined in, meeting her rhythm. The couch felt like a cloud under her side. She could feel the thoughts flying from her mind, a drumbeat of wings merging with her pulse, and then her head was empty and her body was everything, crying out, loving it. Explosions started deep inside her, building, building, *yes! Yes! Yes!*

Her body soared in euphoric warmth, a place where no pain could come, no pain had ever been.

He stayed in her a long time, stroking her, telling her that he loved her, that he wanted to be with her always. She loved him too, oh yes. She did not have to be alone any more. It was the most wonderful feeling she had ever had.

She really wanted to believe it.

Jeff lay with Sharon, feeling her breath against his ear. He ached with love for her, afraid to move, wanting to stop time forever in this glow.

But he had to be at the hospital in twenty minutes.

He rolled gently away from her and padded to the bedroom. Pulling a sheet from the bed, he returned and draped it over her, gazing down at her sleeping form. Her dark glossy hair veiled her eyes; one hand was tucked against her chin. She looked utterly at peace, like a sleeping child.

Dear Jesus, how he loved her.

You're so afraid, he thought, aren't you? Not just that you'll be like your mother, but that some man will come along and prove he's better than your father.

Sadness welled up in him. She worshiped a false memory, a father who was entirely fine and noble, who had been driven away, without any choice, by his wife's insanity. She believed it because she could not bear to believe the truth—that dear old Dad hadn't just left her mother, he had left her too. As a little girl, she wouldn't have been able to bear that pain. Instead, she had channeled all her energy against the one thing she could safely hate—her mother's illness. It had made her what she was today, a highly motivated and dedicated physician.

It had also made her alone and deathly afraid.

Jeff felt a surge of fury at her father, for running out, quitting, ramming himself into a brick wall. Bastard! he thought. She was just a little girl. But she had no chance to mourn or be angry. She was too busy taking care of your wife.

Jeff gathered up his clothes and put them on. He wanted so much to help Sharon, but she was afraid of that, too—*"Do me a favor and don't tell me."*

Okay, not tonight, Sharon, but soon. You don't have to take care of your mom anymore, they're doing that in MHU. I'm going to help you find the old pain and let it out. Weeping or rage—whatever it takes. You need to hate him, just for a little while. Then you need to forgive him.

And then maybe you can believe I won't leave you.

Jeff wrote a note on his prescription pad: *Need O$_2$. Gone to ER. Check your lips—you have been warned.* He signed it *LoveLoveLove, Jeff.*

He tucked the sheet against her chin and pulled it over her feet and slipped out quietly.

* * *

Sharon was at the door to MHU again, trying to get out. The key wouldn't fit. She heard the footsteps in the short hallway behind her.

"Come on, Sharon, back to your room."

The hands closed on her arms. She tried to tell them it was a mistake, but she couldn't squeeze her voice through the strangling pressure in her throat.

A phone started ringing.

The hands released her.

She was lying on the floor, gray fog swirling around her as the phone went on ringing.

She woke, startled, disoriented, feeling her hands clutching a sweat-soaked sheet. Why was she lying on her couch? The phone rang again. She snatched the receiver, feeling her tension smooth out in relief. Just a dream, just the same old stupid dream.

"Hello, and thank you," she said.

"Sharon?"

Jeff! She was gladder than she could have imagined to hear his voice, but before she could say anything, he said, "Listen, I'm sorry if I woke you, but I figured you'd want to hear this. I just saw your friend Brittina down in ER and she says there was a bit of a flap up in MHU tonight—"

"Mom!" Sharon said, frightened.

"No, not your mother. I'm sorry. I should have thought of that. No, it was Frank Greene. Apparently he pitched a royal fit up there this evening, then checked himself out AMA. Nurse Taylor called his family and told them to pick him up, but by the time they got there, he was gone. Now his wife is up there in quite a state. Seems Frank didn't come home."

Sharon felt a horrified shock of recognition, the feeling of things falling into place. Meg and Brian, she thought. And now Frank.

Oh, God. Poor Frank. What have they done to you?

12

AT EIGHT A.M. Sharon hurried out of her apartment and stood blinking in the dazzling sunlight, feeling like a mole that had suddenly popped up from a long stay underground. How could she have slept so deeply with Frank missing? The thirty straight hours on duty must have caught up with her. She peered around. Everything looked a little strange, the street too black, the colors of the parked cars too harsh.

Jeff's Buick rolled up, the sun gleaming off the rich maroon finish, paining her eyes. She slid in beside him.

He leaned over and kissed her. It felt very nice.

"Right on time," she said. "Thanks. Sorry to bother you, but this is important."

"No problem."

"I checked my lips," she told him. "You're a better person than I am."

"You're not out of the woods yet," he promised.

She said, "About last night . . ."

He looked at her, serious, waiting.

She felt a jumble of love and anxiety. "I think we may have gotten a little ahead of ourselves," she said. "And it was my doing. I practically dragged you up."

"Yes, I was quite offended," he said.

She laughed. "The point is—" She stopped. She didn't know what the point was.

He took her hands. "Do you want to explain last night, or make it go away?"

"I never want it to go away."

He looked relieved. "Good. Listen, you've been afraid of love for a long time. You can't ditch that overnight. But you don't have to let your fear scare you."

Sharon saw love and caring in his eyes. It had a wonderful, soothing effect on her. She realized suddenly what a good psychiatrist he might make, the calm kindness, the clear, simple way he had of thinking and talking. She wanted to take that part of him into her. She wanted to give him whatever it was that he loved in her.

But first she had to beat the fear.

She kissed him on the cheek. "Here's the address."

As he pulled out of the parking lot, she noticed the dark rings under his eyes, his slumped shoulders. Concern swept over her. "Are you too tired to drive?"

"A doctor's never too tired to drive," he said, "or to putt." He gave a huge yawn, popping his jaw. "But if you don't mind, I'll just stay in the car and count the capillaries in my eyelids while you comfort Mrs. Greene."

"That's good." Sharon wondered what he would say when she told him she wanted to go straight from Mrs. Greene's to the police. Better not drop that on him yet. Jeff didn't know Frank the way she did. Unless Mrs. Greene could give her a damn good explanation about where Frank might be, she was going to the police, and if that didn't work, she would do whatever she had to do, because she was not going to let them have Frank Greene.

Jeff glanced over at her. "Of course, you plan on more than comforting her, don't you?"

Sharon looked at him, surprised. "Am I that transparent?"

"You're one of the least transparent people I know. But I'm the guy who ripped off Frank's file for you, remember?

Just be careful not to let Mrs. Greene think that anyone at Adams Memorial could have stopped her husband from leaving."

"Come on, Jeff. First his blood test is missing, then he has a psychotic break, which I never saw coming, even though I've lived for twenty-seven years with a schizophrenic and been trained for five of those years on how to spot the signs. Then Frank tells me they're drugging him, and shortly after that he walks out of MHU and disappears. Don't you think that's just a tad suspicious?"

"I respect your judgment on the strangeness of his going psychotic," Jeff said. "But the idea that someone up there is drugging him seems too fantastic to me; I'm sorry. And people go missing every day all over a city this big. I'm sure a fair proportion of them take off from mental wards."

Sharon started to feel annoyed at him, then realized he had just made an excellent point. Did the police keep records on people who were missing from mental wards? If so, she might be able to pin down whether what was happening at Adams Memorial was unusual.

Jeff craned his neck to see a street sign, then turned down a shaded avenue lined with modest duplexes. "Here it is." He pulled to the curb, settled back in his seat, and closed his eyes. Sharon looked at him uneasily, wondering what he was feeling. He didn't seem to see Frank's disappearance the way she did, and that bothered her. She wished she knew whether he thought she was being paranoid. But she was afraid to ask.

Jeff's mouth sagged open in a soft snore.

Sharon smiled. He didn't seem terribly worried.

The evidence that something bad had happened to Frank was there in Norma Greene's tearful eyes, and all around her in the house. Frank and Norma's closeness shone from the photos on the tables: Norma and Frank out on a sun-smitten golf course, Frank standing behind her, helping her swing; the two of them at the edge of a picnic crowd, biting into each other's hot dogs; together on some distant beach with palm trees, standing very close, their arms around each other.

Norma Greene said that she had contacted the police and talked to a Detective Poulson, a huge man, very nice, but that she wasn't sure he had really believed her.

Walking back to the car, Sharon felt a real sense of urgency. Jeff was still asleep. She tried to nudge him over so she could drive, but he woke up with a start.

"Get in back," she said, "Sleep. I'm driving."

He clambered into the back seat. She pulled away from the curb and drove around the block, waiting until she heard his breathing even out before she asked him, "Jeff, you don't mind if we stop off at the police station first, do you?"

"Nnnnk," he said.

At the Third District police station, Sharon left Jeff sleeping in the back seat and hurried inside. The small entry lobby was cool, dim and quiet, not at all like the police stations she remembered from *Cagney and Lacey.* No muscular punks in holding cages or strings of prostitutes handcuffed together. A couple of young guys sat smoking on benches along the walls. An older white man in a loud plaid jacket leaned against the counter reading a newspaper. The only thing she recognized from TV and the movies was a sergeant sitting behind the counter. He was bald and wore glasses; except for the uniform, he looked more like a dentist.

Sharon told him who she was. "Is Detective Poulson in?" she asked.

"What would this be in reference to, Dr. Francis?"

"In reference to a missing person case," she said, feeling a little silly at getting sucked into using his jargon.

"And what case might that be?"

"Frank Greene." Having a sudden idea, she added, "And Meg Andreason."

He turned to a glowing computer screen and his fingers

ditted busily for a moment. "Okay," he said. "That's Poulson, all right."

"Both cases?" she said, wanting to nail it down.

"Yup."

Sharon felt a stir of hope. Maybe the police were starting to make something of this after all.

The desk sergeant lifted the counter door. "Fourth row back, Doctor. Third desk from the left. Big man, you can't miss him."

Sharon walked back through a large room partitioned with wood and frosted glass into a warren of office cubbyholes, the kind one expects to see in the editorial room of a big newspaper. She ticked off the rows and desks. That must be Poulson—he was every bit as big as Norma Greene had said. His shoulders were broad as a door, stretching his blue blazer tight across his back.

"Detective Poulson?"

His chair screeched as he turned. His belly was almost as broad as his back, and just as solid-looking. His skin was a dark blue-black, with a sheen that made his craggy face look like carved onyx.

"Help you?" he said in a bass smoker's growl.

Sharon introduced herself and told him about her connection to Meg and Frank Greene.

"Yeah, Doctor. I think I've got your name somewhere in my notes. Greene's therapist, so you must know him pretty well. You come in to tell me where he might be?"

"Sorry."

"Don't tell me," he groaned. "You came in to climb on my back about it."

"Yes, I did, but that's not all." She swallowed, suddenly nervous.

"So?"

"I think there may be a suspicious pattern about these disappearances."

"All two of them?" he said without smiling.

She felt a small letdown. If Poulson was making anything special out of the two cases, he wasn't letting on.

But he wasn't laughing, either.

"There might be at least one other—that I know of." She told him about Brian and pointed out the fact that both Meg and Frank had signed out AMA. She didn't mention Valois; she didn't have enough for that yet, and it would be better if Poulson found the connection himself. While she talked, Poulson tapped a pencil against his teeth, *tink tink,* making her think of a xylophone.

"So you think it's suspicious," he said when she had finished. "Dr. Francis, we get missing persons all the time; I'm sure you know that. Tell you something else, a lot of them walked right out of mental hospitals just before they disappeared. Usually turn up in a few days wandering around. Or—hate to say it—we find 'em dead. Floaters, or wintertime, they wander off to the wrong place and freeze."

"You said mental hospitals, especially. Do you keep statistics on the number of missing persons from area psychiatric wards?"

"Don't know. I can tell you off the top of my head that Community, up the street here, has been losing about seven a month off the unlocked wards. Another six a month actually manage to bug out from the so-called lockups, if you can believe that."

Sharon was stunned. Thirteen people a month, just from one hospital? She searched her memory, combing back through months of morning reports on MHU. Okay, sure, people did take off every now and then, AMA, or when a staff member had the door open. A few had even been her patients. The point was, none of them had run away or disappeared after leaving.

But what about Brittina's patients, or Kamensky's, or Austin's or Tom's? She didn't follow them. And she wasn't at the hospital every day. The truth was, there could be eight or nine "escapes" a month from Adams Memorial and she wouldn't register it.

"Yeah," Poulson said, "they bug out. Then if they don't come home the hospital or family comes here and gets an 'escape warrant' from us. But all that means is, we happen to spot the person, we return them to the hospital. Unless, of course, they're considered dangerous. But not too many psychos are in the easy-out places to begin with. Most of the people who go on the run turn up in a day or two, alive or dead, without any help from us. If not, the family asks for missing person status. And, since you no doubt know it anyway, I'll admit that doesn't buy you much either."

"I can understand that—"

"Good. A lot of people can't."

"But these people, Meg and Frank—they're different."

"Dr. Francis, *everyone's* different. Nobody's dog bites, and nobody's husband or wife or kid would ever run away. Trust me." He gave her a sweet smile that transformed his tough, homely face.

She saw that it was no use. She would never convince Poulson using this approach.

Damn—what a perfect setup it was. If for some deep dark reason you want to snatch people, but you don't want the police to get too excited, who do you take?

Mental patients.

Mental patients might do anything, right? Certainly it's nothing to get alarmed about if one or two run off.

Wrong, Sharon thought fiercely, but she knew how hard it would be to convince the average person of that, let alone a cop with lots of other, more serious-looking cases on his desk.

"I'll make you a deal," she said. "I'm Frank Greene's doctor, and I *know* that he wouldn't just run off. But it won't do any good to keep saying that to you if you won't believe it. So just let me prove it to you."

He sighed with an air of patient suffering. "Now how you going to do that?"

"You try to find some numbers and names for me: the

people who go missing from area mental wards. Yearly, monthly, however you keep it."

"Even if I've got that, what good would it do you?"

"Plenty, if your stats also keep track of who turns up again."

"I still don't see—"

"I'll check your names against the Adams Memorial census for the past year. Then I'll see how many people *stay* missing from Adams mental wards, compared to those who stay missing from other area mental hospitals."

Poulson gave her a measuring look. "You're kind of clever, you know that?"

"Thank you."

"But say you get a few more from Adams. It's just numbers. Numbers like that are always different. The Bullets play Boston. Bullets score a hundred ten and Boston scores eighty-nine. I guarantee it doesn't prove diddly squat."

"Yeah, but if it's the average over twenty games, or sixteen area hospitals, it proves a lot. In statistical research, 'significant difference' has a mathematically precise meaning. You've been trained as a cop, I've been trained as a researcher. I know how to *prove* if the lost-and-found rate for Adams Memorial is too far off the average of other hospitals to be due to chance. I'll run an F test—"

Poulson burst out laughing. "An *F* test? What, aside from what my dirty mind can imagine, is an F test?"

Sharon hesitated, searching for a way to explain. "An F test is a statistical technique for determining whether something might be *causing* differences among the averages of various groups of numbers, or whether those differences are just due to chance alone. In this process, the variance is included in the—"

Poulson held up a hand. "Okay, okay. I'll take your word for it. I didn't know doctors were experts in math, too."

"They're usually not. But I knew back in college that when I became a psychiatrist, I'd want to be able to evaluate other people's psychological research, and maybe even do some myself. For most of that research, you've got to really understand and be good at statistical analysis to find out whether your results are significant. So in college I took several classes in statistics."

"Do you always plan that far ahead?"

Sharon felt suddenly uncomfortable. "You're kind of clever yourself, aren't you?"

Sharon got the printouts into the car without waking Jeff and headed back to the hospital, a little discouraged. Poulson's list had the names of all missing persons in Washington, but there was no list for just the mental patients. She could match Poulson's names against Adams Memorial's MHU records, but she wouldn't know the norms for the other area mental hospitals unless they would let her access their central computers, which was even more unlikely than it would be time consuming.

At least Poulson had given her a second list with the names of missing people who had turned up again, an overall list, for the whole city. She would prefer to check Adams psych patients strictly against their counterparts in other city hospitals. On the other hand, one could probably assume that psychiatric runaways tended to turn up again more often than those missing from the population at large, if for no other reason than lack of competence. As Poulson had put it, "Most of these people turn up in a day or two, alive or dead." She shuddered. The point was, she should expect to find that fewer people *stayed* missing from Adams, compared to the general population. If she found out there were more, it would make her point that much stronger.

Sharon drove back to the hospital with a slightly breathless feeling in her chest. As she pulled into the parking lot, an eerie sense of alienness swept over her, as though she was seeing Adams Memorial for the first time. The sunstruck windows made every room seem on fire; the tall central section towered above her like a stone monster that might leap to life any second.

The crazy load of paranoia in the image disturbed her. Come on. Someone in there might be dangerous, deadly even, but the hospital itself was not. The hospital was good, the hospital was fine—it had to be or she couldn't keep walking into it every day.

Sharon peered up at the penthouse, wondering if the chief administrator, Judith Acheson, was up there now behind the opaque golden windows, looking down at the maroon Buick. She felt a powerful urge to turn the car around and drive away fast, to keep going until she could no longer see even the top of the hospital.

She turned and wakened Jeff. "Want me to drive you home and pick you up later?"

He looked at his watch. "What'd you do, coast back here in first gear?"

"I took the scenic route." She didn't want to launch into lengthy explanations. She wanted to get on the psych services terminal and compare Poulson's printouts to the record of patients at Adams Memorial. Right now, nothing in the world seemed quite so important as that, not even being completely honest with Jeff. She felt a twinge of guilt but suppressed it. She could fill Jeff in later.

He said he didn't want to go home, the bed in his on-call room was closer. She kissed him good-bye and hopped out, hoping he wouldn't notice the printouts in her hand.

Fortunately, Jenkins had recently bought a new optical scanner for the psych services terminal. Sharon ran it over the lists Detective Poulson had given her, transferring the text into the memory of the hospital's mainframe. Then she instructed the mainframe to cross-match the list with the MHU patient register for the past year. There was a slight delay and she felt her stomach tighten. A lot of the information on patients in the mainframe memory, such as medical charts, could not be accessed by office terminals. But surely that did not include mere census information. The screen began to scroll up and Sharon sighed in relief. She pushed print and watched the names inch line by line from the printer.

Sixty-three names from Poulson's list of missing persons had been patients at Adam's Memorial MHU or psych services. Sharon checked the names against Poulson's found-again list.

Only twenty of the sixty-three had turned up again.

The skin along Sharon's scalp crawled. Jesus!

She cautioned herself: she wouldn't know for sure until she compared the Adams ratio to that for the total list. A simple T test would be enough.

But T test or no T test, she'd bet her rent that the number of missing persons from Adams who stayed missing was significantly higher.

Sharon felt a little sick to her stomach. She thought of Norma Greene, surrounded by her photos of herself and Frank, hoping and praying they were not all she had left.

"What's up, Sharon?"

She turned, startled. It was Jenkins, standing in the doorway. Either she had been more engrossed than she thought, or he had a little sneaker on the tip of his cane. She said, "Just double-checking some statistics in an article I read." Switching off the computer, she tore off the hard copy and folded it, trying to act nonchalant.

"You're not on duty in MHU today?"

"I got someone to cover for me." If it's any of your business.

"And yet you're here. I take it you're not ill." He was staring at the printouts. Sharon began to sweat.

"I feel fine."

She brushed past him and hurried down the hall, feeling his eyes on her back. It gave her the creeps. In her office, she shoved the printouts in her desk drawer and stared at the door, waiting for Jenkins and his cane to swing into sight. They didn't.

She sank into her chair, taking out the printouts again, feeling scared, more scared even than when Brian had sprung from the booth and grabbed her. Brian had been after her, the sick photos proved that. But a bigger fish—a real shark—had come along and gobbled Brian up with hardly a ripple, and Frank and Meg, too.

And now she was poking into it, churning up the waters. How long before that same shark came gliding along behind her?

A cold knot of fear formed in her stomach. I need help, she thought.

I need Mark Pendleton.

13

FRANK GREENE SAT on the table and looked
around the cell, thinking, I'm not afraid. Realizing it,
he felt pride—and relief. Hell, he'd been through tough
times before. Of course, that had been years ago, nineteen
hundred and forty-four, to be exact. When he'd got so
gummy-legged scared there in the mental ward, he'd been
afraid he'd lost it for good, his ability to suck it up and be
brave.

Messing with a man's mind . . .

He shuddered. It was the worst thing you could do. The
bastards had made him crazy, but now that was over. His
craziness had served their purposes, making sure no one
would bother to look for him much. Even poor Norma must
think he had run off because he was nuts.

No one in the world was going to think that son of a bitch
Conroy had bushwhacked him when he had walked out of
MHU. Same son of a bitch who explained how he could
check himself out in the first place.

Oh, it was neat all right.

But now he was here, and it wasn't the worst, no sir.

Normandy had been the worst. When the front flap of
that damn LST had folded down and the sergeant had
yelled, Go, GO! and you jumped in and tried to run while
the water dragged at your chest and legs and the Kraut bul-

lets plopped all around you like murdering hailstones; that was the worst.

GI piss is probably still washing up on that damn beach, Frank thought.

But I got there and I got out again and I'm going to get out of this.

He looked up at the ventilation duct. Nope, definitely too small to wiggle through. Forget the door, too. It was solid core, probably at least two inches on the dead bolt, and set in a steel masonry frame. Some of the carpenters he knew might be able to pick that bad boy with a belt buckle, but he couldn't, so there was no sense messing with it anymore.

That left the wall.

Frank walked over and bent down carefully to where he had felt the draft. Pain knifed through his back. Gritting his teeth, he lay down on his side and drew one knee up. Better. He held the back of his hand to the junction of floor and wall and felt the trickle of air, still there. Had to be a chipped cinder block behind the wood paneling. They must not have backfilled properly. Probably left some pretty big waste in there, some plywood offcuts maybe, so that the dirt didn't fill in good, letting air all the way down from the surface.

In dirt, where air could go, a man could dig.

Hell, he had always wanted to dig a foxhole from the bottom up.

But first he had to remove some of that cinder block.

Pushing himself up from the floor sent pain jagging along his spine. Frank sat, bracing his back against the wall, waiting out the pain. Who am I kidding? he thought. I'm an old man with a messed-up back.

Yeah, but you still got twice the grip of a thirty-year-old man, from squeezing them tin snips all those years. He held up his forearms and flexed his hands. He could get them blocks out.

He heard someone bump against the door outside, and fear flooded up him. Too late! he thought, but he sprang up, feeling his back scream with pain as he hurried to the table. A key slid into the dead bolt; he parked himself on the table again, his head spinning.

The dead bolt slid back so smoothly he could barely hear it, and the door opened. Conroy, the rotten bastard. Even looked like a Kraut: that short blond hair, the square Jerry jaw.

"Brought you supper, Frank." Conroy held out a tray.

Frank took it and looked at the bowl of soup. "Didn't I order steak?"

Conroy laughed. "Sorry about that."

"Any chance you could bring me a TV in here?" That's good, Frank thought. Make him think old Frank was just going to lie here doing nothing.

Conroy laughed again. "I'm afraid we aren't quite as posh as Adams Memorial here."

"I'd settle for a bed. How'm I supposed to sleep on this hard table with my back hurting me the way it does?"

Conroy sobered. "I wish I could help you, but I don't make the rules here. There . . . there's a reason for the table. And you should be glad your back's hurting. It saves you from something worse."

Frank felt a chill. "What could be worse?"

But Conroy backed out and locked the door without saying anything else. Kid had actually looked a little ashamed there for a minute. Sorry, but I'm just following orders. Yeah, Frank thought sourly, now where've we heard that before?

He set the tray on the floor. Supper. Conroy shouldn't have told him that. Soup every meal, no sunlight down here, he had lost track of time. Hope to hell it meant they were going to leave him be for the night. Because he was going to need about all of it.

First he needed a chisel, and his hosts had been kind enough to provide him one. Frank gripped the side of the table and started to ease it over. Heavy bastard—watch your back. His grip slipped a little and he yanked back; pain ripped up through his shoulder and down the back of one leg. He let the table down and staggered away, gasping. Deep breaths, that's it.

Gradually the fire in his nerves died down.

Kneeling by the table, he unbolted one leg and slid out the diagonal bracket that had fastened the apron and leg together. The bracket was good strong steel, with two ends almost as sharp as a cold chisel. The freed leg would make a decent sledge. Frank eased his shirt off, grimacing as pain shot up his back again. He tied the shirt around the thick end of the leg. That ought to keep it quiet if he didn't pound too hard with it.

He rested a minute, then bent to the thin sheet of wood paneling. It resisted at first, but then he felt the glue pulling underneath like taffy. Cinder block was probably damp, keeping the glue from ever setting right. The whole four-by-eight panel popped free with a soft, sucking *plop*. He set it aside and inspected the mortar between the cinder blocks. His spirits rose. It looked pretty sandy. Whoever had built this place—and it sure hadn't been Chuck Conroy by himself—wouldn't have wanted to file no blueprint with the county, and they wouldn't want a bunch of laborers either, who would blab about the job over their beers. They had laid the block themselves and had mixed a bit too much sand into the mortar.

Frank set the edge of the bracket against the mortar line and tapped it with the wrapped table leg. Small hunks of mortar showered out. He felt a surge of excitement. Hot damn! This might work after all.

Frank worked and rested, worked and rested. He kept his back to the tray on his table-bed, but he could smell the soup—a rich bouillon and beef smell. Damn, he was hungry. He would give anything to eat that soup, but that was how they had got him in the MHU, putting the crazy-making drugs in his food. At the least they had probably put some dope in this soup to make him sleep. He might have to eat soon, but he would hold out as long as he could.

Frank worked some more, then backed away stiff-legged from the wall and looked at the block. One almost done. Got to rest. How much time had passed? At least three hours.

And only one block?

His heart sank. He felt his exhaustion suddenly, eating at his bones. His back was a solid mass of pain. No matter which way he turned, it hurt him. This is a damn fool thing you're trying, he thought. You aren't ever going to make it. And even if you do, you won't have no strength left to dig dirt with.

He sat down on the floor and looked with longing at the soup. Norma, honey, I tried, I tried.

Frank heard a faint scream. The hairs stood up on his neck. The scream came again, from the vent. He got to his feet and stared up at the grate, not believing what he had heard. The scream had sounded like his name.

He dragged the three-legged table over to the wall and clambered up on it carefully, keeping away from the corner with the missing leg. He pressed his ear to the vent.

For a few seconds he could hear nothing.

"Oh, God, help me, *help,* HELP, HELP, FRANK!"

Holy Virgin Mary, it sounded like Brian!

A buzzing whine echoed suddenly down the vent. A saw! Frank thought, horrified. The voice screamed again, high as a gut-shot rabbit, and he knew in his heart it was Brian and that he was dying.

The whine of the saw rose sharply in pitch, like it was biting into wood, and the blubbering scream cut off.

Nausea pushed up in Frank's throat. He backed away from the vent, almost falling off the table. Dear Lord Jesus, Brian. Poor damn kid.

Why would they tell Brian they had me locked up here too, Frank wondered. They wouldn't, and yet Brian had called out for him, because they were killing him, and he went crazy, flat-out panicked, wanting someone to save him.

Frank shuddered, stabbed through with a memory: that day Royal Thompson got himself shot reconnoitering that bombed-out farmhouse in France. After the shot, Royal started screaming for his mother, screaming, "Ma! Ma!" and then his voice cut off—the bastard Germans had bayonetted him.

Brian didn't scream for his ma, Frank thought. All he had was me, and I didn't even know it. He probably didn't either, until just then, when they killed him. Oh, you fucking bastards!

Frank felt tears pouring down his face. He got down from the table. A furious energy flooded his muscles. He rammed the table leg into the cinder block he had been working on. The block busted loose and plopped down behind the wall.

Frank blinked away his tears and peered, dumbfounded, through the opening into blackness. Jesus, Mary and Joseph, it wasn't just a bad fill job, there was all kind of space behind this wall. He felt the draft on his face now. It had an odd smell, like very old, rotting timbers. What did they do, build this thing in an old mine tunnel?

The little hairs on Frank's arms and neck prickled up again. What it smelled like was them old World War I sapper tunnels his outfit had run across. Marching inland, one of the men had fallen right through to his hip, and there it was. Nobody had wanted to go down. Frank didn't want to either, but Goldstein had ridden him until he took his flashlight and went. He'd found a hip and leg bone wrapped in a few scraps of gray wool, all that was left of a dead Kraut from the first war.

The same Kraut he kept seeing when they drugged him in MHU. Frank shuddered again. Forget drugs, he told himself angrily. Sons of bitches had just murdered a poor dumb kid. And I'm next, he thought, if I don't get into this hole quick.

He fit the table leg into the opening and jacked furiously at the next block, trying to break the grip of the mortar. At first it wouldn't budge, then suddenly it broke loose. He pushed it through and kept working until he had an opening big enough to crawl through.

He started in, then stopped, struck by an idea. With all the empty space beyond the wall, he wouldn't have to throw dirt into the cell when he dug. What if he put the table back together, swept the mortar dust into this hole, and pulled the sheet of paneling back behind him?

It would give him a lot more time to dig and escape.

Frank felt a savage grin twisting his face. He imagined Conroy unlocking the door. Hell! Where's Frank? Where in hell did he go? He was right here, and now he's gone. Must've picked the lock; how'd the stupid old bastard do that?

Yeah! That was the nice thing about a slick new dead bolt like the one on this door—when you turned your key in it, you could barely feel anything. Once Conroy had unlocked it and got his shock about Frank being gone, he wouldn't be able to remember whether his key had actually run the bolt back or if it had already been picked open. He'd have to decide it had been left picked open, because no one would pick the damn lock, escape, and then hold himself up by picking it shut again.

They would run all over the place looking for him, never thinking he might still be in the cell, behind the wall.

They had slapped on the paneling to keep people from picking at the mortar, but that had been a real mistake. It gave old Frank an extra edge.

He put the table back together and used his shirt to sweep the cement dust through the hole. He reached too far and almost yelled as pain chewed up his backbone. Damn this gol-damn back! He finished sweeping with small, careful movements, making sure the floor was completely clean. Then he took the paneling and stuck one edge along its original seam with the next panel. He pushed about half of it back into the taffylike glue, getting it stuck again. Flexing the unstuck side of the panel as little as possible, he squeezed backward through the hole.

He took a last look at the light. Going to miss the light all right; hope it's not for too long.

He let the unstuck side of the panel spring back against the wall around the hole. Blackness poured over him. He felt as if he were suffocating, standing at the bottom of a well full of black water. He made himself breathe. Turning his back on the hole, he put a hand out in front of his face. Two steps brought him up against a dirt wall. On one side the wall converged sharply with the cinder block, leaving no room to pass. He felt along in the other direction until his hand found a vertical piece of square-cut timber.

Old mining tunnel, he thought. Whoever built this place didn't even need a bulldozer—

He realized with surprise that he could see again.

There was a smidgen of light. Turning, he located the pale source about twenty feet off and down low. Damn. Just a hole in the cinder block. That was probably where the draft was coming from, not from topside but from inside.

He tried to keep his spirits up. Maybe he could still dig out the top. Get down there, he thought, where that light is, and see what you can see.

He made his way to the light, the tunnel narrowing in on him until he could barely squeeze along. He eased himself down, pain ripping at his back, until he was on his side where the light was leaking out. It was another chink where the mortar had fallen out of the cinder block. They clearly hadn't bothered to put any paneling on the other side.

Frank put his eye to the hole. A gleaming tile floor stretched away from him to the skirts of a far wall. Close to his eye, the floor was shadowed, probably overhung by a table or something. That would explain why no one had noticed the hole to plug it.

A foot swung into the shaded area close in front of him. The foot was wrapped in a blue paper slipper, like the ones doctors wore in operating rooms. Frank heard water running close overhead. Must be a sink above the hole.

The foot edged backward into the light and Frank saw that the toe was spattered with blood.

He rolled over onto his back, swallowing hard, sick to his stomach again. Slowly the nausea passed and his eyes readjusted to the dark; the roof of the tunnel swam at the edge of visibility. Straining, he could make out cross timbers, big suckers, running over the cinder block on one side, resting on the vertical timber braces on the other. Tree roots crawled down between the cross braces like stalactites in a cave.

Frank felt the last of his hope bleeding out. It was all over. The roof and wall timbers were set too close together to dig through. He wasn't locked in the cell anymore, but he was just as trapped as he had been before. Pinned in next to a human slaughterhouse that was dug in better than Hitler's bunker. No laborers to tell the tale, either, not even a bulldozer operator. Probably no one but Conroy and whoever was giving Conroy his orders even knew this place was here.

And no one at all knew old Frank Greene hadn't just run off because he was nuts.

Except maybe Sharon Francis.

Frank clung to the sudden thread of hope. That last time he had seen Dr. Francis, she'd believed him—he had seen it in her eyes. Maybe this very minute she was trying to figure out what had really happened to him. Maybe she'd be able to do it. She was a very smart young woman. And she cared.

Frank felt a pang of hunger and was amazed at himself. How could he have any appetite at all?

Because it had been too damn long since he had eaten. He wished now that he had polished off that soup, even if it had dope in it. Hell, especially if it had dope in it. Might as well sleep. His back hurt like hell, and time was going to start dragging on real soon in here. The only chance he had was if Sharon or someone busted this place wide open. Otherwise, he was going to die here. Or they would find him and drag him back inside and buzz-saw him like they had Brian.

Frank felt another hunger forming inside him—for light. He turned back to the hole. The foot was gone now. He gazed with longing at the gleaming tiles. Without the bloody foot, they looked good, a piece of the normal world to cling to.

The light went out.

No! Frank thought. He pressed his eye against the hole, feeling the rough cinder block grind against his forehead, but only blackness poured into his brain.

He closed his eyes and saw the beach at Normandy and realized that it hadn't been the worst after all.

14

"**H**OW DID YOU prepare the chicken?" Mark asked the minute Sharon opened the door.

"I let it talk to its priest," she said. And whatever happened to hello?

Mark looked confused. "No, I mean for the wine. I should have asked you before I came." He held out a bottle of Soave.

"That's fine," she said. "Thank you. Come on in." She walked ahead of him, conscious that her joke was just the kind of thing Jeff would have said. Here she was with Jeff inside her, and earnest, intense Mark standing in her living room. What the hell was she doing?

"Speaking of chicken, it's almost ready. Why don't you sit down?" She pointed to her little table in the dining alcove and fled into the kitchenette.

I'm getting help from a cop, she told herself. If I tell Jeff, he'll just plunge into the same trouble right beside me, and then I can feel scared *and* guilty. Jeff knows about neurology and about holding babies and loving. Mark knows about criminals and what to do to stop them.

She carried the chicken from the oven to the table.

"Do you have a corkscrew?" Mark asked.

Sharon saw the wine sitting on the table. Nuts. She should have stashed it somewhere.

"Uh, sure." She hurried back to the kitchen, feeling anxious. She didn't want to drink wine with Mark, she wanted to consult with him, and dinner was supposed to be the pay-off—just dinner. If only she had the money, she could take him to a restaurant. Then if he ordered wine, she could give the right signal by not having any herself.

She handed him the corkscrew, and he opened the wine expertly, pouring some into both their water glasses, giving her the bigger slug. "A toast," he said, and she was afraid he was going to say, to us, but he just said, "to your health."

"Dig in," she said brightly, handing him a plate.

Mark leaned forward, reaching for the salt and as his coat opened she saw his gun, the dark, scored butt curving from a canvas shoulder holster. She was surprised by the feeling of reassurance it gave her. "Have you ever killed a man?" she asked, astonished at herself.

But he didn't seem offended. "I almost killed my own father," he said.

A chill shot up her spine. She took a sip of wine, cupping the glass, needing to do something with her hands. If she and Mark were going to skip the small talk, they should be discussing Frank and Meg, and the incredible, frightening bottom line on Poulson's missing persons numbers.

Almost killed my own father.

She could not stop the memory: the day the policeman came to the house to break the news about Dad. All she had been able to think was that she had killed him. Crying, sobbing, knowing if she had been the right sort of daughter, he wouldn't have left, would never have smashed his car into the wall, would still be alive.

Alive, and together with her and Mom.

Sharon realized Mark was gazing at her, waiting for her to respond. "Your father seems to have made a remarkable recovery." She tried for a light tone and failed.

"Better than you know," Mark said. "But for six months after it happened, he was, for all intents and purposes, a dead man."

"What did you do? Accidentally shoot him?"

Mark gave a sharp laugh. "No. I used bad judgment. Bad judgment has killed more people than guns ever will." He picked up his glass and drained it. He took the wine and poured, his knuckles white around the neck of the bottle. A little muscle in his jaw was jumping. The barely suppressed anger made Sharon uneasy. Then he took a deep breath and eased it out, swirling the wine gently in his glass, as if it were fine brandy.

"What happened?" Sharon said.

For a moment, he just looked at her, his strange, pale eyes full of pain.

"I'm sorry," she said. "You don't have to—"

"I want to tell you," he said softly. "We were way back in the woods. West Virginia. Pop had finally agreed to go roughing it with me. He didn't like the idea, but I'd been after him for years. 'Come on, Pop, just the two of us. Nothing but the birds and raccoons and squirrels, the fresh air. You'll love it.' " Mark's voice was bitter with self-mockery. "So he gave in. We took a couple of small packs, water and some dried food. No guns, just my bow, and all I carried for that were a few target arrows."

"Target arrows?"

"Yeah. No barbs, so you can pull 'em out again. Pop's like you when it comes to hunting, so I figured I'd just shoot a few stumps for practice. Before we were through, I'd have given my right hand for a gun."

He paused, took a few swallows of wine, as if nerving himself to continue. "First day it was great. I showed Pop how to dig hip holes for his sleeping bag, where to camp to avoid the bugs. He helped me build a snug lean-to. We had a fire that night, some old pine wood that burned hot, cracking and popping. He and I talked about Mother, really talked for the first time since she'd died. She'd been dead about a year—cancer—and it had been pretty tough on him."

Sharon felt a pang. "Just on him?"

Mark looked away. "Mother and I weren't . . . close."

She heard new tension in his voice. How much more lay behind that cryptic statement?

He looked at her and said, "You don't approve, I can see it in your face. But you don't understand, either. Mother never let up. Wanted me to be a doctor, like Pop. Always exerting her little pressures, trying to steer me, then denying it whenever I'd confront her with it. 'I want you to be whatever you want, Mark. But I can't think of anything finer or nobler than being a physician.' " His voice was suddenly high and cool, a dead woman's voice, from the past. Sharon's skin crawled, but then he gave a wry laugh. "I survived it. And you can see how much good all the pressure did. Fortunately, Pop understood what was going on and always gave me room. But Mother . . ."

He trailed off. Sharon wondered if he would say anything good about his mother. If he could not, then it had been a very deep rift indeed, one that must have colored everything he was now. A boy and his mother, a deep but difficult bond, which among other things shaped the way a man thought of all women.

What *did* Mark think of women?

Sharon recalled dancing with him at the party. He had danced expertly, and held her with complete propriety. And at Brian's apartment, he had never once tried to touch her, not even when she was reeling with shock from Brian's filthy photo montage of her. If Jeff had been there, he would probably have tried to take her in his arms . . .

But it would have been wrong.

At that horrible moment, her skin would have screamed at any man's touch. What Mark had done had been exactly right: she had needed silence from him then, and calmness, and later his strong, almost mystical words of encouragement. Had Mark understood that, or had he simply been restrained by his own limits, trapped behind his own iron wall forbidding the emotional touch or feel of women?

Just as her own fears had made her hold men off for so long. Sharon felt a sudden—deep sympathy for Mark.

"Sounds like your mom wanted two of your father," she said.

"Exactly."

"Then she must have loved him very much."

"And he her," Mark admitted. "But we talked about a lot of other things, too."

She realized he was back to that night in the woods with his father. He was not to be diverted; for some reason he really needed to tell her this.

"We sat across the fire from each other," he said. "It was great. The crickets were singing and there was a swamp over the next hill, so we could hear the bullfrogs croaking. I remember it was almost a full moon, so bright it cast shadows. I woke up several times that night, looking across the clearing at Pop, listening to him snore. He looked like a big lumpy walrus, hunched up in his sleeping bag. I listened to the frogs and crickets and watched an owl through the trees. It was the finest night of my life. I had no idea what would happen the next day."

There was terrible pain on Mark's face now. Sharon felt a lump rising in her throat. On impulse, she reached across and touched his hand. It lay still as a stone, and she quickly withdrew.

"We were walking down a steep hill. There're always leaves on the ground, the top layer from the last fall, then underneath the previous year's, and so on until you hit a layer of slime. I should have told Pop to watch his step, or cut him a stick. Better yet, I should have taken the longer route, around the ridges, instead of trying to go straight across. Anyway, he slipped and fell. His feet shot out in front of him, and he smacked down on his back. His spine hit a big rock. He screamed, and then he passed out from the pain. I had never heard my father scream. It shocked me. I knelt beside him—I was crying. I thought he was dead."

The image shook Sharon: kindly, funny Dr. Pendleton lying hurt and screaming, his son weeping beside him. "Horrible," she said.

Mark finished his wine. His eyes took on a haunted, faraway look. "As soon as Pop came around he screamed again. He begged me not to move him. But we were almost two days deep in the woods, with only the water we could carry. By the time I could get out and lead anyone back in to him, he'd be out of water and unable to get more. And we'd be no further ahead—whoever came would still have to carry him a good ways over the uneven ground. The forest was so thick there was no way to get a medevac chopper down in there. If I'd had a gun, I could have started firing it at regular intervals. Someone might have heard us and come. But I didn't have a gun.

"So I picked Pop up and carried him. He cried out at every step. He passed out a number of times. I tried to get as far as I could each time before he came to again." Mark's face was white.

Sharon felt horrified for him. "How awful."

"Two operations," Mark said. "Six months of pain. The neurosurgeon said if the injury had been a few millimeters higher, or if I'd carried him another few hundred feet, Pop wouldn't have moved for the rest of his life." Mark shuddered. "A paraplegic. That would have been the end for Pop. Worse than if I'd killed him."

"But he's all right now," Sharon said, feeling the need to reassure him.

He looked up at her. "Yes. He's fine. No pain, no problems. But it was too close. If I'd hurt him permanently, I don't think I could have lived with it."

She struggled for something to say.

Mark gave a bleak laugh. "Listen to me. Not very pleasant dinner conversation, I'm afraid."

"I'm glad you told me."

Mark looked at her, his eyes unreadable. "I've never told anyone. But I knew that you'd understand."

Sharon felt suddenly uncomfortable. Definitely time to change the subject.

As if he had read her mind, Mark said, "But enough of that. It's time I earned this great dinner. How can I help you?"

Sharon told him about Meg and then Frank disappearing AMA, and said she thought Brian might be part of it too. "I'm scared."

He sat back in his chair, looking grim. "I don't blame you. That's pretty heavy stuff."

She nodded, grateful. He was going to take her seriously—as, indeed, he seemed to take all things.

"I see now why you asked me if I'd ever killed anyone," Mark said. "I guess I got sidetracked, baring my soul about Pop. The answer is, I've never fired my gun at a human being. Red Falls is a pretty quiet little town. My most serious arrest so far was old Warren Dyreson, who shot up the local tavern. But he came along meek as a lamb when I showed up."

"How about investigations? Did you ever have a missing person in Red Falls?"

"One or two, I guess. Kids packing a sandwich and running away from home. They show up the next day, tired and hungry. Nothing like what you're talking about. Sharon, do you have any other evidence?"

"As a matter of fact, I've saved the most important thing for last." Leaving the dishes in the sink, she brought out Poulson's printouts and spread them on the table, along with her scribblings from the analysis she had run on the psych services terminal after Jenkins had gone home for the day. She explained the printouts and her computations to him. "Sixty-three people connected with Adams Memorial psychology or psychiatry services have gone missing in the past year. Forty-three of them are still missing. A certain percentage of these can be subtracted as just ordinary missing persons cases, but that still leaves about twenty people too many. I statistically compared the numbers for Adams to the overall rate at which the city's missing persons turn up again. The bottom line is this: people who disappear from Adams Memorial Hospital are less likely to show up again than missing persons in general. The difference is significant at the point-oh-one level."

Mark looked up from the printouts with a slight frown. "I'm afraid I don't know what that means."

"It means there is only one chance in a hundred that the difference between Adams Memorial and the city in general is due to chance alone. It means that there's something different about Adams Memorial. Something—or someone— is causing our psychiatric patients to disappear."

Mark's face was pale. "Christ. Who'd you talk to at the police station?"

"A Detective Poulson."

"And I assume you've gotten back to him on this. What did he say?"

"He said, 'Hmmmm.' "

"That's all?"

"I'm afraid he wasn't terribly impressed. In your own way, you cops are terrific scientists, but you're trained to deduce things, to work on individual cases, not aggregate samples. You do play certain probabilities: a man is killed, you check to see if anyone took a big insurance policy out on him, did he have a fight with his wife, things like that. But most cops are not tuned in to the scientific techniques of analysis that establish those connections in the first place, as I've done here with these numbers. Cause and effect, that's what cops care about. What I was telling Poulson about with my analysis was just effect. These printouts don't tell you a thing about the cause."

"So what *do* you think is causing it?"

"I don't have a clue," Sharon said, exasperated. "And until I do, I don't think Poulson is going to do more than raise his eyebrows."

"I hate to say this, but as a cop, I can understand his position."

Sharon battled frustration. "Mark, people *are* disappearing from Adams Memorial. The only thing we don't know is who's taking them, and why. Somebody's got to do something!"

Mark's mouth curved into a smile. "You're something else," he said, "you know that? I felt it the first time I ever saw you. Everyone else was standing there staring, but you ran into that den of baboons and grabbed the big hairy thing by the wrist and broke its grip. Then Brian. Most people would go somewhere and cower; you went after him, tracked him right into his den."

Sharon felt oddly defensive. Was he saying she tilted at windmills? She was only doing what any sane, concerned person, confronted with this data, would do. Wasn't she?

"Do you think I'm wrong?"

"I think you are one hell of a woman."

She flushed, pleased.

"Okay," Mark said briskly. "You've convinced me. But the trouble is, as you put it, we haven't a clue. You asked for my professional opinion, so let me tell you the first thing, as a cop, I ask myself, is what is causing the disappearances deliberate—something criminal?"

She looked at him, puzzled. "What else could it be?"

"I don't know. Maybe for some reason more of the people who are likely to take off in the first place go to Adams Memorial. For instance, suppose Adams had the best reputation in the area for treating teenagers. So more of them go there. We also know that teenagers as a group are the most likely to take off and not show up again."

Sharon was impressed with his reasoning. But Adams was not particularly known for treating teenagers. And he was forgetting the rest of it. "Mark, Brian is still missing— I checked just before you came over. He wouldn't carry a morbid joke this far. That means I *did* see a man in that booth, not just a pair of pants. And Poulson won't believe this, but I *knew* Frank—"

She stopped, realizing she'd used the past tense. It made

her feel disloyal. Don't write Frank off, she thought. He's still alive, and you're going to find him.

"I'm Frank's therapist," she finished. "He'd never run off, just leave his wife like this."

Mark nodded. "What are you going to do?"

"I was hoping you might have some suggestions."

"I do. I suggest that I go to this Detective Poulson and have a talk with him."

"Fantastic. But what about me?"

"Look, to be blunt, cops as a rule don't much care for shrinks. All they hear from you guys is that poor LeRoy or Johnny cut loose with their knife or Uzi because they had rotten childhoods, or because they were temporarily insane. Cops have seen too many of their most vicious collars sent to mental hospitals, where your colleagues, no offense, spring them again after six months. But I'm a member of Poulson's club. He'll give me a better hearing if I come in alone, cop to cop."

"Right," Sharon said, "Good."

"Maybe I can get him to put at least a two-man team of detectives on this." Mark gathered up the printouts. Sharon felt a pang of reluctance, not wanting to part with them. But of course he was right.

"You'll let me know what he says?" she asked.

"Of course. I'll try to see him tonight. If not, then tomorrow, as soon as he's available. I should be getting back to you tomorrow evening."

"Terrific."

Mark held out his hand. "Thanks for a great dinner."

Sharon shook his hand. He held hers an extra second, then let go and went to the door, almost hurrying. His odd shyness touched her.

At the door he turned and looked at her longingly, and she knew suddenly from his eyes that he wanted her. She felt a hot charge along her nerves, and then the perverse beginnings of arousal. She tried to suppress the feeling. She did not want her body to feel this way, but her body didn't care what she wanted. Say something, she thought, chill things out, but her throat felt too dry to speak.

"Good-bye," Mark said, and slipped out, closing the door gently after him.

Sharon drifted over to the sink, half in a daze, and went to work on the dishes. She could feel her hands trembling, a lingering echo of arousal, disturbing her. She did not love Mark, she loved Jeff.

But something about Mark fascinated her. She leaned on the sink, watching the sudsy water circle into a vortex and disappear down the drain.

Forget it, she thought. He's out of here. Everything went all right. You've got help now, and that's what you wanted.

Sharon forced her mind back to the missing people. Not just Frank and Meg and Brian, she thought. Fifteen to twenty-five others. Why are they being taken? Why *these* particular people?

They were all connected with psychiatry or psychology at Adams. That made it more likely that the police wouldn't press too hard to find them.

But that still didn't answer the question of *why* they were being taken. What did they all have that someone wanted? Just among Brian, Meg, and Frank there were three different diagnoses, different ages, even different circumstances of disappearance.

There must be another link.

Sharon went to her bedroom and rolled out Dad's weights, going through her warm-ups, her mind floating in a strange, off-center way. She wrapped her hands around the steel bar where Dad's hands had fit so many times, feeling his power flowing into her. She put an extra ten on each end and pushed the weight upward, and just like that, she had it.

Frank Greene's blood test!

What if the test result had been taken out of the chart and the lab computer not because it might have showed he was being drugged into craziness, but because it showed something else? Something special about Frank that, say, Dr. Valois was looking for. When it had turned up on the test, Valois had marked him out for kidnapping.

What if Valois or someone at Adams Memorial was doing illegal research on human subjects?

Sharon dropped the weight and began pacing around the room, feeling suddenly sick and afraid. Dear God, Adams Memorial was a research hospital. At least half of the doctors there were actively involved in research, a lot of them with human subjects. But all of that research was very rigorously controlled. The first rule was that the patient must give informed consent, and the second was that he must suffer no harm.

What if someone had grown impatient with those rules? Someone who thought he was on to something big and that the means would justify the end?

I've got to find Frank's blood test, Sharon thought.

Then she realized she had to do more: she now had a complete list of names of missing people connected with Adams Memorial. If she could get into records, she could pull their files and look for blood tests. If tests were missing from all or most of the charts, that would tell her something.

If they weren't, she could look at them, try to find some value or set of values that was the same for all the missing people, and that would tell her even more.

She stopped pacing and sat on the bed, excited. At last, here was something really important she could do. If she could find out why these people were being taken, she would be a giant step closer to knowing who was taking them. Different medical researchers would be interested in different things. An oncologist would be interested in the presence of T cells, for example; a surgeon might be interested in tissue rejection factors.

And a psychiatrist would be interested in brain chemicals in the blood. A savage excitement gripped Sharon. Valois, she thought. You've really gone after me lately, haven't you? Have I been too persistent about Frank Greene? And you're one of the most active researchers at Adams Memorial. Over thirty journal articles published—oh, yes, I've read them all.

If it's you, Valois, I'm going to know it, and this time I'll be the one to cut you down.

Hang on, Frank, Sharon thought.

15

A NERVOUS DREAD gripped Sharon as she slid her father's barbell back under the bed. Breaking into records—did she really have the guts? If only she could use the normal source of patient information, the computer room. It was always open—if a former patient was readmitted, any resident could get a printout of that patient's old chart, even at three A.M. But Sharon wanted to pore over the private charts of forty-some *former* patients. For that, the computer supervisor would require clearance from administration. At worst, admin would consider her theory—and her—crazy. At best, they would deliberate for days. Even if they miraculously agreed as soon as she could ask, the clearance committee wouldn't be in until eight thirty tomorrow morning. Twelve hours. Frank, wherever he was, might not have twelve hours left, let alone days. That left the records room, where all retired charts were warehoused. Records was closed this late. If she could break in. . . .

Sharon felt an ache in the pit of her stomach. She wished that Mark were still there. If she had thought of it before he left, she could have asked him to help. . . .

Forget it. Mark had already taken too many risks for her. He was a cop, not a cat burglar. If he were caught breaking into records, it might end his career.

It's just me and me, kid, Sharon thought.

She took a deep breath and eased it out. Nine P.M.—things should be pretty quiet at the hospital by now. Records had been closed for four hours, and the only other thing down in that part of the basement was a bunch of storage rooms. She would need the names of the missing, the sublist she had copied from the printout before Mark came over. She would also need sneakers, and something to jimmy the lock. After watching Mark use his credit card on Brian's door, she could probably do it.

Except that she didn't have any credit cards.

Sharon hurried to her bedroom, pulling open drawers until she found the flexible plastic ruler that said ALLSTATE. She rummaged in her closet for her sneakers, breaking into a flustered sweat when she couldn't find them. Come on, come *on* . . .

They were in her office at the hospital. She would have to go there first.

Biking over, Sharon pulled the hot, thick air deep into her lungs, emptying her mind. Don't think. Just do it.

As she hurried in the main entrance, Sharon almost ran into Denise. She tried to get past with a "Hi," but Denise wanted to schmooze about Sharon's performance filling in at outpatient. Sharon had trouble tracking the words—something about "as good as my R-threes" and "keep on this way and you're a sure thing for chief yourself." Sharon knew she should be delighted, but all she could think of was getting past Denise, getting to her office, getting it done.

At last Denise let her go with a final pat on the shoulder. Sharon bypassed the elevator, hurrying up the stairs to psych services. She yanked open her office door—

And froze. Judith Acheson was sitting at her desk, reading a sheaf of computer printouts.

Sharon stared at her, horrified. *That's the printout I pulled from Jenkins's computer.* No. Calm down. Mark took that an hour ago.

Acheson smiled up at her. "Dr. Francis. I thought that was you I saw pedaling into the parking lot. I was about to leave, so I decided to drop by on my way down, see how you're doing."

"Fine," Sharon said. Her voice sounded too high.

"Do you have something you have to do right now?"

"No." Just break into your Records room. "No, no . . ."

"I'm sorry, is this desk yours?" Acheson got up and went around the desks, seating herself in Austin's chair. Sharon went to her own chair and sank into it. That's it, she thought. I can't do it.

Acheson dropped her stack of printouts into her briefcase and gazed around the cramped, cluttered office, her eyes alight, as if she were viewing the inside of a cathedral. "You know, there was always a part of me that wanted to be a physician. The excitement, the knowledge that you were helping people, the glamour of the white coat."

Sharon did not know what to say, so she kept quiet. She noticed that her file drawer was open, the one with the rough drafts of patient intakes. Had it been open when she left? Austin must have used it and forgotten to close it.

"Even this," Acheson said, gesturing around the office. "So Spartan, and yet so *real.* You must love being a doctor very much."

Sharon nodded. Her heart hammered against her chest. She felt as if her forehead were running a marquee message: I'M GOING TO BREAK INTO RECORDS. She wanted to scream, What do you *want*?

"Me," Acheson said, "I get the fancy office—and a ceaseless load of paperwork." She tapped her briefcase. "All the headaches medical science can't cure. Just today I got a call from a police detective."

Sharon felt sweat popping out on her face.

"It seems one of my employees came to see him about people disappearing from Adams Memorial."

Oh God, Sharon thought. Here it comes.

"He wouldn't tell me who brought this idea to him. . . ."

Sharon felt a surge of relief. She kept her face neutral, feeling Acheson's gaze boring into her.

"I was quite concerned, of course, but the detective assured me there was no real evidence that anything was wrong. I told him to keep me posted, let me know if this person came to him again, and he agreed to do that." Acheson leaned back in Austin's chair. "This person probably didn't realize that people disappear all over this city all the time. And that there are beat reporters who do nothing else but hang around police stations, eavesdropping for possible headlines. Can you imagine them? 'Patients Vanishing From Adams Memorial.' " Acheson shook her head.

"At least it would solve our bed shortage." *No!* Sharon thought. You didn't say that.

Acheson gazed at her, then smiled. "And our office space problem." She looked around again. "You know, Sharon, if I could do it, I'd trade places with you in a second. I know it can be hard in your line of work, too, but I hope you appreciate what you've got."

"I do," Sharon said.

Acheson stood, smiling. "Well, I've taken up enough of your time. If you have any problems, Sharon, you come to me, all right? I want to hear your problems. I'm here to listen—and to help."

Sharon stood too. "Thank you."

Acheson closed the door behind her. Sharon sank back into her chair. I can't do it, she thought. I can't do it.

I've got to do it.

Acheson doesn't *know* anything; Detective Poulson kept my name out of it, thank God for that. Acheson homed in on me because I called Meg's parents, but I'm still officially in the clear.

Sharon pushed the file drawer shut and slipped her sneakers on. Her fingers fumbled at the laces and she realized how much Acheson's little visit had shaken her. The timing— the woman was positively fey.

Sharon walked to the east wing of the hospital and took the stairs to the basement so she wouldn't meet anyone on the elevator. The basement hall was dim and hushed. She hurried down it toward records, feeling a prickly tension in the back of her neck. She did not like being in the basement again. Ever since Brian had jumped her, or fallen on her, she had managed to avoid it. Of course, she was on the other side of the hospital from the PT corridor, and there were no curtained booths here, but it was just as creepy, with its bare, concrete floor and scaly pipes snaking back and forth overhead.

And if they caught her down here tonight, Judith Acheson would have office space for one more resident.

Sharon's stomach plunged like she'd hit bottom on a roller coaster, but she thought of Frank and kept walking. At the door she pulled out the Allstate ruler from the waistband of her slacks. Her mouth went dry. This was it. Here's hoping she had good hands. Slipping the ruler into the crease of the door, she worked it around the latch the way she had seen Mark do. The bolt snicked back. She blew out her breath. All right!

Inside, she stood a moment, orienting herself. Light from the hall soaked through the opaque pebbled glass in the door, revealing a service counter running the width of the room in front of her. She looked beyond it down a wide, center aisle. Receding rows of library-type stacks ran left and right off the aisle.

She took out her little flashlight. As she started to twist it on, she heard a distant *thump-thump* outside: the double doors at the end of the hall. Someone was coming! She crouched, terrified. Footsteps approached, leather soles scraping on the concrete—a man's walk. A door opened, then banged shut. Then another door, closer along the hall. She heard keys jingling. The night watchman.

She looked around wildly for a place to hide. At the end of the room she saw a door marked PRIVATE. She tiptoed to it and tried the knob. It was open. The footsteps outside drew closer. She slipped through the door and found herself in a small rest room, just a sink and two stalls.

The door to records opened and light sliced through the

crack under the rest room door. The footsteps came toward her. She sprang into the nearer stall, eased the seat back, and stood on the porcelain, bracing her hands on the wall, hunching down as the rest room door opened. Light blazed above her head, half blinding her. She glimpsed big feet under her stall door, and then the stall next to her shuddered as the man pushed inside. She could feel her pulse ripping at her throat. Her palms turned greasy against the cold walls of the stall.

The man whistled softly, and she heard a splashing stream hit the toilet. Then he flushed; under cover of the whooshing water she drew a deep breath and let it out.

He stood outside in front of the sink. As the flush bubbled away into silence, she heard him whistling again—"Hail to the Redskins." Through the crack in the stall door she could see his back swaying in time to the tune. Her hands started slipping on the walls. She felt sick to her stomach with fear. Go away, she thought. Go, go, *go*.

He went, flipping off the light in the rest room.

Sharon stayed where she was, trembling. God, the luck of the draw. Fifty-fifty that he chooses her stall. Or maybe forty-sixty—some people take the end stall by choice.

Being a Redskins fan wouldn't have saved her.

But you're okay, she thought, so just calm down.

She listened. The silence was complete.

She groped her way out of the rest room. The diffuse light from the hall was enough to get her through the flip-up door in the counter. The stacks, shielded from the door, were totally dark. Her sense of smell sharpened suddenly, making her aware of dust, old paper, and a tinge of mildew, biting high in her nostrils.

She felt her way deep into the first row, then switched on the bright, narrow beam of the penlight, hoping the stacks would screen all trace of it from the hall door. She played the light along the stack, familiarizing herself with the system. Rows and rows of charts stuffed into cardboard expanding files bulged high and low from the metal shelves.

They were arranged alphabetically, and within each letter, by year going back five years. Plenty; Poulson's list only went back a year.

Sharon took out her list of the forty people who had stayed missing. Step one: check the termination sheet of each chart on her list and pull only those patients who had checked out against medical advice. Normally, with AMA being such a state secret, that probably wouldn't be more than six or seven out of the forty. If her theory was right, it would be more like twenty-six or twenty-seven—all but a few of them victims of the kidnapper. She could disregard the rest of the charts as normal missing persons cases. One or two might actually be victims too, like Brian. And a few of the AMAs would not be victims. But she had to have some way to winnow out the bulk of "normal" disappearances. Grabbing people right after they went AMA, like Meg and Frank, was a terrific setup, and the kidnapper would want to use it as much as he could.

Sharon moved up and down through the stacks, pulling the AMA charts and piling them at the end of the back row of stacks, as far as possible from the door. The pile grew past seven to ten, then fifteen, and she began to feel excited. There were definitely too many AMAs. She finished her list and settled cross-legged in front of the charts she had pulled, wedging her flashlight between two files on the bottom shelf so that it illuminated the pile of charts. She counted the charts, her excitement mounting. Twenty-four. Her theory was proving out.

She picked up Meg Andreason's file, feeling a feverish urgency. Halfway into the chart she found a request for a blood test scribbled among the daily notes.

Three pages later, she found the pink test printout from hematology.

She felt a small let-down. If Meg had been snatched because of something in her blood, no one had bothered to remove the blood test. That didn't seem to mesh with Frank's case.

Then she saw how it might work: whoever was snatching people might have removed the test while Meg's chart was active. But they would actually be safer if they slipped it back in just before the charts got locked away in records. Most of the charts there would never be looked at again, but in this age of malpractice lawsuits, a clerk no doubt made sure each chart was complete before it was consigned to probable oblivion. If blood tests were missing, it would definitely arouse attention.

For the lab computer, on the other hand, it would be safer to permanently delete the blood tests, as had been done for Frank. Hospital researchers were always using the data in the various lab computers to screen for trends or baselines, something a computer could do in seconds at the touch of a key. If the blood tests of missing patients *were* similar on one or more key values, and were allowed to remain in hematology's computer, they might easily get lumped together and highlighted on someone's screening search.

Sharon felt encouraged. Meg's blood test would be her key. If her theory was correct, she ought to be able to find at least one blood value in the great majority of these charts that matched up closely with Meg's.

If she found it, she would be hot on the kidnapper's trail.

Sharon bent to the charts, pulling and stacking the blood tests. When she finished, she gazed at the top one and realized she had a big problem. There were over thirty different values on each blood test—potassium, creatinine, cholesterol, and so on. To find possible matches, she would have to start with the top value, glucose, and look through at least half of the tests to see if the numbers on that value were matching up. She would have to do that over and over, working her way down through the thirty values until she found at least one match. Her brain was not a computer; it could not find trends in seconds. It would take hours.

Suddenly she felt very tense again. When was the night watchman going to come back by? She had been lucky last time. The longer she stayed here, the thinner she was stretching that luck.

I've got to steal the blood tests, she thought.

She had a sinking feeling. Terrific. Not just breaking and entering, but theft.

Still, Frank was out there somewhere, and maybe Meg and Brian, and some of the others, too. What was a little larceny compared to that?

Sharon stuck the sheaf of blood tests into her blouse and started refiling the chart folders, hurrying up and down the rows, resisting the temptation to shove them back in willy-nilly.

Finally all the charts were back in their proper places. As she switched off her flashlight and started to walk out the center aisle, she saw a shadow on the window. Her heart leapt and started to pound.

A man, standing just outside the door!

Rigid with fright, Sharon stared at the silhouette—a head and shoulders etched sharp and black against the opaque glass. She had the uncanny feeling he could see her. No, impossible—he must have heard her, some little noise she had made putting the files back.

The night watchman again?

No, this man had crept up in complete silence.

Hide! Sharon thought.

But she was too terrified to move. There was something hideous about the total stillness of the black shape. It was unearthly, demonic.

The image began to fade. Gradually it softened and blurred, thinning like smoke until it wasn't there.

She stared at the milky glass, feeling dazed, like a sleep-walker suddenly waking to find herself wandering an unfamiliar back yard in the middle of the night.

Had she imagined it?

She didn't want to move, but she had to know. She crept to the door, eased it open, and looked both ways down the long hallway.

It was empty.

Sharon felt her insides stretching to nothing. Little spots winked like black fireflies in her vision. Dear Jesus, she thought. Maybe Valois was right. Maybe I am going crazy.

Her mind went blank with fear.

"She didn't know I was there," Conroy said into the phone. "I stood at the door and listened. She was walking back and forth, probably checking the . . . the information. When I didn't hear that anymore, I backed off and got out of there fast. Once you get through the double doors, there's a bunch of spare laundry carts—"

A cold, inhuman sound came at the other end of the line, very short, cutting him off. Conroy broke into a sweat. Phone taps, he thought. I shouldn't have said laundry carts. "I, uh, hid there. She came tearing out behind me, crying."

"Crying?" Hand said in his buzzing, cancerous voice.

Conroy shuddered. "Yeah, you know. Sobbing a little. She was running like a maniac, like all she wanted to do was get out of there."

"She saw you."

"No, I swear it."

"Shut up. You have no idea how smart and resourceful this woman is. When she ran by you, did she have any information in her hands?"

"No." Conroy wished Hand would let him off the hook. He needed to go home now, go home and shoot up and forget tonight. It had been eerie, looking through the glass, not being able to see her, but knowing suddenly that she was there, staring at the window. The fact was, with the hall lights behind him she probably *had* seen his shadow on the glass, but no way was he going to admit that to Hand. She hadn't seen his face, and that was all that counted.

"Any signs of our missing contributor?"

Conroy felt a jolt of fear. Frank. Still missing. He had been hoping the old bastard would turn up after all, still somewhere down in the lab. But that was bullshit. We checked everywhere, Conroy thought, even the cooler. And if Frank's smart enough to pick the lock on his cell, he's plenty smart enough to find his way out of the lab.

"Amber Jack?"

The use of his code name steadied him a little, making him feel stronger, more in control. "Nothing. He hasn't shown up at his house, or anywhere else."

"Okay," Hand said. "Good. If he'd made it, we'd know it by now."

Know it, hell, Conroy thought. They would have arrested my ass. I should have run, taken off for Canada, or Mexico.

But he knew if he had, Hand would be hunting him now. If he ever ran, for any reason, Hand would track him to the ends of the earth and slit him open. Conroy shuddered. Better the cops than Hand.

Relax, he thought. Hand's right. Frank's had more than enough time to bring the cops down on me, or on the lab. Maybe his heart gave out after he got topside and he dragged himself off somewhere and died. He's an old man, and he must have been scared shitless, running, stressing himself.

Forget it, we're clear.

"The woman," Hand said. "Did you have the sense to go back in behind her?"

"Yes sir. She left the door unlocked. I didn't even have to pick it. I looked for which ones had the dust off. I stopped after ten. Seven were subjects we'd sent along."

There was a long pause. Conroy knew what was coming and felt cold all over.

Hand said, "Send her along too. We'll do it the slow way."

"Yes sir." Conroy hung up, sickened. The slow way. Poor Sharon. But Hand was right. She was perfect for it.

16

JEFF FELT GROUCHY and deprived as he shaved the rat's head. Sharon had been due in the lab at six. It was half past, and still no Sharon. With her resident duties up in MHU, she wasn't able to grab that many hours in lab. He had counted on seeing her this evening, springing for dinner after the necropsy. Where was she?

He picked up the little saw and thumbed the switch. The circular blade buzzed to life, settling into a steady high-pitched whine. Poising the whirling blade over the rat's skull, he tried to ready his hand. One slip, one millimeter too deep through the skull, and he would nick the brain. Fragile chemical chains would fly apart in a spray of tissue, maybe the very stuff he was looking for.

He waited, sweat oozing into his surgical gloves.

Not only was Sharon late this evening, but yesterday evening was fishy as hell too. When he'd decided to drop by her office last night, who should he see there but Judith Acheson—at nine in the evening, yet. What the hell was going on? Too bad his beeper had gone off, or he could have hung around and found out.

Jeff glanced at the lab door. It stayed closed.

The hell with it. He bent over the rat and pressed the blade down. The mechanical whine rose as it ate through the bone, grating on his nerves. In its wake, the spinning blade sucked up half-clotted blood, leaving a dark glistening halo behind the cut. He picked up one of the pieces of gauze he had cut for Sharon to use assisting him. Trying to wipe the blood away, he smeared some on his fingertips.

Maybe Sharon had just chickened out. She had done the daily observations on this study; knowing her, she'd become friends with all the rats. Maybe she had just decided she didn't want to watch them die.

That could be it. Feeling a little better, Jeff guided the saw through the final millimeter of the circular cut. He picked up his forceps and gripped the blood-slick edges of the skull plate. Wiggling it gently, he broke the surface tension that glued it to the brain, and it popped free with a moist, sucking noise. He inspected the smooth, pinkish-white mass of the brain and was relieved to see that he had done it right. No nicks, despite himself. He let his hands take over, clipping the brain for extraction—

And realized suddenly why Sharon wasn't there.

Not the rats—she wouldn't like seeing them die, but she had been through that sort of thing before, in med school. The truth was, she probably still had her mind on the Frank Greene thing. Jeff had a sinking feeling. If that was it, things were starting to get out of hand. When a resident skipped out two days in a row, he or she was heading for trouble.

Jeff thought back over the past few days. No one thing she had said or done about Frank seemed that far out, but add it all up, and what did you have? She'd as much as said that Louis Valois was drugging and kidnapping MHU patients.

And her mother's a paranoid schiz.

Jeff's face prickled. He stepped back from the necropsy table, startled that he could have been so dense. Sharon wasn't *getting* into trouble, she was *in* trouble. And what had he done to help her out of it? Dozed off in the backseat. Forget the necropsy, he thought. Get your butt in gear and go after her.

"How's it going?"

Damn! Dr. Pendleton, behind him. "Just started," Jeff said, making himself bend over the rat again. He started tying off the brain stem.

"Didn't we schedule Sharon to assist?"

"She's a little late. Probably blew a tire on that old bike of hers." Jeff felt a cold weight in his stomach. If he could only believe that. He cut the brain stem and lifted the brain out, depositing it in a petrie dish.

"Gently, gently—that's it. So what do you think? This particular rat gonna win us a Nobel Prize?"

"We wish."

Pendleton patted him on the shoulder. "Don't be glum, lad. I know this is a hell of a blunderbuss way to go about it, but it's all we've got. You figure out an acceptable way to get at the neurochemicals in a living brain, you let me know so I can steal the credit."

Jeff forced a smile.

"After the blender, don't centrifuge it too long," Pendleton cautioned. "The stuff we're after now breaks down pretty fast."

"I will—ah, won't." Just tell him, Jeff thought. You're worried about Sharon, you've got to put the necropsy off a day. He'll understand . . . maybe.

"Well, my class awaits. Let me know if anything interesting turns up."

"Right." Jeff kept the relief from his voice. That's right, this is Wednesday. Pendleton's neurobiology class met until nine. Jeff watched him out the door, then unpinned the rat and dropped it into a necropsy bag, brain and all. Thirty-nine other rats on the study, plenty of brains to mash up and sift through.

The only thing that mattered right now was Sharon.

Sharon lay watching the rain. It pelted the window and ran down in wavering streaks. Evening already. It would be dark soon. She had stayed in bed all day. After sleeping all last night. *Get up*, she commanded herself, but she couldn't seem to move. She had slept half the day, too, slept too deeply, and now her muscles felt dead. A huge lump swam in her throat.

At least she hadn't had the dream.

She shut her eyes and saw the black silhouette in her mind, hovering there on the window, like a vampire coming to take her soul. And she had opened the door for it. But it hadn't been out there.

Because it was inside her.

She felt a chill of horror. Was this what she would tell her psychiatrist? Vampires are trying to get into my soul.

If only she had waited to open that door. Then she could assume the man was real and had simply walked away.

Sharon lay on the bed, her mind blank, feeling time drag and leap, crawl and race. The phone rang and rang, finally stopping.

So what are you going to do now? she thought. Wait until they come and get you? Or get yourself back together and go in and try to act like a psychiatrist, until you see something else that isn't there, or hear voices.

Or go back to trying to prove that Dr. Valois is picking off MHU patients, one by one.

The trouble was, she still believed that.

But she couldn't trust what she believed anymore.

Her teeth began to chatter. She pulled the covers up around her. They were damp with her sweat. She couldn't really be cold, but she was. You're doing it to yourself, said a tiny voice, far back in her mind. You're so afraid you can't think.

Sharon felt a thin edge of anger and used it to kick the covers off and sit up. She planted her feet on the bare wood floor, then ran out of steam, gazing out the window. The rain gurgled hypnotically, coursing down the drainpipe. She watched the raindrops slide and waver down the windowpane.

She had a dizzy sensation of falling and dug her nails into the bedspread.

Do something.

She dropped to her knees by the bed and grabbed the barbell, rolling it out. She ran her hands along the scored bar, feeling a faint electricity, the aura of Dad's touch that had not died in all the years since he'd been gone. *Help me,* she thought.

She peeled off her nightgown and dressed in shorts and T-shirt, then settled on the floor, stretching, bending, pulling in deep breaths. The lump in her throat shrank a little; she could feel her heart stutter to life inside her. She bent over the bar, squeezing, adjusting her grip until it felt right, then swung the bar up to her chest and held it, gulping air. She pushed it up, gritting her teeth until she'd raised it all the way, arms locked over her head.

"Yeah!"

Sharon eased the barbell back to her chin.

The doorbell rang.

She felt a sharp dismay. Who could that be? She thrust the weight up again.

Knocking started and went on and on.

Go *away.*

"Sharon, it's me, Jeff."

His voice came to her dimly through the wood and the dead air of the apartment. She felt her arms trembling suddenly under the weights. Not Jeff. She couldn't let him see her like this. She lowered the weight to the floor, easing it down, trying to make no sound, but at the last second the bar slipped from her hands and the weight banged down on the floor, as if it had a will of its own.

"Sharon, please. I hear you. Let me in."

She trudged to the door and opened it. Jeff was standing there, his long white medical coat soaked with rain, his hair slicked down over his forehead. His eyes burned into her, luminous with concern. She felt herself leaning into him, putting her arms around him, pulling him close.

"Hey, hey!" He cradled her neck in his hands, hugging her head to his chest. He smelled like wet grass and starch from the hospital laundry. It was going to break her heart and his, but she loved him so much. How could she stop?

He let go with one arm and closed the door behind himself. Sharon stood back and looked at him.

He took her by the shoulders. "I was worried about you. Why didn't you come in? Are you sick? Look at you, you're sweating." He put the back of his hand to her head. "You've got a fever." He steered her back toward her bedroom, stopping when he saw the weights. "Whose are those?"

She felt suddenly irritated. What made him think they weren't hers? She went over to the barbell, lifted it to her chest, pressed it up, gazing into his eyes, sucking air through her teeth.

"Christ, Sharon."

She lowered the weight again. He seemed dumbfounded. "You don't have a fever, you've been working out."

"Does this mean I don't get a note from my doctor?"

He looked mystified. "You stayed home from the hospital today to lift weights?"

God, Jeff, she thought. Are you being thick? Or is it me. *Probably me.* "No. I stayed home from the hospital because I need . . . a mental health day."

Jeff looked a little scared. He let go of her hands and bent over the weights, examining them, running a hand along the fine-grooved bar. "These look old."

"They were my dad's."

"Really? That's right, he wanted to be an Olympic weight lifter, didn't he?"

Sharon frowned, trying to remember if she had ever mentioned that to Jeff. Then she realized that he had gotten it from reading Mom's chart. She said, "He would have made it, too, if it hadn't been for me. I came along just nine months and two weeks after Dad married Mom. He had to quit college and go to work. No more coach, no more weight room, no more regular training. All he had were these."

Jeff nodded as if he understood, but she could see that he didn't.

"He was a big man, a pure mesomorph. You should have seen his muscles. His back was like a V. His biceps were huge, his shoulders. He had a neck like this." Sharon held her hands out.

"But it didn't make him strong where it counted, did it," Jeff said gently.

She felt suddenly very cold and rigid inside. "What does that mean?"

"Nothing. I'm sorry. Forget it. Have you eaten anything today? C'mon, let me take you to dinner."

"Finish what you were saying."

Jeff tried to take her hands but she pulled away. An icy fury rose in her. It scared her, but she didn't know how to stop it.

"I know you loved your father very much," Jeff said softly. "It must have hurt like hell when he left you."

"Don't play psychologist with me."

"I'm not playing."

"And he didn't leave me, he left Mom."

"Oh, I see. He took you with him."

"You know what I mean. You don't realize the way Mom was back then. A saint couldn't have stayed with her."

"You stayed. And many times, when she was acting paranoid and crazy, it must have seemed that she didn't love you. But your father, he always loved you, right? He said so. He took you places, gave you things, even after he left you. It would have destroyed you if you felt he might not really love you either."

Sharon felt a stab of grief, and then the anger rebounded, twisting cold through her insides. Why was Jeff doing this to her? "He did love me."

"I'm sure he did, as much as he was able. You don't have to hate him, you know. You can be furious without hating."

"I don't know what you're talking about."

"He left you with two terrible gifts—you're afraid to love

a man, and you're terrified that you'll end up like your mother. That can end. But only if you'll finally take a real look at your father, without the blinders. Only if you understand that he left *you,* too, and that there are men in this world who are better than—"

Sharon slapped Jeff.

He stumbled a step to the side, leaning over, then righted himself slowly. The feel of his jaw tingled in her hand. She was stunned at herself, too shocked to speak. He rubbed his chin and gazed at her. His bleak expression tore at her heart.

"I'm sorry, Jeff. Oh, God, I'm so sorry."

"No sweat. I was thinking of switching to baby food through a straw anyway."

She could hear the anger beneath the joke. There was a strange look in his eyes and she knew she had hurt him badly, not just his jaw.

"You must hate me," she said.

"Is that what you want? For the two of us to reenact the whole sorry past? I've got to leave you, don't I, or you'll be forced to finally see that your dad *didn't* have to leave your mom. You're even willing to *be* your mother, if it'll save you from feeling the pain your father gave you—that fucking bastard!"

Sharon felt the words tearing into her like knives. I deserve it, she thought. But I can't take it, not just now. "I think you'd better leave," she said.

He looked at her for a long moment, then turned and stalked out the door. Sharon stared at the closed door, not believing what she had done. She loved him, needed him desperately, and she had hurt him, then sent him away.

Maybe he was still outside. She hurried to the door and threw it open, but the stairway had swallowed him. It yawned emptily up at her. No, she thought. Come back. She ran down the steps and out, hurrying through the slanting downpour, looking for Jeff's car. She circled the block, searching in the gray, fading daylight, but the Buick wasn't there. He was gone. She had driven him away, just like Mom had Dad.

"You're wrong!" she shouted. "It's not what I want!"

Tears welled up and poured down her face, mingling with the rain. She walked back upstairs, feeling very heavy, pushing her legs to take the next step and the next. Looking up, she saw her door standing wide open. She hurried the rest of the way, locking the door behind her, leaning against it.

Not what she wanted and yet, in a horrid way, it had to be. It had to happen now, while there was still time, before she lost it completely and had no strength to deal with the pain of his walking away. Because he was not a better man than her father, he was *not*. And he would leave her.

Oh, maybe not at first. When she started rambling about vampires and people being stolen from MHU, he would hide his pain and pat her hand. He would take her to the hospital, carry her stupid cardboard suitcase for her. And he'd visit her, but the visits would grow fewer, further between, because there was just no way a person who loved you could really stand it. Not Dad, not Jeff, not anyone.

Sure, she had stayed with Mom, but that was different. That's the way it was with parents and children. First they took care of you, and then you took care of them. She'd just had to start taking care of Mom a little earlier than most.

But a marriage was something else.

At least this had come before Jeff and she could get married. He was free and clear. It wouldn't be such a . . . burden.

Sharon burst into tears again, leaning against the door, hitting it softly with her fists until the tears were gone and she had no more. She knew she was feeling sorry for herself, but damn it, she deserved it. All in all, this had been a pretty shitty day.

A weary depression settled over her. She doubted everything. Were people really disappearing from Adams Memorial? If she could see shadows that weren't there, how could she be sure of anything? She should've waited before she opened that door, long enough for a real man casting a real shadow to get down that long hall and away. But she had been scared out of her mind, and . . .

Scared out of her mind.

She had a sudden memory from college: the time she'd studied all night before the biochem final, then gone in scared silly that she would flunk. Sure enough, she had sat there at the desk, her stomach churning, looking at question after question, recognizing nothing, having no clue how to answer. That's it, she'd thought. Zero out of a hundred.

Strangely, she felt the massive load of fear draining out of her. Suddenly she smelled benzene and acetic acid from the lab down the hall. Her fingers registered the light pitting of the wooden desk under her fingertips. She became aware of a cardinal chirping outside the window. Relaxing, she thought about going back to the dorm, petting her illegal cat Soot, and reading *Dune*. Hey, at least she didn't have to study tonight!

She found herself looking at the first question again. She started writing.

She ended up getting a ninety-seven on the final.

Sharon sat up straight on the bed, feeling her mind sharpen and focus. Fear *is* the mind killer, she thought. Fear can make you so you can't think, don't know your own name. What do you want to bet it could also make you unable to tell how much time is passing? I could have stood there staring at that door a lot longer than I—

Something creaked.

She turned toward the door, startled, but no one was there. Her closet door was open about an inch. The line of blackness sliced through her brain, stirring the little hairs on the back of her neck.

She always closed that door.

She didn't like closet doors standing open. One of the many things she had learned from Mom.

She had left her front door wide open while she ran

around looking for Jeff. Someone could have slipped in here and hidden. Fear prickled through her in a slow, cold wave. She looked around for a weapon. There, one of the weights. She picked up a ten-pounder and went toward the closet door, holding the weight ready. She jerked the door open. The closet was empty.

Turning back to her bed, she saw that the last of the daylight had faded into night. The dark, naked window spooked her some more. She tossed the weight onto her bed and closed the drapes, then sat on the bed, facing the door to her bedroom. She tuned into the contact of the floor with the bare soles of her feet, monitoring for the tiny vibrations of other feet creeping around beyond the bedroom door. Her nerves buzzed with alarm, sensing a hidden presence. Suddenly she understood why paranoid schizophrenics sometimes wrapped their ankles in tin foil to keep out the alien radio waves. It had never seemed very funny to her, and it was less funny now.

She felt a tremor through her heels, heard the creak again—*Under the bed!* She jerked her feet up, looking between her knees as a hand thrust out from under the bed, grasping for her ankle and missing. A chill shot through her. She twisted back and rolled across the bed. The man slid out and sprang up into a half crouch between her and the door. His head gleamed like a huge golden bullet, the nose mashed over, eyes pulled down at the corners into mournful slits. He was big, muscular.

She saw with alarm that he had a syringe in one hand, and in the other something that looked like a pen.

Very slowly, he raised one foot onto the bed. Her lungs jerked inside her; her head rang with fear. He was going to come across the bed, lunge over the foot at her if she tried to go around it. She felt one of the weights against her foot, but if she tried to get it, he would lunge as soon as she bent down.

Sharon grabbed for it, and as he sprang across the bed she spun it up at him, a fiver. It smacked him in the thigh.

His foot slipped on the covers and she dashed past him, racing through the living room for the door. She heard him behind her as she went out, heard his feet thundering on the steps behind her, the sound driving straight into her ears. She screamed and ran, head down. *Don't trip!*

She burst out the front of the building and heard him right behind her, too close. She turned, dodging as she saw him leap, but he caught her with one arm and spun her down with him into the shrubs beside the stoop. The bushes crushed down behind her, cushioning her. He landed on his feet and pushed the pen against her shoulder, as though it were a knife. She yelled, punching out at him, but the soft bushes absorbed the blows through her back. He stared at the pen, then cursed, stuffing it in his pocket as he threw a leg over her waist, straddling her. She saw his other arm raise, the syringe gleaming yellow in the porch light.

She rolled a shoulder into him, feeling his fist plunge past. He struck again, but she grabbed his wrist, stopping the syringe an inch from her shoulder. She squeezed hard, grinding his bones together. He yelped and tried to jerk away.

She forced his wrist back, staring into his face, hating him now, wanting to gouge out his eyes, to kill him.

He snatched the syringe with his free hand and stabbed down. Pain sparked in her shoulder, and she screamed in panic. Digging through the bushes with her feet, she found solid ground and heaved him off to the side. He scrambled up and rammed the syringe at her again. She felt it hit her breast, but there was no sharp prick this time.

She kicked him in the crotch. He stumbled, bent over, into the bushes and floundered onto his face. She kicked him again, in the ribs, feeling a dull pain in her toe.

He dragged himself up through the bushes and ran.

Sharon chased him, a savage rage pumping through her. She followed him half a block, then became aware of the sidewalk ripping her bare feet. He was running like a panicked dog, faster than she could, pulling away.

And she was being a fool.

Sharon stopped, panting, and watched him run until he was out of sight.

She laughed, exhilirated. She headed back to her apartment, running, veering onto the grass beside the sidewalk to cushion her feet. The grass looked blue-black in the night. It was wet from the rain, cool and cleansing. She loped along, feeling like a lionness, strong and invincible. The night glittered in halos around the streetlights; it tasted sweet in her lungs.

She climbed the stairs back to her apartment and locked the door behind her. Going into the bathroom, she looked in the mirror. The syringe needle stuck out of her shoulder, bent almost at a right angle. The point had gone in, but then her deltoid muscle had tensed, turning so rigid it had stopped the needle, bending it. A new fringe benefit to pumping iron! The bastard had had no chance to unload the shot into her.

Sharon jerked the needle out and flung it into the sink.

She stared at herself in the mirror, seeing a completely new person, her hair plastered to her face and wonder in her eyes. She grinned at the face in the mirror. "You're not crazy, Sharon Kelly Francis," she said. "They really are out to get you."

Frank heard water dripping. His throat squirmed in a dry swallow. He did not move. He knew it was a dream. He dreamed about water every time he dozed off, thought about it every minute he was awake, longed for it, imagining how it would taste, how it would feel going down his throat. Every time light came through the hole beside his eye, he waited for feet to appear, listening for the sound of the sink above his head, hoping that some water would splash on the floor and drip through the hole where he could lick it. But it never did. Only a few feet, but it might as well be a thousand miles.

Frank tried to take his mind off the water, figure out how much time had passed since he escaped—if you could call it that—through the hole in the cinder block wall. Awful hard to tell here in the dark, especially when he kept dozing off. Let's see, that time back in the war, they'd all had to go without water for twenty-four hours. Did his throat and tongue feel better right now, or worse than that time?

Worse, but not a lot worse. So let's say thirty hours—and here he was thinking about water again.

Jesus, it was so real. He could hear the water plinking down near his head in luscious fat drops, tormenting him. He could smell it, a clean, thin scent mixed with the odor of dirt.

God, don't torture me this way.

The sound continued.

Frank reached up and touched his face gingerly in the darkness, trying to tell if his eyes were open. They were. He was not dreaming—or if he was, he was dreaming his eyes were open.

Plink, plink, plink.

He rolled over in the dark, crawling over the floor, feeling first dry dirt, then mud—*mud!*

He scrabbled into position so that the water hit his cheek, then dripped into his open mouth, blooming on his tongue, sliding down his throat in delicious, quicksilver threads.

It must be raining up top!

God, oh God in heaven, thank you!

He had trouble swallowing at first, but as the parched tissue of his throat absorbed the water, it became easier. He swallowed mouthful after mouthful. It was the most wonderful feeling he had ever had.

I'm going to live, he thought. Norma, I'm still living, I'm still here.

He wondered if Dr. Francis would ever come.

No, he thought, stop that, stop thinking about it. Drink the water, enjoy what you got.

17

SHARON CAME DOWN quickly from her high. She had driven the guy off, but he might come back any minute to finish what he'd started, and she might not be so good—and so lucky—next time.

She called the police.

While she waited for them, she thought of the big bastard with the nylon stocking on his head, hoping he wouldn't come back before the cops got around to her. Once the police arrived, she quickly realized she might as well not have bothered them. No broken door or picked lock, just a few bruises that she could have gotten slipping in the shower, and a suspicious-looking needle. She couldn't give them much of a description, either.

"Sorry, ma'am," said the woman cop, "but I don't think there's enough here to get protection for you on this. You got some people you can stay with tonight? That's what I'd do, I was you. He comes back, you call us."

Right, Sharon thought. I'll ring you up while he's sticking the needle in me.

She took the blood tests she had stolen from records and rode her bike to outpatient, pumping the pedals hard, looking back over her shoulder every block. When she went inside she found Austin already there, standing outside one

212

of the therapy rooms with a cup of coffee. He grinned and waved at her with the cup, spilling some coffee.

"Hi, Austin. What are you doing down here?"

"Filling in for Mike. You know, that R-three who broke his leg in two places. He stepped in front of an ambulance that hadn't quite stopped. He's still in traction."

Sharon knew very well. Austin seemed to forget that she too had been taking Mike's slot off and on for weeks. She felt a small sense of betrayal. Why had Denise called Austin?

Because you've been out of it for two days.

"Oops," Austin said, looking toward the entrance. "I think this is my nine o'clock coming."

Sharon locked herself into the empty therapy room next to Austin and listened to his voice drone soothingly on the other side of the wall. Safe. No one was going to find her tucked away here. And if they did, she would yell and Austin would hear her. There were plenty of other people around, too: patients, staff, the receptionist, and now and then a night watchman. Outpatient would be busy right up until ten, and she could stay later if she wanted, spend the night here.

Sharon spread the twenty-six blood tests in front of her on the table, wishing Jeff were there to help evaluate them.

Oh, Jeff, she thought. What happened?

But she knew what had happened, had waited for it to happen. No, she couldn't call Jeff. Even if he could forgive her, they would just start sinking into the same quicksand all over again. To turn the old joke on its head, just because someone really was after her didn't mean she wasn't paranoid. The hard truth was that if she weren't, she would never have latched on to this in the first place. Look what she had started with: Mom's crazy-sounding talk about Meg, talk most people would have justifiably ignored. Most people got a little paranoid at times; maybe that's all this was. Or maybe she was heading for a paranoid schiz blowup. Until she knew which, she had nothing to offer Jeff—and herself—but pain, more pain, and worse pain.

Sharon thought of Jeff and herself only two nights ago, making love in her apartment. The memory was still fresh, his arms around her, his voice murmuring words of love in her ear. She swallowed hard, holding back tears. Then she jumped up and hit the table with her fist. Austin's voice broke off in the next room. A second later she heard rapping on her door.

"Sharon, you all right in there?"

She got herself under control with an effort. "Fine. Thanks."

Sharon waited until she heard Austin's voice through the wall again, then sat down and dried her eyes. Toughen up, she told herself. These tests, damn it, are your most important problem now. If the bastards who nailed these people get you, you won't have to worry about getting back with Jeff or going crazy or anything else.

Sharon applied herself to the tests, starting with the first blood value, glucose. The first five patients were enough to tell her there was no agreement, no pattern for that value. She moved on to the next. After an hour, she found what she was looking for: the blood urea nitrogen values agreed very closely across patients. Excitement hit her like a shot of caffeine. She bent over the tests, working more quickly. There—the same thing for monocytes! She worked through to the last value, but there were no other matchups.

Sitting back, she controlled her excitement and thought about what she had found: the twenty-six blood tests had been ordered by twelve different doctors. No pattern there, and no reason there should be one. Blood tests were routine in a hospital. Anyone could look at them once they were in the chart.

But someone dangerous had looked at these blood tests.

Someone looking for a very specific pattern—and a very strange one. Her excitement broke through again. It was there in twenty-three out of the twenty-six tests. BUN val-

ues between twenty and twenty-five. An absence of monocytes. A weird double signature.

Okay, BUN, blood urea nitrogen: that had to do with
kidney function. Values between twenty and twenty-five
were at the high end of the normal range. As for the monocytes, these twenty-three people might or might not be defi-
cient. The value was just a sampling count per hundred, and
monocytes were uncommon enough that none might show
up even when the person tested was completely normal.
High BUN, low monocytes; the pattern was stunningly
clear.

Trouble was, it didn't point beyond itself. There was no
medical condition characterized by such a pattern—no
known condition.

Maybe the two values were correlated with some third
condition, *X,* that no one knew was related.

No one but the person who had snatched these patients.

The bad news was that the blood tests were not going
to tell her the medical specialty of the kidnapper—not unless she learned something new. The good news was that,
statistically, this was very compelling proof that someone
with medical knowledge was kidnapping people from
Adams Memorial based on their blood tests. Same narrow
range for all twenty-three people, same high-low pattern.
Assume the other three cases were people who checked out
AMA and then disappeared on their own. If she'd drawn
the twenty-three tests at random, the odds of finding this
pattern in all twenty-three would be less than one in a thousand. Detective Poulson wouldn't have to take her word on
that—any competent statistician would back her up all the
way.

But if she took it to Poulson, her career was over.

Sharon felt suddenly cold. Everything she had worked
for, gone. Maybe Poulson could overlook the fact that she
broke into a locked room in the hospital and stole confidential records protected by law. But he was going to need the
help and cooperation of hospital administration to investi-

gate staff doctors, and he wasn't going to get it unless he told them why he was suspicious. Poulson would have to go to Judith Acheson. And when he did, "I just happen to have twenty-six blood tests from your confidential records room," wasn't going to do it.

Sharon hugged her elbows and bent over the table, feeling as if an icicle had been rammed into her stomach. Jesus, she couldn't. She had to be a psychiatrist; there was nothing else for her.

But Frank. He had been gone only a couple of days. He might still be alive. And if she didn't do something, there would be others.

And tonight had marked her as one of them.

The murmuring voices stopped on the other side of the wall. Sharon checked her watch. Ten o'clock.

A soft rapping came at her door. "It's me, Austin."

She got up and let him in.

"Closing time," Austin said. "Walk you to your bike?"

"No thanks, I'm going to hang out here awhile."

He looked past her at the pile of blood tests on the table. "Want to talk about it?"

She saw shy hope in his eyes. Her heart warmed to him. Dear Austin. Maybe he would get over being thick, and loving people who couldn't love him back, and talking to his patients when he should be listening. Maybe he would end up a good psychiatrist. Probably not. Either way, she would miss him if . . .

"Just a knotty research problem," she said.

"Blood tests. You tracking a vampire?"

She thought of the shadow on the glass. "Sort of."

"Well, good night."

"Good night, Austin."

Sharon followed him to the door. When he was gone she picked up the receptionist's phone and dialed.

"Detective Poulson," said the gravelly bass voice.

She swallowed. This was it, the beginning of the end for her.

"Hello?"

"This is Dr. Francis. I need to talk to you. I've got hard proof that someone's kidnapping people from Adams Memorial."

"More statistics?" His voice was several shades cooler.

"That's right. Could I see you tonight?"

"No chance. I've got a real live murder on my hands. You know, the kind with bodies and blood and like that."

Sharon clenched the phone, feeling stung. What was the matter with him? Suddenly she realized what it might be. Maybe using Mark had backfired, rubbed Poulson the wrong way. "Did Mark Pendleton talk to you?"

"Yeah, last night. An impressive young man. Seems to think the world of you."

"What did you think about the numbers?"

"I'm studying them. Look, Doctor, I gotta go."

"Hang on," Sharon said, desperate. "Detective Poulson, this is important too. I'm talking about twenty-three people. Some of them are almost certainly dead, even if you can't see the blood and bodies. And some of them, like Frank Greene, might survive—if we act fast."

A heavy sigh slipped along the line. "Tomorrow at ten. It's the best I can do."

Her heart sank. Twelve more hours.

But it was still quicker than trying to start from scratch with someone else at the police department. "Can you pick me up in the back parking lot of the hospital?" The silence stretched and she felt herself flushing. "I don't have a car," she explained.

"Fine." His voice was warmer, and Sharon realized he pitied her. She hung up, her face burning.

Forget it. Poulson could pity her, wish she would get off his back—anything he wanted, as long as he listened. Ten o'clock. Twelve more hours.

One last chance to go to work, act like a psychiatrist.

Suddenly she could hear the silence all around her, feel

it eating into her bones. Maybe she should walk over to emergency. There would be people there all night.

She sprang up and hurried out through the darkened halls of outpatient, cutting across through one of the medical wards. The corridor was on night lighting. The low, honeyed ambience gave her a peaceful feeling. Night had descended on the hospital. Sharon inhaled, sorting out the unique mix of smells: the pleasant piney scent of floor cleaner from down the hall where the janitor was mopping, hand lotion from the nurses' station, and the chalky, medicinal odor of the morning meds, now being laid out in their trays.

Passing the patients' rooms, Sharon listened to the small sighs and snores of people slipping into sleep. She felt a strong, proprietary warmth toward them. She loved being in this place, being needed. She had come here wanting more than anything else to treat schizophrenia, and if things went as she now expected, she would leave without ever doing it. But there was plenty else for her to do here, even on wards like this, far from MHU. The people in these rooms had to battle not just illness, but fear, confusion and depression, the erosion of spirit and will. Tomorrow morning she'd be back here for her once-a-week rounds. Would it be for the last time?

She felt a deep sadness and suppressed it. So make it good, she thought. And then whatever happens, happens.

Emergency was bustling. Eight people, including a mother with a squalling baby, sat in the orange plastic seats, waiting to see a doctor. Sharon stuck her head into the treatment area, scanning the booths, getting a look at the residents. None of them was Jeff.

Disappointed, she sat down in one of the seats and waited for morning rounds.

Make it good, Sharon reminded herself as she started morning rounds on the medical ward.

She tried, but she had trouble concentrating.

Mr. Nuñez said that he wasn't frightened about his stomach surgery tomorrow, that he was just fine, and she was in with her next patient before his hands, clutching the sheets, registered with her. She doubled back as soon as she could and tried to comfort Mr. Nuñez, but the moment had passed, and he had shoved the fear deeper, where neither of them could get at it. She left again, feeling terrible.

Doctors and nurses flowed by her in the hall, their faces bright blurs. Some of them spoke to her, and she heard herself answer.

In Mrs. Abernathy's room she asked about the stomach and had to be reminded that it was a collapsed lung and it was doing much better, thank you, dear. Sharon was furious with herself, but she covered up and chatted with Mrs. Abernathy, found out about her arthritis and got her signed up in a pain group. That was more like it.

Back out in the hall, Sharon wondered who Jenkins would get to replace her in pain group. He sure wouldn't want to run it by himself. Maybe Mrs. Abernathy wouldn't get therapy at all.

Sharon fought off a wave of depression and checked the last chart. Mrs. Criley, room 116, at the other end of the ward. Look cheerful, she thought. Criley's a colostomy patient, depressed as hell, and the last thing she needs is a depressed therapist.

Turning into Criley's room, Sharon walked through the short entry hall and stopped. The privacy curtain was drawn around the bed.

"Mrs. Criley?"

No answer. Sharon inched the curtain aside. The bed was empty. It was mussed, but there was something not quite right about it. Where was the knitting that always sat on the bed table? And the juice cans? Mrs. Criley was a hoarder—her table always had at least four or five of the little cans of apple and grape juice from the hospital kitchen. The bed table was empty.

The hairs prickled on Sharon's neck. Hey, she thought,

take it easy. Criley was transferred to another room, that's all, and someone forgot and put her chart back in the wrong slot.

Sharon started to turn. There was a squeak behind her—Tennis shoes—and the bathroom door of the room flashed through her mind, the way it had looked as she'd passed: almost closed, dark when it should have been lit. *Trap!* she thought. Then something soft touched the base of her skull. A shock went through her. The room jerked and slid out of focus.

Sharon hovered in dimness, fighting to hold on to the room, make it come clear again. She could feel hands under her armpits, lifting her onto the bed. She tried to move her arms, kick out with her legs, but she couldn't seem to push the commands through to her muscles. A dull ache started up at the base of her skull.

Little black dots swam on her retinas, and she realized she was staring at the acoustical tiles in the ceiling. A white coat sleeve flashed over her eyes and a hand gripped her shoulder and rolled her over onto her face. She felt very numb and confused. She'd been doing something . . . yes—rounds! What happened?

Fingers wound into her hair and she felt her head being pulled back. She gulped air, and then a hand clapped over her mouth. Fear spurted through her. A knee pressed into her back, pinning her down against the mattress. She felt the hand stuffing a pill in her mouth. *He's drugging me!* She tried to spit it out, but the hand pulled up against her chin, arching her neck. Her throat convulsed, and she felt the pill sliding down dry.

Sharon screamed, but the hand jerked up on her chin, clamping her teeth together, strangling the sound down to nothing.

She forced her head down against the hand, raising her own hand to claw at it. The man dropped onto her, flattening her into the bed, pressing the sheet into her mouth. She bucked, gagging, and he let her move her head to the side a little. Fighting the weight on her back, she sucked at the air, getting just enough to keep from passing out. She could feel the sharp lump of the pill working its way down her throat. What was it? What was it going to do to her?

"Just be quiet," whispered a voice in her ear. "I'm not going to hurt you if you don't fight."

Sharon saw his arm beside her face, the white sleeve pulled up, revealing a mat of blond hair. His arm turned and she glimpsed two small needle marks along a bulging vein.

She gathered herself and tried to throw him off, but she had no strength. It took everything she had just to breathe.

Feeling strange. Hard to remember what was happening. Must be the drug. . . .

"Sharon?" The voice echoed inside her skull.

"Huh?" she grunted.

"Do you want to get up?"

She considered the question for a long time and could not think of an answer.

After a while, she sat up on the bed, breathing deeply. Just . . . felt . . . so . . . weird.

Little strings sawed back and forth inside her brain.

She saw movement at the door, a woman coming in, walking toward her. The woman held a knife, all covered in blood. Sharon started screaming, and then she realized with horror that the woman was her.

18

"WHO ARE YOU?" Sharon's throat felt thick. She could barely squeeze the words out.

Her twin with the knife advanced, grinning. *I think you know.* It spoke in a man's voice, deep and friendly. She could actually see the sound, a warm orange vapor curling from its mouth. The vapor streamed down around the knife, turning a chill blue as it sparkled along the blade. I'm hallucinating, she thought. That man forced a pill down my throat. Angel dust, or maybe LSD.

You don't want to know, the image went on, *but you do know.* There *was* something eerily familiar about the voice.

Think, Sharon. You'll figure it out. It advanced another step on her.

"Keep away from me!"

The twin kept moving in. It held the knife out, aiming the point at Sharon's neck. She jerked the privacy curtain shut between them and pulled her feet up onto the bed. Suddenly she remembered the man who had forced the pill down her throat. Could he see this too? She glanced over, but he wasn't there. She stared, stunned, at the spot where he had been. Spinning around on the bed, she searched the white enclosure within the privacy curtain. He was gone, leaving her alone with it.

Cold with terror, she turned back to the curtain. A blood-red point appeared in the middle and stretched toward her. The curtain pulled with it, then seemed to melt onto it, turning transparent, revealing the knife blade. The hand gripping the knife followed, then the arm, and then above it the curtain molded into a death mask, taking on color as her own face melted toward her through the curtain. It had to be a hallucination, it *had* to be, but she could smell the blood on the knife blade, a decayed, melony sweetness. The bed trembled under her, and she realized she was shaking.

The twin's mouth opened and the deep voice eddied out again, mocking. *Why does the knife scare you, Sharon? It's your knife. You're the killer.*

"No."

Oh yes.

She watched, frozen, as the thing oozed the rest of the way through and stood inside the white tent with her. *You killed me, Sharon,* said the deep voice. Something stirred in the depths of her mind, like a giant eel brushing under her in dark water. Her body shuddered, out of control. "Go away!"

But I can't *go away. Never ever.* The thing grinned and lunged at her with the knife. She shrieked and rolled off the bed. Jumping up, she got tangled in the curtain, ripping the material from the curtain rod. She flung the curtain down and stumbled over it as the thing came up behind her, stabbing. She dodged the knife and lunged past her twin for the door. The light of the hall beckoned in a bright rectangle, but as she ran toward it, it dwindled. The sound of warm laughter followed her, and she screamed, fighting to get to the distant light, but she was suspended, her feet brushing impotently at the floor, and then the door sprang forward, ripping over her head, spilling her into a crazily twisted hallway.

A woman in white was running toward her. Nurse Radomsky. "Look out!" Sharon yelled. "It's back there!"

Radomsky caught her and held her. "Sharon? What's back there?"

"I am. I'm coming. I've got a knife!" Sharon realized with horror that she was talking crazy. It wasn't real, it was the pill, she must get hold of herself—

Strange, chaotic thoughts flashed through her head. Her heart felt as if it were bursting. Radomsky steered her over to the wall. Sharon grabbed the big flattened rail along the wall. She did not want to look back, but she had to. Forcing her head around, she saw it bearing down on the two of them, its bloody knife raised. It ran in utter silence, slipping forward as smoothly as a water snake. Sharon saw that its eyes—her eyes—had turned reptilian, vertical black slits set in brilliant green. It wanted her to think it was only a hallucination so it could catch her and kill her. She screamed and tore away from Radomsky. "Run!"

Radomsky stood staring where she pointed. Sharon grabbed her hand. "It'll kill you too!" She ran, pulling the nurse after her, seeing more people in white ahead: Stan Quinlan, a resident, and two nurse anesthetists.

"Grab her," shouted Radomsky. "She's hallucinating."

"No!" Sharon screamed. "It's real, it's real, CAN'T YOU SEE?"

"There's nothing there, Sharon." Quinlan took a step toward her, holding out his arms. She let go of Radomsky's hand and feinted to one side, but Quinlan lunged and grabbed her. Sharon brought her hands up inside his grip, knocking his arms apart, hearing him gasp. She shoved him over a gurney and ran past, jerking up short, feeling her white coat tighten across her chest. Someone had grabbed the back of it. She tore free with a ripping sound and sprinted away from them.

There—the door to the stairwell! She pushed through and ran up the stairs, hooking the rail to spin herself through the squared landings, pulling her way up the straightaways. Her breath tore at her throat and her legs began to ache, and then she was at the top. She burst through a low door and found herself in open air.

She stood disoriented, gazing down. Gravel stretched away from her feet. Looking up, she saw a brilliant sky, so blue it jumped and crackled before her eyes. The horizon was impossibly close, a low, straight line of brick.

You're on the roof, said a voice in her mind. Just take it easy. Sit down and rest.

But she couldn't rest, it was chasing her—Watch out!

Sharon turned and saw herself coming through the door.

You can't run from us, Sharon. The thing gave her a sad, mocking smile, then thrust the knife out. Sharon leapt back. It thrust again and she backed away, terrified, groping behind her, knowing the low wall could not be far, and beyond it, a long, dizzy plunge to her death.

The door banged open and Quinlan stepped through. His face was white. "Sharon, stop!"

The thing with the knife took another step toward her, ignoring Quinlan.

"Get it away from me!"

"Just take it easy. No one's going to hurt you—Sharon, stop!"

"It'll get me!"

"No. I won't let it," Quinlan said.

One of the nurse anesthetists came through behind him, followed by two big men in orderly dress. "Christ," said one of them, "she's going over."

Sharon felt stone scrape against her calves and stopped. Looking over her shoulder, she saw the side of the building plunging down to a small patch of green bordered by cement. Her stomach went hollow. She stared with dread fascination at the cars, bright as beetles, nestled together in the parking lot. She felt her legs pressing harder against the low wall. A high whine sang in her ears. Far below, the base of the building swung toward her, and she knew she was falling, and then fingers clamped around her arms.

"Shit!"

"Got her. Jesus, she's strong—hang on!"

Sharon realized she was fighting them and stopped, letting them lower her to the gravel. The stones seemed to crawl like insects beneath her. She smelled dirty water and tar. A face hovered above her, a dark nub haloed by the blazing, turquoise sky.

"Now take it easy, Sharon." Quinlan. "Everything's going to be all right."

"Did you get her?"

"Don't worry," he answered.

Sharon grabbed his arm, easing up as she saw him wince. "Did you *get* her?"

Quinlan nodded, looking uncomfortable. Relief filled her. Another head joined Quinlan's, and then the sky rolled to the side and she saw the gravel stretching away from her. The crawling sensation vanished beneath her. Relieved, she kept her eyes on the stones so they wouldn't turn back into bugs. She felt a prick in her hip and the stones blurred and faded. It was all right. Quinlan had gotten. . . .

" . . . aron?"

"She can't hear you, man. Quinlan shot a load of Demerol into her."

"Demerol?"

"One of the N/As gave it to him. It was all they had on them. It'll hold her until she gets to MHU."

"MHU? Who admitted her?"

"Dr. Valois. He was down in ER on call and he did her paperwork himself."

"*Damn!*"

The anguish in the voice pried at Sharon, making her open her eyes. She could feel little jolts through her back, see recessed lights flowing up from her feet to disappear above her head. Everything glowed fuzzily around the edges. She felt fine, very good indeed. A dinner plate drifted into sight, hovering over her. Jeff's face was painted on it. The painted mouth moved. "Sharon?"

Not a plate. Jeff. Sharon tried to say his name, but felt only a low gurgle in her throat.

"It's okay, I'm right here. I'll stay with you." The face gave her a stark smile.

I'm going to MHU, Sharon thought. Tiny alarms went off in her head, but she could not think why. It would be all right. Any port in a storm. She giggled. And besides, she felt fine, now.

The recessed lights divided into pairs as they passed over her head. Mitosis, she thought, that's how my twin was made, by splitting off me. Nasty thing. What's its problem, anyway? Giving me a real attitude. Sharon giggled again. A faraway voice said, "Don't worry, that's just the Demerol."

The voices buzzed back and forth like flies on a lazy summer day. Sharon felt a draft; the cart bumped something and the smell of floor wax and disinfectant hit her nostrils. She heard a door clang shut, sending a ripple of echoes off tile. MHU. She felt a sluggish anxiety that faded quickly.

Rolling onto something soft.

Straps across her chest and thighs.

Someone squeezing her hand, babbling something, why didn't they speak Eng . . .

Sharon dreamed that someone was giving her a pill. Making her take it, shoving it down her throat. She wanted to open her eyes, fight, but her eyelids seemed gummed together. She couldn't even scream; the air huffed uselessly past her vocal cords. The pill inched down her throat. She could feel a trickle of water down her cheek, and then the dream faded and it was soft and dark as the inside of a coffin.

A hand squeezed her shoulder. Someone kept saying her name, over and over, until she had to open her eyes. Jeff.

"Hi," he said.

She felt a dull pleasure, mixed with anxiety. He looked so good to her. But there was something she had to say, a warning, and she could not think what it was.

So try hello. Her voice cracked, paining her throat.

"Here, I'll get you some water." Jeff jumped up and disappeared, returning in a minute with a brimming glass. She tried to sit up but couldn't. Looking down, she saw the edge of the top strap. Dread welled up in her.

"Jeff, what . . . " She could not go on. So *dry*. Jeff lifted her head gently and held the glass to her lips. She gulped until it was empty, feeling the parched tissues of her mouth soak up the glorious wetness.

She pushed at the top strap. "What is this?"

"Just a precaution. They didn't want you to roll out of bed."

Liar! She felt a rush of panic. "Get them off me."

His face grew bleak.

"Get them off, get them OFF!" She started lunging against the straps.

"Wait! I'll do it." Jeff undid the straps.

Sharon sat up, rubbing her wrists, feeling some of the fear recede.

"Do you remember why you're here?" Jeff said.

"Of course I . . ."

She realized she did *not* remember. Her mind was blank. She tried to force it, but nothing would come. She had been on rounds this morning—was this still the same day? She looked out the window and saw that the sun was low. Morning or night? Which day? Her fear mounted again.

"When did I . . . ?"

"This morning. You were finishing your rounds."

Good, she hadn't lost much, then. She had been on rounds, and then . . . and then . . . She strained to remember, feeling sweat break out on her forehead.

"It's all right."

"No!" she said fiercely. "Just hold on." But nothing more would come to her.

She shuddered.

"Are you cold? I'll get a blanket."

And then she remembered. "Jeff, they drugged me."

His face was very somber. "Who?"

"A man. I never saw his face. He grabbed me in Mrs. Criley's room. He forced a pill or a capsule down my throat. It was one of the hallucinogens, PCP or LSD, maybe both. . . . " Sharon could see that he didn't believe her. Her heart sank. Dear God, if she couldn't convince Jeff, she was lost.

Beyond Jeff's shoulder, she saw her own face gazing down, grinning. Her twin, raising its knife over Jeff's head. "Look out!" she screamed.

Jeff jumped up and whirled. He turned back slowly. "There's nothing there." He gave a shaky laugh. "Jesus, you scared me."

Sharon could still see the thing behind him. It mimed a kiss at her. Her heart pounded. "It . . . it's not there? Are you sure?"

"Yes," Jeff said. "What are you seeing?"

She told him.

"Well, don't worry. You're hallucinating, just like you said. I'll tell Dr.—the doctor."

Sharon had a sudden, horrid suspicion. "Dr. Valois?"

Jeff took her hand. "It's routine, you know that. You don't already have a doctor, so Valois, as chief, will assign you one. You're only with him till then, and I'll make sure he assigns you as quickly as possible. Who would you like? Tilgen? Or a woman, Soames, maybe or—"

"No one. I'm not crazy. I'm hallucinating because of the damn *pill!* You've got to get me out."

"No one says you're crazy. But you're having trouble with reality right now. There's no reason for anyone to drug you—you're imagining that, too. Sharon, you've got to trust me."

"No! *You've* got to trust me. They're going to keep drugging me, just like they did Frank!"

"Sharon," he said gently, "you've been afraid of this for most of your life. It's happened, but you can fight it. We can fight it together. The first thing you must realize is that it's an illness, not a pill—and definitely not someone trying to get you. I'm going to do everything I can to help you, but you've got to help yourself, too."

A terrible sense of urgency filled Sharon. "Jeff, I'm not going to beg. Either you believe me or you don't. But what I said is true. You have to get me out of this hospital, not just away from Valois."

Jeff said nothing. He looked miserable.

She jerked her hand away from him, frantic with frustration. Behind his shoulder, her twin laughed silently. She tried to ignore it. She felt hysteria swelling inside her. She had to make Jeff listen, but he wouldn't listen, *couldn't* listen.

Dr. Valois walked in behind Jeff, followed by Chuck Conroy. Valois was wearing a look of concern. "I think it would be best if you let her rest now," Valois said.

"No!" Sharon shouted at Jeff. "He's going to get me, just like he got the others."

"Dr. Valois," Jeff said, "let's get her assigned right away. How about Dr. Soames?"

Valois gave him a cold look. "Dr. . . . Harrad, isn't it? I'm sure I can make that decision without help, thank you."

"I have a strong interest in this case."

"Do you? Are you an immediate family member?"

Jeff flushed. "I'm sure you know I'm not."

"You have a brief from the court, then, making you Dr. Francis's guardian?"

"Get it, Jeff," Sharon said. "Get a court order, do whatever you have to do."

Jeff jerked his hand at her, low to his side where Valois couldn't see it, signaling her to hush up. "Dr. Valois, Dr. Francis is my fiancée. It would be wise if you understood that and let me in on any decision making."

"And I think it would be wise if you go now," Valois said.

"Fiancée or not, you are a resident in this hospital. I suggest that you remember your place. For now, Dr. Francis is my patient, and I'll do whatever I think best. You may see her at normal visiting hours."

Jeff stared at Valois like he was about to punch him; Sharon felt a jolt of alarm. Arguing with him could finish Jeff as a resident. "Jeff, it's all right. Go on, get out of here."

He gave her a look full of pain. "I'll be back. Don't worry." He stalked past Valois and out.

Sure, Sharon thought hopelessly. You'll be back, and you'll still think I'm crazy, and each day it'll get a little bit harder to tell people that sweet lie about me being your fiancée.

Dr. Valois sat down beside her, patting her shoulder. She felt a surge of revulsion. "Get out of here," she gasped. "Leave me alone. I know what you're doing. You stay away from me."

"It's all right," Valois said soothingly. "We're going to give you some medication that will make you feel better. You just rest, and tomorrow we'll talk." He turned and indicated Conroy. "You know Chuck."

Conroy gave her a sheepish little wave.

Sharon's skin crawled. My God, she thought. Of course. Chuck. You're the one in the nylon mask; you're Valois's muscle. Mom was right.

"Chuck will help look after you," Valois said. "I know you're very scared and confused right now, but it'll get better." He patted her shoulder again. She squirmed away from him, cold with terror. He smiled down at her and she knew he had her, had her right where he wanted her, and there wasn't a thing she could do about it.

19

SHARON CLOSED HER EYES, sickened, but she could still see her twin, standing at the foot of her bed, using the knife to shred skin off its hand. Against the darkness of her eyelids, blood ran bright from its fingers.

"Well, Ollie, this is a fine mess."

Sharon opened her eyes and saw Brittina standing in the doorway. The twin, with its bleeding hand, was gone.

"How you doing, kid?"

Before Sharon could answer, Brittina held up a plastic bag. "I was going to bring you posies, but then I decided you'd rather have these."

"Brazil nuts."

Brittina snapped her fingers. "I can't ever trip you up, can I? You're just too sharp for me."

Sharon felt a burst of gratitude for Brittina, so powerful that it shook her. The MHU attendings and nurses and the other residents had been coming by to say hello or wish her a quick recovery, but none of them had quite managed to be themselves, because they could no longer see her as herself. The invisible wall had dropped between them; they were still on the sane side, she suddenly was crazy. But not Brittina, bless her. Brittina, who had clawed her way from a Detroit ghetto into a mostly white medical school and knew what it was to try to be herself when so many people around her kept seeing only a color.

"I don't belong in here," Sharon said. "You've got to help me."

Brittina sobered. "Sharon, I will help you, any chance I get. But you *do* belong in here, just for the time being."

Sharon's heart sank. Suddenly Brittina was Dr. Wallace, psychiatric resident. What else could she be?

A terrible weariness came over Sharon. "Thanks for the nuts. They can keep me company." She realized how bitter it sounded and tried to smile.

Brittina set the bag on her bed table. "I didn't mean it as a statement, Dr. Francis. They're just food. Don't try to psychoanalyze them." She leaned over and kissed Sharon on the forehead. "Get well. I miss you."

And then she was gone.

Have you figured out who I am yet?

Sharon saw with a jolt of alarm that her twin was back, standing where Brittina had been. She wanted to cry out for Brittina, beg her to come back, but the cry stuck in her throat. She would have to fight this out herself. This was not real, this thing before her. It was a drug-induced hallucination. She must ignore it.

Had Brittina been a hallucination too? Sharon looked at the bed table. The bag of nuts was there. She picked it up and hugged it to her chest.

Come on, Sharon. You're not trying.

"You're no one," she whispered.

Thanks to you, the twin answered in Dad's deep warm voice. It changed before her eyes, becoming Dad, looking the way he had looked just before he'd left, his grin sad and uncertain. His skin seemed gray, his big shoulders bowed, as though he carried a huge, invisible weight that he could neither raise above him nor drop. He said, *Why did you kill me, Sharon?*

Grief tore at her throat. "I didn't mean to. What did I do?"

"Oh, honey, you *are* here. I thought they were lying."

Dad vanished; beyond where he had stood, Sharon saw her mother standing in the doorway. Her face was filled with pain.

Sharon blinked, disoriented. First Dad, then Mom—no wait, this was MHU. Mom was really here, really standing there now, not another hallucination.

Gently her mother pried the bag of nuts from her fingers and put it back on the bed table. Then she leaned down and hugged her. Sharon hugged back, feeling her face grow hot with shame. She hated for Mom to see her like this.

Was this how Mom had felt all these years?

No, worse.

Sharon clung to her, appalled for both of them. This was the woman who had put the bottle in her mouth, changed her diapers, held her fingers when she took her first step. And then Ellen Francis had lost control of herself, and daughter had become mother. Even with all my love, Sharon thought, how that must have hurt her.

But the shame—for both of them, now—was here, built into this place, in the locking doors, the staff that could give permission or withhold it, kindly, parental people who controlled their lives.

Mental illness was nothing to be ashamed of, but anyone who thought it wasn't humiliating had never been there.

I'm a psychiatrist, damn it, Sharon told herself, just like Brittina and Dr. Valois. I'm the parent, not the child.

But it was useless. She felt like weeping from mortification, but she would not let herself. It was the last bit of control she had.

Her mother sat down on the bed and studied her face. "I heard you talking when I came in. Who were you talking to?"

"No one," Sharon said. "Myself."

Ellen took her daughter's hand. "Honey, you don't have to be embarrassed. I've talked for years to people who weren't there. Was it your father?"

Sharon felt the grief again, a sharp knot in her throat. She cursed the drug, the havoc it was playing on her emotions. She did not want to discuss this.

Ellen looked away. "You don't have to tell me."

"Yes, it was Dad."

Her mother nodded sadly. "I see him a lot. He's not real."

"I know that." Sharon sat up, feeling a dread fascination. "How did you know I was talking to Dad?"

"I heard you say, 'What did I do?' I used to say that a lot, too, when I imagined I was talking to Ed."

Sharon hugged Mom again, feeling Mom's heart beat against her. Warmth and security flowed into Sharon, and she wondered if something deep in her brain remembered this rhythm, the first she had ever felt, so powerful and soothing. "What did he say?" she asked.

"The same as when he was alive: 'It's not you, Ellen, it's not even me. Something happened in the jungle. All I know is I used to be strong, but I'm not anymore.'"

Sharon's throat burned. She felt tears pushing up around her eyes, threatening to spill. That was the real Ed Francis, Sharon thought, the way Mom knew him—and I never did. She longed to see her mother's version of him. She wouldn't care if it turned out to be an illusion if she could only believe for a moment that he was real and back with her. She would remind him of their night at the circus, and he would laugh and tell her that he loved her.

"Why did he go?" Sharon's voice shook. Dear God, why had she never, in all her life, asked her mother that question?

Ellen pulled away gently from her embrace, took a tissue from her robe, and patted at Sharon's eyes. "At the end there he couldn't stay in a house, dear. I remember he came by once a few weeks after he left. You were in school. He told me he'd been sleeping in fields. Over in Vietnam, he slept in foxholes and bunkers, of course. One night a VC sneaked in and rolled a grenade into a bunker where two of your father's friends were sleeping. After that, he slept on the open ground, wouldn't come down, even during attacks. I don't think he was afraid; I think he felt he shouldn't be alive when those friends were dead. Anyway, after they sent him home, he'd make little sounds in his throat when he was sleeping at night. He'd jerk up in bed, sweating and staring. Then he'd have to dress and go out."

Sharon was riveted by her mother's words, as though they were an alien language she had heard many times and suddenly understood. "I never knew. I mean, I knew he was depressed after he was sent home, but never like that."

"Ed and I didn't want to worry you, honey. But I should have told you. Your father loved both of us, as much as he was able. We didn't make him leave . . . *neither* of us."

There was no accusation in her mother's voice, and yet Sharon understood what she was saying. "I never blamed you," she said. "But I did blame the schizophrenia."

Her mother patted her hand. "I know. It's okay."

Sharon searched her mother's face with dawning realization. She seemed perfectly sane right now. It was as if there was no craziness in her at all. It reminded Sharon of right after Dad had died, when Mom had pulled herself together and seemed well. She took care of me for a while, Sharon thought, and then she slipped back and I took care of her, and now it's full circle again. She sees her daughter lying in a bed like hers. How it must horrify her. But she's being strong for me.

Sharon squeezed her mother's hands. "God, Mom, I really love you, you know that?"

"I love you too, honey. More than anything."

Holding her hands, looking into her eyes, Sharon knew it couldn't last, this show of strength, any more than it had the other times. It might be over in the next minute, the next hour. Mom was still a paranoid schizophrenic. Sharon could hate the schizophrenia all she wanted, but it was time she accepted the fact: Mom didn't *have* it, she *was* it—along with a lot of other things, some beautiful and some not.

An incredible feeling of peace flowed through Sharon. Beyond her mother's shoulder she saw a giant teddy bear. It winked at her. She groaned.

Ellen squeezed her, hanging on, as if she knew what was happening. "It's not real."

"I know," Sharon replied. "But it's a big improvement."

The bear wavered and disappeared.

It's probably LSD, Sharon thought. It would give me the hallucinations, just like PCP, but PCP might also make me violent, which they don't need. They want me crazy, but they don't want me hard to handle.

Sharon realized with pleasure that she was thinking pretty clearly and had been, despite the intermittant hallucinations, for several hours. The distorting effect of the drug must be weakening inside her. Maybe the effort of concentrating, talking to Mom, had helped. She could probably help herself even more by exercising a little. Letting go of her mother, she swung her legs out of bed. The sudden movement made her head spin. She stared down at the floor, seeing a shower of sparks that faded slowly. She could feel the rounded steel bars of the lowered side guard against the backs of her thighs. The floor seemed very far away. Her feet dangled above it, reminding her of when she was a child.

Even the beds in here made you feel like a four-year-old.

Sharon took her mother's arm and jumped down. "Help me. I want to walk around a little." Leaning on her mother, Sharon circled the room, around and around. Gradually she felt stronger, more clear-headed. She sat down again, sweating but encouraged.

Her mother gazed at her with terrible sadness. Sharon wondered if she should tell her. Which could she stand better? Sharon wondered. That I'm schizophrenic, or that someone is drugging me to make me look schizophrenic?

Sharon realized suddenly that she had no choice. If she didn't get out of MHU, she was going to disappear, just like

Meg, and that was something neither her mother *nor* she could stand.

"I'm not schizophrenic," Sharon said. "I'm seeing things because someone is keeping me drugged on LSD."

Mom looked at her with alarm. "Drugging you? Who?"

"The same people who kidnapped your friend Meg: Dr. Valois and Conroy. They did it so that I would be brought in here. As soon as they can, they're going to kidnap me, just like they did Meg—unless we can stop them."

A fierce light came into Mom's eyes. "Conroy! I knew it! And Dr. Valois, you say? But I always thought he was so nice."

"He's been kidnapping people from MHU. I think he's using them in experiments."

Mom looked horrified, and Sharon felt a sudden powerful sense of unreality. What she was saying sounded crazy, even to herself.

"We've got to get out of here," Ellen said.

Sharon almost laughed. Her mother believed her. She was talking crazy and her mother was the only one who believed her.

"My sentiments exactly," Sharon said.

"You want to check out AMA?"

"No, we can't. Remember, that's how Meg and several of the others got taken. You have to go to the nurses for AMA, and then they call Valois. If we did it now, he'd keep us tied up in paperwork long enough to set up the kidnapping. When we stepped out the door, they'd be waiting."

"Then what can we do?"

"We're going to break out of here."

"All right."

Sharon felt a little jolt of alarm at what she was saying, then realized she was right. She had to get her mother free, too. Ellen Francis needed to be in a mental ward right now, but not this one, not as long as Valois was running his deadly little side program. She couldn't take everyone with her, but she wasn't leaving without her mother. "I'll need your help."

Suddenly, Ellen looked doubtful. "I'll try. But you know, sweetie, sometimes I get confused."

"I know. But try to be strong a little longer. Between the two of us, we'll make it. We've got to. I'll come down to your room and—"

"Hello, ladies."

Valois was standing in the doorway. He gave them a patronizing smile. "Visiting your daughter, I see. Good, Ellen, good."

Anger flamed up in Sharon. "I didn't hear you knock."

"Now Sharon. You're in a hospital, you know. And I'm your doctor."

"I want another doctor."

"Yes, you've made that quite clear. We're going to do all we can to help you, Sharon. But you must help us, not fight us. Ask your mother. She knows. She's been doing very well lately, and I'm sure you'll do just fine too."

His pretense of concern sickened Sharon. Did he think she didn't know what he was doing to her? If he hadn't known she was getting close to him, she wouldn't be here now to begin with, and both of them knew it.

He must be keeping up appearances for her mother.

"Are you still seeing things?" he asked.

Sharon hesitated, then realized she must say yes or Valois would dose her again. And she had better watch what else she said to him too. Valois was the one person who knew she wasn't crazy; accusing him would do no good, and it might well alarm him enough to make him step up his measures against her. She had to just play it cool with him until she could get out of there.

"Sharon?"

"Yes, I'm still seeing things." *You know I am, you bastard.*

Valois nodded. "Well, your medication should help with that."

A young man in a blue dentist-type jacket came in behind Valois, and he turned. "Ah, here we are." Sharon saw that the man was carrying a test tube rack and syringe. He was from labs. He was going to draw her blood!

Fear surged through her. She got out of bed and started for the door. Valois cut her off. "Whoa—easy does it. We just need a few cc's of blood for the lab, Sharon."

"No!"

"It's routine. What's the matter, are you afraid of needles?"

"Yes," Sharon said. This was it. Valois wanted to know what kind of research subject she would make. But it didn't matter what her test said. One way or the other, once he had the data, she was going to disappear, just like the others.

Somehow she had to stall him.

Sharon felt her mother's fingers clenching her arm; she realized that her terror was contagious. She forced herself to speak calmly. "Dr. Valois, I'm perfectly healthy. I don't need a blood test."

"I'm afraid I must insist." His eyes were hard now.

"You have no right to take blood from me if I refuse."

Valois ignored her and took her mother's arm. "Ellen, I think it would be better if you went back to your room now."

"No, I want to stay." Ellen's voice was tremulous.

"Please do as I say."

"It's all right," Sharon told her mother. "I'll be fine. You go ahead and we'll talk later."

Her mother clung to her. Sharon forced a smile and patted her hand. "Later, Mom. I'll come to your room."

Ellen gave her daughter a kiss and shuffled out. The technician came over to Sharon and started to wrap her arm with the piece of tubing. She shoved him onto the bed.

"Sharon!" Valois said sharply. "All right, Tom. Come along." Valois helped the technician off the bed and walked out, closing the door. Sharon heard the key turn in the lock.

Dread filled her. He'll be back, she thought. Do something! She inspected the windows, testing the wire mesh with her fingers. It was thick and solidly anchored.

If only she had a phone. But MHU didn't let patients with active psychoses have phones—usually with good reason.

Sharon saw movement in the corners of the ceiling; when she raised her head to look, blue faces winked out. She spun, trying to catch one of the faces, but each time she looked it disappeared.

The door opened again and Valois came back in with the blood technician and two big orderlies. His dark eyes glittered. Terror swelled in Sharon.

"Hold her," Valois said.

20

F RANK COULD HEAR the rat in the darkness. Its claws made dainty ticking noises on the hard ground around the drying mudhole. The rat was getting closer, bolder.

Frank's head spun with fear and desire. He could feel a dry pulse in his tongue and knew his mouth would be watering if he had the spit. Food, he thought feverishly, and realized that the rat must be thinking the same thing about him.

If only he could see it.

What if he was too weak to grab it?

Frank thought about testing his hand, seeing if it would move after his having to keep still all this time. But if he went to twitching, he would scare the rat off, and there might not be another chance, because he was getting weak.

Frank felt a feather touch on his ankle and knew it was the rat's whiskers. What if it bit him and had rabies?

Frank felt a crazed laugh pushing up his throat. He held it back with an effort. He was getting set to eat the damn thing if he could, and he was worried about rabies? If he didn't get this rat, he wasn't going to have time to die of rabies. It wasn't so much the meat—he could live a fair time longer without that. It was the moisture. He needed the rat's blood.

Odd thing was, wanting it didn't make him sick. No, if

he could get this rat, it would make him the happiest man alive.

Frank felt the rat nuzzling at his pocket. A thrill went through him. It was only a foot from his hand now. If it stuck its head a little farther into the pocket, he would have it for sure.

The nuzzling stopped. Frank felt the rat's whiskers tickle his fingers. He grabbed the rat, rolling to his knees, twisting its head as it bit him. It kicked once and was still.

Frank raised his head and stared up into the darkness, feeling a dry prickle at the backs of his eyeballs. He could smell the moisture in the rat. That's what it was, not blood, moisture. Thank you, God, Frank thought.

After the technician left with her blood sample, Sharon forced herself back to calmness. All right. She had done all she could and Valois had won another round anyway. But the fight wasn't over yet. Her mind was growing clearer by the hour. Now she must use that clarity to think, to plan.

The first thing was to get her clothes back.

Sharon headed for the nurses' station. The three-to-eleven shift had just come on. Sharon's heart sank when she saw the charge nurse. It was Erin Schmidt, a real hardass with the patients. Schmidt ignored her, talking to a couple of nurses aides. Sharon leaned on the lower half of the Dutch door, waiting until the conversation hit a lull.

"Nurse Schmidt, could I get dressed?"

Schmidt turned and eyed her. "I don't know, Sharon. I understand you gave the blood people some trouble."

Sharon gave her a sheepish grin. "I know. I'm sorry. It's just that I hate needles. I'm fine now, really." She hated the wheedling note in her voice, felt angry at Schmidt for making her beg. But it seemed to satisfy Schmidt. She nodded to one of the aides, who took her down to the end of the commons and let her into her locker. Sharon selected a shirt and a pair of slacks and took them to her room. She dressed quickly and went back out for a walk on the ward, getting her blood moving, savoring the feel of it pumping through her. It felt good to have normal clothes on again, and to be able to *think*.

She must make sure she kept on being able to think. How had they been getting the LSD into her? Probably the food; that would be the easiest way.

Okay, she thought. No more eating till you're out of here.

And how do we get out?

Maybe after supper, when things quiet down, Mom can create a diversion, get Schmidt out of the station. Then I could sneak in and use the phone to call the police.

And tell them what? That I'm a mental patient who needs help escaping from MHU? Sharon suppressed a groan. Even Detective Poulson wouldn't buy that—if she was lucky enough to be able to reach him in the first place.

She thought of Jeff and felt a mixture of hope and doubt. Would he help them? Jeff thought she'd had a schizophrenic break. He didn't believe her about Valois.

He doesn't have to believe me, she thought desperately. I'll tell him that if he loves me, he must do what I ask this once, do it for me, no matter what he thinks.

Suddenly Sharon noticed three of her patients standing ahead of her. They were huddled close together, talking. One of them glanced over his shoulder at her, then away again, quickly. Sharon blushed, realizing they were talking about her. God, what must they think, seeing her now as one of them. They must be wondering if she had been crazy all along, while she was treating them.

She fled in humiliation, hurrying to her mother's room. There, she worked out an escape plan, refining it, making Ellen repeat it back to her and rehearse it.

When her mother seemed clear on her part, Sharon slipped back to her own room. She noticed the Brazil nuts Brittina had brought sitting on the bed table. Good—if she was going to skip supper, she would need energy. Sharon ate a handful of the nuts, wondering if Schmidt would let her refuse to eat. Maybe if she said she was sick to her stomach—

"Hello."

Sharon turned and was surprised to see Judith Acheson standing in the doorway. She was wearing a dark blue suit with padded shoulders that made her look like a weight lifter.

"Mrs. Acheson."

"Please; Judith. How are you feeling?" Acheson walked over to her and offered her hand. Sharon put the bag of nuts down and shook hands with Acheson, feeling a sense of unreality.

"I feel all right."

Acheson gazed at her with frank curiosity. "They say you were hallucinating."

Resentment stabbed through Sharon. What gives you the right to rub my face in that? she wondered. You may be chief administrator of this hospital, but you're not my friend, and we don't know each other that well.

And why do you care, anyway?

"That's right, Judith. I was hallucinating."

"I just wanted you to know," Acheson said smoothly, "that I'm behind you one hundred percent. I'll see that you get whatever care you need, for as long as you need it. Don't worry about the cost."

"Thank you." Sharon wanted to tell Judith Acheson to stuff her care, that she was not sick. That it was Acheson's hospital that had a horrible sickness buried deep inside it. Something held her back. What was the use? This *was* Acheson's hospital, and whatever was happening here was at least partly her fault.

"Take as long as you want," Acheson said. "Don't think about anything but getting well, do you understand? Just leave everything to us."

"Leave everything to you."

"I think that would be best, don't you?"

"Thanks for stopping by," Sharon said.

* * *

They weren't happy about it, but they let her skip supper. They made her sit there with the others, but they didn't make her eat. After supper Sharon went back to her room and sat on her bed, growing more and more worried.

Did she really have to break out tonight?

Valois had gotten her blood around two o'clock, and now it was almost nine. Hematology was closed, but it had had three hours to screen the blood before it shut down for the day. If they weren't backed up today, they might have gotten to it, which would mean that Valois could get the report as early as tomorrow morning. Whatever the blood test showed, as soon as Valois knew that he had a valid screening, he would move to take her out of MHU.

Sharon went to her door and looked out at the commons area. It was beginning to quiet down for the evening. A couple of the older men were playing a game of pool. Two young women who had gone into depressions following miscarriages were playing Ping-Pong in a lethargic way, one or the other of them continually walking after the escaped ball. Only three other patients were in the commons, sitting on the Naugahyde sofas, reading old magazines. Dinner had been cleared away; the cart with dirty dishes and trays had trundled by a few minutes ago. In a little over two hours the boneyard shift would begin, and Conroy would come on duty.

Conroy would be looking to dose her.

Fear rippled through Sharon. In the report at shift change, Conroy would find out she had skipped supper and was overdue. One shock from his taser pen—or whatever it was and she would lie there like a frozen log. He could stuff the pill down her throat and she wouldn't even be able to squeak. All very neat and tidy, no injections or bruises for the nurses to see in the morning.

Or maybe, if Valois trusted that the lab wouldn't botch the blood test, he would simply have Conroy grab her tonight. Conroy could wait until the duty nurse took her nap at around three in the morning. The resident was usually snoozing in the on-call room by then. Then all Conroy would have to do was give her a good jolt from the taser and lug her out the door for Valois to pick up. Make up some story later about how she bashed him and took his key.

She really had to get out tonight.

Okay, do it. Sharon felt a choking nervousness. She walked down to her mother's room, praying silently, let her be okay.

Ellen Francis was sitting on her bed, her face vacant. She had put her hospital gown on over her faded housedress and was fiddling absently with the ties.

Sharon felt a cold dread in her stomach. "Mom?"

Her mother turned slowly, and her face lit up. "Sweetie!" She looked down at her hospital gown and said, "Oh, dear."

Sharon felt a small relief. At least her mother realized what she had done. "Here, let me help you with that." Sharon worked the gown off her mother's shoulders. "You remember what we talked about?"

Ellen nodded.

"Do you feel up to it?"

"Uh-huh." Her eyes were scared but rational. "Don't be nervous, honey. I'll fool them, you'll see."

"I'm sure you will."

But Sharon felt terribly nervous. She got as close as she dared to the nurses' station, then watched her mother walk out to the pool table. One of the old men was about to make a shot. Ellen flopped across the green felt in front of him, scattering the balls, then sliding to the floor. Sharon watched with approval. A touch melodramatic, but quite good, actually.

The man who had been about to shoot bent over Ellen while the other waved at the station, fidgeting in agitation. "Nurse! Nurse!" His voice was froggy, as though he seldom used it, but loud as a foghorn. Nurse Schmidt charged out of the station, her shoes clopping fast on the tile. Sharon hurried in. The phone was on the counter by the meds. She dropped to her hands and knees, keeping below the long window, and crawled over, lowering the phone to the floor. She dialed Jeff's apartment. One ring, two, three, *come on* . . .

"Hello, I'm sorry I can't come to the phone right now . . . "

His answering machine! Sharon cursed softly and pushed the disconnect. He must be on call tonight.

She dialed neurology and found out Jeff was on call—and had been called to emergency. Frantically, she dialed ER.

"Emergency, Nila Downs speaking."

"Jeff Harrad please."

"Who's calling?"

"Mrs. Harrad—his mother."

"Oh, yes. He was here, but now he's up in surgery, Mrs. Harrad. There was a big car crash, and—"

Sharon heard footsteps approaching the door. She pushed the disconnect, scooted under the counter, and pulled the big wastebasket over to hide her. Through a tiny gap between the top of the trash bucket and the bottom of the counter, she could see a man's plaid shirt. One of the patients. She heard the door creak as he leaned on it. Then it creaked again and the plaid shirt disappeared; the footsteps receded. Sharon snatched up the phone again, fighting panic. No Jeff. What was she going to do?

Mark!

But she couldn't remember his number.

She dialed information and got his home number, then asked for the number of the Red Falls PD, too. The floor was dusty; she wet her finger and traced both numbers on the tile. Home first. She waited in an agony of impatience through six rings. Damn, damn, *damn!* Schmidt wouldn't leave the station for long—she might even be headed back this minute.

Sharon dialed the Red Falls police, gave her name, and said she had to speak to the chief right away.

Seconds dragged by.

"Sharon?"

Her heart leapt. "Mark, listen carefully. I have no time
to explain. I've been locked up in MHU at Adams. I'm not
crazy—they drugged me. I need your help."

There was a short pause. "What do you want me to do?"

Just like that! He was so professional. "I'm going to break
out of here with my mother. I can't sign out AMA—the
people who drugged me are watching for that. I need you
to pick me up. I'll explain everything then."

"I can be there in forty-five minutes if I use my siren,"
Mark said. "Don't leave before then; since you're breaking
out, they'll consider you dangerous, at least to yourself, and
they'll come right after you. As soon as you're out, go
straight to the park in back of the hospital. Check the time
as soon as you hang up. I'll see you in forty-five."

"Okay. Good-bye."

Mark had already hung up. *Bless you,* Sharon thought
fervently. She slipped the phone back onto the counter and
listened. A babble of voice came from a dozen feet away.
They were coming back! She scuttled across to the door,
opened it and slid out, rising as she closed it.

She saw a crowd of patients stalled halfway from the pool
tables to the nurses' station. Through their legs she could
see her mother sitting on the tile. She must have gotten up,
moved with the crowd, then swooned again.

Sharon suppressed a grin. Mom deserved an Oscar.

Now all we have to do is break out.

Sobered, Sharon hurried to the group, forcing her way
in and kneeling beside Ellen. Her eyes focused on Sharon,
and she groaned. "Sweetie?"

Perfect! Sharon thought.

"You were great out there," Sharon told her mother.

Ellen nodded. She got up from her bed and paced to the
window, her face strained. "How much longer?"

"Five minutes. It's better that Mark waits for us a minute or two than if we have to wait for him."

"They'll be wanting our clothes for the night any minute now." Ellen turned back from the window. "I *was* pretty good, wasn't I?"

Sharon laughed, a jag of nervous tension rippling through her. "All right, it's almost time. Now just let me take care of it. All you have to do is stick with me." A nerve throbbed in the pit of her stomach.

Ellen squeezed her hands. "You'll do fine, honey. Whatever you do, you always do it well."

Sharon gave her a peck on the cheek. "Let's go."

Nurse Schmidt had her nose buried in one of the patient charts. She looked up with a slight frown. "It's time for bed. You'd better get changed, Sharon."

"Dr. Francis to you, Nurse." Sharon felt her heart pounding in her throat. She slid her hand over the edge of the Dutch door, popped the lower half open.

"Hey, you can't—*awk!*"

Sharon's hand caught her under the chin. She forced Schmidt down in her seat, easily overcoming the resistance of her legs. "Your keys. Give them to me."

"This isn't necessary," Schmidt choked out. "You can leave if you—"

"The keys!" Sharon gave a little squeeze and Schmidt's eyes rolled up in her head. Crap! Sharon let go, but it was too late; Schmidt flopped to the floor. Sharon knelt beside her, scared, then she saw the nurse's chest rising and falling under the white uniform.

"Hurry!" Ellen hissed. "The orderly just came out of one of the rooms . . . okay, now he's going into the next."

Sharon unbuckled Schmidt's belt and slipped off the key lariat. She hurried her mother into the short back corridor that housed Valois's office. The hall was empty. The steel door waited at the end. She rushed to it, breathless, and thrust the key in, getting a déjà vu flash of her nightmare

—*What if it won't turn*—but it turned easily. She yanked the door open, feeling a rush of exhiliration. Free!

The short mezzanine beyond the door looked deserted. Sharon couldn't see all the way down the stairway, but no sound came from it, nor from the entry foyer below. She took her mother's hand and led her out. As they passed through, a man stepped from behind the door—Conroy!— and she saw the pen pointed at her.

"Look out!" Ellen cried.

Sharon felt a huge shock and then the world spun away into blackness.

21

DARKNESS. A droning hum.

Her legs jerking on their own, her heels bumping on something springy. Where were her hands? Couldn't feel them, and her elbows and shoulders hurt. Go back to sleep. Lose the pain, wake up later, later.

The back of Sharon's head bounced, shocking her awake. She opened her eyes. It was still dark. Fear knifed through her. *Where am I?*

That whining sound—tires, close under her head. Hot as hell, her clothes sticking to her. Lying on her back, wrists tied behind her, jacking her shoulders forward. Hands numb. Ankles tied too.

Sharon felt a surge of panic and fought it with deep, measured breaths. She rolled partly onto one shoulder, levering her body off her wrists. There was a little slack in the ropes. She twisted her wrists and flexed her fingers until she felt the prickle of returning circulation. Her eyes began to pick features from the dimness. Struts and a roof close overhead, curving at the corners. A van.

And before?

Conroy, she thought. He shocked me out with that damn taser pen. He was waiting for Mom and me—*Mom!*

Sharon called out to her softly.

"Sweetie? Oh, thank God!" Her mother's voice was high and scared.

Sharon felt a rush of relief. "Are you okay?"

"I was afraid they'd killed you," Ellen whispered.

"I'm fine; how about you?"

"There were two of them. Conroy, and the other had a mask. They threatened to kill you if I screamed. They took us here and then they tied me up."

Waiting for us! How did they know?

Sharon made out her mother's dim outline hunched in a corner of the van. Why was it so dark in here? No rear windows; a solid partition sealed the cab off from the rear of the van. They must have done it to protect the driver against attack from behind.

Others had lain there before them.

A faint, stale odor hung in the van—sweat soured by fear. Sharon had a sudden, horrid vision of bodies piled in a dark place, Frank Greene sprawled on top, his dead eyes staring at her. She felt her fear building up to hysteria. Damn it, HOW DID THEY KNOW TO BE WAITING FOR US?

The phone, she thought. Valois was in his office and he picked up when I called Mark. Now just calm down!

"Mom, are your hands tied in front or in back?"

"In front. Honey, I'm scared."

"I know. I'm going to try to get us out of here. Be brave now—I need your help. My hands are tied in back. I'm going to scrunch over there, and I want you to untie me."

"I'll try." Her mother's voice had a whining, half connected sound that worried Sharon. She sat up and spun herself around. Still sitting, she drew her heels to her rump and pushed off, covering the distance to her mother like an inchworm. The effort brought sweat pouring down her face. She cursed. It was baking in here. They must have left the van sitting in the sun all day.

Sharon pushed her hands back toward Mom. "There— can you reach the knots?"

"Uh-huh."

She felt her mother's fingers picking and fretting at the ropes. She clamped her wrists together, trying to create some slack for Mom to work with. Time crawled by; a choking tension rose in Sharon's throat, but she knew if she tried to hurry her, her mother might freeze up. Finally the ropes loosened a little. Sharon pulled and yanked until her hands slid free. Bending forward, she picked at the knots at her ankles. Come on, come on . . . *there!*

She kicked the ropes off and untied her mother.

Ellen sat rubbing slowly at her wrists. She seemed very sluggish, distant. Sharon patted her on the cheek. "We're going to get out, Mom. Just hang on while I check things out."

Sharon moved to the back of the van and tried the handles. Locked.

What next? Sharon thought. Wait and try to jump them when the doors open? But "them" could easily be more than two, once we get where we're going. And they'll be ready.

Stop the van now, as soon as you can, while it's just two of them.

Bracing a hand on the rear doors, she bent, stretching and twisting to get her blood flowing.

When she was ready, she got down on her back on the floor at the rear of the van, cocking her legs, setting her feet against the doors. "Mom," she said softly. "I'm going to yell at them. Don't say anything or move until I tell you to, all right?"

Her mother made a small sound in the back of her throat.

"Help!" Sharon yelled. "My mother—she's suffocating!"

Nothing happened. The van kept rolling.

"Help!" she screamed. "HELP! I THINK SHE'S DEAD!"

The van screeched to a halt. A muffled curse came from beyond the bulkhead. Sharon heard the door slam. She drew her knees tight, ready to kick out. She could hear her blood singing against her eardrums. *Come on.*

A sliver of light appeared between her feet. The doors swung open and she kicked out with both feet, catching Conroy in the face, feeling a sickening crunch through the heel of her shoe. Conroy flew backward, landing on his back in the roadway. He lay very still, not making a sound.

Sharon scrambled up and motioned frantically to her mother.

Ellen did not move.

Sharon ran to her, grabbing her hand and pulling her up. Her mother allowed herself to be jerked along like a marionette. Not now, Sharon thought, agonized, please not now! At the rear of the van, her mother plopped down and sat dangling her legs out, refusing to be pulled farther. In the moonlight, her face was smooth, her eyes distant.

"Jack and Jill fell down the hill," she chanted.

Sharon heard the van's front door open, then a sharp, sliding click: a clip being rammed into an automatic. She felt an instant of terror, and then her mind focused. She could run for help—without Mom—or stay here and remain a captive.

She gave her mother's hands a quick squeeze. "I'll be back." Her mother gave no sign of having heard.

The van shifted on its shocks; the driver was getting down!

Sharon glanced left and right. A dark mass of trees rose on either side of the road. She scrambled down a short weedy grade into the woods. A yell came behind her, then the loud report of a gun. The bullet passed her ear with a rattle of ripping leaves. Adrenaline kicked through her and she ran full out in panic. Leafy branches nicked her face, slapped at her shirt and slacks. Moonlight filtered down through the trees; she searched desperately for a path, but there was none.

She hit a downslope, dodging trees, feeling her legs start to jerk out of control. Darkened roots and stones jarred her feet. Slow down! she thought, but the man was too close, crashing through the bushes just behind her.

She blinked and flinched as a branch lashed her face. Another gunshot, close behind her. Again she heard the bullet rip past.

The air seemed to thicken, dragging at her legs, slowing them. Her pulse hammered in her throat. He was still behind her, not gaining, but not falling back either.

Her foot hit a loose rock; pain jabbed up her leg and she went down, biting back a scream, tumbling headlong into a bush. She curled into a ball, half crazy with pain, gripping her leg above the ankle.

He ran past, less than ten feet away, continuing on for a ways, then stopping. Sharon groped around to find a rock and hurled it as far as she could. It crashed through the trees and he went after it.

Pain shot up her leg in raw bursts, clawing into her brain. Tears poured from her eyes. She listened for the man. He was running back toward her, charging through the bushes. A circle of moonlight illuminated the ground next to her, creating a hazy bronze glow on the forest floor. She looked up through the bush. Leaves spiralled above her, glinting like dimes suspended in free fall.

Terrified that he would see her face in the moonlight, she pressed her face into the ground. Wet leaves clung to her cheek, cooling her face. The smoky scent of them seemed to soothe the pain a little.

He was close now. Walking. Stalking her, compressing the leaves in slow, carefully plotted steps. She could hear him panting softly. A chill ran up her spine.

He stopped a few feet from her.

Crickets began to chir. His stillness unnerved her. What was he doing? She imagined his head swiveling in the moonlight above her, like the head of a wolf sniffing out its game.

Valois? You bastard, is it you?

Pain pulsed in her like a raw, red beacon. Surely he could feel it, smell it.

And then he moved on, his footsteps crunching away from her. She almost groaned in relief. He searched for her in widening circles, kicking bushes. He never said anything, not even muttering a curse. His silence seemed grotesque—single-minded and inhuman.

At last he moved off toward the road.

Sharon felt a tiny, strained gratitude, swallowed up in the white-hot pain of her ankle. In the distance, the engine of the van revved up, filtering through the trees, muffled in the heavy night air. She wondered if Conroy was on his feet again. She had really smashed his face, broken his nose for sure.

Thinking about it gave her a savage pleasure. She pushed herself up, careful not to make any noise, standing gingerly on her good leg and grabbing the bush for support. As soon as they were gone, she would hobble back to the road—

No. That's what they'd expect her to do.

One of them might wait, nail her as she struggled up out of the woods.

She would go the other way, then. There had to be another road somewhere, or a house. All she really had to do was get to a phone, call the police and let them take it from there.

She bent and probed the ankle, letting the pain wash through her, not fighting it. The joint was starting to swell. It's just a sprain, she told herself. People walk on sprains all the time.

Gritting her teeth, she lowered the injured foot to the ground and eased a little weight onto it. Pain washed through her, but it was not too bad. Not too bad—*Jesus, it was awful.*

She heard a distant rumble—the van driving off, fading into the distance. Taking Mom with it. Tears sprang to Sharon's eyes. Fiercely, she blinked them away. She must be strong now, stronger than she had ever been.

She fell to her knees and searched through the leaves until she found a limb stout enough to make a crutch. But it had no fork, nothing to set against her armpit. She searched again, finding a shorter piece of branch. Lining the short branch up against the long one, she made them flush at one end. Pulling her belt off, she strapped it tightly around both pieces about a foot down from the flush ends. Then she pried the two pieces apart at the top, making a fork. Setting the fork under her armpit, she took a step. Better. It still hurt like hell, but she could walk.

She picked her way through the bushes and trees, away from the road, moving slowly, concentrating on where she could plant the crutch, where to put her foot next. The crickets sang around her. The throaty call of an owl sounded in the distance. *Who?* it said.

Valois, Sharon thought.

The real question is why.

C'mon, where are the houses? Or a road, anything.

She began to feel heavy. No matter how she pushed, she seemed to be going slower. You're exhausted, she thought.

No, I'm fine.

She pushed on. A little farther, then she could rest.

No, not yet. Not yet.

Sharon saw a big tree, bathed in moonlight. It looked like a sentinel, standing with its arms spread protectively. She hobbled to it and lowered herself to the ground.

What are you doing? Get up!

She leaned back against the tree, her head woozy with pain. So tired. Just a little rest and then she would go on.

Sharon tipped her head back against the tree trunk. It seemed to stretch up into infinity, crowned with milky radiance, its leafy branches poised in stillness under the hot August moon.

"I was better off crazy," she said to the tree.

The pearly leaves melted into each other. She felt herself slipping away. Hang on, she thought. Don't fall asleep. . . .

Sleep . . .

22

JEFF STARED in shock at Dr. Valois. "They what?"

"They broke out together, last night. Sharon choked Nurse Schmidt and took her keys. By the time the orderly realized something was wrong, they were long gone."

"Choked—" Jeff could not believe what he was hearing. "No. She wouldn't do that."

"She did, though."

Jeff stared down at Sharon's bed, stricken by the rumpled sheets, the pillow that had cradled her head. His chest was tight; he could barely breathe. "For God's sake, why didn't you call me?"

"We've been over that before," Valois said. "You're not a relative, and Sharon has a right to confidentiality."

"Damn it, Valois—" Jeff made an effort to keep his temper. "Dr. Valois, you know I've been here every chance I had. I was trying to get her transferred to another hospital. You know that too, and you know damn well how I feel about her. Twelve hours, out there alone all night—"

"Her mother was with her."

"Christ, how much help do you think her mother would be? All that time, I could have been looking for them." Jeff felt himself slipping over the edge. "So help me, Valois, if anything's happened to either of them, you're going to answer to me."

"Watch your tone, Harrad. I don't have to take crap like that from a resident—"

"Fuck resident. You think that matters to me with her out there in the streets in her condition?"

"I guess if she'd thought she needed you she could have found a pay phone 'out there' and called you," Valois said.

Jeff felt something snap inside him, bunching his fist, launching his arm—

And then a vise closed on his wrist, stopping him dead.

He looked down, startled, and saw a huge, black hand encircling the sleeve of his medical jacket.

"Gentlemen, if I may interrupt for a second."

Something about the iron grip made Jeff's fury evaporate. As if sensing it, the big man released his wrist and gave a polite nod, as if nothing had happened. "I'm Detective Poulson."

"Jeff Harrad." Alarm shot through him. "Is she—"

"Hold on: I have no idea how or where she is."

"Then why are you here?"

"I called the police," Valois said. "For some reason, they sent a full-fledged detective."

"I just have a few questions," Poulson said to Jeff. "Maybe you can help Dr. Valois here answer them." He turned to Valois. "You said on the phone that Sharon Francis is dangerous?"

"Definitely."

"That's bullshit," Jeff said. "Sharon wouldn't hurt a fly." Suddenly he remembered the time she'd slapped him. "Unless it hurt her first."

"Please excuse Dr. Harrad," Valois said coldly. "I'm afraid he is not in a position to be objective."

Poulson said, "As it happens, I know Dr. Francis. That's why you got you a 'full-fledged detective' here. She seemed like a very nice young woman to me, not the violent type at all."

"I didn't realize you were a trained psychiatrist, Poulson. Sharon Francis is paranoid and delusional. She choked a nurse unconscious in order to escape. Those are the facts. I did not make them up."

Jeff felt sick. *Sharon, what's happening to you?*

Poulson looked at Dr. Valois. "Are you aware that she was investigating disappearances from this mental ward?"

"Investigating?" Valois said. "You make her sound like a police officer. She is a severely disturbed young woman."

"Not so disturbed that she hadn't put together some evidence. She took on some data from our police computers and showed that your little operation here leads the city in unsolved disappearances. So what? I tell myself. Somebody's got to be highest; luck of the draw. Then Sharon called me saying she had found more proof. But when I came by the hospital to pick her up, she wasn't there, and I find out she's been locked away up here. Don't mind telling you gents, that bothered me. I got a nasty, suspicious mind; comes from wearing my hats too small. Then today, call comes in says Adams Memorial has a dangerous escapee. Desk sergeant punches the escapee's name into his computer, finds out she's in my jacket. So here I am."

Poulson sucked air through his teeth. "See, the way I'm starting to look at this, Dr. Francis says people are being snatched from this place, and she starts to get warm on who, and presto, she gets slapped into this place and then snatched herself."

Valois gave a disbelieving laugh. "Don't be an idiot."

Poulson moved just a little, almost inperceptibly, but Jeff realized he was squaring on Valois. Keep talking, Valois, he thought. I'd like to see this.

Valois held up his hands. "I beg your pardon, Detective. But statistics can easily lie. She manipulated them to fit her delusion."

Poulson gazed at him. "Yeah, so I've been told. Seems like all of Sharon's friends think she's a little fugazi."

Jeff said, "What do you mean, all of her friends?"

"She had some hick town cop bring the numbers in to me. He spent the whole appointment dropping little hints that Sharon was a great kid, but that she didn't quite have both oars in the water."

Mark, Jeff thought with a sinking sensation. She was seeing Mark Pendleton.

"How much more evidence do you need, Detective?" Valois said.

Poulson turned to Jeff. "How do you see this?"

"Just in the last few days, Sharon has been confused at times," Jeff said miserably. "But she's definitely *not* violent."

"Confused." Poulson shook his head with a disgusted I've-been-had look.

"Did you hear what I said, Detective? She's not violent. She needs help. If you can find her, just treat her with normal respect, and she'll give you no trouble."

Poulson held up his hands. "Hold on, son. I'm not going to find her. I can't even spare the people to look. If she's not dangerous, and Dr. Valois here isn't selling his patients for cat food—"

"I resent that."

Poulson wheeled on Valois. "I don't give a rat's ass what you resent, Doctor. I don't like you. But fortunately for you, that doesn't make you Doctor Mengele either. If I were you, I'd quit while I was ahead. Dr. Francis isn't dangerous, you're not dangerous, fine. This is Washington! I've got twenty-three jackets on my desk right now that *are* dangerous."

Valois's face was red but he didn't say anything.

Jeff turned away, unable to keep his mind on Poulson and Valois anymore. He was vaguely aware of them stomping off in opposite directions, and then he was alone in Sharon's room. He looked at the empty bed, his heart aching. What should he do? Go home and wait for a call, or go looking for her? Go looking—he could page his phone periodically and play back any messages. He would start now, go by her apartment. She probably wouldn't go back there if she really wanted to stay out of the hospital, but who knew. If she wasn't there, he would drive around the hospital, widening out as he went. If she was hiding out nearby, it was a pretty long shot that he'd find her, but maybe she would recognize the Buick and come out.

If she was able.

Adams Memorial was in the midst of one of the worst neighborhoods in the city. The murder rate in Washington D.C. was now averaging over one a day, and for a lot of the victims, the nearest stop was Adams Memorial.

A terrible urgency filled Jeff as he ran out of MHU.

23

SHARON AWOKE with a start. The sun was shining. Birds were singing. "Oh, *no*," she groaned. Despair filled her. She had slept all night. They could have driven Mom four hundred miles away by now.

She sat against the tree trunk, too stricken to move. Her back ached from pressing against the hard wood all night. Her ankle felt numb and heavy; she could feel the swelling coiled around the joint like a python, ready to squeeze if she moved.

Her mother could even be dead.

Sharon's stomach plunged inside her. If she had kept going last night . . .

No. She had passed out, for God's sake. She had been drained of everything.

But, thanks to the sleep, she had regained some of her energy.

Sharon saw the crutch lying beside her in the leaves and pulled it to her, feeling a warning throb in her ankle. Using the crutch and the tree trunk for support, she hauled herself up. Her ankle blazed with pain. "Screw you," she told it. "You're not going to stop me, so just shut up."

She gazed around, trying to get her bearings. The woods looked very different in daylight, expanded and shaped by the light and color. Better get her directions straight; she couldn't afford to waste time blundering back the way she had come. There, those marks in the dirt from her crutch: they led back through a gap in a thicket.

Sharon set off the other way. Pain jabbed her with every step. She clung to the crutch and pushed on, sweating. Her armpit, already sore from its workout last night, throbbed against the fork of the crutch. She tried switching to the other side, but that put too much weight on the bad ankle.

What she needed were wings—and six aspirin. She plodded through the trees, imagining the tablets in her mouth, dry and slightly bitter. Then a nice glass of water to wash it down.

Water. A vicious thirst rose in her throat. How long since she had had anything to drink? Over twelve hours, long enough to sweat it all out and then some. At least it was cooler this morning—so far. She looked up through the trees and saw that the sky was whitening with haze. Right. Going to be another hot one.

Never mind. You'll find a house soon.

Sharon remembered Mark's story about being marooned in the forest with his Dad, three days from anywhere. Surely these woods couldn't be that big. She wasn't that far from the Washington metro area, a million and a half people.

She'd settle for just one of them. Or a phone.

A small, grayish bird with a black peak lit on a branch ahead and started chirping at her.

"Oh, shut up," she muttered, and the bird flew off again.

She slogged on in black depression. If only Mark had arranged to meet them at the door of MHU instead of down in the lot.

Why hadn't he?

Because his father's standing would be badly damaged within the hospital if Mark were caught helping two people escape from MHU. Damn it, anyway.

Black spots danced suddenly in front of Sharon's eyes. I'm passing out! she thought, alarmed, then realized it was only a cloud of gnats. They swarmed around her face, homing in on her sweat and the moisture of her eyeballs. She swatted at them in a petulant fury, but they only retreated an inch and zoomed in again.

She stopped and leaned on her crutch, discouraged. She had been walking an hour, and there were no roads, no houses. . . .

Just that telephone pole!

Sharon stared ahead through the sun-scorched trees, holding the pole with her eyes, afraid it might disappear. No, it was there—a beautiful, tall pole, with wires. Hot dog! She hurried toward it, flinging the crutch forward and swinging through, panting with exertion and excitement. The woods opened up abruptly, divided by a grassy right-of-way that stretched out of sight in either direction. Telephone poles marched down the center of the cleared lane in a lovely, straight line. All she had to do was follow the poles and she would find civilization.

Energy pumped into her. She plowed ahead through the cleared right-of-way, making much better time on the smooth terrain. The ground rose gradually, then more steeply. She pushed herself to the crest and looked down, blinking sweat from her eyes. A long, cleared valley spread before her. In the middle stood a house, a grand, white house, surrounded by tidy outbuildings. She felt a rush of joy.

The house had pillars and wings. Behind it was a swimming pool . . .

Sharon stared, incredulous. There, to the side, was the greenhouse. Grant Pendleton's house!

She hurried down the hill, barely feeling the jolts in her ankle, eagerly making out each landmark: the tall windows, two big oak trees she had passed with Dr. Pendleton coming in the night of the party. She headed for the long gravel access road that led in to the house's circular drive. This time of day Dr. Pendleton would be at the hospital, but he had household staff. They would remember her and let her in, help her call the police.

What an incredible coincidence, breaking free so close to Pendleton's . . .

Sharon stopped, staring at the house. What if it wasn't a coincidence?

She sank down in the tall grass, stunned, petrified by what she was thinking. No, not Pendleton. Valois was the kidnapper. Valois and Conroy . . .

Unless Conroy was working for Pendleton.

Sharon realized with a sinking feeling that it could just as easily work that way. Look at Frank Greene's case: Frank had been Pendleton's patient before he had been Valois's. It was Pendleton who had insisted on sending Frank to MHU. How many others might that have been true of?

No, she thought. Pendleton is almost like a father to me. He's a good man, not the type who would—

The door to the house opened and she saw Grant Pendleton walk out on the porch. Dread seized her; she dropped low, watching him over the tall grass. His snowy hair fanned and ruffled in the breeze. He was dressed in a white lab coat. He stared up the access road for a minute, then frowned at his watch and went back inside.

What was he doing home on a weekday, wearing a lab coat? Obviously waiting for someone. The van?

Mark!

Sharon felt as if she had been kicked in the stomach.

It all fit so neatly. She had set Mom and herself up. She had called Mark to come and get them, and that's exactly what he'd done. Mark had been the man in the mask.

Sharon's mind reeled. *Wouldn't it be fairer to take from humans?* That's what Mark had said at the party. They had been talking about lab rats, about killing them, cutting their skulls open—

Jesus, their *skulls.*

She heard the hum of a motor and knew, even before she looked up, that it was the van. Watching it hurtle up the access road, she wondered if her mother was still inside. No, they had had lots of time to leave her off here and go back out looking for the one that got away.

The van roared into the circular drive and braked sharply to a stop. Dr. Pendleton strode from the house again as Mark rounded the front of the van to meet him. Conroy got down from the passenger side, walking with wounded slowness.

A bitter taste rose in Sharon's mouth. What a great psychiatrist she was. Valois didn't like her, Valois was out to get her, so Valois must be the kidnapper. Sure, and almost twenty-five percent of Americans still thought the sun revolved around the Earth. She had made the facts fit her theory, instead of building her theory from the facts. A detective might be able to get away with that most of the time, but it was lousy science.

Still, it had gotten her this far, hadn't it?

So what was she going to do about it?

Sharon saw Mark disappear around the front of the van; he reappeared, carrying a long bow. A chill ran up her spine. He had been out hunting her. She stared at the long bow. It curved wickedly. She could sense the humming tension in it, the promise of death. Her knees felt suddenly weak. She could almost feel the arrow driving into her back.

Then she got angry.

She stared down at Mark. I really liked you, she thought. If it hadn't been for Jeff, I might even have fallen in love with you. And now you want to kill me?

Well first you've got to catch me.

Sharon flattened herself in the grass, thinking furiously. She had to go for help. As soon as they left or went inside, she should back out of here, try to find another house, call the police.

But what would she tell them? That Mark had kidnapped her and Mom? Hard to prove. And where had they hidden Mom? She wouldn't be able to tell the police where to look.

Anyway, here, the police was Mark. The Pendletons, scions of Red Falls, would just deny everything.

Poulson?

He had seen the evidence; Mark had taken it to him—

Sharon groaned. Perfect. Mark had no doubt convinced Poulson she was a mental case: Let's humor her. Then they had made it come true. Now, as an escapee from a mental ward, she would have about as much chance of getting the truth across to Poulson as a chimp playing charades.

Red Falls was way outside D.C. jurisdiction anyway. Red Falls belonged to Mark.

Dr. Pendleton walked away from the van toward the distant greenhouse. Sharon watched Mark and Conroy follow him, the three of them dwindling into a halo of light reflected from the greenhouse's opaque glass. They went into the greenhouse.

And stayed there.

Sharon felt a surge of adrenaline. The greenhouse didn't look big enough to hide a lab. But it was plenty big enough to hide an entrance. Her mother was in there! She was Pendleton's new experimental animal, and he had just reported for work.

Sharon struggled to her feet, galvanized, and hobbled down the hill. The ankle had started to stiffen. The pain was terrible, breaking her into a fresh sweat. At the door to the greenhouse she paused to catch her breath. Her clothes were soaked. She leaned against the wall and pressed her ear to the glass. She could hear the torpid buzz of a fly inside, nothing else. She slid the door back an inch and looked in. The men were not there.

She went in. The place was hot, smelling of manure and straw. Boxed plants lined a center aisle. Bars of hazy sunlight, dancing with dust motes, poured down through the milky panels of glass. The floor was bare packed earth.

Where had they hidden the entrance?

Sharon saw several large wooden crates against the back wall. Limping over, she pulled them away from the wall.

The first two were heavy; the one in the corner flipped over easily. Beneath it was the trapdoor.

All right, Sharon thought. You've found it, Sherlock. Now go call the police.

Outside again, she stopped. What if Dr. Pendleton was this second strapping her mother down on some operating table?

Sharon stared back at the greenhouse with a sinking feeling. What could she do against three men, three murderers?

If she had a gun . . .

Sharon remembered Mark's automatic. He had shot at her last night. Maybe the gun was still in the van. She hurried over to it. It was locked. She found a rock and smashed the side window, wincing at the noise. The gun was under the seat.

Sharon inspected the gun as she hobbled back into the greenhouse. It seemed to have several safeties. Were they on or off? How did you tell? Better leave them as they were.

She stuck the gun in the waistband of her pants and pulled the trapdoor open. An aluminum ladder dropped straight down. In the yellow glare of a bare, hanging bulb, she could make out a rough wooden floor about eight feet below. Several loading pallets had been pushed together to make the floor. Around the margins she could see bare, packed dirt.

Sharon took a deep breath and climbed down, using her arms to keep the weight off her ankle. Through the rungs she saw what looked like an old mining tunnel, dwindling away into blackness. The air was musty and dead. It smelled of rot. The yawning blackness of the tunnel made her neck prickle. She stalled on the ladder, gazing back up at the warm square of greenhouse light, fighting the urge to climb back up there and out, get as far away from this awful place as she could.

Forcing herself down again, she eased her weight onto the makeshift wooden floor and turned her back on the tunnel. In front of her, the chamber was walled off in cinder block. In one corner stood a small generator and a sealed twenty-gallon drum that was probably gasoline. The generator was silent—probably just a backup power system. Beside the gasoline drum, a single door stood open a few inches. Light shone through the opening; she detected the low hum of air conditioning.

Sharon pulled the gun from her waistband and held it down at her side. She felt stiff with fear. Her throat was so dry she couldn't swallow.

She pulled the door open. The musty smell vanished in a tide of cool, scrubbed air tinged with the scent of antiseptic. A hallway led straight away from her to the gleaming metal door of a walk-in cooler about fifty feet away. Along the left wall at regular intervals were six doors. Bare bulbs glowed from a ceiling of buttressed concrete. The walls were cinder block and the floor was made of pressure-treated timbers, big as railroad ties but smoother. She could see a few cracks between the timbers. They must have been laid right on the ground and the moisture beneath had started to warp them.

A chill went through her. How long had this place been here?

Never mind that. Where were Dr. Pendleton and the others?

They must have gone into one of the rooms.

Sharon felt her pulse throbbing in her throat. All right, *go!*

Returning the gun to her waistband, she settled the crutch under her arm and moved carefully to the first door in the corridor. Pressing her ear against it, she heard muffled male voices inside. One of them laughed, and she recognized Grant Pendleton. She hurried to the next door and the next, hearing only silence behind them, trying the knobs. Locked. Mom, where are you? Sharon fought the urge to call out to her.

The fourth doorway was set with double doors—unlocked. Pushing one open, she saw a small operating room with a steel gurney rolled under a big surgery light. The floor was tile. Beyond the gurney was a scrub sink.

Water!

The sight of the sink made her conscious again of her thirst. She hurried across and fitted her mouth to the long spigot. The water gurgled through her lips, bathing her throat. God, it tasted wonderful! She gulped greedily, feeling the parched tissues swell, sucking at the spigot until her stomach was full. As she turned to leave, she saw that the cart stationed beneath the surgery light was not a gurney but a modified pathologist's table; it had a slight pitch, and there was a drain at the foot.

The head of the table was stained with blood.

Sharon felt sick to her stomach. Mom . . . *no!*

Frantic, she hurried back into the hall. The gleaming door at the end held her gaze. She hobbled toward it, filled with dread. Mom, *no Mom, no*—

Sharon pulled the door open. Inside, on the floor, were bodies. Rows of frozen human bodies, some stacked on top of each other. The heads—*Oh, God!*

Sharon sank to her knees, stunned.

The tops of the skulls had been sawed off. The brains had been removed.

The room tilted and spun around her. With a fierce effort, she clung to consciousness. She looked at the nearest body. The corpse's skin was the color of wax. Swallowing hard, she made herself look at the face.

Not Mom. This woman was much younger, with blond hair, frozen now into reddened, ropy strands. Meg?

Sharon crawled through the bodies, half crazed. She found Brian. His eyes stared at her like clouded marbles, frozen forever in an expression of pop-eyed rage. Sharon remembered how he had shaved his head to impress her. Now the top edge of bone was visible all around.

She leaned over and threw up onto the floor. In the cold, steam rose from the pooled water she had just drunk.

Wouldn't it be fairer if we took from humans? Oh Christ God you BASTARDS!

The cold of the room began to penetrate. Her hands and feet were going numb. Mom wasn't here, and neither was Frank. Sharon began to recover from the shock. The blood in the operating room was not her mother's—not yet.

Outside, the hall was still empty. There were two doors beyond the O.R. She tried them both, but they were locked. Frustrated, Sharon tried to think. Her mother must be behind one of these doors. Did she dare tap on them, try to get a response?

No, Dr. Pendleton and the others might hear her. Besides, knowing which door hid her mother would do her no good without a key. But she didn't dare leave to call the police either—not with Dr. Pendleton down here, only steps from her mother and that O.R. If only there were a phone down here—

The O.R.! Sharon thought.

She hurried to the double doors, looked inside again, and there it was, on a counter across from the sink.

Picking up the receiver, she heard the warm, wonderful drone of a dial tone. She punched Jeff's number. *Please be there.*

His machine answered.

Sharon cursed silently, forcing herself to wait for the message tone.

"Jeff," she said, "this is Sharon. I'm at Dr. Pendleton's estate near Red Falls. He's got a secret lab here. He kidnapped Mom and me, and Mom is in here somewhere. I need your help, fast. Please, Jeff, I know it sounds crazy, but you've got to believe me—"

A hand shot past her face and punched the disconnect. She screamed and jumped back, pulling the gun from her waistband as she whirled around. It was Mark. She aimed the gun at his face.

"Hello, Sharon." His eyes shone, fixing on the gun.

"Take me to my mother, or I'll shoot you."

"Will you?" He reached for the gun. She pulled the trigger. Nothing happened. The safety!

With a high, brittle laugh, he snatched the gun away, flipped one of the safeties and pointed it at her.

She spat in his face.

24

J EFF PULLED TO THE CURB and tried to see into the alley. The sidewalk in front blazed in the sun, numbing his retinas, making the narrow canyon between the buildings seem dark as night. Squinting, he could just make out two shapes, about ten feet in, hunched against one wall. Hope stirred in him; he reached for the car door handle and then the shapes wavered and crawled into focus: trash cans.

He felt himself sagging inside. A sickly-sweet odor of decay penetrated the cool scrubbed air of the Buick. He shuddered, sensing death in the smell.

He turned from the window, setting his jaw. *She's all right. You'll find her.* Rolling his shoulders, he forced the stiff muscles of his neck to relax.

Maybe he should check Sharon's apartment again.

He reached for the gearshift, then stopped. If Sharon had gone back home, she was safe. As long as she was out here with the pimps, pushers, and street thugs she wasn't. The maintenance man at her apartment would call if she came back, a sweet old guy, genuinely concerned. Out here was where Sharon needed him, Jeff decided. Best to keep searching the streets and checking the answering machine.

Jeff glanced at his watch. Three ten. He realized, startled, that he had been driving around for over six hours. It was forty minutes since he had checked for messages.

Scanning ahead, he spotted a pay phone outside a Laundromat. He pulled forward and parked. Stepping into the brutal afternoon sun, he broke instantly into a sweat. The air prickled down his throat, hot and foul with exhaust. As he approached the Laundromat he checked the long, dirty window, just in case. Inside, a row of dryers gazed back at him, winking in agitation, as if trying to draw his attention to something. But there was nothing to see. Six people who were not Sharon sat around in plastic chairs, avoiding the sun. Their faces looked lifeless and cyanotic under the blue-white fluorescents. He looked away, angry that he kept seeing death everywhere, smelling it, sensing it.

She's alive, damn it.

He wiped his forehead with his sleeve, feeling the humid heat rush at once to the dry spot. Dialing home, he gave the receiver a burst from his tone key. Please, he thought, *please.*

The high, agitated voice of Dr. Billings, chief of training, blustered in his ear. Where had Jeff been? Eight medical students had wasted an hour waiting for him. If he thought this wasn't serious, he had another think coming. The voice groused on and on. Jeff burned with impatience. He didn't give a flying fuck about the medical students or about Billings. Get off the damn tape, he thought. I only want to hear one voice on this tape—

And then he did.

"I'm at Dr. Pendleton's estate," she said, "near Red Falls." Jeff's heart leapt; he pressed the phone to his ear, not daring to breathe. "He's got a secret lab here," Sharon's voice went on. "He kidnapped Mom and me, and Mom is in here somewhere. I need your help, fast. Please, Jeff, I know it sounds crazy, but you've got to believe me."

Pendleton's!

Jeff was filled with exhiliration. Talking crazy, yeah, but alive and safe and he knew where. Gonna be all right now! Just call Pendleton's, tell his butler or whoever that Sharon and her mother were there somewhere and to please find her and watch after her until he got there.

Jeff started to punch in Pendleton's number, then felt a sharp prick in his back. What the—? Go away. He punched two more digits.

"Drop the phone, white boy," hissed a voice behind him. No! Jeff thought. I've got to call Sharon.

The point dug into his back. *Shit.* He hung up the phone.

"Don't turn around. Just gimme your wallet."

"Sure. Here." Jeff pulled his wallet out as fast as he could and held it up. A hand snatched it away from behind him.

"Just stay like you are—don't turn around, or I'll stick you."

"Fine." Just take it and go, Jeff thought. *Hurry up.* The knife point stayed pressed in his back. He seethed with frustration. He had to get moving before Sharon wandered off someplace else. "Uh, could you hurry it up?"

"Say what? You *crazy,* man?"

"My girlfriend—"

"You shut your face or you won't never be hurrying again." Jeff realized dimly that he should be scared, but all he wanted was for the man to get it *done.*

"Now empty your pockets."

Jeff dug into his pockets and pulled out his change. "Can I keep just one quarter?"

"I don't give a fuck about your quarters. Where's your car keys?"

Jeff stared at the contents of his hand—all change and no keys. Yes, where were they?

A hand patted down his pockets. "C'mon, c'mon. Don't tell me you conned no cabby into bringing you to this part of town."

Jeff felt a small relief. The mugger didn't know the Buick was his. "Bus," he said.

"Bus? You *are* crazy, you pale muhfucker." The knife hand reached past his face, severing the steel-wrapped phone cord in one easy slice. The receiver dropped to the pavement and shattered. "Don't want you callin' the man as soon as I leave, do we."

Jeff stared down, horrified, at the broken receiver. "You son of a bitch!" He whirled and smashed the mugger in the face, feeling the knife slash through the side of his shirt. The man dropped flat on his back, his nose spurting blood. Jeff bent over, seeing everything in a red haze of anger, and snatched his wallet back. The knife was lying beside the man.

Jeff snatched it up too. "You want to cut people, go to med school like the rest of us."

He turned and ran for his car. Three women had inched out the Laundromat door and were staring at him with fascination, as if he suddenly had two heads. He stopped. "Is there another phone in there?"

One of the woman shook her head. "That dude bad news, man! You lucky you ain't the one bleeding on the sidewalk there. You best go back and kill him or get yourself *outta* here."

Jeff ran to his car and slid in. His keys were right in the ignition where he'd left them. His face flushed cold. *Christ.* What an *idiot.* But it had saved him.

Okay, forget that. Ten minutes to home. He could call Pendleton's from there. Maybe they had already discovered Sharon and he could tell her to stay there, he was coming.

He tossed the mugger's knife onto the passenger seat and took off, tires squealing on the hot pavement. He pressed the speed limit, thinking about her, about what he would say when he got to Pendleton's.

How had Sharon gotten clear out there?

And why?

Who cared? All that mattered was that she was off the streets and out of danger.

Jeff pulled up in front of his town house and saw with irritation that someone had parked in his spot. He found another space a few units down and hurried back. At the door, he froze.

The door was open a crack, the wood around the lock splintered. He stared at it, stunned. Robbed twice in one day?

He slipped inside and stood in the foyer, listening.

A plastic click came from the den. Keeping to the carpet, he crept to the den door. It was ajar. Inside, a man with his back to him was bent over his answering machine.

He was stealing the message tape out of the machine.

Jeff stared at him, dumbfounded. Why?

Suddenly he realized what it meant and almost cried out in shock. *Sharon was telling the truth.* She was in danger. This guy could only be here because someone at Pendleton's estate had overheard her blowing the whistle. They were hoping to get the tape before he could hear it.

She isn't crazy! Jeff thought. She's been telling the truth all along. He felt a huge relief, and then shame.

Yeah, and you treated her like a lunatic.

Forget that—she's in deep trouble.

Jeff stared, alarmed, at the man tampering with his answering machine. If they had overheard Sharon then they had probably caught her too.

And this bastard would know all about it.

Jeff felt fury rising in him. He charged, but the man heard him and turned—Chuck Conroy, from MHU.

Conroy pointed a gun at him and yelled, "Stop!"

Jeff stopped. He could feel his arms trembling with the desire to choke Conroy, beat his face in—

Jesus, someone had already made a start. Conroy's nose looked very fat, and both eyes were black.

Jeff said, "Give me the gun, Chuck."

"Just chill out, Dr. Harrad." Chuck's voice was labored and nasal.

Jeff felt his muscles straining, but Conroy was just far enough away to shoot easily before Jeff could close the gap. "What have you done with her?"

"Turn around." Jeff saw that Conroy's pupils were abnormally constricted. *Drugs?* Conroy sniffled, as though he had a cold. His hands were trembling. *Withdrawal.*

"Just take it easy, Chuck. Are you strung out? Maybe I could—"

"No!" A look of longing crossed Chuck's face. "No. Hand would kill me. Now turn around—I'm serious."

Jeff hesitated, feeling the beginnings of fear. Did the son of a bitch actually have the guts to shoot him? Conroy jerked the gun at him and he turned around, the nerves in his spine crawling. Damn it, he couldn't get shot now, he had to get Sharon out of this.

"Chuck, wait a minute. I know you're in trouble, but I can help you. If you tell me where she is, I promise I'll do all I can with the pol—"

The world exploded and shrank into blackness.

25

I T'S ALL ABOUT PAIN, isn't it?" Sharon said. "This lab. The horrible things you've done." She felt numb, cut off from her feelings. Being up close to Grant Pendleton, seeing his face, hearing his voice, had a strange, narcotizing effect. His old self kept breaking through what she now knew about him, making her mind flicker like a computer stuck on a massive, insoluble calculation.

Dr. Pendleton straightened and gazed at her, his finger still resting on her ankle. "What makes you say pain? Just because I'm doing some rat endorphin studies at Adams—"

"Your back." Her voice sounded very far away to her. She needed to feel something, terror, rage, disgust.

He frowned. "Where did you hear that story?"

"From your son. He told me the surgery had taken care of it, but it didn't, did it? I should have realized. He was so agitated when he told me. The horror and guilt seemed very fresh in him. Those feelings would have receded at least a little by now if you had really recovered." Sharon stared at Pendleton. She had worked for this man, liked him, *admired* him. He had been her mentor, the doctor who had taken her under his wing after Valois had tried to smash her. At times, she had felt almost like his daughter. And this same man had butchered over twenty people for their brains and left them stacked in a cooler like sides of beef. She couldn't seem to comprehend it.

"You'd still be in pain," she said, "wouldn't you? Except you found a way to get rid of it."

"You're even smarter than I thought, Sharon."

"If I were smart, I wouldn't be sitting here now."

"Oh, don't sell yourself short. You've been extremely resourceful." He bent over her ankle again, exposing the top of his head. She had the sudden impulse to drive her fist into the white hair, smash him senseless. Adrenaline surged through her. She clenched her fist. *Hit him, then run. . . .*

No. Mark was in the hall—Dr. Pendleton had told him to wait there. She wouldn't get two steps. She forced her fist to relax.

I can't run yet anyway, she thought. Not till I find Mom.

Pendleton tut-tutted. "This looks quite bad."

"A few weeks of rest and I'll be good as new."

"A few weeks? I'm afraid not."

I'm afraid not, Sharon, because you're not going to be alive in a few weeks. But her voice came out normally, calm, denying everything. "Come on, it's only a sprain—"

"Broken."

She had a sudden, shaky feeling, as if she had almost stepped on a fallen power line. Broken! If she had known that, she never would have been able to get this far. She would still be lying out in the woods somewhere. Safe.

And Mom might, this minute, be headed for the cooler.

Sharon felt sick with fear. Jeff, she thought, trying to muster some optimism. Maybe he had checked his answering machine by now. But even if he had, and he came rushing right out here, how would he know where to look? She hadn't had time to tell him where the lab was before Mark had cut her off. Jeff could be walking above her this minute, and neither of them would ever know it. She might as well be on another planet. She felt the fear swelling inside her, pushing her to the edge of panic. She fought to regain her calm. Thinking was what she needed now, not feeling. It was all up to her.

Pendleton looked up at her, watching her face as he probed. "This must hurt a very great deal."

"I'll live. Right?"

Pendleton gave her a tolerant smile, not bothering to answer. He was being gentle, but every time he touched her ankle in a new place, waves of pain shot up her leg. Clenching the edge of the table, she leaned back against the wall. Suddenly, Pendleton pressed hard. Pain blazed through her. She shouted and the room went gray. Slowly it swam back into focus. Her ankle throbbed viciously. She felt a dam breaking inside her, releasing all her pent-up terror. She stared at Pendleton, horrified. His face seemed bright and too flat, like a picture torn from a book. And then she saw him as he was, the stranger behind the familiar mask. A mass murderer.

And she was his next victim.

He grunted. "Amazing. I believe I would have passed out just then. It's broken, all right. And you walked all the way from the highway on this ankle. Over the rough ground, up and down those hills, all by yourself?"

"No, I was . . . carried by beavers with little barrels of cognac around their necks."

He smiled. "I'm impressed that you can keep your wit even at a time like this. I know this must be very shocking to you. But after you understand everything, you may feel different. I sincerely hope so, for all of our sakes."

A way out? Sharon felt hope stirring in her. She gave a rigid nod.

He seemed encouraged. "Listen carefully, Sharon, and hear me out, because it is your only chance—and your mother's. The best I can offer you is that you can't leave here, at least not for a long time, until I'm sure of you. But we could make you comfortable, Mark and I, and challenge your mind, give you work—important work. Are you willing to listen, and to try and understand?"

She nodded again, not trusting herself to speak.

"Good. The first thing you must understand is pain. You have some now, and that will help you. When I squeezed your ankle just then, it wasn't from spite. I want you to remember that instant of terrible pain, multiply it by ten, and lodge it in the middle of your spine. Then imagine trying to live with it year after year. Imagine taking stronger and stronger drugs until you're shooting up heroin. Feel the addiction growing stronger in your veins every day—feel your sense of self submerging so deeply into the drug that you can't speak a coherent sentence, can't do the work that means more to you than anything else in the world.

"I'm not asking you to pity me. I turned away from pity years ago—pity from others and my own self-pity, and finally, pity for those I've had to use up. But I'm still a healer. Understand that. I have healed a thousand backs in my time, destroyed much more pain than I've caused. And, if I'm successful, I am going to end all unnecessary pain."

He paused. Sharon knew she should say something. But what? He was a highly intelligent man. He would quickly see through any fake enthusiasm. "I'm listening." There was a tremor in her voice, but surely he must expect that.

"Fine. You too are a physician. And you too have dedicated your life to an important cause—dealing a blow to schizophrenia. Commendable. But if you can overcome your fear and horror now, your disgust for me, you'll have a chance to help in something even more important. Extreme pain is more debilitating than, even, schizophrenia. I know. A schizophrenic can dream, plan. He can eat his dinner and enjoy it. At night he can doze off in comfort.

"But pain . . . " He closed his eyes and rocked on his heels, as if seized by terrible memories. "Chronic pain reduces you to total impotence as a human being. Throughout history men have suffered it, gone mad with it."

Like you, Sharon thought. And then she wondered. *Was* Pendleton insane? Or could a man truly rationalize even this, forgive himself this much? Or worse yet, believe he had done right.

"Until now," Pendleton went on, "humanity has had no choice but to suffer pain. I was *given* a choice, Sharon. Several years ago I found that when I injected a certain fraction of liquified tissue from the pituitary area of a rat brain into the broken backs of other rats, it destroyed all pain for hours. The injured rats ate and slept again, and even played. Hidden in that liquified brain tissue was a master biochemical, as far above endorphins and the other known painkillers of the body as a diamond is above cut glass. I called that hidden substance gamma lipoprotein. Unlike heroin and all the other painkillers to date, gamma lipoprotein produces no side effects and no addiction.

"But I'm getting a little ahead of myself. While I was still working with rats, I found that the gamma lipoprotein of certain rats relieved rat pain longer than identical doses from other rats. I called the longer-lasting version of gamma lipoprotein, gamma prime. Certain humans produce prime too. When I first started using humans, I examined blood tests of my prime producers and found a double signature that distinguished them from all other subjects—"

"High blood urea nitrogen paired with low monocytes," Sharon said.

He frowned. "Yes. That was very clever of you, getting on to the files."

She realized she had made a mistake. She didn't want him thinking about that, about how she had pursued him, how she might yet bring him down if he let her live.

"If you found this in rats," she said quickly, "why are you . . . using human beings to get it?" Sweat popped out on her forehead. She had almost said MURDERING.

But Pendleton did not seem to notice.

"Believe me, Sharon, I've studied every research animal available. They *all* have gamma lipoprotein. And in every case, it works only in the specific animal it came from."

"So synthesize it."

"I'm a neurosurgeon, not a neurochemist—and I'm sure you see why I can't go out and find a neurochemist to work with me on this," he added dryly. "Gamma lipoprotein is an extremely complex chain, with literally hundreds of amino acids. I've tried over and over to analyze the complete chain, but I'm still too clumsy at it. It keeps breaking up during measurement."

Sharon felt sick. Pendleton had murdered twenty people, stolen twenty human brains, and he still didn't even know what he was taking from them. Disgust filled her. She thought of Dr. Jenkins—a miserable twit, but he had learned to live with his pain. With all his inadequacies, he was a hundred times the man Pendleton was.

Pendleton was looking expectantly at her; she realized what he must want her to ask. "Instead of using the brain," she said, "why not isolate it from blood samples? If gamma lipoprotein kills pain, it must be carried in the bloodstream."

"Unfortunately, gamma lipoprotein can't cross the blood-brain barrier. It's present only in the brain. It never leaves the brain, never enters the body's bloodstream."

"Then how—"

"Think, Sharon. Pain occurs *only* inside the brain; you learned that in med school. The hurt you *seem* to feel at an injury site is an illusion, a ventriloquist's trick by which your brain tells you what part of you is injured."

"Yes. So why does gamma lipoprotein work when you inject it into an injury?" She realized with dismay that, along with her fear, she was starting to actually feel some interest. Pendleton had hooked her curiosity just the smallest bit, and he was using it to sanitize himself, to draw her away from the horror of what he had done. She felt dirty for even discussing it with him.

But what choice did she have?

"Good question," Pendleton said. "You're showing why I think you can be a help to me. Clearly, gamma lipoprotein not only works outside the brain—it works better. The capillaries, of course, pick it up wherever you inject it and circulate it through the whole body. Apparently, if it hits any synapses trying to send a pain signal, it blocks the neurotransmitters right there. If the signal can't reach the brain, it can never be interpreted in the first place, and there is no pain—none at all. Isn't it beautiful!"

She nodded. "Yes . . . beautiful!" *Don't overdo it.*

"You can see what I've got to do," he said, "I've got to synthesize gamma lipoprotein. Then we won't need anymore human subjects."

We, she thought, and felt a wave of disgust.

He eyed her. "Don't kid yourself, Sharon. You won't be any gladder for that than I will. In the meantime, you've got to remember how important this is. To end all human pain . . . I don't like to sound melodramatic, but it will truly be the most important breakthrough in the history of medical science."

Sharon felt a sudden, deep sadness, not for him but for what he had so mercilessly destroyed in himself—the Grant Pendleton that was still there on the surface, now only a kindly veneer that hid his true self to eyes like hers. In its power to conceal, his kindness actually made him more monstrous. The Bible talked about the mark of the beast. But there were no marks on Pendleton's forehead or hands. Even a dumb rabbit knows the shadow of the hawk, Sharon thought, and runs from it. What is there to protect us?

Pendleton took a syringe and vial from the pocket of his lab coat.

She felt a rush of alarm. "No—wait!"

But before she could move, Pendleton seized her foot. She yelped from the pain, trying to pull away, but he plunged the needle into the swollen area. She felt a thin, hot wire of pain—

And then coolness rushed through the ankle, up her leg, through her whole body. The pain in the injured tissue dwindled and shrank. It felt as if it were plunging down and out through her heel. In seconds, every trace of pain was gone. The relief was incredible, beyond anything she could have imagined. She looked at her ankle, half believing it might have started to heal. It still looked like hell. It was badly swollen, the skin dark blue and purple.

But all of the pain was gone.

Suddenly she thought of Brian that night in group, his rage at the agony in his head. *Why don't you go out and find a painkiller that really works?* And now someone had, and it had cost Brian and a lot of other people their lives.

A sick horror filled her. This stuff Pendleton had just shot into her ankle had come from one of the corpses in the cooler. One of the emptied skulls, maybe even Brian's. She felt herself trembling and hugged her arms to her chest. You bastard!

She realized Pendleton was eyeing her expectantly. She tried to keep all horror from her voice. "The pain is gone. Remarkable."

"Yes." Pendleton pulled a cigarette lighter from the pocket of his lab coat. Rolling up his sleeve, he flicked on the lighter and held the flame against his skin at the inside of his elbow. Sharon heard herself gasp. Pendleton held the flame against his skin for several seconds. His face was serene, but there was an odd light in his eyes. At last he snuffed the lighter. Sharon gazed at the reddened patch of skin, sickened. Around it were a number of older, blistered scars, and she realized he did this often, putting the flame against his skin, testing his God-like immunity to pain.

She felt a twinge of nausea. "What . . . what about getting human brains assigned to you from autopsies? That can be arranged, can't it?"

"Come on, Sharon. Don't you think I tried that?"

She nodded energetically, realizing her mistake. Panic welled up in her. She wasn't doing this right, wasn't convincing him, and she had to, she *had* to.

"Gamma lipoprotein," he said reprovingly, "is present only during intense pain. Apparently there is a triggering mechanism in the pituitary. When it recognizes pain, it orders gamma lipoprotein to be made from simpler chemical chains. At other times gamma lipoprotein doesn't exist. Think of a firefly in the night, landing on your hand. If you can crush it while it is lit, its remains will glow on your finger. But if you are a fraction slow, your finger is covered with only a dull smear."

She shuddered at the grotesque analogy. Then the deeper meaning sank in, and a cold horror filled her. "You mean you . . . tortured all those people as you killed them?"

Pendleton sighed. "You're not with me, are you, Sharon? You can never be with me."

Her throat went dry. "I . . . just want to understand."

"I had to hurt only one or two of the subjects," Pendleton said in a flat voice. "Most of them already had pain, and it was enough merely to give no anesthesia at the time of surgery."

Revulsion swept through her. "Oh, my God," she mumbled. "All those people." She closed her eyes, but she could not shut out the terrible images: Meg lying on the table, hearing the saw come down, screaming as it cut through her forehead and ground down into bone. "You bastard."

She started to shake, the fear swirling up in her like a whirlwind, raw and cold, beyond control. There had never been a chance that he would let her live, or her mother either. Oh, he might actually have believed he was giving them a chance, but he couldn't, not really. Deep down inside, he had never truly convinced himself that his terrible acts could be justified. So, in the end, he would be incapable of believing he had convinced anyone else.

Sharon stared at him, petrified. "What have you done with my mother?"

"She is in no pain."

Alarm shot through Sharon. She pushed herself up from the bed and grabbed Pendleton's lapels. "What does that mean?"

He stepped back, looking surprised. "Oh, I see. No, she's

not dead. She's resting in one of the rooms." He waved a hand around the little cell.

She let go of him, feeling a small relief. She realized with surprise that she was standing, putting her full weight on the ankle, without the slightest pain. And what Pendleton had said about side effects was true; her head felt completely clear—no blurring of the senses, no drowsiness. Her state of awareness and her ankle both felt completely normal.

But no matter how it felt, the ankle *was* broken.

She sat again, squeamish at the thought of splintered bones grinding together. "How long will my mother *stay* alive?"

He looked sad. "I hate to lose you. Your mother has led a useless, unproductive life. But you—"

"Get out."

"Now, Sharon—"

"GET OUT!" she screamed.

He walked to the door. "Try to calm yourself. Getting hysterical will only make it all worse. I'll be back."

She turned away from him, hearing the door close, then sensing that she was still not alone. She looked up and saw Mark, gazing at her with a hard smile.

"Hi," he said. He locked the door behind him, put the key in his pocket and started to unbutton his shirt.

Dread rose in her. "What are you doing?"

"Take your clothes off."

"Forget it." She squared herself on the table, angry and offended, readying herself to fight him. He peeled his shirt off, revealing planes of muscle on his chest, lean slashes of bicep running down to corded forearms. Her heart sank. Mark hit the weights, too. It was written in every crease and bulge of his chest and arms. He pumped iron. He was bigger than her, well fed and rested; no broken bones.

She didn't have a chance.

"I mean you only honor," he said.

"Stay away from me, I'm warning you."

He slipped his pants off, folding them, putting them on

the floor by the door. He stood before her in just his briefs, gazing at her with his unnerving, pale gray eyes. "Do you know about the Masai, Sharon? They hunt the lion only with their spears. As the Masai hunt the lion, the lion hunts them. If the Masai win they eat the lion's heart. Not from cruelty or barbarism, oh no; they do it out of respect, to take the strength and courage of the lion into themselves. You are a true lionness, Sharon. You were hunting me, and then I was hunting you. I have great respect for you. But the hunt is over. I've caught you, and now you're mine."

Frank dreamed he heard Sharon Francis's voice. A murmur, as if it came from another room. A second voice answered. The voices murmured back and forth for awhile. In his dream, he listened fondly, feeling needles of pain as his parched lips pulled into a smile. Dr. Francis had come to get him. She was talking to them, asking them where he was.

But they did not *know* where he was.

Anxiety bunched in Frank's stomach. He struggled to open his eyes. He must wake up, call out to her.

And then he realized that he was awake.

And the voices were still murmuring.

His heart began to pound. He pressed his eye eagerly to the hole, but it was dark in the surgery, and then he realized that the voices were coming from the direction of his feet. He rolled to his side, wincing as pain shot through his stiffened back. With a fierce effort, he made it to his knees and crawled toward the sound. It was coming from the cell he had been in. His heart pounded with excitement. Dr. Francis *was* here!

He crawled faster, feeling the strength of desperation flood through him. Pushing his tongue against his teeth, he tasted a shred of the rat still stuck there. He was pretty thirsty again, but not like he had been. And that was all over now.

The voices were quite clear now. He realized that he recognized the other one. Dr. Pendleton!

Frank's jaw dropped open. Dr. Pendleton and Dr. Francis, both here? He grinned, feeling warmed in the darkness: his two doctors, come to rescue him.

They had started arguing. "Get out!" Dr. Francis said.

Dr. Pendleton mumbled something, and then Dr. Francis shouted it again: "GET OUT!"

Frank listened, stunned. A door slammed beyond the thin paneling that covered his exit hole. Then another voice, one he didn't recognize. Dr. Francis answering, sounding scared.

They had her, too—*Dr. Pendleton* had her! Frank thought, sickened, of the saw whining, of Brian screaming his name through the vent. He felt the strength of fury rising in him. He put his hand against the paneling.

Dr. Francis screamed.

With a hoarse bellow, Frank broke back into his cell.

26

SHARON PUSHED Mark's hands away from her blouse. He shoved her back on the table and she screamed.

A savage bellow came from behind Mark.

He whirled around and Sharon sat up, confused, looking toward the sound. A section of the wall paneling flew back, revealing gray cinder block—broken through near the floor. A man staggered up from the hole, batting the flimsy panel aside. Sharon stared, astonished, Mark frozen at the edge of her vision. The man hardly looked human. He was hunched over. His face was filthy, his mouth caked with blood. She could see only the whites of his eyes and his bared teeth.

"Green!" Mark gasped.

The word made no sense to Sharon. She kicked out with her good leg, smashing Mark in the back. He went down on one knee, shouting in pain. The wild man from the wall grabbed him around the waist, bending him over backward to the floor.

"Run, Sharon!"

Greene. "Frank!" she yelled, dumbfounded.

"I've got him," Frank shouted. "Run! Get help!"

She slid off the table and jumped on Mark, scratching at his eyes. His fist shot out from the tangle of limbs, smacking her shoulder, knocking her back. She felt no pain, but it shocked her brain into action. Her kick hadn't hurt Mark much—he would break free of Frank in seconds. Get out, now! she told herself.

She fell to her knees by the door, tearing at the pockets of Mark's pants for his key, fumbling it out, pushing it into the cylinder lock.

"Hurry!" Frank gasped behind her.

"Let go, old man!"

Sharon heard a fist thud into bone. Frank gave an anguished grunt. She felt the bolt slide back and shouldered her way out the door. "I'll be back, Frank!" she shouted.

She sprinted down the hall toward the exit. Grant Pendleton came through the door of the anteroom just as she reached it. His eyes widened. She punched him in the stomach and he doubled over, gasping. She pushed by him and clawed her way up the ladder into the greenhouse and out the door, running for all she was worth. Outside, she headed up the long slope toward the treeline, taking the same route she had taken coming down. Her mind was a jumble: Frank, alive—in the *wall*. Incredible.

Jesus, poor Frank, he had looked awful.

The hill steepened; her breath tore in her lungs. She felt the ground thudding under her feet. Her bad ankle felt just like her good one; her legs were strong with panic.

"SHARON!"

She glanced back over her shoulder. Mark was standing beside the greenhouse, and she realized with horror that he was holding his bow, drawing it back.

She feinted to one side and pushed off the good ankle in the other direction, seeing the arrow flash past her and stick in the hillside ahead. She ran with new terror, a horrid itch crawling between her shoulder blades. The air seemed to hum. She dodged left, then right, but no arrow came. The trees at the top were only yards away.

He doesn't have another arrow, she thought. I'm going to make it!

Then she felt a piercing thud in her back and the ground slammed up into her face and wrapped around her and she knew that she was finished.

A dull pain throbbed at the back of Jeff's neck. He stared out the windshield of his Buick, trying to knit his scrambled thoughts back together. Beside him in the driver's seat, Conroy sniffed.

How long have I been out? Jeff wondered.

The horizon ahead of him registered, a thin line of deep rose, the only color left in a dense, ultramarine sky. On either side of the car, dark woods flowed back from the sidewash of the high beams. Jeff's heart sank. It had been late afternoon when Conroy hit him. A couple of hours had passed.

Where was Sharon right now? What were they doing to her?

Jeff felt a surge of fear for her, and then disgust at his own impotence. He clamped his wrists together behind him, trying to ease the biting pressure of the rope. His shoulders ached from the effort, but if he gave it up, the cords would cut off the circulation in his fingers again, and he would have no chance to work free.

Chuck glanced over at him.

"Where are we?"

"Out in Virginia," Conroy said. "Route Two Thirty-one. You have a nice nap?"

"Where are we headed?"

"Not much farther."

"Ten thousand bucks, Chuck. All you gotta do is stop the car and let me out."

Chuck grunted. "Thanks, Dr. Harrad. But money's no good to me if I'm dead."

"Who would kill you? Dr. Pendleton?"

"Not him. His son."

"Mark," Jeff muttered, appalled. A galling bitterness filled him. There was always something odd about that bastard, he thought. I should have recognized it and warned Sharon—

He realized he was being absurd.

"Please. He likes to be called Hand. And you can call me Amber Jack." Conroy's voice was sardonic, but Jeff could hear a note of pride, too.

"Amberjack? That's a fish, isn't it?"

Conroy glanced at him, frowning. "A fish? No shit? That fucker. I should have known he was laying something stupid on me, even though he made it sound neat." Conroy seemed genuinely aggrieved.

Jeff was aware, suddenly, of the gritty surface of the floor, pressing against the soles of his feet. Conroy must have taken his shoes and socks to slow him down in case he managed to get out of the car. The thoroughness of it unnerved him. It was too slick, something only a professional killer would think of.

"Help me, Chuck, and you'll be safe. We'll put his ass in jail."

Chuck laughed, a brittle, scared sound. "You don't know him. But I've done a little research. Markie boy has killed three people 'in the line of duty,' just in the little town of Red Falls. Two other guys he didn't like 'hung themselves,' in Mark's jail. Guy like him could get me from jail as easily as you sew up a cut lip. He makes his old man look like Mother Teresa."

Jeff realized with a chill that Conroy was talking too freely. "You're going to kill me, aren't you?"

"Just take it easy."

"Answer me."

Conroy sniffed. "Hell no, I'm not going to kill you."

Yeah, but Mark is, isn't he? Route 231—that was the last leg to Grant Pendleton's house. *Sharon!* Jeff thought, then felt a stab of fear for both of them. He was headed for the right place, all right, but the wrong outcome.

Jeff gazed ahead through the windshield. Could he somehow signal an oncoming car?

The narrow road was empty.

Jeff poked his fingers down into the crack of the seat, trying to bring his elbows together to create more slack. His index finger hit something solid. He traced his fingertip along it. What . . . ?

A knife?

The mugger, this afternoon—Jeff had taken the guy's knife and thrown it on the seat, and here it was!

He felt a surge of hope. Straightening his body, he eased his hands deeper. The knife teased him, slithering away at the tips of his squirming fingers. Conroy glanced over at him and he froze.

"You can't shake loose, Doc, so you may as well sit back and enjoy the ride. By the way, I like your wheels. You fix this baby up yourself?"

"Yeah." Jeff started talking about the Buick, telling Conroy how he had found the car sitting behind an old gas station and given the owner eight hundred dollars for it, how he had restored it, step by step. Covering his small movements with a flow of words, he shifted his weight along the seat, his fingers tracking the knife, his nerves boiling with an agony of hope and dread. Come on, come on . . .

Got you.

Gingerly, he eased the knife up from the crack, finding the switch button with his thumb. He pushed it, coughing to cover the snick as the blade popped out. He glanced at Conroy, terrified that he had heard the sound, but Conroy nodded encouragement. "So when you lost the keys, what did you do?"

"One of my patients, a guy I stitched up in ER one night, taught me how to hot-wire it. I drove it around for a while that way. Then I found a whole steering column, complete with key, at the junkyard."

Conroy laughed appreciatively, as if they were two buddies out for a drive. He drew in a long, shuddering sniff. Strung out, Jeff thought. He needs a fix. He's probably half crazy from it.

Jeff talked some more about the car, bringing the sharp blade to bear on the cord, feeling the point prick his wrist. He remembered how easily it had sliced through the steel-sheathed phone cable. *Just don't cut your wrists,* he told himself shakily.

Jeff shifted his weight on the seat, using the movement to cover a sawing thrust.

The blade sliced cleanly through the cords. With a savage grunt, Jeff whipped the knife up, pressing the blade against Conroy's throat. Conroy gasped.

"Stop the car."

Instead, Conroy stepped on the accelerator. The car lunged forward.

"Christ!" Jeff shouted.

"Drop the knife, or I'll crash us."

"You're *crazy!*"

"You get away, Hand will fucking kill me, DROP THE FUCKING KNIFE!"

Jeff felt frozen with terror. The Buick careened down the road, swerving toward the trees. "Look OUT!" Jeff yelled. *Too late—*

Sharon lay face down on the ground, feeling no pain, only the pressure of the arrow in her lower side, a shearing path of tension that pulled the wound one way below her stomach and the other at her lower back. She must be lying on the arrow, pushing it over. No pain, but the twisted feeling was dreadful, yanking at the nerves of her spine. She rolled onto her side and the arrow straightened itself inside her, relieving the pressure.

Looking down at her stomach, she felt a queasy shock. The arrow stuck out half a foot from her lower abdomen. Depending on where it had entered her back, it could have punched through either a kidney or her small intestine. She saw that the point was small and blunt, and she realized it was a target arrow, like Mark had told her about. It must have been the only kind handy as he ran out after her. The point shone red, and she could feel blood coursing down her side. It soaked into her shirt in a dark, widening stain.

Reaching around to her back, she grasped the shaft and yanked the arrow out, flinging it away. There was no pain, but her head felt light for a few seconds. She pulled a deep breath, feeling the oxygen hit her brain, clearing it a little.

Mark! He must be heading up the hill toward her.

Could she still run?

She pushed herself to her feet and looked down the hill. Mark had started after her. Adrenaline slammed into her legs; she turned and sprinted up the last few yards. Topping the rise, she ran on into the woods, staggering, fighting through the trees. A loud, high whine filled her ears. Distantly, she felt her knees fold and hit the ground. She teetered at the top of a mountain that plunged away steeply on all sides. The air was thin and cold in her lungs. She sucked at it, clinging to consciousness.

Losing blood, she thought.

She put her head down between her knees, and the faintness passed. Getting up again, she pressed a hand over the wound and walked deeper into the woods, keeping a slow, steady pace. If she took it easy, just put one foot in front of the other, she could get in deep enough that Mark would never find her.

She became aware of a crust forming on her hand where it pressed her side. The blood must be clotting. She tried not to think about her intestines. If one had been punctured, she was as good as dead. The massive infection would kill her.

But not right away. It might take as long as a day or two for the infection to build to a fatal level. For the first few hours, she would still be able to function. Time enough to get help for Frank and Mom. They're still okay, she told herself. Pendleton won't kill them while there's still a chance I could bring the cops down on him.

She pushed her way through a patch of low bushes, amazed at the way her broken ankle was bearing up. She felt almost normal. As dreadful as its extraction was, gamma lipoprotein was also truly incredible. She had never understood how profoundly pain could shut a person down—and how the lack of it could make even a terrible injury seem like nothing. Broken ankle, arrow through the gut, but she didn't feel either one.

It was more than just not feeling it. She knew, consciously, that she had been badly wounded, but apparently her conscious mind had a lot less to do with her mental and emotional response to the wounds than she would have thought. It must be some other, nonconscious part of her brain that was supposed to depress, scare, and immobilize her, and that part *didn't* know that the wound existed.

She felt a dizzy moment of euphoria. I'm going to get you out, Mom, she thought. And you, Frank. Just watch me!

Pushing deeper into the protection of the trees, she felt her optimism growing. Mark must be somewhere behind her, but she was moving quietly and there was no way he would be able to see her, or know which way she went.

Speaking of that, which way *was* she going?

Sharon peered through the woods. Her route this morning would be the best way back out, or at least the one she was surest of. But she couldn't find anything familiar.

Never mind. Just go.

When she tried speeding up a little, her knees went spongy and she had to slow down again. Pushing too hard would only cause her heart to beat faster and harder, putting pressure on the crusted patch of blood she could feel hardening beneath her palm.

A distant howl rose behind her, then died away.

She stopped, uncertain, then heard it again. Dogs, at least two of them. A chill ran up her spine. The cover of the woods would mean nothing to the dogs. They would follow their noses, not their eyes.

A scene from dozens of old movies flashed through her

mind: a man in prison clothes, wading upstream, as the hounds barked.

But there was no stream here.

She lengthened her strides, searching for a place to hide. Or would the dogs just corner her if she did that?

The dogs howled again, then set up an excited barking. They had found her scent. Dread filled her. They would be on her soon.

The ground rose a little and Sharon saw a dark slash between two trees. A cave? She veered toward it, stumbling. The slash took on a yawning, dark depth—yes, it was a cave. She dropped to her knees and crawled in, feeling an overhanging ledge of rock scrape her back. She burrowed deeper, desperate, thinking of the dogs behind her. The cave narrowed quickly, ending in a damp wall of earth that smelled of dirt and mushrooms. She touched the wall; it was sticky like clay and veined through with slick tree roots.

She listened anxiously for the dogs. Their barking swelled, then suddenly began to recede. She scrunched around, wild with sudden hope, facing the gash of light from the entrance.

Yes, they were going away!

A huge relief swelled in her. She cocked her head, listening, picking up fading yaps and warbling howls. They still sounded determined, as though they were right on her trail, but they were going away. Stupid dogs! What could they be after?

Suddenly, she realized what was happening: she had run back into the woods where she'd come out that morning. Both trails were fresh: the dogs were being drawn off by the earlier one. With any luck, they would track her all the way back to the highway.

She laughed aloud. The damp womb of earth sucked up her voice. The light slit of the entrance danced and wavered before her eyes.

Come on, she thought. Get out of here and get going.

But she felt so weak, so tired, and she could still hear the dogs. Better to wait a few minutes, rest, and when she couldn't hear them anymore . . .

Sharon came to with a start, hearing the loud chir of crickets. Another sound lingered in her memory, fading before she could identify it. So dark. Where was she? Panic swelled in her, and then the smells registered: damp earth, mushrooms. The cave.

She had passed out. While she'd been unconscious, night had fallen.

I've got to get out of here, she thought.

She started to move, then heard a soft, snuffling whisper. Her hackles rose. It was the sound that had roused her. A dog, out there, *close.*

She pulled her legs under her; pain swept up from her ankle and she froze, gasping.

The painkiller was wearing off.

Gritting her teeth, she crawled to the entrance. Her side started throbbing too. She could feel the pain eating its way through her.

She heard a crackle through the leaves, too light and fast for a man, and then the dog howled, raising goose bumps on her arms. She scrambled forward, but it leapt into the entrance, trapping her.

27

JEFF PULLED THE KNIFE away from Conroy's throat as the Buick crashed off the road and sideswiped a tree, hurling him back against the passenger door, knocking the wind out of him. Dimly, he felt the car shudder to a stop. He sucked in a breath and shook his head, trying to clear it. He saw that the driver's door had been torn off by the tree. Outlined in the ragged opening was Conroy, pushing himself off the wheel, digging in his coat—

The gun!

Jeff lunged at him, slashing at his hand, seeing the gun fly up against the windshield as Conroy screamed. The gun slid along the dash toward Jeff and he grabbed for it, feeling the car lurch as Conroy leapt free.

Jeff got the gun and slithered across the seat and out the driver's-side door. Bright moonlight bathed Conroy's back as he ran into the woods.

"Stop, or I'll shoot!"

Conroy kept running. Jeff aimed at him, but his finger refused to squeeze the trigger. Conroy disappeared amid the trees.

Disgusted, Jeff stuck the gun in his pocket. He should have shot the slimy bastard. They were very close to Pendleton's. Conroy would cut across through the woods and warn them.

Not if I get there first, Jeff thought grimly.

He looked back up at the weed-choked margin of the road. The grade up to it wasn't steep at all; if he could get the car restarted, he should be able to drive right out. He lunged back into the Buick, shifted into neutral. He found the gas pedal with his bare foot and twisted the key in the ignition. The engine chattered, then kicked over.

"Attababy!" Shifting back into gear, he eased the gas pedal down. The left rear tire spun with a loud, flapping shriek.

Jeff's heart sank. He let up on the gas and popped his glove compartment, taking out his flashlight. Leaning out, he shone it on the rear wheel. The tire dangled in ribbons on the rim.

"Shit!" Jeff shouted.

Sharon stared, petrified, at the black silhouette of the bloodhound in the mouth of the cave. It had her neatly boxed in. How long before Mark got here?

The dog raised its muzzle and howled, sending a cold shock up her spine. She clambered up from the hole, gasping at the pain in her ankle.

"Good dog," she whispered. "Go find Mark. Find Mark!"

The dog stayed where it was, howling at her. Moonlight gleamed off the whites of its mournful eyes.

She turned and hobbled away, the broken ankle hammering bolts of pain into her brain. She pressed a hand against her side. Bleeding again. Her abdominal muscles burned where she had pulled the arrow out.

Forget that, she thought. Run. Get back to the road as fast as you can. If you can do it with gamma lipoprotein, you can do it without.

Sharon broke into a staggering run. Pain raged into her head, white hot, blinding her. She dropped and rolled to her side, gulping at the air.

Get up, they'll kill you, *get up!*

Sharon pushed to her knees. Sweat burst from her forehead, filling her eyes. She crawled, dragging the ankle after her. The dog followed behind her, yapping, barking, and then she heard feet ripping toward her through the leaves. She dropped flat, but there was nothing to hide her. Mark's feet appeared in front of her face.

"Sharon."

She rolled over, peering up at his dark silhouette.

"You've done very well," he said. "I salute you. For your reward, I'll let you see your mother before you die, as soon as we get back. I'll have Dad give you another shot."

Sharon's mouth went dry. Another shot. She could almost feel it flowing into her, warm, like Mark's voice, smooth as silk, driving out the pain. A fierce hunger welled up in her throat.

"Go to hell," she said.

Let her still be alive, Jeff thought, agonized.

He pressed the accelerator down a little, feeling a mushy response from the rear of the car. How had he let the spare get so low?

Never mind, he was back on the road, he was rolling.

But it had taken him too long; a half hour to change the tire and coax the car up out of the slippery sea of grass onto the road.

He pressed the accelerator down another fraction, feeling the hot rubber press into the tiny raw grass cuts on his bare foot. The Buick shuddered and shimmied forward on the partially deflated spare. The speedometer said forty. Air whipped at his side through the gaping hole left by the torn-off door.

Hurry. Please God, I've got to hurry—

A deer swelled, transfixed, in the headlights, eyes gleaming like gold ingots. Jeff flicked the lights off for a second, then on again, the beam catching the back end of the deer soaring off the road just in front of the car. Sweat broke out on his face.

He hunched over the wheel, seeing the trees flick by in the sidewash of the headlights. Getting close now—there! Pendleton's arched gateway made a distant white speck in the headlights; Jeff eased the car down to twenty. As the white arch loomed, he saw a man at the gate, closing it.

Conroy.

Jeff felt his face twist in a savage grin. All right, Chuck baby, my turn! He swung in at the gate, catching Conroy full in the lights, and saw him shield his face with an up-flung arm. Jeff felt his teeth clenching. He steered into Conroy, savoring the solid *thunk* as he went down.

Jeff stopped the car and leapt out. Dimly he felt the gravel stab his feet as he ran to Conroy's side. Conroy lay moaning and writhing in the grass. One leg was bent at an odd angle. Jeff knelt beside him and tried to grab him by the hair, but it was too short. He got hold of Conroy's ears instead and jerked his head up, feeling a hot satisfaction as Conroy's eyes widened in fear.

"Where is she?"

"My leg! I think it's busted!"

Jeff let go of one ear and slapped him. "WHERE IS SHE?"

"No way, man, no way."

Jeff stood and planted his bare foot on Conroy's leg.

"No, please, Doc. You can't. He'll kill me."

"*I'll* kill you."

Conroy stared at him. "You wouldn't. You're too— AACCKK!"

Jeff jammed his foot down on the leg, feeling bone grate. Conroy arched and went limp.

"Shit!" Jeff said. He stared down at Conroy, feeling queasy himself. So much for the Hippocratic oath. And so much for getting any quick information out of Conroy.

Jeff got back into the Buick. He killed the headlights and rolled the car slowly through the gate. Easy does it—no sense letting them know he was coming. At the end of the drive, the grand house waited. Several lights were on in the west wing, and the white-columned portico gleamed in the security lights.

Jeff patted the gun in his pocket. Who needs Conroy anyway? he thought, looking at the house. Sharon has to be in there somewhere.

28

SHARON'S SKIN CRAWLED at Mark's touch. He held her between himself and the ladder, one arm across her back, the other under her knees, his hands gripping the rails. She tried to ready herself as he dropped down another step. Her side jolted against him, bringing a raw burst of pain. Sweat ran into her eyes. She bit the insides of her lips, holding her mouth shut, knowing the next step down would make her scream. Then she realized they had hit bottom.

Mark turned toward the door in the cinder block. He looked at her face and held her still. The hole in her side burned like a red-hot iron. Tears flooded her eyes, blurring the door and the generator and drum of gasoline beside it.

"Put me down. I can walk now."

"I don't think so," he said.

"Please!" Sharon tried to keep the revulsion from her voice, but she didn't want him touching her, holding her. She would crawl if she had to.

He eased her to the floor and gave her his arm. Sharon let him support her through the door and into the hall. Then she pulled away and leaned against the cinder block wall. Keeping her weight off the ankle didn't do much good; it hammered with constant, steady pain—her reward, no doubt, for running on it. She inched along, slower than she had to, conscious of the operating room ahead. She stopped beside the cell they had kept her in before, but Mark pointed to the O.R.

A sick fear rose inside her. With an effort, she controlled her voice. "You said I could see my mother."

"That was before you told me to go to hell."

"Where is she?" Sharon whispered.

"One of the cells. What does it matter?"

Still alive. Sharon felt a little better. "And Frank?"

Mark gave a harsh laugh. "That tough old bird? He really had us fooled. Do you know that he stayed back there for days in a dark covered ditch not much bigger than a grave? He may be old, but he's a real badger, Sharon."

Sharon looked at Mark, sickened. "Badgers, lionesses," she said. "The hunter and the hunted. Such quaint, romantic lies you tell yourself to keep from facing what you are. What Frank did—he must have been starving out there in the dark, dying of thirst, but he would rather do it than come inside to you. Can you really not comprehend what it says about you and your father?"

His pale eyes bored into her. "And what does it say?"

"That you're maniacs—monsters."

The skin around his eyes whitened. "Into the surgery, Sharon. I'm sure Pop will want to do you right now. You're too full of pain to waste it."

Her stomach went hollow. Mark grabbed her arm and dragged her into the surgery, pushing her up onto the steel table. Distantly, she heard herself crying out with pain. Her head floated. *Hang . . . on.* Through a blur of tears, she saw him dialing the phone.

"Mark!" she gasped.

He hung up and turned to her, looking irritated.

"If you were on this table, I'd let you see your father." He frowned, considering it.

"It won't take that much longer. She is my mother, Mark. She's been everything to me."

Mark's hand dropped from the phone. Sharon felt a rush

of relief. She would see her mother, live a few more minutes. There was that one point of contact between them, just that one little bit of humanity left in Mark. His father was everything to him: holding on to that had cost him all the rest.

Mark helped her up and walked with her down the hall, stopping at the second to last door. "Want to see Frank, too? He's in there." He nodded at the door.

Sharon hesitated, torn. She wanted to see him, but it might be better for him if she didn't. Let him think she had gotten away. Let him hope a little longer.

"No," she said quietly.

Mark shrugged. "If it's any comfort to you, he'll be around a few more days. We've got to fatten him up a little. Fasting like he did out there diminishes the capacity for pain, and for making gamma lipoprotein."

Sharon shuddered. "You don't fatten him up," she snapped. "He's not some animal. . ." She trailed off. What was the use?

Mark shrugged, unlocking the last door in the hall and helping her in. Her mother was lying on the bed, apparently asleep. Her face looked peaceful. A lump formed in Sharon's throat.

"I'll give you about fifteen minutes," Mark said.

Sharon heard the lock whisper shut behind her. Leaning on the wall, she made her way to the foot of the bed, and then along the side, sinking to her knees. Her mother stirred and looked at her vacantly. "Honey?"

Sharon tried to say something, but her voice wouldn't work. Her mother reached out, and Sharon crawled onto the bed with her. It was like those times long ago. Mom smelled of sweat, not lavender, but her hugging arms had never felt so good.

Our last storm, Sharon thought.

Her mother patted her back, stroked her hair. Tears scalded Sharon's throat, but she would not sob. One of her mother's hands settled near the entry wound in her back. Even the light pressure hurt, but Sharon held still, enduring it, unwilling to end the moment. As she hugged her mother back, she realized suddenly that with all the pain from the wound, she still hadn't grown ill from it. Why? By now the infection should be spreading, she should have a raging fever.

What did it matter? She was going to die anyway.

She would die to relieve Pendleton's back pain for a few hours or days. She would never become an attending physician, never work with schizophrenics, never again ride her bike or feel the wind through her hair. In time, Jeff would forget her and marry someone else. Life would go on, people would laugh and joke, and it would be as though she had never been.

In her mind she saw a pair of shoes she had had when she was little, black patent leather, with rounded toes. Dad had gotten them for her, and some little white socks to wear with them. How she had loved putting them on, polishing the shiny black toes with Kleenex, pretending she was a princess going to a dance. Whatever happened to those shoes?

She heard footsteps outside the door. The lock turned again and the door opened. She felt her body going rigid, Mom's hand clenching her neck. No, not yet, *please.*

"Sharon?" Grant Pendleton's voice. He cleared his throat. "I'm afraid it's time."

Her mother clutched at her, but she pulled away, determined to be brave. Gently, she disengaged her mother's hands, gazing down into her sweet face, so full of fear. "It's all right, Mom. I'm fine now. I love you. I always have. You—"

A hand grabbed Sharon's arm. "Come along."

"Let her finish, Pop."

Pendleton released her. Her mind spun. I'll never see Mom again, she thought. I have to tell her how I feel. Dear God, there's so much, how can I say it all? "You've done your very best, always, and fought as hard as you could," Sharon said. "I'm proud of you."

Tears spilled from her mother's eyes. Sharon kissed her and stood up, ignoring the pain. How pointless that her body should still be warning her she was hurt, telling her to take care of herself. Pendleton took one of her arms and Mark the other. At the door, she sensed movement behind her, and then her mother hit Pendleton's back, jarring him loose from her.

"Run, Sharon!"

Before Sharon could move, Mark grabbed her, pinning her arms behind her. Struggling hard, she could see her mother clinging to Pendleton's back, her legs wrapped around his waist, her arms around his neck, choking him as he lumbered around trying to shake her off.

"Mark," Pendleton squeaked. "Help!"

Sharon twisted in Mark's grip, fighting him with all she had. He spun her around and slugged her just under the ribs. She staggered back, trying to breathe, and sat down hard on the floor. Mark pulled her mother off Pendleton's back, throwing her down on the bed, handcuffing her wrist to the iron footboard.

Sharon's lungs opened and she sucked in air.

"Damn woman," Pendleton shouted at Ellen Francis. "I think you injured my back."

Sharon looked up at him, incredulous. "You *think*? When will you know? When you turn the wrong way some day, or lift something you shouldn't and cut your spinal cord and fall on your filthy, Nazi face? You don't even know if your back is broken. And for this you became a mass murderer?"

"Shut up!" Mark snarled. She felt his hand clutching her hair, jerking her to her feet.

"Bring her to surgery," Dr. Pendleton said coldly. Mark grabbed her wrist and jacked it up behind her, forcing her through the door and down the hall behind his father. Her ankle thumped against the tiles, sending distant shock waves through her. The air felt very cold on her skin. Her throat was dry. This is it, she thought. Show them some strength now.

Mark shoved her into the O.R. and flung her onto the table as his father went to the sink. The steel of the table was chilly against her back. She tried to sit up, her body still determined to fight, but Mark shoved her back easily and cinched straps over her legs, waist and chest, yanking them so tight she could barely squirm. Circling to the head of the table, he grabbed her hair again. She closed her eyes, but they opened again at once, demanding to see, tracking Grant Pendleton's every move. He pulled on a pair of surgical gloves, letting the cuffs snap against his wrists, a terrible sound, zigzagging along her nerves.

Pendleton picked up a bone saw, like the ones in his lab at the hospital. Sharon's stomach knotted inside her. The small, circular blade gleamed, bright and terrifying. She felt herself sinking into a huge, cold vacuum of horror. She wanted to say something, taunt him, but her mouth was too dry, her tongue paralyzed.

He flicked the saw on, filling the room with a sharp, high whine that kicked and raged through her muscles. She clenched her teeth, focusing all her strength, bucking hard against the straps. They held. Pain flamed in the roots of her hair as Mark pulled her head down hard against the table. Dr. Pendleton held the saw up, and with his free hand touched a point just above her eyebrows . . . *God, GOD*—

She heard a deafening bang; Mark's hand pulled free from her hair. She saw the whirling blade swing away from her as Grant Pendleton wheeled toward the door. Mark's face swung into view, upside down over hers, falling toward her in slow motion, his eyes wide and baffled. She jerked her head to the side as his forehead thumped onto the table beside her. He slid away and clattered to the floor.

"OH MY GOD!" Pendleton screamed.

"Sharon!"

Jeff! She twisted on the table, wild with hope, and saw

him at the door, a gun in his hand. He shot Mark! Pendleton raised the saw.

"Look out!" Sharon screamed.

Pendleton bellowed and charged Jeff. He seemed insane with rage and grief. The gun went off again and the saw flew from Pendleton's hand. He plowed into Jeff, knocking him over. Sharon strained against the straps, desperate to help Jeff. Pendleton staggered up and rushed out the door. As it swung shut behind him, she glimpsed a splash of red, high on the shoulder of his lab coat. He had been hit, but the bullet hadn't fazed him—he hadn't even cried out.

Of course not—he was full of gamma lipoprotein.

Alarms went off in Sharon's mind. Where was he going?

Jeff was up, bending over her, undoing the straps. His fingers stopped for an instant as he looked at her side. His face blanched, but he said nothing.

"It's all right," she said. "Hurry!"

He got the last strap off and helped her sit up. His eyes glistened. "Sharon—"

"We've got to get Mom and Frank!" She squeezed Jeff's hand, wanting to hug him, but there was no time. "Follow me!"

Sharon took one step and her ankle buckled under her. Pain burst in her side as her knees slammed down on the floor. She felt Jeff's arm around her, pulling her up. Her legs refused to help. "Damn it, come *on!*" she shouted. Fury surged through her, whipping strength into her legs. "This way!"

Grabbing hold of his shoulder, Sharon half leaned on Jeff as she pulled him into the corridor. She glanced both ways. Pendleton wasn't in the hallway, but the exit door was ajar, spilling light from the anteroom. She could see one edge of the ladder, but she couldn't see him. She hoped he was already out and running, but something told her he wasn't.

"This way!" She pulled Jeff away from the exit toward the cooler, keeping her arm around his neck for support. "C'mon, go—I'll keep up." She swung her good leg forward, desperate to get Mom and Frank, get out of this hole in the ground before—

"JEFF!"

Pendleton's voice. Dread seized Sharon. She turned, feeling Jeff stop beside her. Pendleton stood at the head of the corridor, leaning on a small drum container. The shoulder of his lab coat was soaked in blood; his face was flushed, his teeth bared in a crazed grin. With a shock, Sharon recognized the drum—the gas supply for the emergency generator. Fear swept through her in icy waves.

Pendleton pushed the drum over. Gas gushed from the opened feed hole at the top, snaking across the wooden floor toward them in shiny, twisting ribbons.

Pendleton held one hand high. A tiny flame flared from the lighter he was holding, the lighter that had left the scars along his arm, the blistered promises that he would never feel pain again. She squeezed Jeff's arm, horrified.

"Dr. Pendleton!" Jeff shouted. "Wait—"

But Pendleton spun the drum sideways with his foot and kicked it toward them. The drum banged along at frightening speed, gas pinwheeling from the whirling hole in the top. Jeff lunged forward, intercepting it. Picking it up, he flung it back up the hall just as Pendleton dropped his lighter. Runners of flame leapt up along the gas-soaked floor toward them, enveloping the drum.

"Jeff!" Sharon screamed.

He rushed back to her, sweeping her up, sprinting away from Pendleton toward the cooler. The drum exploded with a huge *whump* behind them, slapping them down in a hot shock wave. Sharon sprawled across the floor, feeling a dim tearing in her side. She scrambled to her knees, adrenaline pumping through her. A wall of smoke boiled down the hall toward them, obscuring Pendleton and everything beyond.

"Are you all right?" Jeff's face was inches from hers, but his voice sounded muffled.

Sharon nodded. He pulled her up with him, jockeying

her toward the smoke. She planted her good foot. "No! Mom and Frank!"

"That fire's only going to get worse—"

"You go."

"Bullshit! Where are they?"

She turned, trying to see the doors, but the smoke caught up with them, billowing around their heads. She held her breath, hoping it would clear away, but it didn't. Groping along the wall, she felt the doors, barely able to see. She took a sip of air and doubled over in a jag of coughing, pain exploding in her side.

"The floor!" Jeff shouted, pulling her down.

The air was clearer there. Sharon gulped it, holding her side, finding the base of the door to Frank's room. "Your gun, Jeff. Shoot the lock."

He did and the door swung open. Frank stumbled out. Jeff pulled him down into the clearer air. Sharon felt a lift at the sight of him. He had managed to clean the blood from around his mouth, but his face was still dirty and his hair stuck up wildly. He grabbed her hand and squeezed. "I knew you'd be back, Dr. Francis."

"The next door," she said to Jeff. Hot pressure waffled over her skin, and she knew the fire was gathering force, the wooden floor feeding the flames. A horrid, trapped feeling gnawed at the back of her brain.

Jeff pressed the muzzle of his gun against the lock.

"Wait!" Sharon shouted. "Mom's on that side of the room, handcuffed to the bed."

Jeff angled the gun the other way and fired. The lock splintered but the door wouldn't open.

He stood and kicked at the door. "Come on, you bastard!" The lock tore free and the door banged open. Sharon crawled through and glimpsed her mother, seated on the bed, pulling at the handcuffs. Smoke rolled in, blotting her out. Sharon lunged through it to her side, grabbing the chain of the handcuffs and twisting it with wild strength, but it wouldn't break.

"Here," Jeff shouted. He stretched the chain over the steel footboard, placed the muzzle of the gun against it, and fired. The bang was hideously loud in the enclosed space, making Sharon's ears ring.

The chain remained unbroken.

"Had my cutters," Frank said, "I'd chop that bad boy in a second."

Jeff pounded the chain with the butt of the gun, and Sharon saw the links blackening, bending, and then the gun went off again and she heard the slap of the slug around the room. She looked at Jeff, horrified. His face was dumb with shock. "Holy shit! Is everyone all right?"

"I think so."

"How do you do," Ellen said. "I'm Ellen Francis, Sharon's mother."

Jeff blinked, and Sharon saw that her mother was holding her hand out to him. Jeff's last blow must have broken the chain. Jeff shook her mother's hand, looking nonplussed. Ellen saw Frank and paled. Frank rubbed self-consciously at his hair.

"Frank Greene, ma'am. I'm one of your daughter's patients."

"Never mind that," Sharon said. "You two pick Mom up."

"I'm perfectly capable of walking," Ellen said.

Sharon thought of her sitting in the van, catatonic, unable to run when her life depended on it, and nodded to Jeff. He swept her mother up in his arms. "Frank, help Sharon," he said.

"Right." Frank took her arm and they staggered back up the hall through the smoke. Sharon saw Jeff's ankles and bare feet. What had happened to his shoes?

Then she saw the flames ahead of them, a solid wall, licking at the ceiling, edging toward them. Her heart sank. Jeff stopped abruptly, stiffening, and Grant Pendleton emerged from the smoke and flames, walking toward them. He was on fire—his lab coat, his hair, his skin, and yet he was walking. Sharon stared at him, appalled. Pendleton could have run away. He was destroying himself too. Why?

The flaming figure stopped, facing them. "Mark," he cried. "Mark, Mark . . . "

Oh, God, Sharon thought. He wants to die with his son.

Pendleton toppled onto his face and disappeared beneath the flames.

"Dear God Almighty," Jeff croaked.

"We've got to go back the other way," Frank said. "Can't no one get through that fire."

"You're right," Sharon said. "There's a cooler back at the end of the hall. It's insulated. We'll wait out the fire. C'mon Jeff." She tugged at his arm and he turned to follow Frank, carrying her mother. The corpses—what would seeing them do to Mom? No choice.

At the door, Sharon turned back to her mother. "There are bodies in here. But we have to go in."

"Bodies?" Ellen said.

Smoke billowed around them, hiding Ellen and Jeff. Sharon grabbed out for her mother, catching a handful of her dress. Frank pulled the cooler door open and helped everyone in. The cold felt wonderful on Sharon's face. Jeff pulled the door shut behind them. "Close your eyes, Mrs. Francis—there's a light switch here, and I need to see the layout, just for a second."

Sharon closed her eyes too.

"God!" Jeff hissed.

She heard the switch snap off again. The bodies, the cupped skulls, flashed in her mind. She felt sick to her stomach.

"Oh, dear," Ellen's voice quavered, and Sharon realized she had not closed her eyes. Her mother began to sob. Sharon pulled her close.

"They don't feel anything."

"Is—is Meg in here?"

"I don't know," Sharon lied. She hugged her mother, thinking of Pendleton crying out for his dead son as the skin burned from his bones. Monsters, both of them, but Mark had loved his father, and his father had loved him.

She felt Jeff's hand squeezing her shoulder. "That hole in your side . . . I'd better check you over."

"In the dark?"

"Listen, by the time you're a third-year resident you've examined at least a thousand people sound asleep with your eyes closed. Just hold still. Were you shot?" The strain in his voice sent a cold tremor through her.

"No. Arrow."

"Really!" His voice brightened. "What range?"

"Around sixty yards."

"Good! The intestines are so slippery that they'll sometimes slide around an intrusion, as long as the entering velocity isn't too great and the projectile isn't too sharp. A bullet's got too much velocity, but in ER I've seen two different guys stabbed in the lower abdomen with no intestinal perforation. The knife was probably pretty dull in each case. Was this a target arrow?"

Sharon pulled his head close and whispered in his ear, "Yes. But let's not worry about it anymore unless we get out of here. I don't want to upset Mom."

Then she realized that Frank and her mother weren't listening. They were talking together; Frank was telling Ellen how he mulched his azaleas. Sharon felt a surge of warmth for him.

There was a sudden silence in the walk-in and she realized that the refrigeration unit had been running and now it had cut off. The fire must have burned through the wiring at some point back in the corridor, cutting all power in the underground lab. The chill began to fade almost at once.

Jeff's arms went around her. She nestled back against him, feeling her muscles spasm as they relaxed. Exhaustion gnawed at her, sucking out the last dregs of her strength. She tried to hang on, knowing it was too soon to let go, but she could feel herself melting against Jeff. If I have to die, she thought, this is the way.

"Why did he keep these bodies?" she whispered to Jeff.

"He's been having me look at the spinal cords of rats for trace endorphins, and I've been finding some. I assume he took the brains because he's looking for some new kind of endorphin. He's probably keeping the bodies as an extra last-ditch source if he runs low on fresh human subjects."

The air became warmer. The heat of Jeff's body began to be uncomfortable, but Sharon did not want to pull away.

"I don't suppose," Jeff said, "there's any point in my trying to apologize for assuming you were crazy."

"You don't?"

He gave a wretched groan and Sharon relented. "I think you redeemed yourself by finding us. How *did* you find us?"

"I thought you were in the house. I was creeping up on it when Pendleton suddenly charged out the front door and headed for the greenhouse. I just followed him."

The air was turning hot now; Sharon had to work to fill her lungs.

"We'd better let go," Jeff said. "We'll stay cooler." He gave her a final squeeze and she moved away. Mom and Frank were no longer talking. Sweat poured from Sharon, soaking her clothes. She couldn't hear the fire, but it must be outside, raging all around them, turning the cooler into an oven. We may die, she thought. After all this.

She wiped at her forehead, feeling the heat inside her now like a baking fever. There was only one hope left—the frozen bodies. The cooler was full of them, and it would take time for those bodies to give up their chill.

If we live, Sharon thought, it will be because of you, Meg, and all you others.

Even you, Brian.

Brian. She tried to cling to the bitter irony of it, but it slipped away in a black haze.

She woke slowly. Someone was shaking her. "I think it's getting cooler," Jeff said.

They waited as long as they could stand it, then opened

the cooler door. Jeff took some shoes from one of the bigger corpses to protect his feet from the hot floor. The tunnel was pitch black, filled with the stench of smoke and slag. Sharon hung on to Jeff's shoulder, picking her way through the rubble, while Frank helped Ellen along. A cool draft brushed Sharon's face. She inhaled deeply, feeling a rush of hope. There must be a hole up ahead, where the ceiling had fallen in.

And they had better find it fast, before the rest of the corridor caved in and buried them.

"There!" Jeff said. "I can see stars!"

A loud cracking noise started in the distance and rumbled toward them. "Quick!" Sharon said. "You and Frank go first. You can pull us up."

She heard him scrambling, then saw his silhouette, very faint, rise into the starlight. Frank followed, and then they pulled Sharon and her mother up. Sharon hung on to Ellen, stumbling away with her through the night. She felt the ground tremble as the rest of the underground complex caved in behind them.

All the strength fled from Sharon and she slumped to the ground. I need water, she thought. I've needed water for days.

She looked back the way they had come. Smoke rose from the chasm of the ruined lab, curling into the night sky like the souls of the dead. She shivered. Her mother and Frank settled in the tall grass beside her.

Jeff cleared his throat. "Mrs. Francis, I know we've just met, but before anything else happens, I'd like to ask for your daughter's hand in marriage."

Sharon felt her heart leap. "Could you take my ankle instead?"

"Mrs. Francis?" Jeff said, ignoring her.

Ellen looked up at him, her eyes dreamy. "Lot's wife turned into a pillar of salt," she said.

"You can ask her again later," Sharon said. "But in the meantime, I accept." Her heart overflowed with love for

Jeff. She took his hands and pulled him down to her. Right there, with Frank and Mom watching, Jeff kissed her lips, then bent and tenderly kissed the hole in her side, and finally her swollen ankle.

It's not gamma lipoprotein, Sharon thought happily. But it will do.

LANDMARK BESTSELLERS

FROM ST. MARTIN'S PAPERBACKS

HOT FLASHES
Barbara Raskin
_____ 91051-7 $4.95 U.S.   _____ 91052-5 $5.95 Can.

MAN OF THE HOUSE
"Tip" O'Neill with William Novak
_____ 91191-2 $4.95 U.S.   _____ 91192-0 $5.95 Can.

FOR THE RECORD
Donald T. Regan
_____ 91518-7 $4.95 U.S.   _____ 91519-5 $5.95 Can.

THE RED WHITE AND BLUE
John Gregory Dunne
_____ 90965-9 $4.95 U.S.   _____ 90966-7 $5.95 Can.

LINDA GOODMAN'S STAR SIGNS
Linda Goodman
_____ 91263-3 $4.95 U.S.   _____ 91264-1 $5.95 Can.

ROCKETS' RED GLARE
Greg Dinallo
_____ 91288-9 $4.50 U.S.   _____ 91289-7 $5.50 Can.

THE FITZGERALDS AND THE KENNEDYS
Doris Kearns Goodwin
_____ 90933-0 $5.95 U.S.   _____ 90934-9 $6.95 Can.

Publishers Book and Audio Mailing Service
P.O. Box 120159, Staten Island, NY 10312-0004

Please send me the book(s) I have checked above. I am enclosing $_____
(please add $1.25 for the first book, and $.25 for each additional book to
cover postage and handling. Send check or money order only—no CODs) or
charge my VISA, MASTERCARD or AMERICAN EXPRESS card.

Card number _____

Expiration date _____ Signature_____

Name _____

Address _____

City _____ State/Zip_____

Please allow six weeks for delivery. Prices subject to change without notice.
Payment in U.S. funds only. New York residents add applicable sales tax.

BEST 1/89

BESTSELLING BOOKS
to Read and Read Again!

HOT FLASHES
Barbara Raskin
_____ 91051-7 $4.95 U.S.   _____ 91052-5 $5.95 Can.

LOOSE ENDS
Barbara Raskin
_____ 91348-6 $4.95 U.S.   _____ 91349-4 $5.95 Can.

BEAUTY
Lewin Joel
_____ 90935-7 $4.50 U.S.   _____ 90936-5 $5.50 Can.

THE FIERCE DISPUTE
Helen Hooven Santmyer
_____ 91028-2 $4.50 U.S.   _____ 91029-0 $5.50 Can.

HERBS AND APPLES
Helen Hooven Santmyer
_____ 90601-3 $4.95 U.S.   _____ 90602-1 $5.95 Can.

AMERICAN EDEN
Marilyn Harris
_____ 91001-0 $4.50 U.S.   _____ 91002-9 $5.50 Can.

JAMES HERRIOT'S DOG STORIES
James Herriot
_____ 90143-7 $4.95 U.S.

Publishers Book and Audio Mailing Service
P.O. Box 120159, Staten Island, NY 10312-0004

Please send me the book(s) I have checked above. I am enclosing $_____
(please add $1.25 for the first book, and $.25 for each additional book to
cover postage and handling. Send check or money order only—no CODs) or
charge my VISA, MASTERCARD or AMERICAN EXPRESS card.

Card number _____

Expiration date _____ Signature_____

Name _____

Address _____

City _____ State/Zip _____

Please allow six weeks for delivery. Prices subject to change without notice.
Payment in U.S. funds only. New York residents add applicable sales tax.

BB 1/89